THE
ARRIVALS

THE
ARRIVALS

a novel

MEG MITCHELL MOORE

A REAGAN ARTHUR BOOK

LITTLE, BROWN AND COMPANY

NEW YORK BOSTON LONDON

Reagan Arthur Books / Little, Brown and Company
Hachette Book Group
237 Park Avenue, New York, NY 10017
www.hachettebookgroup.com

First Edition: May 2011

Reagan Arthur Books is an imprint of Little, Brown and Company, a division of Hachette Book Group, Inc. The Reagan Arthur Books name and logo are trademarks of Hachette Book Group, Inc.

The publisher is not responsible for websites (or their content) that are not owned by the publisher.

The characters and events in this book are fictitious. Any similarity to real persons, living or dead, is coincidental and not intended by the author.

Excerpt from *Bread and Jam for Frances* by Russell Hoban. Copyright © 1964 by Russell C. Hoban; renewed 1992 by Russell C. Hoban.

Library of Congress Cataloging-in-Publication Data
Moore, Meg Mitchell.
The arrivals : a novel / Meg Mitchell Moore.— 1st ed.
p. cm.
ISBN 978-0-316-09771-0
1. Adult children—Family relationships—Fiction.   2. Vermont—Fiction.
3. Domestic fiction.   I. Title.

PS3613.O5653A89 2011
813'.6—dc22   2010038837

10 9 8 7 6 5 4 3 2 1

RRD-IN

Printed in the United States of America

For Brian, my anchor

JUNE

It was eight thirty in the morning, June, a Saturday, and the sunlight was coming in the kitchen window at such an angle that William's granddaughter, Olivia, had to shield her eyes with one hand while she bent her head to sip from the straw in her glass of orange juice. In a couple of minutes the sun would shift and begin to move over the garden, out of Olivia's eyes — William had sat at that table for too many years not to know that — but even so he rose and pulled the cord on the shade, lowering it six inches.

Sitting back down, he pushed aside a stack of coloring pages on which Olivia, who had been up for two and a half hours already, had begun making halfhearted scribbles and swirls and even, in the corner of one sheet of paper, a small triangular object that she claimed was a dog. He opened the front section of the *Burlington Free Press,* unwittingly setting the sports section on top of a small puddle of orange juice.

Olivia watched him. She was three, but she would tell you with no small amount of dignity that she was three and five-eighths. William, who had been the one to get up with her, was on his fourth cup of coffee. A fifth was not out of the question. At the stove, Ginny, his wife, was scrambling the eggs Olivia had requested for breakfast.

"Well," he said, "when do you suppose Lillian will be down?"

"I don't know," Ginny said without turning around. She extracted the saltshaker from its berth in the spice cupboard and shook. "Eventually, I'm sure. I'm surprised the baby is still sleeping."

"That baby cries *all the time*," said Olivia. She screwed up her tiny, perfect nose. "He's a bad baby."

"He's not a *bad* baby," said William. "He's your brother. That's just what babies do: they cry. You cried too, when you were a baby."

"I did?" asked Olivia airily. "I bet I didn't."

"Oh, you *did*," said William. "You cried all the time. You cried oceans."

Ginny carried the plates to the table and set them down before William and Olivia.

"No toast yet," she said. "I'm working on it."

"I don't like scrambled eggs," said Olivia.

"You liked them yesterday," said Ginny. "Five minutes ago, when I asked you what you wanted for breakfast, you liked them then, too."

"But I don't like them any*more*," Olivia said implacably. "I like soft-boiled."

Lillian had called two days ago to let them know she was coming. Not to ask them if it was all right if she came, but to tell them. William listened to Ginny's end of the phone conversation from the deck, where he had the Red Sox game on the old portable television, a beer in his hand. He was looking out over the garden, still tentative in early summer.

"All of you, then?" he heard Ginny say. "The whole kit and caboodle?" Then a pause. Then "Oh, I see," but in a way that said she didn't see. At last she appeared at the door, flushed from her energetic dinner preparations, faintly flustered.

"They're coming," she said. "Lillian and the children. Tomorrow!" And off she went in a frenzy of arrangements, which took her long past their usual bedtime. There were fresh sheets to put on the beds, and the Pack 'n Play to set up for the baby in Lillian's old room. A last-minute trip to the grocery store, to purchase the very eggs at which Olivia was now turning up her nose.

Later, in the semidarkness of their bedroom — the moon was full, or nearly so — William finally had an opportunity to ask her.

"Why just Lillian and the children? Why not Tom?"

"He has to work, I suppose." Ginny was on her side, turned toward him, her hands settled tidily under her chin.

"Over the weekend? He has to work over the weekend?"

"I got the impression Lillian might stay a bit longer. Have a bit of a vacation." Ginny's eyes were closed. Her words came out in a fragmented way; it was as if she were speaking through a net. She wore a sleeveless nightgown of a color that had once been a vibrant blue but had long ago faded to muted gray.

"How long?" He was thinking of the weekend plans that would now have to be changed: the dinner with Hal and Maria canceled or postponed, the Sunday papers unread, the Saturday-afternoon baseball game unwatched.

"I don't know," Ginny said. "But shame on you for asking. You should be happy to have her."

"Mmmmh," said William.

Lillian was the oldest of their three children. She had left home ages ago. William supposed he could begin counting her absence when she went off to Boston College as a freshman, with a giant paisley duffel bag and a tangle of auburn hair. Though there had been a brief postcollegiate stint when something — a lack of money, a broken heart, a lost job — had driven her back home for six months, during which she'd slept away the days in the very bed in which she now reposed and passed the evenings in a sullen state in front of the television or out with friends, returning from those outings in a state of mild hysteria or ebullience.

Lillian had been gone from them for so long, in fact, that sometimes, despite not-infrequent visits, William found it difficult to call her image to mind, and when he did it was an outdated picture that presented itself. A girl on a soccer field with two missing teeth and scabbed knees, not a woman who had transformed herself—effortlessly, it seemed, almost magically—from befuddled youth to capable adult and mother. Witness Olivia here on the stool beside him, witness the baby asleep in the room upstairs.

So why did he still feel this irksome responsibility toward Lillian, this desire to protect her? And protect her from what? Because, now that she was here, it turned out that despite his initial lack of enthusiasm, despite the concern about the paper and the game and the plans, nothing made him happier, nothing made him feel safer and more at ease with the world, than having one of his children under his roof once again.

"I'll go and look in on them," he said now, standing.

"You haven't eaten your eggs." Ginny's voice rose an octave. "Is *nobody* going to eat these eggs I cooked?"

"*I'm* not," said Olivia with great cheer.

"I'll have a look, and then I'll eat."

"Don't, William. If the baby's sleeping—well, you'll only make things worse. And the eggs won't keep. Nothing drearier than cold eggs."

"What's 'drearier'?" interjected Olivia.

"Worse," said Ginny. "Nothing *worse* than cold eggs."

"I'll go and listen, then," William said. "Outside the door."

And he did exactly that. Ginny had put Lillian in her old room, which she done over as a guest room, with a cheerful flowered comforter and a vase of pastel marbles on the white dresser. Olivia was deposited in Rachel's old room, which remained much as

Rachel had left it, in a state of organized chaos, with a Kurt Cobain poster on the back of the closet door. Stephen's old room they had done up as absolutely nothing, and as a result it had become the receptacle of myriad suitcases, once-used mailers with bubble wrap sticking out of them, winter boots packed in boxes after the spring thaw had come, however late and reluctantly, to Vermont.

William paused outside the door. They had lived for so long in this house, the bunch of them, that he failed, mostly, to take in any of the details. For example: in this hallway, with its various nicks and chips, evidence of the children's (and then later Olivia's) propensity for banging things inappropriately against the walls, hung a school portrait for each of the children. Here was Rachel, toothy, dark-haired, eagerly leaning toward the camera. Stephen, the year he got his braces, pulling his lips forward purposefully to hide them, his cowlick standing at attention.

And here, next to Stephen, was Lillian. She must have been in junior high in this picture. You could see, even there in the dim light of the hallway, despite the age of the picture, the luminous skin, the beauty emerging from the little girl.

From downstairs came Ginny's voice, strident now. "William? William! What are you doing? I told you, these eggs aren't going to keep!"

He could hear Ginny as clearly as if she had been speaking through a megaphone aimed directly at his ear. That was one of the strange and delightful things about this house, the way the sound carried from one place to another, even if the first place was geographically distant from the second.

But in addition to Ginny's voice, something else. He could hear the sound—muffled but unmistakable, familiar, even, in a way that he would not have thought possible, this many years removed from when he had last heard it—of his daughter crying.

Lillian woke in her childhood bed. Beside her, in the Pack 'n Play, the baby had begun to make tiny, mewling noises, which Lillian tried to ignore. She opened her eyes just a fraction, but it was enough to see the pale strips of sunlight coming through the slats in the blinds.

She lay still, as still as possible, forcing her breathing to become deep and even, willing the baby back to sleep. He had woken three times in the night, twice to nurse and once for no discernable reason—belly full, diaper dry, that time—and on each occasion she had consulted the numbers on the digital clock that sat on the pristine white nightstand. Just after midnight, then two, then three.

She had turned on the lamp that last time, and studied the baby in the glow the bulb cast over the room. He was three months old now. He had lost the boneless look his body had had at the beginning of life, when he had curled like a semicircle on her chest to nap; he had lost, too, the alien shape to his head with which he had emerged from her womb, blinking and whimpering, then fixing her and Tom with an uncompromising stare that seemed to say, *Well, here I am. What are you going to do with me now?*

What, indeed!

What they were going to do to with him, with the baby, Baby Philip, who might one day (but so far hadn't) become a Phil, was upend his tiny universe before he'd even had a chance to become accustomed to it. Or rather, that's what Tom was going to do. Tom was going to drink a few too many gin and tonics at the company party in May and sleep with his assistant, a snub-nosed snowboarder named Nina, while Lillian sat at home with leaky breasts and dark circles under her eyes, blithely unaware, nearly comatose, watching an episode of *Supernanny* and eating chocolate chip Breyers straight from the container.

Which transgression Lillian was going to learn about from a (formerly) dear friend of hers named Marianne, who had attended the party with her own husband, a leader of the product development team at the same company, and who had come to Lillian contritely and had, in painstaking detail, laid out the scene.

"He was awfully drunk," Marianne had said. "It was that kind of a party. People did crazy things, all sorts of crazy things. He wasn't the only one, not by a long shot. You know that type of party: the office party gone awry."

"I'm not sure I do," Lillian had said coolly. "I haven't worked in an office since before Olivia was born."

"Well, for example—"

"That's it," said Lillian. "I don't need to hear any more."

"He wasn't the only one," said Marianne. "If that helps."

"It doesn't," said Lillian.

"We're going, then," she said to Tom fiercely later that day— God, only Thursday, just two days ago. "I'm taking the children, and I'm going." There was some satisfaction in saying this, in watching the color rise to his cheeks—those pale Irish cheeks, quick, like hers, to display exposure to sun or alcohol or embarrassment—but not enough.

She had packed like a person in a movie, quickly and dramatically, pulling suitcases onto the bed, emptying the contents of drawers into them without considering her choices. (So it was that when she unpacked she discovered that she had brought along an old red shawl she had worn over a black dress years ago to a friend's wedding. Not quite vintage, she supposed, fingering it later in the quiet of the guest room. But certainly outdated. And pantyhose. She'd brought pantyhose! In June, to Vermont!)

Tom was remorseful, appropriately chagrined, embarrassed, all of the things he should have been. He didn't try to get them to stay. (If he had, Lillian thought partway through the four-hour drive north, she might have acquiesced, her anger and hurt considerable but not necessarily strong enough to negate the effort of transporting the two children on her own.)

Olivia had been finger-painting in the yard in a plastic smock. When Lillian went to fetch her, the little girl was completely absorbed in her work, smearing alternating circles of blue and green on the page. Watching her for a moment, Lillian was filled with such a fierce love, such a desire to envelop and protect, that she hardly knew what to do next.

Now, in the guest room, which was formerly her room but which now bore very little resemblance to the room in which she remembered sipping from a purloined bottle of vodka her best friend, Heather, had procured from her mother's liquor cabinet, and in which she had spent numerous hours talking and listening to that very same Heather on her pink Princess phone (back when phones tethered you firmly to your location), Lillian pushed herself up on her elbows. Four minutes past eight. The baby, having settled himself again after his initial murmurings, was still asleep. Lillian could hear her mother's voice from downstairs, and Olivia's too, and a low baritone that belonged unmistakably to her father.

"Wake up," she whispered to Philip. It was time for a feeding— she could feel the tightness in her breasts that meant the ducts were filling. "Wake up," she whispered again. "I'm ready for you now."

But he slept on undeterred, curling a fist, raising it to his mouth, letting it fall again. She watched his chest move in and out, imagined the inner workings of his body, the astonishing efficiency with which his heart moved the blood around to the proper places.

Her sister, Rachel, seven years younger, not yet thirty, had driven up from New York City in a rented Impala to meet Philip four hours after he was born. Lillian had sat with sweaty, limp hair, watching Rachel, who looked particularly put together and glamorous, hold Philip. "God," Rachel said. "He looks so vulnerable."

She worked for a casting director in New York City; she had, in her years in Manhattan, adopted a brisk, no-nonsense way of talking that was a far cry from the volubility she had shown as a child. "I mean, Lilly, I think he's adorable. The fingernails and all of that — really, so tiny and perfect! But I wouldn't know what to do with him, day after day after day."

Then, in the flush after childbirth, in the brief stage of elation before the real fatigue set in, Lillian had felt pity for her younger sister, who had recently ended a relationship and was, as Ginny liked to say, "foundering." But now she thought that maybe her sister had the right idea after all: all that free time, all that *Sex and the City* posturing, all those brunches at sidewalk cafés.

The business with Tom was so awful, really so impossible to contemplate, that if Lillian let herself think too much about it she feared she might crumble, rendering herself incapable of taking care of either of her children. Which was partly — no, *mostly* — why she had come to Vermont, to be taken care of herself, and to deliver Olivia and Philip into the loving and doting arms of their grandparents.

Not that they were going to find that out. She would never — she would not, she would *absolutely not* — tell her parents. Nor would she tell Rachel, nor her brother, Stephen, whose wife, Jane, was expecting a baby later that summer, and who was so wrapped up in attending to her considerable needs that even if she told him her tale of woe he wouldn't have much time to absorb it.

Maybe, after all, she would tell Heather. Or maybe she wouldn't tell Heather. Maybe she would soldier through on her own, like those hardy and relentless women from long ago, working the fields in faded dresses and wide-brimmed hats, shouldering the burdens of the household while the husbands were off fighting in wars. Doing whatever they could, these women, to ensure the survival of the family.

She hadn't cried yet. Not when she told Tom she was leaving, not when she packed the car, not when she'd caught sight of her pouchy stomach in the bathroom mirror as she looked for the little cap shaped like a duck that was meant to go on top of Olivia's toothbrush. Not when she bent down to Olivia and told her to pick out three of her favorite toys and collect all of her bathing suits because they might be staying a little while.

"*All* my bathing suits?" Olivia's eyes grew wide.

"Yes, all of them."

She hadn't cried then, nor had she cried pulling out of the driveway or saying good-bye to the dog, who twice hopped into the back of the station wagon, thinking she was going along with them, but whom she entrusted to Tom because whatever his failings in the marriage department he was devoted to the dog.

But now, in the quiet of the room, surrounded by the things that were familiar and yet decidedly not so, it all began to seep out: the sorrow, the grief, the humiliation. Softly, with the pillow pressed to her nose, with her abdominal muscles clenched to keep the shaking of her shoulders to a minimum, Lillian began to cry.

⁕

The car eased through traffic on the West Side Highway. Beside Stephen, Jane closed her eyes. He put his hand on her arm and she let it stay there until he had to shift the car into a lower gear. Traffic had stopped.

"Okay?"

"Mmmm," she said. "Tired."

This impromptu trip to see his parents had been Stephen's idea, to get them out of the city. Which really meant to get *him* out of the city, or, more specifically, out of the apartment. He worked there, in their massive Tribeca loft, reviewing business books for a variety of publications, many of them obscure. He didn't, he often thought, know as much about business as he should for someone thus employed, but he was a good enough writer that he could generally fake it. Occasionally he took on a bit of freelance editing. The loft was big and open, with soaring windows, and, sitting in the corner that he had claimed as his home office, looking out at the trendy furniture boutiques and funky art galleries, he could nearly pretend that he was in an altogether different building from the place where he ate and slept. He said, if anyone asked (and they rarely did), that he took on the extra editing to pay the bills, but the truth was (and probably most people who inquired already knew this) that it was really Jane's job that paid the bills. His work provided something more akin to pocket money.

Jane worked as a managing director in midtown, in an office so sleek and so quietly stylish that each time he visited it Stephen came away with the feeling that he had been to a foreign country. The muted gray letters on the glossy black front of the building, the expensive art hanging on the walls, Jane's pale, graceful assistant with the emerald eyes: all of these spoke to Stephen of a world so immaculate and precise, so tidily prosperous, that he, with his overflowing desk and piles of books stamped with Post-it notes, could never hope to join it.

"So wonderful," his mother had said during a recent phone conversation, "that Jane enjoys her work so much. It will be a real adjustment for her when the baby comes." He had not, at that moment, or in any moment since then, corrected his mother. He had not told her that Jane was planning to return to work three weeks after the baby's birth. He had not told her that he himself, Stephen, with a master's degree (in English Literature, to be sure, but a master's degree nonetheless), was going to take a hiatus from working to care for the baby full-time.

He and Jane had talked about it *ad nauseam* (literally, it seemed to Stephen, because even into the middle of her second trimester Jane had suffered from bouts of morning sickness). They had agreed on the plan, they were both completely on board with it, and really it was a financial no-brainer, but even so Stephen found that he carried the plan around with him like a burden—like a terrible secret, which he had so far been able to divulge to nobody. Not to his friend Gareth, with whom he ran six miles every Saturday morning, not to either of his sisters, and certainly not to his mother.

Jane's mother was an altogether different story. Robin, a divorced psychologist with her own practice in midtown, was all for the arrangement in a way that Ginny certainly would never be.

"That's it," Robin said approvingly, as the three of them sat over dinner in a restaurant near her office one Thursday evening not long ago. "Enough of this rubbish with gender roles. You two do what's best for you, and never mind what the rest of the world says about it." Robin had blondish hair cut in a stylish manner, all angles and points, and she had, in the way that seemed unique to women of a certain age in Manhattan, failed to age a minute since Stephen had first met her, seven years ago.

"Though," she'd added patiently, laying a soothing hand on top of Stephen's, "you'll have to stop referring to the poor thing as *it*."

"I'll try," he had said.

Stephen, for all the time he spent waiting for and preparing for the baby's arrival, had not managed to develop an actual picture of what his days would entail once the baby turned from an *it* to a he or a she and acquired a name, a personality, clothes.

Sometimes, at lunch, he walked to a small, fenced-in playground near their building and sat with his wax-paper-wrapped sandwich to observe the children and caregivers he saw there. Mainly he saw foreign nannies of indeterminate origin, but occasionally the children were accompanied by their own mothers: smart-looking women in their midthirties, drinking from stainless-steel Starbucks mugs and comparing the features and faults of their strollers. Rarely did he see a father, and when he did it was typically a harried, expensively dressed bag of stress, typing frantically into a BlackBerry and glancing up intermittently to survey the action on the playground — clearly a stand-in for the regular caregiver.

Stephen had read all the requisite books about parenting that seemed to him to offer useful advice. He had learned — as much as one can learn from a book — all about diapering and feeding and burping, about the Back to Sleep campaign and the Ferber method and Dr. Spock's advice on soothing a teething baby. He was ready for the tremendous change that was going to come into their lives.

He was not, he was realizing, quite so ready for the changes in Jane. She had entered pregnancy as if entering a cocoon, protecting herself from the newly perceived dangers in the outside world. Caffeine. Mercury in fish. Bacteria lurking in seemingly benign slices of lunch meat or rounds of Brie. He watched her sometimes, when they were sitting in front of the television or when they went out to dinner, and on her small sharp features he could see evidence that she was pulling herself inward, girding herself for the battle she and the baby were going to wage against the world.

Now, in her seventh month, she had emerged from the cocoon into something altogether more brittle and unknowable, despite the new roundness in her breasts, the swell of her belly underneath the smart maternity pantsuits she wore to work.

They were on the New York State Thruway now. Jane opened her eyes and said, without turning her head toward him, "You should call them."

"I will, when we get a bit closer."

"But—"

"I *will*, when we get closer."

"We just don't want to show up there without any notice."

"Why? Who needs notice? They're always asking us to come up for a weekend. Every week I get an invitation. It will be good for you, you'll see. We'll do the sights of Burlington."

Jane, a lifelong New Yorker, snorted. "Such as they are."

"Such as they are!" he said ebulliently. "I'll take you to a cheese farm or something. Give you a taste of country life. We'll eat samples!"

"I can't eat soft cheeses."

"Well, then, the Ben and Jerry's factory. Free samples there too."

She laughed, reluctantly. "Still. I don't think they mean for us to show up without telling them first. Anyone wants notice before having overnight guests. Just call them. Please? Stephen? I don't want to just...*arrive*. I already feel conspicuous, dragging this belly around. I look awful. I don't want to show up uninvited on top of it. You know how your mother makes me feel—"

"We're always invited. A standing invitation. And I think you look beautiful," he said loyally. (He did think so.) "And my mother loves you to pieces." (She didn't.) But he relented, and said, just before Jane closed her eyes to fall properly asleep, "Fine. I'll call them. In just a few minutes. Promise."

But they hit a dead zone and his phone first lost reception, and then it lost its charge altogether, and they were making such good time that the act of stopping to find a pay phone seemed, in this day and age, anachronistic to the point of being foolish. So he just drove on and beside him Jane slept, her lips parted, a slight wheezing sound coming from her nose, both hands laid protectively over her belly.

"Hello," Stephen said softly to the baby inside her, the baby he couldn't quite picture but whom he already loved deeply, devotedly. "Hello, you little life-changer. Hello, thunderstorm."

They had to put the extra leaf in the dining room table for dinner that night to accommodate the lot of them. Ginny made lasagna and a green salad and sent William out at the last minute to Shaw's for a loaf of bread. He returned with two, having been unable to choose. William stepped out of the den when Lillian began to nurse Philip. "It's okay, Dad," Lillian said. "It's not a big deal. People do it in public all the time these days." But to him it was strange and inappropriate, this glimpse of the intimate, almost animal exchange of milk to mouth, the naked display of need and satiety. The slurping sounds! No, he would rather hover over Ginny in the kitchen, watching her slice the carrots, attack the cucumbers.

"I'm *hungry*," said Olivia from the den. "When's dinner?"

"Don't whine, Olivia. Just talk in your regular voice," said Lillian.

"But I'm *hungry*."

"That's still a whine." William could hear the sharp edge in Lillian's voice.

"I'm moving as fast as I can," said Ginny to the salad bowl. "William, will you set the table?"

But Stephen was already setting the table. Jane sat in one of the dining room chairs, tapping away at her BlackBerry.

"What's that?" asked Olivia, sidling up to her.

"I'm just doing some work," said Jane. She looked up briefly and considered Olivia with a combination of indulgence and anxiety.

"No, what's that *thing?*"

"It's called a BlackBerry."

Olivia thought about this. "No, it's *not,*" she said finally, authoritatively. "A blackberry is a fruit. Like a blueberry."

Jane was already looking back at the screen. "I know. It's funny, right? But this is also a BlackBerry."

"Olivia!" called Lillian from the den. "Stop bothering people."

"I'm not bothering! I'm helping."

Jane, frowning at the BlackBerry, said nothing.

At last they were all seated, the lasagna parceled out, the salad served, milk poured into Olivia's cup, wine into William's and Ginny's and Stephen's, water into Lillian's and Jane's.

"Grace?" said Ginny, and Jane, who had begun eating, put down her fork and folded her hands in her lap.

"Bless us, O Lord," began William. Only Ginny and William said the grace. Surely, thought William, this was an unnecessary rudeness on the part of his children, who had grown up saying that prayer nightly. Surely they had not forgotten each and every word.

Olivia ate her lasagna in typical three-year-old fashion, picking it apart and sorting the different types of food into disparate piles: a tiny mound of sauce, ribbons of noodles, a heap of ground beef.

"Oh, just *eat* it, Liv," said Lillian.

"In groups," said Olivia. "Not all together."

Philip, in his car seat next to Lillian's chair, squawked.

"Not you again," she said tenderly. "You wait. *I'm* eating." And then to Jane, and partly to Stephen, "Eat all you can now. You'll never sit down to a full meal again, I can promise you that."

"Oh, now," said Stephen. "Never?"

"Maybe when they're off to college," said Lillian.

Jane had set her BlackBerry on her lap before the meal began, under her napkin. Every now and then it vibrated, and she lifted the napkin to look at it.

"Sorry," she said. "I don't mean to be rude. But there's an incredible amount going on right now."

"It's a Saturday evening," said Ginny. "Surely there's nothing going on *now?*"

"There's always something going on," said Stephen. "You know what they say: the markets are always open somewhere."

"Really?" said Lillian. She had taken Philip out of his seat and was holding him awkwardly with one arm while she attempted to eat with the other hand. "Do they say that?"

"Or about to open," added Jane.

"In Japan," whispered Stephen, "it's already tomorrow."

William studied Jane. She was not beautiful. She was, in fact, perhaps the *least* beautiful of the girls and women Stephen had brought home over the years; her eyes were too small, her forehead too low, for true beauty. But William could see how there might be something lovely about her when she was working, something engaging and winsome about her utter certainty.

"How's your work going, Stephen?" asked William.

Stephen turned his head away from the baby to cough. "Okay," he said. "It's a living, I guess. Well, sort of. Part of a living." He glanced at Jane.

"You have a baby in your belly," said Olivia to Jane.

"That's right," said Jane. "And soon I will have a little baby, just like your baby brother there. Except it might be a girl. We don't know." She rubbed a hand in a circular motion on her stomach.

"And your work, Jane?" said William.

"Fine," she said. "Busy, always busy. But that's how I like it." She smiled; she had flawless teeth, very white and straight. William knew from his own children's orthodontist bills that this was an expensive smile.

"You love it, right?" said Lillian. She put down her fork and lifted Philip over her shoulder.

"Lillian," said Ginny. "You've eaten nothing. Give him to me."

"He's fine." Lillian kept her eyes on Jane, who was nodding eagerly.

"I do! I really do. I feel like—like every day I'm accomplishing something."

"Wow," said Lillian, steering Olivia's hands toward her fork. "I can't imagine feeling that way. Like I'm accomplishing something."

"Lillian!" said Ginny. "Look at your children. Of course you're accomplishing something." To Jane she said, "Will it be difficult to cut back your hours, Jane, once the baby is born?" Ginny reached over William for the salad bowl.

Jane looked hastily at Stephen. "The thing is," she began.

"It's not like that anymore," said Stephen. "With technology. You don't have to take any time off, really, not if you don't want to."

Ginny put the salad bowl down and stared at Stephen. "But why would you not want to?"

"Well—"

"I mean, surely you get a maternity leave?"

"Of course," said Jane.

"And then?"

"Ginny," said William. "We don't have to talk about all this now."

"But I want to talk about it," said Ginny. "I'm curious. I'm a curious and concerned grandmother-to-be."

"Cloth!" said Lillian suddenly. "Somebody get me a cloth!" Philip had unloaded his last meal onto her shirt.

"I will," said Stephen. "Tell me where."

"Bag," said Lillian. "Diaper bag, in the den. Yellow cloth. Hurry."

"For heaven's sake, use your napkin," said William.

"No!" said Ginny. "Don't use the napkin. Those came straight out of the dryer."

Stephen returned with the cloth, and Philip, reacting to the commotion, began to cry.

The BlackBerry buzzed again. Jane looked at it and laid it on top of the table.

"Jane," said Ginny, with exaggerated politeness. "I wonder if we couldn't turn that off, just for dinner. And finish this conversation."

"Mom!" said Stephen. "Easy."

"What? It's not a lot to ask."

"I want bread," said Olivia, reaching over her cup toward the basket.

"Careful!" said William and Ginny together. But it was too late: Olivia's arm hit the cup and knocked it over. For an instant they all watched as a pool of milk spread along the table and underneath Jane's BlackBerry.

"Shit," Jane said softly, then snatched it from the table and examined it for possible damage.

"I'll get paper towels," said William.

"I'm sorry," said Olivia, looking first to her mother, then to Ginny. Her mouth quivered.

"That's okay, sweetie," said Lillian. She looked pointedly at her mother. "It was an accident. And you should have had a sippy cup."

"I'm sorry," said Olivia again, this time in a whisper. Her shoulders bent toward each other, and her neck stuck forward. She looked to William like a little bird who was about to start pecking at something.

"She's three!" said Ginny. "She perfectly capable of using a regular cup." To Olivia she said, "It's okay, really." Olivia nodded.

William returned with the paper towels. "You know what they say about the spilled milk and the crying."

"Dad," said Lillian, shifting Philip. "Not now."

"It's not working," Jane whispered to Stephen. "I think maybe—"

"Heaven forbid," said Ginny quietly, watching her, mopping at the spill.

"No, really, it's not working—"

"It's okay," said Stephen. "Maybe it needs to dry out."

"It's not okay!" Jane stood abruptly, but it was clear that she had misjudged the size of her belly; she knocked against the table and the wineglasses shuddered. She stopped for a second, as if waiting for them to fall. When they didn't, she pushed her chair in deliberately, gathered her plate of lasagna in one hand and her BlackBerry in the other, and, leaving her water glass, leaving her salad, leaving her husband, and leaving the astonished audience, the mass of wet paper towels, and the now-quiet Philip, who had nuzzled into Lillian's neck and gone to sleep, she stomped off toward the den.

"Mom," said Stephen plaintively.

"What?" Ginny had returned from the kitchen with a full sippy cup of milk for Olivia, who accepted it and drank it, eyes wide, taking in the scene before her.

"You could go easier. She's my wife. She's stressed out. She's pregnant. And she's a guest."

"I know all that," said Ginny. "But—"

"But nothing," said Stephen. "We're only going to be here for two days. Can't we just have an easy visit?"

※

Lillian found Jane later on the deck, staring out into the dark yard. The deck lights were on, casting shadows on the table and on Jane's face and, beyond, on the woods that backed up against their yard.

"Here," Lillian said, offering a bottle of bug spray. "It can get pretty bad out here. I don't want you to get mauled."

"Thanks," said Jane. She took the bottle and peered at it in the darkness.

"Oh, Jesus," said Lillian. "I didn't even check it out. Is there some kind of special spray you're supposed to use when you're pregnant? I mean, I never did, but—"

"I don't know," said Jane. "But I'll use this. The mosquitoes love me."

"You must have a fast metabolism."

"Really? Is that a thing?"

"I heard it once. I don't know if it's true."

Lillian watched as Jane covered her bare arms with the spray. "You're carrying really well," she said.

"Ugh. I feel enormous."

"Well, you don't look it. You look fantastic." Lillian paused. "I'm sorry about all that, back there." She gestured toward the house. "I don't blame you for walking out, frankly. I'd have done the same thing in your situation."

"Really?" said Jane. "Well, I'm embarrassed. That isn't my typical behavior. I just can't seem to keep my emotions in line anymore. And my BlackBerry is fine, by the way. A lot of fuss over nothing."

"Perfectly normal," said Lillian. "Me too, with the nursing. I'm all over the place. Really, it takes almost nothing to set me off. And my mother—well, I can see why the two of you might rub each other the wrong way." She couldn't see Jane's face clearly, but she sensed a shift in her posture. That had come out the wrong way, probably, what she'd just said.

After a moment Jane said, "How are you with Tom's parents?"

Lillian slapped a mosquito in the air, and Jane slid the spray bottle back over to her. "We don't see them much. They retired in Florida and took up golf. They come up twice a year, and they keep talking, ominously, about how we'll have to take a trip to Disney World together sometime soon. But really they're very low mainte- nance. Freakishly tanned, but low maintenance."

"Your mother and my mother are complete opposites," said Jane. "They couldn't be more different. It confuses me."

"Your mother is...what? A doctor or something, right?"

"A therapist. Hard-driving, works a million hours a day, wouldn't have it any other way. The phone used to ring at two, three in the morning all the time. That was normal. That's what I grew up around. I think I can count the meals she cooked me on one hand."

"That's funny," said Lillian. "When I was young, in junior high school, I used to be so jealous of my friend Heather, because her mother worked, so she came home to an empty house. She got to do whatever she wanted until six o' clock, when her parents got home. God, I envied her! It wasn't until I had my own kids, really, that I appreciated what a blessing it was, having my mother around."

They sat there for a few moments and Lillian drank in the silence. Olivia had gone up with William to have her bath and Philip was taking his evening catnap. From a distance, low and musical, the sounds of a cricket came to her. She remembered how strange it seemed when she was a child, that one cricket could sound like thousands.

"Well, don't let it get to you," she continued. "She wants everyone to be happy, that's all. She just wants things to be happy and simple."

"I guess so," said Jane. "As if that's possible."

Lillian rose. "I think I should go in. Olivia is up way past her bedtime. She's teetering. I should be there when she loses it." Then, as she was about to push open the screen door, she said, "Tom cheated on me."

"*What?*"

"That's why I'm here. I left him. I ran away."

"You *did?*"

She sat back down. "I don't know why I just told you that. I wasn't going to tell anyone. That was my plan, don't tell anyone." She felt a thud in her stomach.

"Don't worry about me," said Jane. "I can keep a secret like nobody you've ever met."

"I don't want my parents to know."

"Of course you don't."

"Or Stephen. Not even Stephen."

"Cross my heart," said Jane, and Lillian could see that she was actually doing it, was actually crossing her heart as if she were a second grader. Lillian liked that. She made a move to rise from the chair, but she paused and said, "What would you have done? In the same situation?"

She expected some equivocation. She expected Jane to ask for the circumstances, the details. But Jane rose too, and it seemed like the cricket's call became stronger and nearer as she stepped closer to Lillian and said, "I would do the exact same thing. I would leave, and I wouldn't look back."

Sunday morning: church. Ginny knocked softly on Lillian's door. From inside she heard a faint rustling. "Lillian?" she said. "Lillian? There's church in forty-five minutes."

Nothing.

"There's a new priest. Father Colin. Visiting from Boston. Father Michael is in the hospital—"

Lillian opened the door. Her eyes looked pink. There were smudges of purple underneath them; she hadn't slept. She emerged from the room and closed the door behind her. "Father *Michael?*" she said. "He's still *alive?*" Father Michael had given her First Communion. He had been ancient then. He had confirmed her; he had heard her first confession; then, seven years ago, on a September day with the sky positively wiped clean of clouds, he had married her and Tom. Thinking about that, her throat caught. She felt embarrassed for herself the way you feel embarrassed for a child who falls down while she's running toward a playground. So much optimism, dashed.

"Alive, yes. But ailing. This new priest, though, you'd like him. He's young—oh, Lillian. You look positively *ragged*."

"Mom! Jesus, what do you expect? The baby was up four times last night—" She crossed her arms over her pajama top.

"Oh," said Ginny. "Well, I am sorry about that. But why don't you get dressed? Come to church with us. You'll feel better."

"I doubt it." Lillian examined a fingernail. Her feet were bare, the toenails painted red. "Is Stephen going? Is *Jane?*"

"I don't know," said Ginny. "I haven't asked them yet. I asked you first. And Jane isn't Catholic, so I doubt it."

"Well," said Lillian. "I'm not going. Take Olivia, if you want."

From downstairs Olivia called, "Take me *where?*"

"To church," called Ginny. "Let's get you dressed."

Lillian stood firm. "I am not going." She opened the door to the bedroom and closed it softly behind her.

*   *   *

In church, with Olivia sitting between her and William, Ginny experienced a feeling of serenity and optimism. Olivia was coloring resolutely on the children's bulletin with a crayon the lady behind them had given her. Father Colin, in the pulpit, was giving the sermon, and though Ginny knew she should have been paying attention she really wasn't; she was admiring his young, handsome face, and the way the light came in through the high square windows of the church, and the familiar faces of the congregation around her.

But the feeling dissipated quickly when they got home. Lillian was pacing the den with Philip, who was crying. She was wearing the same pajamas she'd been wearing when they left. Stephen and Jane were reading the *New York Times* at the kitchen table. They must have been out to buy the paper, and its presence at the table made Ginny feel inferior, made all of Vermont, indeed, feel inferior. The kitchen, with pieces of Lillian's breast pump scattered around it, seemed small and cluttered.

Later that day Ginny escaped to the basement: laundry. The washer and dryer were new, front loading, cranberry red; an indulgence Ginny had allowed herself a few months ago when the old washing machine had sputtered, sighed, and succumbed finally and dramatically to old age.

"My God," Lillian had said the day before, coming down with a pile of Philip's damp and sour-smelling onesies (he was a champion spitter). "Flashy, aren't they?"

And Ginny, having no patience for what, long ago, when Lillian was in high school, with a row of glittering studs in each ear and blue mascara turning her lovely eyelashes into something bright and ghastly, she had privately termed her oldest child's *superior attitude,* had pressed her lips together, saying nothing.

The washing machine and dryer were supremely efficient, with Energy Star labels to prove it; they had the incredible ability to figure out how large a load was without Ginny's having to tell them a thing; they fit together handsomely in a way that the old washing machine and dryer, purchased long ago but at different times and from different manufacturers, never had done. They made her happy, and they turned laundry from a dreaded chore into a rather pleasurable task, and she was not—she was *not*—going to let Lillian take away that pleasure from her.

Ginny moved a mass of damp towels into the dryer. She had a load of whites ready to fold. William's whites, as it happened, had become rather gray; surely, she told him, it wouldn't put them under financially to invest in a few new T-shirts or a couple of nice short-sleeved knits, the kind with collars and a logo of some sort over the pocket. But William was not much of a shopper and didn't see the point in spending money on something that he only planned to dirty.

And dirty them he would, to be sure. Since selling his landscaping company and moving into semiretirement William had begun to spend much of his time in their garden, which, over the decades, had been often neglected to allow William to focus on other people's gardens and yards.

"You know what they say!" he'd said cheerfully for much of their early married life, pulling at a weed in the bed of salvia that was crying out for a pruning. "The cobbler's children have no shoes. Or is it the tailor's children have no clothes?"

And Ginny, grimly chopping carrots or mopping up spilled juice, had not answered.

Ginny peeled off a dryer sheet from the stack and tossed it into the dryer, then for good measure another one. There had been a time in her life when laundry had been her greatest source of stress and anxiety, when she felt that she could have reduced her sleeping time to three hours a night and still would not get everything in the various hampers throughout the house sorted, carted to the basement, washed, folded, and put away before they all filled up again. Since the children had cleared out—really that was only five years ago, if you counted the postcollege stints when Rachel took over Lillian's old room, preferring it, always, then and now, to her own, smaller room just down the hall—her attitude toward the task had changed considerably.

Now Ginny found laundry to be calming and satisfying; she took care with stains and hand-washables; she carried the stacks of folded clothes up the stairs with a sense of vigor and purpose and put them away immediately.

Yesterday, soon after Jane and Stephen arrived, and before the disastrous dinner, Jane had produced a small bag of laundry from her smart black rolling overnight bag and asked Ginny if she minded if she washed it while they were there.

"Of course not," said Ginny.

"I hope that's all right. The machine in our building—"

"Broken again," interjected Stephen. "It's *always* broken."

"I don't know how you people live that way, sharing a machine with strangers," said Ginny, holding out her hand for the bag.

"Oh, well. We don't," said Jane. "We usually send it out. To the wash and fold. But I didn't know we were coming"—here Ginny looked pointedly at Stephen—"and I need a few things for the week, and there won't be time when we get back."

"The wash and fold! Even worse," said Ginny. "Other people touching your underwear. That doesn't bother you?"

"They don't care, Mom," said Stephen. He rubbed his hand in a circle on Jane's back. "It's New York City. Everything is anonymous."

"Anonymous," said Ginny. She thought of Rachel, shacking up with that man who had broken her heart, poor Rachel with her career anxiety and her expensive, impractical shoes and handbags and her enormous rent. "Even so, I shouldn't think I'd want anyone else washing *my* underwear." She realized after she'd spoken how sharp her voice sounded; she'd meant her comments mostly as an entrée into conversation but found that suddenly she was committed to a point of view and felt she had to press on, arguing a topic on which she truly had no strong feelings. She did not, at the end of the day, care what Jane and Stephen did with their laundry.

She kept her hand out insistently until finally Jane said, "Oh, heavens. I didn't mean for you to do it! I was only asking if I could use your machine."

"Of course I knew what you meant," said Ginny briskly, mildly irritated (she hadn't, after all, been sure). "But I've got some going in tomorrow anyway. I'll add yours to it."

This, precisely, was the effect that Jane had on Ginny, that she'd always had on her, from the sticky Friday evening in July eight years ago when Ginny, who had been canning tomatoes in the kitchen, and who was splattered with red tomato guts and little bits of seeds, had opened the door to find her only son standing on the porch, holding the hand of a woman with small sharp features and a simple, elegant haircut that even to Ginny's untrained eye looked expensive and said, in an uncharacteristically giddy voice, "Mom? I'd like you to meet the girl I'm going to marry."

Jane set Ginny off balance, that day and for all days that followed.

They said, didn't they, that you never really lost your sons, as a mother. You lost your daughters, because they became absorbed into another man's house, into a family of their own, but your sons always remained loyal to you. They said that every woman should have at least one son for precisely that reason.

Now here was Jane, with her gold wristwatch, with her business degree and her lucrative career, with Stephen's baby taking shape inside that bulging stomach on the tiny frame—here was Jane, making Ginny feel as though she'd broken one of the most important rules of motherhood, making her feel as though, despite all her precautions, despite her careful attempts at loving and granting privacy, she'd lost her son.

She tried to call up the sensation of peace and harmony she'd felt during Mass. During Communion, Father Colin bent down to Olivia and had laid his hands on her head to bless her. Ginny could tell, from the startled way Olivia looked at the priest, that this was not a common occurrence. Most likely the child hadn't been in a church since she'd been baptized, and here was Philip, three months old, and no sign of a baptism being planned for him.

Now, in the basement, Ginny realized that she had forgotten to mix Jane's laundry in with theirs; she'd have to put in a separate load after all. Perhaps she would have been better off letting Jane handle it herself. She opened the bag and unloaded its contents into a basket. Jane's underwear wasn't in there, that was true, but a few pairs of Stephen's boxer shorts were. One pair was covered with little yellow ducks, and another had mocha-colored coffee cups scattered across it.

Ducks! For a man of thirty-four. This was an absurdity. Surely Jane had bought those for Stephen. Ginny couldn't imagine Stephen going to any sort of trouble to choose decorations for his boxer shorts. As a child, and later as a teenager, he had been the sort of boy to care very little what clothes he put on or how his hair was cut or combed; even in high school, when he had begun to attract the attention of a series of girls — all of them, it seemed to Ginny, similarly sprayed and glossed and poured into tight jeans with zippers at the ankle — he had done so despite (or maybe because of) his complete lack of fussiness or awareness of his appearance.

With the machine comfortably chugging away she was free to go upstairs, but she didn't want to. Stephen and Jane had retreated to the den with the rest of the paper. Lillian was upstairs nursing the baby — Lillian was always, it seemed, upstairs nursing the baby — and Olivia was out in the yard with William, playing an elaborate game involving a pink rubber ball and three princess dolls leaning against the pines. Occasionally Ginny could see two white sparkly-sneakered feet run past the rectangular basement window; she could also, in the pauses between the washing machine gurgles, make out William's voice and Olivia's high giggle.

Really, William's patience with his granddaughter was endless, commendable, even, Ginny sometimes admitted privately, enviable.

She didn't feel like joining them. She felt like sitting. So she sat for a moment in an old black rocker that had once lived, by turns, in each of the children's rooms. It was this chair in which she had read *Goodnight Moon* to each of them, in which she had comforted them and rocked each of them to sleep. Sitting there she could almost feel Rachel's head nuzzle into her neck; she could smell the baby shampoo in Lillian's soft duckling hair.

Most of the basement was cluttered and chaotic, a microcosm of their family life, all its histories and warts and honors. There, for example, was the trophy Stephen had won in the state cross-country championships his senior year in high school, in which he took third. There was the cardboard box of jelly jars, some with lids and some without, that Ginny had begun saving for some sort of school project for Rachel and then, out of habit, had continued saving. There was the disorderly stack of mismatched curtains removed from numerous rooms in the house during assorted painting undertakings. Surely they would never be hung again; they were variously dirty or torn or hopelessly out of fashion — but still they remained.

Now she let her eyes roam past the washing area to the shadows of the rest of the basement. It was appalling to her, when she really stopped to look around, how much *stuff* they had accumulated since they'd moved into the house thirty-five years prior, when she was pregnant with Stephen and Lillian was just a toddler. There was the elderly ten-speed, yellowy brown, that Lillian had taken to riding back and forth to friends' houses the summer she was thirteen. There was the jumble of metal and cords with which William had once aspired to build a reading lamp for the den. There was the heap of paintings Rachel had created one humid August, shutting herself in an empty bay of the garage with an easel and canvases and white tubes of oil paint on which the names of the colors were written in a deep and foreboding black: burnt sienna, cobalt teal, Portland gray deep.

Suddenly she felt a thrust of nostalgia so powerful it was like a pain: nostalgia for Rachel's intensity that August; for Stephen's running singlets, draped over the back of the chair in his room; for the sight of Lillian's hair blowing out behind her as she careened into the driveway on her bike.

She knew, of course, that she could appreciate these details, the textures of her children's childhoods, only in hindsight. She remembered how annoying it had been to peel the singlets from the chair; she remembered how the damp from the sweat of them had warped the wood and how cross she'd been about that, throwing them all in an angry heap in the middle of Stephen's room. She remembered how often Lillian, out on the bike, had been late for dinner that summer, and she remembered the frustration she had felt trying to remove oil paint from the fabric of one of the dining room chairs.

In the moment, you were often too tired to enjoy watching your children turn into people. It was such a busy time, so demanding. There was always somebody with a science project due the next day, always a lesson or a practice to get to, always a meal to cook or a stray mitten to find.

And then suddenly everyone had cleared out, flung themselves into the big world, two of them to New York City, Lillian to Massachusetts, calling, sure, e-mailing often, even visiting, but they were gone, truly gone, replaced by the silence — beautiful and blessed, of course, but still, sometimes, she had to admit, strange and unnatural.

She heard a footfall on the stairs.

"Mom? You down here?" Lillian appeared, holding the baby, walking carefully. Philip was wrapped in a pale green blanket; he was sleeping with one red fist raised toward his head, as though he had succumbed to slumber in the middle of a cheer.

Most of Lillian's baby weight was gone, except for a soft part around her normally slender middle, but Ginny could see that her face looked rather drawn and gray; the lavender circles around her eyes were still there. She wore no makeup, and there was a child's red barrette holding her hair haphazardly back from her face. "What are you doing?"

"Nothing," said Ginny. "Overseeing the laundry."

Lillian made a small face of disapproval or irritation. "I almost slipped on the stairs," she said. "Maybe you should think about carpeting them."

"Carpeting the cellar stairs?"

"Maybe. Oh, I don't know. Don't listen to me. I slept for about a minute last night."

"You poor thing," said Ginny.

"And I'm dying for a coffee—but that goes right into the breast milk, and it's not worth the risk, messing him up for sleep—"

"Surely a little bit won't hurt him. Half a cup?"

"Maybe. I don't know."

"I could put another pot on."

Lillian sighed deeply and dramatically. "Don't go to the trouble, just for me. Only if you were going to make some."

"Well, I wasn't. I've had mine."

"Then never mind."

"But it's no trouble. It's just coffee."

"I don't know. No, forget it. I don't want it."

For an instant Ginny saw the teenaged Lillian standing before her, with her neon earrings and her identically dressed friend Heather, both of their expressions slightly derisive.

"Sweetheart," she said, and Lillian's shoulders twitched.

Ginny peered at the baby. "Sleeping," said Lillian. "Until I put him down. Then—bam! Awake."

"Try the car seat."

"I did! He woke up."

"The Pack 'n Play?"

"Same."

"The BabyBjörn?"

"Hurts my back."

"Adjust the straps?"

"Tried. Didn't help."

The dryer buzzed. Ginny rose from the chair and opened the

door, pulling out the warm towels. "So delicious," she said to Lillian. "Isn't it? A pile of warm towels. Smell."

"I guess," said Lillian, not smelling. She looked down at the baby and chewed the outside of her lip.

"Oh, honey. He needs to learn to sleep by himself. Otherwise you'll end up with—"

"With what?"

"With a very grumpy disposition."

"For me or him?"

"Either. Both."

"Ha." Lillian rolled her eyes. "I might be stuck with that anyway." She surveyed the basement, the various mountains and piles. "What are you keeping all this around for—all this junk?"

Ginny ignored the question. "It's okay to let him cry a little bit, you know. So he gets used to going to sleep. I did that with all of you children."

"I bet you did," said Lillian, smiling wanly.

Ginny shook out one of the towels and picked a ball of lint off it, not looking at Lillian.

"I know you're right," said Lillian. "I know that, I do. I'm just not sure how to do it. It was so much easier with Olivia. Why was it so much easier?" She sat down heavily on the last basement stair, the motion disturbing Philip briefly but not fully awakening him.

Ginny thought about that. She wiped at the outside of the detergent bottle, where some of the contents had leaked. "Well, she was all you had to do. She was your universe." Lillian looked pained. "You could afford to hold her all day."

"I know."

"But this one... you just can't. You've got too many other things to do. You've got to put him down."

Lillian took a deep breath. "I know. I mean, I know that, in my

head. But he's still so small. And it just feels wrong, when everything is so—"

"So what?" Ginny folded the last of a stack of towels and moved
the stack into the waiting laundry basket, then moved the basket to
the foot of the stairs.

"I don't know," said Lillian. "Nothing. I'm just tired. I'm *so*
tired, Mom. Do you mind if I sneak in a nap?"

"Of course not," said Ginny, minding a great deal. She had
wanted to put the laundry away, then straighten the kitchen, then
pop out to Shaw's for more fruit. Olivia had eaten it all.

"If you mind, I'll go ask Dad."

"I don't mind," said Ginny. "Not at all. And anyway Dad's in
the yard with Olivia."

"Oh," said Lillian. Then, "That's sweet. He's good with her."

"He is," said Ginny, smiling hard at the towels before she turned
to take Philip from Lillian. She watched her daughter carefully. She
looked…what? More than tired, beyond exhausted. *Defeated.*
Ginny felt a swell of tenderness, of protectiveness. It wasn't easy,
any of it.

"Chin up, my girl!" she said. It was an exhortation left over from
her own mother, which in turn Ginny said often to her children.
They had uniformly disliked it when she'd said it to them, had given
over to sneers and unadulterated sighs. And still she'd kept saying
it, believing, somehow, as her mother had before her, in the refrain,
in the ability of people to will themselves out of despair.

"Right," said Lillian. Ginny watched her slow progress up the
stairs, then turned her attention to the baby in her arms.

"Philip," she said softly. She sat again in the old rocker. If she
closed her eyes, if she ignored the damp smell of the basement and
the chug of the washing machine, she could imagine that she was
in one of her children's bedrooms sometime in the distant past.
She adjusted Philip so that his head fit exactly in the crook of her

arm. He shifted but remained asleep; his breath came steadily, resolutely. His head was hard against her arm.

You never forgot, once you'd had children, how to hold a baby. You could almost never hold a baby without believing, for an instant, that it was yours. Philip's weight in her arms was steady, unwavering. She looked at the tiny web of blood vessels on his eyelids, at his pale lashes, at his small pursed lips. *Philip.*

⁘

Rachel wasn't expecting anyone on a Sunday so when her door buzzer first sounded she ignored it. When Marcus moved out she had scratched his name off the label next to the buzzer downstairs and in the process — out of negligence or anger or overzealousness, or possibly all three — had scratched off part of her name. Since then she got the occasional errant ring.

She had been out earlier in the day for the paper and a coffee. She hadn't bothered to do anything with her hair, and she hadn't taken any care with her clothes. She found a crumpled pair of yoga pants and a tattered sweatshirt in the bottom of her closet, and these she donned quickly, almost haughtily, as though by wearing them she was somehow punishing the society that had wronged her. She was reading an article about the upcoming Tony Awards in the *Times. In the Heights, August: Osage County, Passing Strange.* She longed to go to the Tony Awards. She longed for her job as a casting assistant to bring her someday close enough to that glittering stage. She put down the arts section and picked up the magazine: a lengthy article about equal parenting. She studied the photographs of pint-sized violin players and children frolicking across large green lawns while their parents looked on adoringly. This had even less to do with her. She put it down.

The buzzer sounded again. She pushed the button on the intercom and waited.

"Babe?"

It was Marcus.

"Babe? Are you there?"

"Marcus?" she said. She felt a flutter in her chest; she had to put her hand on top of her heart and press down to rid herself of the sensation of impending cardiac arrest.

"Yup. Are you going to let me up? Or should I stand here until the lady with the dancing dogs comes in?" The lady with the dancing dogs had been their neighbor; she had a pair of poodles that sometimes walked half a block on their hind legs. True story.

Trying to ignore the waves of trepidation that washed over her, she pressed to let Marcus in.

Their previous meeting, a month earlier, had been disastrous, from Rachel's point of view. Marcus had come to sign a paper that allowed Rachel to close a joint checking account they had opened—stupidly, nearsightedly, it turned out, but nonetheless there it was. Marcus worked as a sales rep for a wine distributor; he had brought a bottle of a new Malbec for her to taste. Taste it she did, and then she tasted more, and soon enough they had tasted most of the bottle, and instead of dealing with the bank account they had gone to bed.

After, they lay on the sheets that she bought six months prior, when they moved into the apartment together. Seeing Marcus once again in the bed reminded her of the unfamiliar state of bliss and joyfulness in which she had resided for a short time back then, and the sense that accompanied it, that after so many years of searching she had found what she'd been looking for.

She hadn't, of course. It turned out that Marcus, despite his sexiness, his generosity, his humor, and the talent he had for laying to rest the panic that occasionally surfaced inside her, was happy to leave things as they were forever. He was happy, indeed, to live eternally the life of twenty-somethings (though he had passed thirty and she was quickly approaching it), that life being a life of permanent impermanence, of being connected but not tethered, allied in mind and spirit but not in name.

One day he had said this to her: "I can stay forever, just like this. *Forever,* Rachel. Or I can go now. But you've got to stop pushing for marriage."

She took a deep breath and, without looking at Marcus, said, "I understand."

She swallowed. "And I think you should go now."

She hadn't really thought, as she said it, that he would.

But he had.

He moved out one Saturday morning three months ago, taking with him not only a giant brown duffel bag and the blender in which he made his protein smoothies, but also her ability to pay the rent without a considerable — really, a *very* considerable, so considerable that if she thought about it too much she developed an ache along the edges of her brain — strain on her finances.

The sex a month ago was not, she was certain, disastrous from Marcus's point of view. Nothing was ever disastrous from Marcus's point of view, and it was that blitheness of spirit, the devil-may-care attitude, the antidote to her neuroticism, that she missed the most. (Neuroticism? She had not grown up neurotic, had she? No, certainly not. So when had she become so?)

He tapped softly on the door, but she had unlocked it after she buzzed him in so it swung open. He looked freshly showered and alluringly tousled, carrying his familiar navy blue gym bag.

"Oh," she said, looking at the bag. "I haven't been to the gym in ages."

"I figured. I was looking for you."

"You were?" Her heart lifted briefly.

"Yeah. I was going to ask you—"

"Yes?" She felt herself stand straighter.

"I thought I left my sneakers behind—the Nike ones, that you use with the iPod?"

"Oh." The only thing Marcus had left behind was a red T-shirt, faded to a sort of apologetic pink, that bore the name of a Fourth of July road race he had run in his hometown several years ago. This T-shirt Rachel had folded carefully and placed in the bottom drawer of her dresser, underneath a pile of tank tops. She had no intention of returning it.

"No," she said. "No, sorry."

"You sure?"

"Sure. You could have called, though. To ask." She thought of adding, *I wouldn't have thought you were calling to woo me back.* But didn't.

"I know," he said. "But I was in the neighborhood. And I thought—" He looked toward the bedroom. She crossed her arms.

"You thought?"

He moved closer. He smelled good; she had forgotten, in the months since she'd lived without him, how good a freshly showered man could smell, and how innocent.

"Listen," he said. "I—"

"You have to go," she said. "Marcus? You have to go."

"Aw, come on, Rach," he said. "Don't be like that."

"Be like what?" she said in a strangled voice.

"Why can't we just have a little fun? That was fun, last time. Right?" He put his hand to the back of her neck and stroked softly with one finger.

"Yes," she said truthfully. "That was fun."

"So why can't we have a little more fun?"

"We can't have a little fun," she said, "because to me it wouldn't be fun, again. To me it would be serious." Still she didn't move away.

"Rachel," he said, sighing regretfully, dropping his hand from her neck, moving backward. "That's your problem, you know? That's your biggest, one and only problem. You take things too seriously. You're missing out by doing that." He shrugged, a small, familiar spasm of his shoulders, and she looked away, because she knew that to let him see her crying now would be a humiliation she couldn't bear to suffer. She looked steadily out the window while he gathered his bag, took one last look around for his shoes, kissed her on the cheek, and let himself out the door.

-'⁄⁄⁄⁄-

Lillian didn't nap. Instead she called Heather, who had grown up around the corner and who had eventually, along with her husband and two sons, taken over her parents' house when they retired to a planned community in Arizona. Once Philip fell asleep she collected him from Ginny and deposited him in the car seat. He was dozing there when Heather arrived.

"Well," said Heather, dropping her purse on a dining room chair, peering into the car seat. "He's *perfect*, Lil."

"I know," said Lillian, smiling. "He is, right?"

"Look at his fingers! The way they float in the air while he's sleeping. I forgot about that."

"I know," said Lillian. "He's delicious. I swear to God I could eat him."

"So could I!" Heather practically shouted. "So could I." She took a step back and reached into her bag for a package wrapped in blue tissue paper.

"Oh!" said Lillian. "But you already—"

"I know. But it's just a little something. For you, really, more than for Philip."

Lillian rustled the tissue paper and pulled out a small square black box. She opened it and found inside a gold charm in the shape of a boy's face in profile.

"Oh, Heather—"

"Someone gave me one for Ethan," said Heather. "And I don't know, I'm not a big charm bracelet person, but I just loved it. See the little cowlick there? God. It just breaks your heart, or something."

"I love it," said Lillian.

"It's engravable," said Heather proudly. "I was going to get it engraved for you, there's a place in Winooski that's actually pretty good, but I wasn't sure what you'd want it to say."

"Heather," said Lillian, and she could feel a quiver beginning in her lip.

"That's a lie," said Heather. "I just ran out of time, really. I would have put his initials, something simple like that, but—"

"Heather."

"Oh, come on. You're not going to cry. Are you? Are you, Lilly? It's just a charm."

"No, I'm not going to cry," said Lillian, but she could feel her eyes filling, and she turned her head away and looked steadily at her shoulder.

"But, then, you're nursing...the hormones."

"It's not the charm," said Lillian. "It's not the hormones."

"Then what?"

Lillian shook her head. "Heather," she said, and she began to cry in earnest. "Heather, I left Tom."

"Oh, sweetie," said Heather. She reached out to Lillian, but Lillian, having heard the back door open, held up her hand.

"Let's just go for a walk," she whispered. "Let's go." She composed her voice enough to call out to her parents. "Philip's right here," she called. "He's sleeping! Just keep an ear out. We're going for a walk."

In the yard next door, Mr. Anderson, who had seemed to Lillian to be old when she was in junior high school and now was positively decrepit, was poking at weeds with a long metal stick.

"Rachel!" he called over. "Out for a walk?"

"Hello, Mr. Anderson," she answered. "It's Lillian. Rachel's my little sister." He cupped a hand to his ear and she shook her head and waved and walked on.

They set off toward the lake, which lay before them, calm and glittering, inviting.

"Say what you want about the ocean," said Lillian. "And Tom says plenty, Massachusetts boy that he is. But I love this lake more than anything."

She and Heather had learned to swim in this lake, the mothers in the neighborhood pooling their money to pay for the services of an instructor. "Remember sitting barefoot at that picnic table?" said Heather, pointing. "Chewing a sandy peanut butter sandwich?"

Lillian nodded. She remembered jumping off the dock. She remembered the annual Fourth of July cookout the neighborhood put on together.

"I still go to that," said Heather. "Every year."

It seemed to Lillian now to have happened so quickly, the transition from what she was then—the carefree girl with the peanut butter sandwich—to what she was now. Did it feel that way to everyone? Was this just life?

In between the sandwich and the infidelity, of course, there were other stages: high school, college, the years after college. Wedding planning, preparing for a baby. And now what was she planning for?

"Tell," said Heather softly. "Tell what happened with Tom."

Tom. She swallowed hard and clenched her fists. She walked faster.

"Tell me," said Heather. "That's what I'm here for."

So Lillian told. "This girl, Heather—you wouldn't believe it if you saw her. She's Tom's assistant. And he *slept* with her."

"Oh, God," said Heather. "Really? That doesn't sound like Tom."

"I know. But he *did*."

"Have you met her?"

"Just once, when I swung by to show Philip off to the crew there. She's *young*, she's really young. I mean, she's just out of college. She's got a snub nose and a perfectly flat stomach. She's got this space between her front teeth—oh, I can't even stand to think about her. She says *like* every other word, she texts people who are standing right across the room from her." Lillian paused, then said, "She seriously, legitimately belongs to another generation. That's how young she is."

Lillian and Heather sat on a bench by the lake, not far from an outcropping of rocks that Lillian remembered climbing on as a child. There was a group of three boys, teenagers, on the dock. They wore long, bright swimming trunks; they were taking turns jumping into the water from the dock. Lillian watched them for a moment, watched their tanned, sinewy bodies, their complete lack of self-consciousness.

"Oh, Jesus, Lilly, I'm sorry. What do you think you'll do?"

Lillian wrapped her arms around her knee. "I don't know. What choice do I have, really?"

Heather lifted her face to the sun and then looked levelly at Lillian. "What choice do you have? Well, you have two choices. Stay, or go. Or make him go. Three choices."

"But the kids—"

"I know," said Heather. "The kids. The kids are huge."

It had come as a surprise to Lillian, motherhood, despite her attempts to prepare beforehand, despite her careful observations of the young mothers in her neighborhood, despite her copious reading of the books her friends who were already mothers had pressed into her hands.

The biggest surprise, in fact, was that her new world, this complex, labyrinthine universe, did not seem to be so different from the world that her mother had inhabited, and that *her* mother, in turn, had inhabited before her. It confused Lillian that that had happened. The world—society, all of it—seemed to be moving forward, the role of women in the workforce, in business and science, seemed to be changing and strengthening, and yet Lillian's current position remained essentially unchanged from what it had been for generations.

There was one notable difference, of course.

"What do you call yourself?" she asked Heather. Heather adjusted her sunglasses and looked out at the lake.

"What do you mean?"

"I mean once you stopped working, to be with Max and Ethan. What do you call yourself?"

"A stay-at-home mother."

"Me too. But isn't that funny? If anyone asked my mother what she did, she would have said, 'I'm a housewife.' Or 'I'm a homemaker.' But we—you, me, everyone in my town—we're stay-at-home mothers. And we'd be insulted if anyone called us housewives. Why is that?"

"I don't know," mused Heather. "To me, a housewife insinuates that you wear some sort of a kerchief wrapped around your head to clean the house."

Lillian laughed. "Or an apron, with piping."

"See?" said Heather. "You haven't forgotten how to laugh."

"But where did that come from, that change? How was it that our mothers' generation found some pride in *making a home,* while for us the housekeeping part of the job seems like a slight?"

"I don't know," said Heather. "I think maybe because we gave up on keeping things clean?"

Lillian thought of her laundry room, perpetually littered with the detritus of Olivia's constant costume changes, and of the kitchen, whose countertops seemed never to be free of a certain unidentifiable stickiness, and whose pantry seemed always to be missing two or more crucial items.

Making a home.

Ha.

She looked away for a second, back at the street, where two little girls a bit older than Olivia were navigating bicycles with training wheels while their mothers trailed behind them, one dragged by an enormous German shepherd.

When she turned back to the lake, she saw two of the teenaged boys standing on the dock and leaning over the water. It seemed like a long time that they stood there, and Lillian felt her heartbeat begin to speed up. The third boy was missing.

"Shit," she heard one of them say.

"Heather." She gripped Heather's arm. She felt in her pockets, but they were empty. "I don't have my cell…"

"Me either," said Heather. "I could run back—or over across the street." She stood. Lillian stood also. She was trying to think if she remembered CPR from the class she had taken at the Y.

Suddenly the third boy launched himself out of the water, spitting like a whale, laughing.

"You asshole," said one of the boys on the dock.

"You total bastard, you suck," said the other.

"Naw, man."

"No, you're an asshole! I though you drowned."

Only he said "drownded."

The boys didn't notice Lillian and Heather. One boy cannonballed off the dock. *Be careful,* Lillian wanted to say. *I grew up here. The rocks are really sharp.*

But they wouldn't want to hear that from her, wouldn't pay her any heed, and anyway Philip was probably due for a feeding.

"I've got to get back," said Heather, stretching.

"Me too," said Lillian. "But I'll walk you to your house first."

After, Lillian didn't feel like going back. Instead of turning toward her house she continued up the hill, through the neighborhoods up toward Route 7. The houses were a little smaller here, and closer together, shabby and well kept intermixed.

She passed the road that led to Burton Snowboards. She thought of the boys jumping into the lake. They'd be snowboarders, she could tell by the easy way they had with their bodies, and by the skateboards they'd left in the grass by the docks.

She passed the turnoff to the rock-climbing gym. When she had grown up here, there had been no rock-climbing gym—only a scrubby field where some kids in high school used to come and drink beer from cans late at night in the summer. She felt suddenly, irrationally angry at the rock-climbing gym for not existing during her youth. Perhaps she would have grown into a different person if it had been there: more daring, more adventurous. Perhaps, instead of marrying and having children, she would have become a fabulously audacious rock climber; perhaps she would have traveled the world, tied to nothing or no one but the mountain.

Then she thought of Olivia a month or so ago, calling down the stairs to Lillian when she was supposed to have been sleeping, with a question she deemed important. "If you have lunch and dinner at the same time, would that be linner?"

"Yes," Lillian said. "Yes, Olivia, that would be linner." And she and Tom had dissolved into giggles.

She could, if she felt like taking a long walk, go all the way downtown from here. She turned left on Pine Street. She calculated how long it would take to get to Church Street—two miles, more or less, if she went by the road. Perhaps longer if she cut down to the bike path, but she'd be walking along the water, which would be nicer. But then she wasn't sure she felt up to dealing with summer crowds on Church Street: all those happy, wholesome families. All that sticky ice cream. And she couldn't be gone from Philip that long.

She came to the church. The parking lot was empty; the noon Mass was long over. In the corner of the parking lot, there were a couple of kids on scooters. The day had grown warm, and Lillian was sweating and thirsty. She had no water with her, and no money to stop at the convenience store across the street. Perhaps if she could just rest for a moment—perhaps if she stepped inside the church. Surely it was cooler in there than it was out here.

Later, after all that had happened that summer, she would remember the way she felt standing outside the heavy wooden door that day. She would remember, too, the way she felt watching the boys on the dock. She would remember the sun beating down over the water, and she would remember the feeling that despite the clarity of the lake, despite the fact that nothing, after all, had happened, the day had turned dark and sinister.

※

William had to go to Williston for some bonemeal to put in the flower beds. Olivia wanted to go along.

"Go," said Ginny. "I'll watch the little one until Lillian returns. Olivia, run and get your sandals."

It took William some time to navigate Olivia's car seat straps. "You know," he told Olivia. "When your mother and your uncle Stephen and aunt Rachel were young, we didn't have all of this. We just threw the kids in the back of the car and hoped for the best."

Once William had pulled out of the neighborhood and onto the highway, he glanced in the rearview mirror. He was startled, for an instant, by how like Lillian at that age Olivia looked: the same flame-colored hair, the same fragile skin, the same thumb sucked in the same unvarying rhythm.

"It's kind of nice to get away from the baby brother for a while, isn't it?" he said in a conspiratorial voice.

Olivia nodded.

"Maybe when we're at the garden center," he continued, "you can pick out a few flowers for your very own pot."

"My very own *pot?*"

"You got it. Would you like that?"

Vigorous nodding from the backseat.

"Okay, then. We'll do it. Olivia's Very Own Pot."

"And I can show my daddy, when he comes."

"Sure."

"Grandpa? When is my daddy coming?"

"I don't know," said William. "I don't know how long you're staying. Do you?"

Olivia shook her head.

"Did your mother say, when you packed up?"

"No. But I brought all my bathing suits."

"Oh yeah?"

"And I have a lot of bathing suits."

"Do you? How many?"

"Thirty. A hundred. Thirty a hundred."

"Wow," said William. "That's a lot, all right."

"I know," said Olivia proudly. "So I guess we're staying a long time."

Lillian pushed open the door of the church. It was dark and heavy—foreboding. You would think that if they really wanted you to go to church they'd make it a little easier to open the door.

She couldn't recall another time in her life when she'd been in a completely empty church. She couldn't recall a time when she'd so wholly taken in the atmosphere of *this* church: the smell of must and incense, and of the bodies that had been there earlier in the day. The worn spots in the carpet up the center aisle. The way the stained glass caught the sunlight and sent it in fragments over the pews. The missalettes leaning in the stands. She could almost feel their tissue-thin paper, and the sturdier pages of the song-books. Not even on her wedding day had she noticed all of this.

Wedding day: Tom. A pinch beneath her breastbone. She took a deep breath. She chose a pew in the center of the church and pulled out the kneeler. She put her head in her hands. *Don't cry,* she told herself. *Don't cry. Just think. Just sit here and think: figure out what to do.*

She didn't hear the door open, and she didn't hear the footsteps coming up the aisle, but she felt a touch on her shoulder and she started, looking up. "Oh," she said. This, then, must be the famous Father Colin. Clerical clothing, young. "I'm sorry, I was walking, and I needed a rest. I thought it would be all right—"

"And it is," he said softly. "The church is always open, whether you're a parishioner or not."

"Oh, I *am,*" she said. "I mean, my parents are. And I was too, a long time ago. I was married here—" She gestured toward the altar.

"How about that," the priest said. It seemed awkward to have him standing there above her, and it would have been odd of her to stand up, so she moved over in the pew and he sat beside her. "Father Colin," he said, extending his hand. He wasn't tall, but his fingers were long and strong, and he had a firm grip. It was the sort of grip Tom's father, a career military officer, would approve of. "A lovely place to be married," he said.

"Ha!" she said. "Lovely, yes." She regarded him for a moment longer and then said, "My mother has been talking about you non-stop. You're practically famous in our house." She corrected herself: "Her house."

He laughed. He didn't sound like a priest when he laughed; he sounded like a regular man, like someone Tom would be friends with. "I'm just the substitute," he said. "I'm just doing my bit, until Father Michael improves. Or... or not."

"Substitute," she said. "That's funny. Do they throw spitballs at you and change seats when your back is turned? Pass notes about you?" He laughed again. She could feel her shoulders slumping forward; she straightened and then, as though in unconscious imitation of her, Father Colin straightened too. "You're young to be a priest," she said.

"We're not born old. We just get that way eventually." He had a way of looking at her that was disarming, as though he could see that there was more going on with her than she let on. The only other person she remembered looking at her that way was an old boyfriend, long before Tom, whose face she could barely call to mind.

"I see." She rubbed her eyes with both fists. "I'm Lillian," she said finally. "My parents were here earlier, with my little girl. The Owens. They're regulars. My mother does all those good-deed things people do when they're retired with time on their hands. Meals-on-wheels and such. I'm sure you'll know her soon if you don't already."

"God bless her," said Father Colin. "It's people like that that make the world go around."

"I know," said Lillian. She sighed. "But it just makes the rest of us feel...well, awful." She looked around. The church was smaller than she'd remembered it being, and older, and it also had a homey quality to it that she'd forgotten about. She had a sudden memory of the church being decorated for Christmas, with poinsettias and evergreen wreaths, the children's choir at the front.

He laughed again—he really seemed to laugh quite a lot. Or maybe she was just especially funny, sitting in a depressed state in an empty church on a hot Sunday afternoon. "It shouldn't make you feel bad. If you have a young child, then you are fulfilling the work of God in that way."

"Yeah?"

"Of course." Father Colin rubbed at a spot on the pew with one finger. "Not everybody can serve God in all ways. That would be asking too much of us."

"I guess that's right." She examined her fingernails. "So where did you come from, Father?"

"Boston. I'm just on loan."

"I thought I heard something in your accent there. I went to BC. And I live down that way now."

"Not local, then?"

"Not anymore. Just visiting." She paused. "A long visit."

"Boston College," he said. "I grew up watching those football games. Born and bred in Southie. I couldn't get rid of the accent if I tried. And believe me, I tried."

That seemed right. He reminded her of certain boys she'd gone to college with: the voice, the open, freckled face, the broad smile. He was about her age, maybe—he could be a year or two in either direction. She could imagine him at a fraternity party, or sitting in the back of the lecture hall. This, despite the clerical collar, despite the way he reached into the pew to straighten the books. There was something proprietary in his air inside the church. She could imagine him standing on the altar, delivering a sermon with conviction and authority. She could see now why her mother had gone on about him. The priests she remembered from her childhood had been aging and stooped. She understood how it would be refreshing and uplifting to have someone young behind the pulpit, how it could make it a little easier to believe.

He rose then. "I'll let you get back to your... to your prayer. Your meditation. Whatever it was you were doing."

"Moping," she said. "But thank you. You stay. I'm going anyway. I've got to get home." She stood.

"Moping. I'm sorry to hear that." Father Colin clasped his hands together and stretched his arms out in front of him. It could have been the gesture of an athlete, not a priest.

"Yes. Well. Long story." Lillian looked to the altar. Had she really stood there next to Tom, in this very church, with their friends gathered behind them? Had they really promised to love each other forever? Had he really broken that vow to her? Had they really agreed to welcome children into the world, and were those very children really at her parents' house, waiting for her to return and continue the charade that everything was normal? It didn't seem possible, suddenly, any of it. Her throat caught.

Father Colin was saying, "For another day, then. It was a pleasure to meet you. Perhaps I'll see you at Mass next week?"

"Oh, maybe. But my baby is very young. It's difficult—"

"I see."

"And I don't think I really belong."

Father Colin squinted at her. "Everyone belongs, who wants to be here. Everyone who believes."

"I'm not sure I'm much of a believer these days," Lillian said. "In anything." She saw something unpleasant cross his face and she said quickly, "I'm sorry. I didn't mean anything by it. I'm just tired lately."

"I understand," he said. "My brother has three little boys.

Believe me, I know what it takes out of you. I know what goes into it." You don't know, thought Lillian, but she appreciated the effort that went into saying so. He extended his hand, and she reached hers out to meet it, but instead of shaking her hand he clasped it and placed his other hand squarely over her the back of her palm.

She found, as she walked home, that she seized on one thing he said: *For another day.* He wanted to hear her story. She wanted to tell him.

She thought about how he clasped her hand at the end, and covered it with his long fingers. She thought about how she could have pulled her hand away, but how she waited for him to release her, because standing there, protected from the heat of the day, protected, for a moment, from the complications of her life, she felt safe.

※

"How long do you think they're staying?" Ginny said to William later that night. They were undressing for bed. Around them the house was quiet—finally, blissfully quiet.

It was nearly eleven, dark everywhere inside the house, but with a beach ball of a moon visible through the skylight in their bedroom.

"Shhh," said William. "They might hear you."

"What? *Who* might?"

"Stephen and Jane."

"Oh, but, William. They're a floor below. And they're off tomorrow, that's what they said. Jane's got to get back to work. I meant Lillian and the kids. How long do you think *they're* staying?"

"Don't know," said William. He was wearing the striped pajamas Ginny had given him the previous Christmas. He rubbed at his eye and turned down the bedspread on his side of the bed.

"Take your best guess." She turned down her side, fluffed the pillows. William held the television remote.

"Read, or eleven o'clock news? Or sleep?"

"Read or sleep. The eleven o'clock news is completely useless."

"Sleep, then."

"So, how long?" She switched off the lamp on the bedside table.

"A week? Two?"

"*Two?*"

"I don't know. What do *you* think? I guess it depends on if Tom is coming up to join them. Is he?"

"What? Coming up?"

"Yes."

"I don't know. I haven't asked her. I guess he is. He usually does. Maybe next weekend, when the workweek is out—"

"I suppose that would be the way to find out, wouldn't it. To ask her directly."

"I suppose," she said. William closed his eyes. They lay there silently for a few minutes until Ginny said, "Isn't it strange, though? That he didn't come this weekend?"

"Not necessarily."

But Ginny persisted. "You don't think?"

"No. No, I don't think it's strange. Maybe he had things to do around the house, things he couldn't get to with the children."

"Maybe," said Ginny. Then, a moment later, "Do you hear something?"

"No."

"Nothing?"

"Nothing."

"Well, I do." She got out of the bed. He could hear her slippers padding down the hallway. In less than a minute she returned. "It's Lillian," she whispered. "She's on the phone."

"Hmmmm."

"Who is she talking to, do you suppose?"

"I don't know. Probably Tom."

"At this hour? No, I don't think so."

"How do you know?"

"I could just tell, just by the way she was talking."

"Must be Heather."

"Oh! I bet it is."

"Why do you care?"

"I don't."

"Not much," he said. He closed his eyes, but on the other side of his eyelids the moon seemed to brighten. Why was it, William wondered, that when you wished for a moon there was none to be had and when you wished for a solid night of sleep it was above your window, as round as a cantaloupe, as insistent as a child? He turned his head to the side on the pillow.

He was nearly asleep when Ginny said, into the darkness, "You've always gotten on better with Jane than I have."

He made a noise of neither disagreement nor agreement.

"Why is that, do you think?"

"I don't know."

"Take a guess," said Ginny. "Why do you think that Jane takes to you more?"

"Not sure," William said. He lifted his head from his pillow and pounded it lightly in the center. "There," he said to the pillow.

"I wish I got on better with her."

"You could."

"How?"

"You could make more of an effort."

He felt her bristle.

"I make an effort *all the time.*" She turned away from him, faced the nightstand.

He kissed her on the shoulder, the shoulder that he knew, even in the darkness, was freckled and soft. "Ginny, my dear. Don't ask a question and then get mad at the answer. It's bad form."

"I'm not getting *mad*."

"You are."

"Well."

He shifted in the bed, then swung his legs over the edge and rose.

"Where are you going?"

"Kitchen," he said. "I'm thirsty."

"You're as bad as Olivia."

"Yes," he said.

One or the other of them had been in three times to Olivia's bedroom since her bedtime: once to take her to the bathroom, once to bring her a cup of water, once to plant a kiss on some imagined scratch on her elbow. Each time Olivia had called they had waited to see if Lillian would reach her first; each time she had not.

"Goodness," said Ginny the third time. "Are we to do this all night long? Do you think she doesn't hear her? Or do you think she hears and she's ignoring?"

"The latter," said William. "But I don't mind." He was reminded, going into Olivia's room, of when his children were young, and the different ways they slept. Stephen always on his stomach, giving in to sleep with complete abandon. Lillian on her back, arms beside her. Rachel on her side, hugging one or another of her stuffed animals to her. She had been a teenager before she'd forsaken the animals. To college she'd brought her green bunny with the long ears, ostensibly to be placed on a shelf or on top of the dresser, as decoration, but he suspected that in times of heartbreak or loneliness the bunny made its way into her bed.

In the kitchen he retrieved a glass of water from the cupboard and filled it from the tap. He drank it standing, looking around. The kitchen looked different at night, illuminated only by the glow of the under-counter light, and the unremitting moonlight coming in through the kitchen window. All surfaces were wiped clean, the toaster was gleaming: the evidence of all the meals eaten that day, all the different people fed and watered, was completely gone, save one lonely colander sitting in the dish drainer. He took the colander and found its spot, nesting it inside other larger colanders.

He felt a flood of affection for Ginny, who had done all of this, who had wiped the counters and sucked up the crumbs from Olivia's animal crackers with the Dustbuster; who had set out the Disney Princess place mat for Olivia's breakfast the next morning. He thought of all the nights and mornings Ginny had done this for him and the children while he went on about his business: providing for them, certainly, but also nourishing his own soul and his own ambition. Entrepreneur. Small-business owner. Qualified success.

Perhaps, after all, it was this great difference between Ginny and Jane that unsettled Ginny; perhaps she looked at Jane over a great chasm of ambition and achievement and felt that she, Ginny, remained forever on the other side of the chasm.

He filled the glass again, then filled one for Ginny, and returned to the bedroom with them. Ginny appeared to be sleeping so he set the glass carefully on the coaster on her nightstand.

Then, instead of getting into bed, he went one more time down the hallway and paused outside Lillian's room. The room was silent; if she had been on the phone, as Ginny said, she was no longer. The door was slightly ajar, which was the only reason he looked in. This room, too, was lit by the moon. Lillian was asleep in her clothes on the top of the bed, shoes too. Beside her Philip was sleeping also, his arms above his head. He wore a one-piece Red Sox pajama outfit. His chest moved up and down, up and down, as rapidly as a bird's. There was something birdlike about the tuft of hair on his little head too, and about the way he worked his mouth in his sleep.

William thought perhaps he should do something. He thought perhaps it wasn't safe, the baby sleeping on the bed like that. He thought about moving him into the Pack 'n Play, but if Philip woke up during the transfer it could result in a disaster for all of them. So in the end he found an afghan on the trunk at the end of the bed, which he laid over Lillian, keeping it carefully away from the baby. Lillian didn't stir when he put the afghan on her, and he backed out of the room, closing the door softly behind him.

When he returned to his bedroom he climbed carefully into bed. Ginny shifted and stirred and when he thought she was close enough to awake that he wouldn't be disturbing her he said, in a stage whisper, "Ginny?"

She sat upright immediately, looking around. "What? What is it?"

"Oh, no—nothing. Nothing big. I didn't mean to wake you. I'm sorry."

"Well, now that you have, let's have it, whatever it was you were going to ask."

"It's nothing, really."

"*Will*iam. I was *sleep*ing. It had better be something."

"All right. Well, I was just wondering."

"Yes?" Ginny switched on the light, saw her glass of water, nodded at William. "Thank you for this." She took a sip.

She switched off the light again, and he felt her settle herself back down on the pillow. He took a deep breath.

"Does Lilly seem different to you?"

"Different? Of course she's different. She's had a child recently. Childbirth always changes a woman."

"I know, but it seems…beyond that. More sad than anything."

"Maybe. It's not our business, though. She'll be fine."

"But we're her parents."

"Yes," she said slowly. "Yes, of course we are." He could feel her waiting for him to fill the silence after she spoke, and when he didn't she patted his arm softly, the way one would pat an old dog, turned carefully away from him, and went off to sleep.

William lay there for a long time, tired but not sleepy, listening to the noises of the house settle around him. He remembered the creaks and groans that his own childhood home had given out at night, he remembered his mother consoling him when the noises frightened him, he remembered the apple scent of the soap she used and the way her cheek felt smooth against his when she leaned down to kiss him good night.

And there was something else he had forgotten, from his children's youth, something he'd never articulated but now felt so strongly it was almost palpable: the peace you feel when you are awake in a house where children are sleeping.

※

Normally Rachel went to the Starbucks closest to her apartment, but she knew that Marcus went there sometimes, and she thought that seeing him might be too damaging to her already fragile state. She nearly swore off coffee altogether but instead decided to choose a location closer to her office, in midtown. This one was less busy than her usual Starbucks, most likely owing to its proximity to another, identical shop, and, being unusually ahead of schedule, and having treated herself to a particularly large and expensive concoction, she decided to take a seat.

She sat at one of the small brown checkerboard tables, between a teenaged girl whispering earnestly into a cell phone and a fiftyish man in a pale gray suit. Were they happy? They looked happy enough. The man was reading the business section of the *Times;* he wore a silver wedding band; his hair was cut neatly but not stylishly; he had the air of a person whose life was considered, ordered, in control. The girl appeared to be going through some sort of teenaged drama, but, as Rachel remembered from her own teen years, sometimes the adrenaline resulting from those dramas could masquerade as happiness.

Was Rachel happy? She didn't feel happy. Had she ever felt happy, apart from the nine months she had spent in a relationship with Marcus and the three months she'd spent sharing the apartment with him? She didn't think so.

If she thought back, very far back, to when she was a child growing up in Vermont, well cared for, the youngest, the most coddled of three children, she thought *maybe* then she had been happy. Riding a bike, perhaps, feeling the wind off Lake Champlain on her face. Or waking up in her bedroom on a Saturday, the whole of the day ahead of her, to spend or squander as she wished. Maybe then she had been happy.

The door opened and the napkin Rachel had set beside her cup blew onto the floor. A woman with short blond hair who was making her way past with her coffee retrieved it. She was familiar in a vague way to Rachel, the way that people on reality television shows look familiar when you see them in a magazine photo spread, outside of their usual milieu.

"Here," said the woman, handing her the napkin. And then, "Don't I . . . ? Aren't you—"

"You're Jane's mother," said Rachel, realizing. "From the wedding, I remember you. I'm Stephen's sister, Rachel."

"Of course. Of course you are. I'm Robin." She tipped her head toward the table. "May I?" She sat without waiting for an answer. When she was settled she took a long drink of her coffee and pointed her kind brown eyes toward her and said, "Now, Rachel. Isn't this funny? All this time, living in the same city, never running into each other. Tell me what you've been up to."

"Well," said Rachel. She thought about lying in bed with Marcus the previous month. She thought about his most recent visit. *You take things too seriously,* he'd said. *That's your biggest, one and only problem.*

"I'm working for a casting director," said Rachel.

"Wonderful!"

She remembered now that Jane's mother was some kind of doctor. A therapist, that was it. She thought about her boss, Tess. In her recent employee review Tess told Rachel that she seemed like she'd lost something over the past year. "You're talented, pet," Tess said. "I just don't think you're *focused* anymore." Tess, who was one of the least nurturing people Rachel had ever known, had a grating habit of calling everyone *pet*.

"Casting!" Robin said approvingly. "Such a glamorous business."

"Sort of," said Rachel. For Tess, it was glamorous. Tess cast famous actors in famous plays; Tess went to the theater so often that she actually complained about going; Tess was married to a publishing executive and lived on the Upper East Side with him and their three-year-old twins, whose care fell almost entirely, as much as Rachel could tell, to the live-in Mexican nanny. "It's not exactly glamorous," said Rachel. "For me. I do a lot of commercials, that sort of thing. But I'm going to be in charge of casting an independent film, later in the summer. That could be a big deal."

"Wonderful!" Robin wore glossy lipstick and a beige pantsuit that Rachel's father, with his slightly old-fashioned way of talking, would have called *sharp.* "A single girl, working in New York. Self-sufficient. The best way to be."

"I guess. It doesn't feel that way, always."

"You're what? Thirty? Thirty-one?"

"Twenty-nine," said Rachel morosely.

"Oh! Twenty-nine. You're practically an infant, still!"

"Not really."

"And I suppose everyone is telling you these are the best years of your life."

"Yes—"

"And they're not."

"No."

"Because you don't feel settled, and you feel that you ought to."

"Yes!"

"Well, don't believe them, is all there is to it."

"Really?"

"Really. It gets better. When I was your age—Lord, it all felt like such a struggle! Deciding whether or not to have a baby. And then being married to someone I shouldn't have been. And then having the baby. And working, trying to get ahead. And wondering if I was caring for the baby properly. And then a divorce. God, I'm glad to be finally done with all *that*. And now I'm about to become a grandmother! Which is unbelievably exciting. I plan to be the best grandmother in the entire city. To make up for all the mistakes I made as a mother."

"Oh, I'm sure you didn't," said Rachel.

"Trust me." Robin opened a small brown bag and drew out a blueberry muffin, which she offered first to Rachel, who shook her head. "I did. But I've come to terms with it."

"Well," said Rachel breathlessly. "In my case—" Later, telling her friend Whitney about the conversation, she felt faintly embarrassed for her honesty, for unloading the contents of her heart so readily in front of this woman who, whatever their connection, was nearly a stranger. But at the time it felt perfectly reasonable.

"In your case?" Robin prompted. Her face fell into creases of understanding and expectation.

"Oh, I've just gone through this breakup."

"Oh. That's hard. That's very hard." Robin nodded sympathetically. This, Rachel figured, must be the way she nodded at patients, because there was something about it that made Rachel want to continue talking.

"And we were living together."

"Ah! Even harder."

"And I can't afford the apartment anymore without him."

Robin sighed and made a small grimace with her mouth. She bit into the muffin. "Well, that's a shame. Only in Manhattan! If you lived in, say, Boise, you'd just keep the apartment on your own without worrying about it. But you can't find the energy to move, I suppose."

"Exactly. Or the time. Or the money."

"So what will you do?"

"I don't know."

"You'll figure something out. People always do. It's the survival instinct."

"I suppose," said Rachel. "But it doesn't feel that way, just at the moment."

"I know, darling. It never does," Robin said seriously. "But there are ways of making it all work out for yourself. I truly believe that."

"Thanks," said Rachel, and after Robin had gone she found that she felt better—infinitesimally maybe, barely a speck, but still better.

Rachel remained in her seat. She drained the last of her coffee and looked for some moments out the window, watching a gaggle of Catholic school girls in plaid skirts and blue kneesocks pass by. They were how old? Fourteen? Fifteen? Newly aware of their effect on men and boys, she could see that by the way they flipped their hair back and forth, and the way one of the girls had rolled her kneesocks all the way down to display her muscular and suntanned calves. You had to live a life of some privilege to have calves so suntanned in the very early stages of the summer.

She was due at work in ten minutes. Pushing open the heavy glass door, she emerged into the evolving Manhattan morning and reached into her bag for her cell phone. Her father would be up for certain, out working in the garden or in his office, at the computer. But the phone rang and rang with no answer and then the answering machine interceded.

"Daddy?" Rachel said, hoping her voice didn't break, hoping her sorrow didn't show through in her voice, hoping Ginny didn't get the message first because it was William she wanted this time, William who would not judge or, if he did, would do so quietly, only in his head, and who would ultimately—of this she was certain—see his way clear to helping her. "Daddy, if you have a second, could you just call me back?"

❋

Lillian took the call from Tom on the back deck. It was Monday morning. Stephen and Jane had gone downtown; Ginny was fiddling in the kitchen; Philip, having been awake much of the night, was napping in the Pack 'n Play. William and Olivia were off to the lake for a swim.

She answered because for the past three days she had allowed herself to entertain the possibility that Tom would be able to offer some sort of apology or explanation that would somehow make it all right again, that would allow her and the children to return home with a modicum of dignity and self-respect. Telling her, somehow, that it had all been a mistake, that she had misunderstood.

"Hey!" said Tom jovially. "How's the trip?" He had called from his work number; she could picture him sitting at his desk, full of Monday morning good intentions. It seemed lifetimes ago that she had had a desk, a job, an office phone, a lunch packed in a Tupperware container and placed alongside other lunches in a communal refrigerator.

Before what she was now (Domestic Lillian, Betrayed Lillian), there had been another Lillian: Professional Lillian. When she met Tom she was working for a high-tech public relations firm in Boston, putting her English major to semi-legitimate use by writing press releases and arranging press interviews for a variety of products whose purpose, truth be told, she never fully understood.

"I told you not to call." She leaned her elbows on the rail of the deck. Through the kitchen window she could see that her mother had ceased her movements to listen. She moved farther from the window.

She had enjoyed her job, had enjoyed, too, the camaraderie among her coworkers, many of whom, like herself, were new to the workforce, were new to living on their own, were sharing apartments with friends, were negotiating life in the city beyond the safety and security of the dorm rooms or parent-subsidized student apartments from which they had come. She had to take on a waitressing job at a restaurant in the South End, that's how little her job paid.

"Lillian! It's been three days."

"But I told you not to call. At all." She looked at her father's garden. She knew that William would have calibrated it carefully so that something in the garden would be blooming all summer. Already the phlox had given way to the bachelor's button—she remembered how funny she thought that name was when she was a child. This talent she had not inherited. Perhaps it came with age, the patience necessary to tend a garden. Or perhaps it would never come to her at all.

"Three days," she said, "is not that long. Considering." It had been at that restaurant where she met Tom, who was out for a business dinner on a damp April Wednesday. He was in sales then. He was transitioning from grunge to grown-up: flat-front khakis replacing torn jeans, Nirvana and Pearl Jam giving way to Elliott Smith.

She looked toward the kitchen window. She couldn't see her mother. She felt Tom switch gears; she could nearly feel his exhalation of breath. "How are the kids?"

"For God's sake," Lillian's friend Amy had said after Lillian and Tom started dating. "Don't get out of control."

"Lillian? I said, 'How are the kids?'"

But she had, after all, gone out of control: she'd gone completely, utterly out of control.

"Don't become one of *those* girls," Amy had said one day, in the overly fluorescent ladies' room at work.

"I won't."

But she did! She became one of those girls. And she didn't care. She was consumed with Tom, ravenous for him, dizzy with it all. Then one day, in the middle of the Common, just to the left of where a bunch of college students were playing a game of Ultimate Frisbee, down on one knee, a black velvet box appearing from his bag, where, to her knowledge, there had been only a bottle of water and a baseball hat, he had proposed to her.

Now, not trying to shroud the sarcasm, she said, "Wonderful. Philip woke up every two hours last night." She was so tired that she found it difficult to focus on anything. The flowers in front of her seemed to have blurred their edges, and the sunlight reflecting off the deck chairs felt like a physical pain.

"Oh, Lilly. That's terrible. I'm sorry."

Her friends were doing it too. There was the summer they went to eight weddings in a row, their bank accounts depleted from buying gifts, their heads aching from too much drinking. Then the baby showers started, one after another, white cake with pink or blue frosting in someone's mother's living room, a stockpile of loot from Babies "R" Us in the corner, all the talk about strollers and diaper brands and day care versus nannies and was formula going to ruin your baby forever or not.

That's what she wanted, she wanted all of that! She wanted to write thank-you notes on little gender-neutral cards featuring a yellow baby buggy or a set of tiny clothes swaying on a clothesline. She wanted to eat saltines in the morning to chase away nausea. She wanted to know what it felt like to have a tiny person growing inside you, multiplying cell by cell.

"Yes, well. You have other things to be sorry about, before that."

Then suddenly the baby shower was hers. *She* was the one sitting in the frilly white chair, pulling pastel wrapping paper from packages of tiny washcloths; *she* was the one cruising the aisles of Magic Beans, looking at strollers that cost more than her first car had cost; *she* was the one watching her husband, newly earnest and responsible, putting together a crib in a pale green bedroom.

"Olivia must be asking about me."

"She's not." That was a lie; Olivia had asked about Tom every day. Lillian told her he was tied up with a major work project and wouldn't be in touch for a while.

"Can I talk to her?"

"She's not here."

"Really?"

"Really. She went swimming. With my dad."

"Oh. Well, when she comes back you can call—"

"Maybe," said Lillian. "But maybe not."

"Come home. I miss you. I miss the kids. It's so quiet—"

"Don't you know," she said, "that I would give anything to be surrounded by quiet. Anything."

"Then come home!"

"It's not quiet for me at home. I have an infant and a three-year-old. It's not quiet for me anywhere!"

"That's all temporary. Come home, and you can rest. I'll take a day off work. You can have a whole day to yourself."

"And I suppose you're going to nurse Philip all day too?"

"You can pump. Pass bottles out to me." She heard the beep of another phone line ringing in his office. She supposed his little slut secretary would answer that one.

"Tom? I have to go. I'm too angry to talk to you. I can't even stand to think about you. I really can't. Maybe in a couple of days, or a week. Yes, a week. You need to give me a week. But not now. I can't talk to you now." She closed the phone and placed it on the table.

She sat in one of the deck chairs and considered the garden: how orderly it looked, all those plants waiting their turn to bloom. How predictable and dependable they were.

Looking back, she wasn't quite sure how it had happened. All of it! Marriage, motherhood, the whole thing. She had always been decisive and methodical; as a child, just ask her mother, she had organized her dolls' clothes by color, and had kept a sharpener in the colored pencil box in case any of the pencils got dull, and had completed her homework and packed it back in her schoolbag nearly as soon as she had finished her afternoon snack.

She folded her arms and used them as a pillow for her head. Wasn't this how they were instructed to rest during the school day in elementary school? She remembered that! How peaceful that was.

"Lilly?" Ginny was standing in the doorway. "Lilly? Is everything okay?"

Lillian didn't look up. She spoke from the depths of her arms. "Yes. Just tired."

"I heard Philip stirring. Do you want me to get him?"

"No." Lillian sighed heavily and stood. "No, I'll get him."

As she passed her mother, Ginny made an uncertain gesture toward her, perhaps wanting to embrace her, but Lillian knew getting through the day—the week, the month!—would require a steely resolve, a careful boxing up and compartmentalizing of emotions, and so she walked on, all the way up the stairs, slowly, purposefully, to the room where her baby waited.

※

The baby was somersaulting, or at least that's how it felt to Jane. The sensation was strange and pleasant to her in the way that riding in a car moving very fast over hilly terrain is strange and pleasant. And it was comforting, too, to know that the baby was all right, was receiving adequate food and liquid and oxygen or whatever it was that it received through the umbilical cord. She made a small gesture toward her abdomen.

"Is it moving?" said Stephen eagerly. They were walking down Church Street on Monday morning—Stephen had persuaded her to take one of her precious vacation days from work so that they could extend their visit to Vermont by a day—and Jane halted, taking one of Stephen's hands and putting it on her stomach. "I can't feel anything!" he said.

"Be patient. You will. I feel something moving—right *here*. Could be his hand or his foot."

They didn't know for sure that the baby was a he, because Stephen had adamantly *not* wanted to find out during the ultrasound and Jane, fighting hard against all her urges to prepare and anticipate, all her unwillingness to brook unnecessary surprises, had acquiesced. But she was nearly certain the baby was a boy. Already she had experienced a few of those pregnancy dreams she had long heard about. In one she was chasing a two-year-old boy around a playground; in another, she held a newborn wrapped in a blue blanket, who looked up at her and with a perfect French accent said, *Bonjour, maman.*

How strange it was to have this other being tethered to her, partaking in each meal and each drink and each taxi or subway ride along with her. On balance, Jane had decided, she liked being pregnant more than she expected to. Once the morning sickness had departed, once her energy had returned, and once her belly had grown enough to accommodate the maternity business suits she had purchased at no small expense, she discovered she possessed feelings she would not have expected herself to possess—feelings of wonder and joy, feelings of protectiveness and responsibility that went far beyond those she felt for her career, for the apartment in which she and Stephen lived, for the furnishings her job had allowed them to put there, for marriage, for her relationship with her mother.

When she took the time to examine these feelings, she knew that part of what was allowing them to exist was the fact that once the baby was born, and once her three scheduled weeks of maternity leave had ended, she would be going back to work, back to sit at her tidy, polished desk, with her telephone and her computer and her cup of coffee and her assistant, Rebecca, at her disposal, while the baby remained safely at home with Stephen, fed and burped and shielded from harm. She did not, truth be told, anticipate that her day-to-day life would change dramatically once the baby came. Stephen's, yes. But not hers.

Then, when Stephen was ready to get back to work, maybe in a year or so, maybe longer, they would employ some sort of a nanny, perhaps a sturdy, grandmotherly type, with a seen-it-all demeanor, and life would go on rather smoothly. Blissfully.

Recently she had visited her closest friend from business school, who had three children and lived in a four-bedroom colonial in

Nyack. "I'll get back to it—working—someday," the friend—her name was Lisa—had said, while she was peeling Play-Doh off the kitchen counter and searching through a cluttered kitchen drawer for a Band-Aid to cover somebody's skinned knee. "When I'm ready." She had worked for some time in marketing at P&G; she had climbed high up the ladder and had been in line for another promotion when she became pregnant with the second child.

Jane had looked with some surprise at Lisa's tousled ponytail, at the sleeve of her white T-shirt, crusted with some sort of indiscernible squash, and had known that this wasn't the truth.

"Don't look at me like that, Janey," said Lisa. "You! So smug and employed." She was smiling, but it was clear to Jane that she didn't think any of this was funny. "Your time will come soon enough," she added. "You'll see. You think it's easy, making these decisions—"

"I don't," said Jane defensively. "I don't think it's easy at all." She just didn't think these decisions pertained to her, particularly, even now, in her pregnant state. But she understood that this was what Stephen's parents expected from her: the house, the children and pets, the clatter and disorder of domestic life.

"They just worry, that's all it is," Stephen told her. "That you'll regret your choices, later on, when it's too late."

"But I haven't got a choice!" Jane's voice rose stridently. "I worked so hard, to get where I am."

"I know you did." They had been married for seven years; he had seen her through the end of business school, and her first job, and then this one, which taxed her and exhilarated her all at once.

"I haven't got a choice. There's nothing to choose *between*. There just *is*."

"I know," he said soothingly. But she wasn't sure, always, that he did know.

Once, when she was in first grade, Jane had been sitting in her bedroom reading when she overheard her mother and a man she was dating talking in the kitchen. The man was tall and broad, with a rumble in his throat when he talked, like a car starting up. Roger, his name was.

"Not a beauty queen, is she," said Roger. "Good thing she's smart."

Jane looked down at her book; she was reading *James and the Giant Peach*. She was the best reader in her first-grade class; her classmates were still making their way haltingly through picture books. James had just spilled the magic beans. She imagined the desperation he felt, scrabbling at the ground.

"Jesus Christ," said her mother. "Roger. What a thing to say." She could tell by her mother's tone, and by the way her voice and the man's voice lowered immediately: they were talking about her.

The words blurred in front of her, but she blinked and wiped her face on her sleeve and read on. The peach started to grow; Aunt Sponge and Aunt Spiker built a fence around it; James, hungry and alone, watched the crowds gather from inside the house.

Some time later her mother came in. "Jane? Jane. What is it?"

"Nothing," she said. She held the book steady in her lap.

Her mother crouched down beside her and met her eyes. "Janey? Tell me."

Roger had laughed after he said it, and that's what bothered her the most.

"*Nothing,*" she said more sharply. And then, because she wanted to hurt her mother, she said savagely, "Just leave me alone." Her mother left, closing the door softly behind her, and although they never spoke of it they both knew Jane had heard.

The next day, Roger was gone. When Jane asked where he'd gone, Robin said, "*I* don't know. But I didn't think he was that nice. Did you, Janey?"

"No," said Jane softly. "I didn't either." She was sad because until she overheard the conversation she had liked Roger; he had taken her and her mother to an Italian restaurant near their building, where she was served a Shirley Temple and was allowed to order off the adult menu and to tuck a big red napkin into the collar of her white shirt to keep the sauce off of it. He had called her "kiddo."

She had never told anyone about it, not even Stephen, but sometimes she thought about it at odd moments, and she remembered the feeling of having something bloom inside her, some sort of perception of how the world worked, of its little cruelties.

Earlier that day, at breakfast, Ginny had watched her checking her BlackBerry and had said, with manufactured bemusement, "Heavens. Something going on already? So early in the morning?"

Stephen had answered for her, exasperatedly, "Mom. There's *always* something going on. And it's not that early." William, who was painting a birdhouse with Olivia on the porch, had looked up sharply and said nothing.

Well, if they were going to fault her for being successful, then so be it. She had not studied so hard at college, had not been at the top of her class at business school, had not worked like a maniac all these years, to be made to feel guilty about all that she had achieved. To be made to feel like an outcast if she answered e-mail each night before bed.

"It's not *guilt* exactly," said Stephen when they were in the car, driving down Pine Street toward the downtown, in search of the cranberry scone that Jane had decided that she wanted. "It's not that they actually want you to feel *bad* about it. It's just that they're not accustomed to your—"

"My what?"

"Your intensity, I suppose. Your drive."

"There's not much I can do about that."

"Nor should you!" said Stephen. "That's what I love you for."

"Well," she said. "I love you too."

The baby moved again. Stephen's face opened in delight. "I felt it this time! I really did!" And standing there in the strengthening summer sunlight, with the tourists just beginning to throng around them, her husband's hand on her belly, Jane caught hold of the thread of a feeling that, if she pulled at it hard enough, she thought just might turn out to be contentment.

Later, after they had looked into some of the shops and sat for a while on a bench in the sun, Jane announced that she had to go to the bathroom.

"Okay," said Stephen sleepily. "I'll be right here waiting." She spent a moment being offended that he wasn't finding the bathroom for her, then set off on her own.

She entered a shop that sold only socks—oodles of them, in all shapes and sizes and colors—and asked the bored, pierced teenager employed there about the bathroom; the girl, looking from Jane's belly to her face and back again, said, "It's not for customers, usually. But I guess you can use it. It's back there."

"Thank you," said Jane, and she thought later that she must have looked quite frightful retreating from the bathroom afterward the way she did, nearly knocking over a giant pile of pet-themed socks.

Stephen was on the bench where she had left him, eyes closed, face lifted to the sun.

"Stephen," she said, and she knew her voice sounded shrill; a few people passing stopped to look at her. So she continued more quietly but no less intently. "Stephen, we have to call the doctor. Something's wrong. There's blood."

☼

Rachel was overseeing the first of three days of auditions for a tampon commercial. She had spent the previous two workdays calling agents, putting out requests for actors, talking about tampons, thinking about tampons.

"I *can't* go to the beach," the girl was supposed to say, casting a glance of longing and regret at her friend. "I have my *period.*" To which the friend would reply, in a voice of experience and reason, that there was a solution the girl hadn't considered: the mighty tampon.

It was astonishing to Rachel, in this day and age, that not everybody knew about tampons, that the company needed to advertise them at all. Weren't they rather a necessity of life, if you were young and female? Did anyone really learn about them from television? Was there actually a target audience for this commercial?

Then again, Rachel felt that way about most of the commercials she worked on. It all seemed unnecessary. It all seemed like a colossal waste of time and money and energy. People would either go to McDonald's or they would not, they would buy a Diet Coke or they would not, they would eat a cracker or they would not: it seemed to Rachel that it would have very little to do with whether a certain commercial had played during *American Idol* or *Desperate Housewives.* She supposed it was this refusal to believe in what she was doing, this inability to pretend that it was remotely important, that ignited the feelings of lassitude and ennui that had lately engulfed her.

In her own defense, though, she had *not* gone into casting to find the perfect spokesperson for a tampon. She had gone into casting because she believed in theater, and because she believed in the power of a good play to change people's lives forever, and because she believed in her own ability to be involved in that process.

And then, as she was limping toward that goal, she had met Marcus, and she hadn't cared for a long time about what she was doing during the day; her time and energy had gone merely into getting *through* the day so she could see Marcus.

In the process she had got stuck where she was. Watching

groups of girls come in and stand in front of her and recite an inane bit of dialogue about a feminine product, while in the next room, she knew, her boss, Tess, was preparing to call actors in for *Streetcar,* and that she had chosen another assistant, the obsequious Stacy, to join her for those auditions. So here was Rachel: peddling Tampax instead of Tennessee Williams!

They broke for lunch. Rachel was due to meet her friend Whitney at the massive Crate & Barrel in SoHo. Rachel told the next person in line, a slight, winsome blonde who looked barely old enough to have gone through puberty, that they would convene again at two o'clock.

The blonde nodded eagerly, and Rachel, looking around for her bag and the water bottle she had set down beside it, calculated in the tip for the driver along with the fare downtown, plus the cost of lunch, which she would have preferred to eat at her desk—quietly, cheaply, in solitude—but which she had promised to eat with Whitney.

She decided the subway was by far the wiser choice. So off she went into the bowels of the station, where she discovered her MetroCard had expired the previous day; she used her ATM card to buy another one, for eighty-one dollars, which brought her bank balance to a new and abysmal low.

She did not allow herself to dwell on how many days remained until her next paycheck would arrive, nor did she think for long about the stack of bills—slim, yes, but nonetheless insidious— that sat on her nightstand in her apartment, held down by a paperweight her sister Lillian had made for her twenty-five years ago at her first sleepaway camp.

Rachel stood on the platform near a couple in shorts and T-shirts consulting a guidebook. On the other side of them a young black woman rested her arms on a stroller in which a sweaty, chubby toddler was sleeping. They had the same coffee-colored skin.

The couple in shorts was possibly Rachel's age and was possibly a year or two older or a year or two younger. Both wore shiny gold wedding bands. There was a possessiveness with which the woman took the man's hand, wrapping her thumb around his wrist, and a languid way with which they studied the book and then the subway map in front of them, as if they had nowhere immediate they were expected to be. *Newlyweds,* Rachel said in her mind. *Honeymoon.* Then, *Midwesterners,* and for a moment she feared she'd said it aloud, for the woman looked up and met her eyes.

Near the honeymooners stood a teenaged boy and girl, with their arms wrapped around each other's waists, listening to an iPod with a shared set of earbuds. The girl's head bobbed in time to the music.

Everywhere, it seemed, were people who were more successful at maintaining a relationship than Rachel was; everywhere were signs that the rest of the world was moving onward and upward while she was not. In fact, here she was, eight years after college had set her on what seemed at the time to be a promising and glittering path, still single, still holding the title of assistant, and unsure for how much longer she'd be able to pay her rent.

For all of these things she blamed Marcus. Unfair, she knew, because most of them, except the rent, were not directly related to him. Still, it was easy to blame Marcus, to *hate* him, even. And on the subway platform, as the train snaked its way in, and as the couple with the iPod moved even closer together, if that was possible, hate him she did.

Two stories high, chewing up a significant amount of real estate, the store — even in the daytime — seemed to glitter with the promise of self-indulgence and decadence. Whitney had instructed Rachel to meet her near the wineglasses, but Whitney was late, so Rachel decided to wait for her in an oversized leather chair that bore a price tag of nearly two thousand dollars.

Even the size of the chair depressed her—it was big enough for two. Before she sat in it she spent a few minutes trying to work up a noble pity for anyone who would buy such a chair, and for the disorder that must certainly exist in their priorities to do so. She studied the specs and learned that the chair reclined—perhaps that accounted in part for the exorbitant price—and suddenly the word *reclined* reminded her of her father, who had asked for and received a La-Z-Boy recliner one Father's Day when Rachel was in elementary school. That recliner, a brown tweedy number with a leg extension—her father was very tall—sat now in her parents' den. Still, this many years later, if William was about, anyone who wanted to sit in it was required first to ask permission and second to surrender the chair the minute he wanted to take possession of it.

But *this* recliner: this recliner would be out of place in her parents' home, where the biggest extravagance was her mother's new washing machine and dryer—Rachel had not seen them yet in person, but had learned all about them in an e-mail—and where Rachel had grown up alternately mortified and impressed by her parents' ability to make do with what they had rather than reach for something bigger and better. She supposed it came with age, that ability. Or perhaps not. Perhaps to some people it never came at all; perhaps to *her* it would never come at all. Her father, in fact, would think that this chair was an absurdity. If he saw the price tag, he would clutch his chest in a theatrical display of shock. He would mime a heart attack. *Nouveau riche,* he would call it, were he playing up his sophisticated side. Or, more basically, *pointless.*

And maybe, long ago, Rachel would have done the same thing. But now: well. She had lived in New York for far too long to be able to recognize the beauty of a simple life. She had surrounded herself too readily with people—Marcus, Whitney, everyone she knew on the Upper West Side—who could afford things that she could not; she had spent too many years trying to fit somewhere she did not belong to be able to dismiss it all with a wave of her hands and a fake heart attack. She had bought into the idea that there existed a natural order to society and class, and she had dedicated herself too fervently to moving herself out of one group and into the next. Because that's what it was: an order. And she was caught at the bottom of it, where forever she would remain, scrabbling to get higher.

Rachel put her hands on one arm of the chair—she could not, from the center of the chair, reach both arms, and her attempt to do so made her feel as small and helpless as a child. Rachel tried to imagine a home she knew that was big enough for the chair in which she now sat: a home in which such a chair would melt seamlessly into its surroundings. If it stood out, she reasoned, it probably didn't belong there at all.

She could, after some reflection, imagine the chair in her sister Lillian's home, which was a stately four-bedroom near Boston, decorated with a mixture of taste and haste from the pages of a Pottery Barn catalog, and from the very store in which she now sat, admiring all around her the glasses and martini shakers, the flambé pans, the glass nesting bowls, and the bamboo salad sets.

She had thought that someday she would own a home suitable for such accessories, but that she would eschew the typical, look beyond the chain stores, and instead decorate with acrylic lounge chairs and rectangular suspension halogen lighting. She had thought, of course, that she would share the home with Marcus, and that they would fill it with two or three lovely children, on whom Rachel would bestow skilled and benevolent care, with the help of some sort of nanny who would allow her to keep rising in the casting world, to see what she believed to be her natural talent through to its fruition. She wanted, basically, to be Tess. With softer edges, and perhaps without the twins. One child at a time seemed like plenty.

Whitney appeared some minutes later. She was carrying a new Coach bag with a soft geometric print; her hair was judiciously moussed and styled; her engagement ring managed, somehow, to twinkle and shimmer enough to garner attention even in *this* store, which must see a hundred new engagement rings pass through its doors each day.

Not that Whitney's ring was exactly new, of course: for one, she had been engaged since the previous September, and for another, her ring had been created from stones that had once adorned a necklace of the maternal grandmother—now dead, but very much remembered and beloved—of Whitney's betrothed, Rob.

Whitney kissed Rachel on the cheek, holding her lightly by the elbow at the same time in a gesture that Rachel, no matter how she tried, despite all her years living in the city, had never been able to master, and said, all in one breath, "Sorry I'm late—a meeting ran over, and then the taxi took years, and then I had to stop downstairs and print out our registry—"

Whitney, then, had felt no compunction about taking a cab.

Whitney shook at Rachel a sheaf of papers she was carrying— this was the aforementioned registry list—whose heft and length proved that Whitney and Rob were on the threshold of obtaining the very existence whose impossibility Rachel had recently (privately, yes, perhaps shamefacedly, but still recently) been bemoaning.

"I was up all night thinking about wineglasses," said Whitney. She rustled the papers. "Can you believe it?"

"I can't." Slowly, reluctantly, Rachel peeled herself from the leather chair and stood next to Whitney.

"Yes! I think we ordered the wrong ones! I think we made a huge mistake."

Rachel was silent, looking over Whitney's shoulder.

"You see? We put the Inga on the registry list, when really that would be a disaster. What we really want is the Mara. I think that's what it's called. I don't know—they all seemed to be named after foreign girls. The Inga, the Mara. It's easy to get confused. Now where is the Mara?"

Rachel summoned every ounce of kindness that she could locate and said, "It *is* easy to get confused."

Whitney didn't hear her; she was running her thumb down one of the registry pages.

"I mean," Rachel continued, "you've still got some time before the wedding. No need to rush into a decision. Something as important as this, you don't want to screw it up."

Whitney looked up then and raised her eyebrows haughtily. "The wedding is in less than four months! But the shower—that's only, what? Twelve weeks away? Eleven? People may have started shopping. I actually *do* need to make a decision."

"I guess so," said Rachel. As maid of honor it was her job, of course, to plan and execute the shower, but she had given over the reins willingly to Whitney's mother, who wanted to hold the event at a particular restaurant near Whitney's family's summer home in Maine and who had promised Rachel that she could take charge of the favors, or perhaps the game to play at the shower, so that she still felt involved.

"A game!" Rachel had said, appalled.

"As long as it's appropriate for a variety of ages," Whitney's mother said, placing two manicured fingers on Rachel's elbow.

Rachel, her bank account reeling from the prospect of buying the three-hundred-dollar bridesmaid dress Whitney had chosen, had been immensely relieved by this turn of events. She hadn't bought the shoes yet, nor had she committed to a wedding gift, nor had she allowed herself to calculate the considerable expense that would be involved in making her way to the town on the coast of Maine where the wedding was to be held and in staying for two nights at the inn whose entire reservoir of rooms had been reserved for the event.

At one time, when Whitney had first become engaged, Rachel had been certain she would be making the trip with Marcus, which meant that she would have someone with whom to share both the expense and the droll moments that were certain to transpire once Rob's family, Whitney's family, and an open bar found themselves in the same room. But now—no.

Whitney's cell phone rang. She removed it from her bag, looked at the number, then shook her head. "My mother. I'm not answering. I'm sure it's something to do with the wedding. She's driving me *crazy.*"

"That must be difficult," said Rachel. If she and Marcus had married, she wouldn't have cared about the actual wedding. She would have been happy to wed in the guts of city hall.

"It is difficult. Particularly with my mother. And then you throw Rob's mother into the mix…I just feel like I'm walking on eggshells. *All the time.*"

"I'm sorry," said Rachel.

They had moved closer to the shelves of wineglasses, and Whitney was examining them, chewing on her lip. In the mirror behind the shelves Rachel could see Whitney's expression, which was both studious and concerned, and eerily reminiscent of the way she used to look during exam weeks at NYU.

How was it, Rachel wondered, that they had both strayed so far from the people they had been then, when then was not so very long ago? *Had* they strayed, in fact? Or was it just that the circumstances around them had transformed so significantly so as to reveal parts of their personalities that had been always present but for the most part had remained hidden? Of course Whitney had always had more money than Rachel. Of *course* she had, it was clear from the first day of their freshman year, when Whitney had arrived at the dorm lugging not one but two outsized pieces of Louis Vuitton luggage, both of them filled with clothing brands that Rachel not only couldn't pronounce but really, truly had never heard of.

Finally Whitney gave a little shout of triumph and lifted a glass toward Rachel. "This is the one! The Mara glass. I knew this was right, I just knew it, but we were rushing through the end of the registering the day we were in here—"

"Well, there you have it," said Rachel.

"And Rob had to be at the hospital, and I was determined to get it all done—"

Rachel made a small grimace that she hoped conveyed sympathy and understanding.

"And the other one just isn't *tapered* enough, don't you think?"

"I do," said Rachel. "I couldn't agree more. Not tapered nearly enough."

Whitney looked admiringly at the glass. "Well, I really do love it." Then she laughed. "Can you believe this is what I've turned into? Rach? Can you believe this is what I've become?" Rachel didn't answer, but Whitney talked through the silence, not noticing. "So let me just make the switch on the computer, and then we're done. I'm starving. Are you starving? What should we do for lunch? Diner, or Mercer Kitchen?"

"Diner," said Rachel immediately.

"Oh, *Rach*," said Whitney, folding the registry pages into her bag.

"What?"

"Is it the money?"

"No," said Rachel shortly.

"My treat," said Whitney.

"No," said Rachel. "I feel like diner food, is all."

"Don't be stupid," said Whitney. "Nobody *feels* like diner food when there's better food to be had."

"No," said Rachel again, without conviction.

Then she allowed herself to be taken to the restaurant, and allowed herself to order a crab cake appetizer, and an entrée of sea scallops with crisp pancetta and lemon crème fraîche.

"Is that all?" said the waitress. She had flawless, milky skin and a fabulously short haircut; Rachel saw her playing Dunyasha or some other Chekhovian heroine. Or perhaps her skin was too perfect for the stage; perhaps all that creaminess would be wasted so far from the audience. Perhaps it was the movies where her future lay.

"That's all," said Rachel.

"No!" said Whitney. "And two glasses of—" She paused, looking at the wine list. "The Pouilly-Fuissé," she said.

"Whit—"

The wine was fourteen dollars a glass.

"*My* treat," Whitney said firmly. She closed the menu and handed it to the waitress and took Rachel's from her and did the same. She looked exhilarated and satisfied, the way Rachel's brother, Stephen, used to look after he'd completed a cross-country race in which he'd done well.

"Thank you," said Rachel. "I appreciate it, I really do. But you really don't have to."

"Of course I don't," said Whitney. "But I can, so why wouldn't I?" Rachel pondered this. For all of her protests, why *shouldn't* Whitney be permitted to treat? Not only had she come from a family with more money than Rachel's, but the family she was marrying into was hardly a disappointment in the financial area. Rob's great-great-grandfather was said to have been instrumental in the development of the flow-through tea bag. There were millions there, somewhere, and at some point a significant part of that would be Whitney's. Rachel, thinking about this, looking hard past Whitney, at the feet and calves of the people moving by on the sidewalk, tried very hard not to hate her best friend. She said, "I shouldn't have a drink before going back to work. I'm in the middle of casting a commercial."

"Oh, *phooey*," said Whitney."

"Right," said Rachel, with some effort. "Phooey."

"Pretend it's nineteen sixty," said Whitney. She leaned conspiratorially toward Rachel over the table. "I've been watching *Mad Men* on DVD while Rob is at the hospital. All of Madison Avenue was drunk back then! It was a hoot. It's a wonder anyone got anything done. Drinking and sex. That's all they did."

"In the office?"

"Sometimes! It's not like that anymore, I can tell you *that* much." Whitney worked for a large advertising agency in midtown; she had been climbing its ranks steadily since they had graduated from college. Recently she had been put in charge of a small but very successful advertising campaign for an energy drink.

When the fourteen-dollar wines arrived, in glasses big enough to comfortably house a goldfish, Rachel took a sip and felt better.

"Good," said Whitney authoritatively.

"Yes," said Rachel without the same conviction. When had it happened, that she'd taken to deferring to Whitney in matters of food and drink? She remembered a time, not so very long ago, in college, when she and Whitney had been more or less on equal footing—when Whitney, whatever money her parents had, had wordlessly agreed to live by Rachel's financial constraints. When dollar drafts at a bar in the East Village were the extent of their treats to themselves. And Rachel didn't think about it much then, but the truth came to her now, as hard and cold as a bullet. Whitney had been slumming it back then. Pretending. While Rachel was just living.

Whitney's cell phone rang again and she picked it up, looked at it, put it back down, and said, "Just Rob."

"Get it," said Rachel. "You might not get another chance to talk to him today." Rob was completing his residency in orthopedics at Columbia Presbyterian; he worked agonizingly long shifts.

"No," said Whitney. "I talk to him all the time. This is more important. I never see you anymore." She leaned over the table and said, "So how are *you?*" The question, and the concern and munificence that accompanied it, appeared to be genuine, and Rachel, who felt suddenly as though she might cry, took another sip of wine.

"I'm okay," she said.

"Yeah?"

"Not great," she conceded. "Not by a long shot. But okay."

Whitney nodded. "And work is?" The waitress appeared with their appetizers, and Rachel and Whitney leaned back from each other to allow room for the giant white plates to be set down before them.

"Work is...work is okay. I mean, screamingly boring right now. I'm casting for a tampon commercial."

Whitney giggled. "Rachel! That's hilarious."

Rachel permitted herself a wan smile. "I suppose it is. But it's not, as they say, what I came to do."

"But it's okay? It's manageable?"

"Yeah. It's manageable. I've got bigger stuff coming up in the next couple of months, if I can keep my head on straight. An independent film."

"Rachel! Really? That's fantastic."

"Yeah. Yeah, it is."

"So...oh, it's *Marcus*. That's what isn't okay."

"Right."

"Oh, Rach." Whitney shook her head sadly. It was the way, Rachel thought, that her mother had shaken her head at her when she was young and had done something careless, something about which she ought to have known better, and had disappointed her.

Rachel took a bite of crab cake.

"Phenomenal, aren't they?" said Whitney eagerly. "I had them last time. I came with Rob and his parents, for brunch. Right after we got engaged."

Rachel nodded, and chewed. It *was* phenomenal, the crab cake, and the sensation that had come upon her, of being well cared for, and of being plied with expensive food she could not afford to buy for herself, and of being looked at with such love and caring by someone whom she had known so intimately that they'd once spent the whole of a six-hour car ride from New York to Vermont not even turning on the radio because they'd had so much to talk about—this sensation was enough suddenly to allow her guard to come sufficiently down so that she said to Whitney, "I slept with Marcus."

*

"Stephen," said Jane. "Don't get in an accident."

"I'm not. I won't." He gripped the wheel. If you had asked him earlier in the day how far the hospital was from Church Street he would have said, Oh, not far, you could walk there if you wanted to, wouldn't take you long. But now, faced with the task of navigating his car through summer traffic, of remembering exactly where to turn so as not to get caught on a one-way street, it felt like miles and miles. It felt like he was driving to another state.

"Main Street?" he said out loud. "Or Colchester Avenue? Shit, they redid all this since I've been here—"

He glanced at Jane. Her face was white. Both hands pressed into her stomach as if by holding on she could keep the baby safe. She looked straight ahead; it seemed to him that she had not even blinked since they got in the car. "Just pick one," she said. "Find it. Stop and ask if you have to."

"No, I don't have to—see? There's the sign for emergency. We're going the right way. The blue sign, right there?"

Jane said nothing.

"Can you feel it?" he asked. "Is it still moving?"

She nodded. He had never seen a look exactly like this one on her face. He had seen fear, of course, but always in combination with something else: fear and impatience, fear and resolve, fear and uncertainty. But this: unadulterated terror. He had never seen it. It frightened him.

"It's going to be okay," he said. "You know that. It's going to be okay."

"Stephen," she said. "Stop saying that. You don't know if it's true."

"Of course I do," he said. But his own voice betrayed him, the falsehood lying just below the surface of the words.

Ahead of him a black SUV stalled at a green light. "Jesus Christ, come *on*," he said, hitting the wheel with his fist. "Come *on*." And at last the SUV spurted forward and so eager was he to follow it that he nearly hit its rear end.

And here it was, finally! The stout red letters against the white building: EMERGENCY. If ever I've experienced an emergency, he thought, this is it.

"It's going to be okay," he said again, pulling over. This time Jane didn't answer because she had already unfastened her seat belt and was on her way out of the car.

"Oh, Rachel," said Whitney. "You didn't. When?"

"I did. A month ago. He came by to have me sign this banking thing, and, well, it just happened."

"Rachel!"

"I know," said Rachel. "It's terrible, and stupid. And even so, I can't help thinking—"

"What?"

"I can't help thinking...I know it sounds idiotic, and like such a cliché, but I can't help thinking that Marcus *was* the one. And I let him get away. And now he's gone."

Whitney put down her fork, then took a great big drink of her wine. She regarded Rachel over the glass, and when she put it down she reached across the table, with the hand that wore the massive, taunting engagement ring, and said, soberly, "Oh, sweetie."

"What?"

"Of course he wasn't the one."

"How do you know?"

"Because if he was, he wouldn't have gone away."

Rachel sighed. She wondered if it was possible to hate a best friend and love her to pieces at the exact same time.

"But."

Whitney stabbed at a piece of radicchio. "But what?"

"What if it's not that simple?"

"What do you mean?"

"Well, love. Commitment. All of it. What's if not so simple as you say it is? What if the right one *can* walk away? And the wrong one can stay?"

"It is, though. It is that simple," said Whitney fiercely. She took a piece of bread from the basket on the table and buttered it with energy and conviction.

"But... don't you think that maybe that's easy for you to say, in your position?"

Whitney wiped her mouth and put her hand to her forehead, in a gesture that reminded Rachel of women in centuries-old paintings. Whitney had lately begun wearing her hair differently, in the sort of cut that you had to keep up with every six weeks or it would all go to hell, but that, when kept up properly, and styled correctly, the way Whitney's was, looked outrageously good. "Because it has to be that simple," she said. "I won't accept it any other way."

Rachel felt an unwelcome pinch of envy. Then, catching sight of herself in the mirror behind Whitney, she wondered if she was getting too old to wear her hair long and straight. It had always been one of her greatest sources of pride, her hair, and the one thing about her physical appearance that was an indisputable positive. Marcus had loved it, and had told her so, nearly every day they were together, and she had promised, one night in bed, one of those nights when she would have promised anything at all, never to cut it. But perhaps the world would take her more seriously if she had shorter hair.

"Listen," said Whitney. "I only know my own situation."

"But your own situation is... pretty good." The waitress appeared and swept away their plates gracefully, as if she were performing in a ballet.

"I suppose it is," said Whitney modestly. She smiled.

The waitress deposited their entrées in front of them and said, in a voice that somehow exhibited ennui and sophistication all at once, "Anything else?"

"No, thank you," said Whitney, and then she looked down and said softly to her plate, "I don't know as much as you think I do, Rach. Don't listen to me, not if what I'm saying is making you upset."

"But." Rachel felt a bit desperate. "You have to know more! Look where you are. And look where I am."

"I don't, though," said Whitney. "I don't know anything. I mean, Rob and I, we can't even——"

"Can't even *what?*" said Rachel, a bit more eagerly than she would have liked.

"We can't even choose a wineglass without getting into a fight."

"Really?" Rachel stopped cutting her scallops——there were only three of them, but they were nearly as big as a baby's head—— and looked inquiringly (hopefully) at Whitney.

"Well, it's not quite *that* bad. But this wedding——and his mother——and *my mother.*" She paused and took another sip of wine. "Good Lord, this is going to my head." There was a little spot of color on each of Whitney's cheeks.

Rachel felt a sudden affection for Whitney, and for the restaurant, and for Manhattan itself, going about all of its weekday business outside the windows. "It all sounds like a bit much," she said kindly.

"It is!" said Whitney. "You can't imagine."

"I know," said Rachel. "I really can't."

"I didn't mean——"

"I know you didn't."

"And I feel like an idiot complaining about it, because really there's nothing to complain about. I'm the luckiest girl in the world."

"It's probably the wine," said Rachel.

"I think you're right," agreed Whitney, draining her glass. "It's the wine. But, God, can you believe how stressed out I let myself get? About *wineglasses?*" She giggled, and Rachel giggled too, and they ate the rest of the meal in that companionable, silent way that only friends who have known each other for a very long time can do.

When they had finished and Whitney had settled the bill, Rachel was nearly late getting back to the auditions. She would have to spend the money on a taxi after all.

In the lobby of the Mercer Hotel, Whitney hugged Rachel and said, into her hair, "Thanks, sweetie."

"But I didn't do anything."

"You listened. And you came with me. I'm so glad to get those stupid glasses taken care of. *Finally*." Whitney squeezed Rachel's arm an extra time and stepped out onto the sidewalk. Rachel watched her arm go up to hail a cab.

She stood for a minute in the lobby of the hotel, which was full of sleek, stylish people moving quickly. Where could they all be going? And what was the rush?

She checked her cell phone; no messages. She checked her office voice mail too — nothing there either. Then she examined the contents of her wallet. She had just enough cash for cab fare back to work.

As she made her way through a throng of people in the doorway, she could feel the momentary good cheer provided by the wine begin to dissolve. It had been hours since she'd called her father, and no call back. This was unusual, and suddenly irritating, even infuriating, for how was he to know that her crisis was merely financial? What if she had been calling him from jail, or from the bottom of a ditch somewhere?

She opened her phone and scrolled through her contact list, looking for her sister Lillian's name.

Lillian might understand. Lillian had once been twenty-nine, childless, unmarried, perhaps unmoored, though Rachel, so many years younger, had certainly been too caught up in her own life to notice what was going on with Lillian. Still, Lillian, before acquiring the marriage and the house and the beautiful children (well, calling the new baby beautiful, *that* was rather generous, but perhaps with time his looks would improve), had possibly at one time felt the way Rachel felt now. And perhaps she could dispense some advice to her younger sister.

Depending on when you caught her, Lillian could either provide a sympathetic ear or be a complete grouch, and you had no idea, until you'd tried, which Lillian you were going to get. But the benefits of the sympathetic Lillian far outweighed the risks of the grouchy one, so, once she had successfully hailed a cab and given the driver the address of her office, she pressed the call button. Lillian was sure to be at home at nearly two o'clock in the afternoon, when Olivia was napping.

Perhaps Lillian, if she were feeling particularly generous, could see her way clear to lending Rachel a bit of money to get her through until the next paycheck. Perhaps at the very least she would have some words of wisdom, something that would allow Rachel to feel that the hill she had ahead of her to climb was not so impossibly tall after all.

⁓∗⁓

"Just do it," said Stephen. He gripped Jane's hand tightly. It seemed suddenly smaller and whiter than it had earlier in the day; it looked and felt like a child's hand. He held Jane's cell phone out to her. He had found the number in the phone's contact list, had scrolled down to it, had done everything but pressed the green button to send the call.

Jane looked steadily at the ceiling, which was white—not surprising in a hospital, of course, but Stephen couldn't help wishing that Jane had something more exotic to look at, something less predictable and mundane. A jungle scene, perhaps, or an ocean motif. She had been looking at the ceiling for a long while, ever since the doctor and nurses had cleared out of the room.

"Call her," said Stephen. "She's your mother. She's going to want to know. She's got a right to know what's going on with you."

"Oh, *rights*," said Jane dismissively. She closed her eyes.

"Come on, Janey, or I'll call her myself."

"She'll be in a session, I'm sure of it. She's back-to-back on Mondays."

"Then you leave a message."

"I can't leave *that* on a message — 'Hello, Mother, here in the hospital, almost lost the baby.'" She put her hands on her stomach. "I'll call her later, I promise. Move the phone, okay?" Shakily, he put the phone back in her bag.

He was still terrified. He couldn't forgive himself for the conviction he'd felt. He'd been certain that they'd lost the baby, and somehow, unbidden, his mind had leaped ahead, had jumped from where they were now to the question of what to do next, how to console Jane, how long it would be until they could try again.

But they hadn't lost the baby. "It's going to be all right," Stephen said now. "You know it is. Right? You know it? Because it is." He had seen the blood on the seat of the car when Jane got up. *Maternal bleeding,* the nurse had told him. Bright red blood like that: *maternal bleeding.* He didn't like the sound of that.

"I guess," she said. "But it's really...it's really terrible. Bed rest! Aside from losing the baby, it's sort of the worst thing that could have happened."

"We'll work it out. You've only got ten weeks. That's not so long."

"Ten weeks! That's forever." She beat her hand lightly on the sheet next to her. "That's unbearable."

"But it could have been so much worse."

"I know that," she said. She began, softly, to cry. She turned her head to the wall.

"Don't," he said. "Janey, *don't.*"

"But," she whispered. "How am I going to make it through? All day, lying down, at home? For *ten weeks?*"

"We'll figure it out. It might not be the whole time. If the placenta—what'd they say? Moves away?"

"Resolves, I think they said."

"Right. Resolves. Then you're fine. You're good to go."

"What about work?"

"We'll figure it out. We'll figure all of it out. You can work from bed."

"How?"

"I don't know, exactly. But I can promise you that we'll figure it out. What's important is that the baby is going to be fine."

"Is *probably* going to be fine. What if it happens again? All the bleeding?"

"Then we'll deal with it. Even if the baby came today, it would be okay. We would take care of it."

"But ten *weeks*." She gathered a handful of the hospital gown in her fists and lifted it to her face. Silently, Stephen handed her a tissue from the box on the table closest to him.

"Thank you," she said morosely. From the depths of her bag her phone began to ring.

"That's work," she said.

"Don't answer."

"Maybe I should—"

"Don't."

"Okay."

He had not yet told her the rest of it, which the doctor, summoning him into the hallway, had discussed with him several minutes ago. The doctor was Indian, with dark hair pulled back into a bun and unlined caramel skin. Young, from the looks of it—maybe his age, give or take. No nonsense. Clearly busy.

"Listen," she'd said, looking at a clipboard, then glancing up at Stephen. "You're visiting family here?"

"Yes, my parents."

"I think it's best she remain."

"In the hospital?" he'd asked.

"For forty-eight hours, yes. So we can confirm the bleeding has stopped. But after that, here in town. For the duration."

He swallowed hard, beginning to understand. "For the duration of—"

"Of the pregnancy. For the duration of the pregnancy, your wife should be resting."

"I'm not sure I—"

The doctor sighed, and made a nearly imperceptible shift of weight. "She should not make the trip back to New York. What if the bleeding were to begin again?"

"She'll never go for that."

The doctor shrugged and met Stephen's eyes. Her eyes were remarkably dark, no makeup. "Sometimes it's not up to us."

"But…are you saying for certain?"

"I am saying for certain that if you want to give this baby the best possible chance, your wife will rest at home in Burlington until she delivers. Which may be in ten weeks, and which may be sooner. The nurses will give you discharge instructions and talk to you about setting up appointments." She shook his hand then, and turned to walk down the hallway.

"Jane?" he said. "One more thing we need to talk about."

She held out her hand. "First, phone," she said. "I'm going to try my mother."

He watched her scroll through the numbers, watched her bite her bottom lip and put her thumbnail between her teeth. After a moment she put down the phone and looked up at Stephen. She touched her hands to her stomach. "She's not picking up. I'll call her when we get back. Do you think we can go soon, Stephen? Is there anything else we need to do? I really just want to go home, to my own bed, back to the city. *Please* take me home."

"How come you're allowed to eat in the den?" Olivia demanded from the kitchen.

"I'm a grown-up," Lillian said. She was holding a cherry Popsicle; Olivia's was grape. "I can be very careful." She was flipping through a gardening magazine that she had found on the coffee table. The photographs in the magazine—the perfect outdoor spaces, the perennial gardens in full bloom, even the advertisement picturing a happy middle-aged couple sharing a bowl of granola—reminded her of all the deficits in her own life. She closed the magazine and put it back where she'd found it.

"Can I eat mine in the den?"

"No. You can eat yours where you are, or outside."

"Why?"

"Grandma's house, Grandma's rules."

"Outside. But I want you to come *with* me."

"All right." They stepped together onto the back deck. Lillian shifted Philip's car seat near the door so that she could see inside it. Miraculously he wasn't sleeping, but he wasn't crying either. He was regarding both of them seriously, sucking on his fist. "Good boy," said Lillian. Olivia crouched down and stuck her head inside the car seat.

"Careful," said Lillian. After she had talked to Tom, Lillian had fed Philip and then handed him to Ginny while she took a half-hour nap. Thirty minutes hadn't been enough to replenish her completely—her reservoirs, after all, were completely dry—but it had helped, and she felt that now she could face the rest of the day.

"I'm just giving him a kiss," said Olivia, and she was; Lillian heard the gentle smacking sound and then Olivia emerged, triumphant, still grasping her Popsicle.

The pots of geraniums on the deck were beginning to droop in the sun. Lillian found a watering can on the deck and filled it from the tap in the kitchen, then held it out to Olivia, who smiled and began serenely to water the deck around the pots.

"In the soil," said Lillian.

William was working in the back garden. Ginny had gone out to do errands. Next to William was parked the old green wheelbarrow Lillian remembered from her youth. She watched William dip his shovel into it, then bring it out.

"When's Daddy coming?" asked Olivia. "Tomorrow?"

"No, not tomorrow."

"Why not?"

"Daddy has to work."

"So, when?"

"I'm not sure," said Lillian.

"What's Grandpa doing?" Olivia's Popsicle was beginning to drip a purple river down her chin.

"Spreading mulch."

"What's malch?"

"Not malch. Mulch."

"Malch."

"It keeps the gardens healthy for the summer. Keeps the weeds away."

"Oh." Olivia worked at her Popsicle for some time. "I don't like the way it smells," she said, then looked squarely at Lillian and said, with a fair amount of indignation, "Grandpa has hair in his nose."

"Does he?" Lillian snorted. "How lovely of you to notice. I suppose you pointed it out to him?"

Olivia nodded. "He said it's because he's old."

"Oh yeah?"

"I wanted to take it out. But he wouldn't let me."

"I expect not."

Olivia finished her Popsicle; she licked the stick until there was no grape left and handed it to Lillian. "Here." Lillian ignored her. *"Here,"* said Olivia again, and this time Lillian took it and put it, with her own, on the table. Lillian peeked inside at Philip: still content, he was looking up at the bright plastic spider hanging from the car seat's handle. She sat down on the bench that wrapped around the inside of the deck.

"I have nothing to do," Olivia said.

"What do you want to do? Hopscotch?" She hoped Olivia didn't say yes to that. She didn't have enough energy for hopscotch.

"No..."

"Color?"

"No..."

"Just sit here in the sun, then?"

"Yes!"

"Come here." Lillian patted the spot beside her on the bench. She closed her eyes. Perhaps Olivia could be persuaded to fall asleep in the sun with her. She was trying to convince herself— and the Popsicles were part of this ploy—that this was merely a vacation, just a little jaunt to visit the family, and that at some point soon they would return home and resume their normal existence. She had found that by keeping her marital wound tightly covered, indeed, by refusing to acknowledge it at all, and by refusing to acknowledge the now rudderless state that accompanied it, it hurt much less.

She thought about her visit to the church the day before, and the unexpected lift she had felt sitting there in the pew talking to Father Colin. There was the way he'd looked at her that had allowed her to believe for a moment that everything would be all right. The feeling had dissipated entirely by the time she got home, of course. But if she thought very hard, and if she imagined herself back in the pew, with the smell of incense that reminded her of sitting beside her siblings, of having both of her parents beside her, of the utter ordinariness and simplicity of a Sunday morning, then she could almost call the sensation back again.

Stephen and Jane, whose unannounced appearance had first surprised her and then, quickly thereafter, offended her—mostly because she felt *they* felt as though she ought to turn over the proper guest room and take the pullout couch in the den—had proved to be much less of an obstruction to her little homecoming fantasy than she had at first feared.

Still, she was glad they were off at the end of the day, glad that she would have her mother's attention back where it belonged, on her and the children. Ginny did tend to *dither* so around Stephen and Jane. Lillian supposed that they all did, in their own way.

But Lillian, this time, had found herself dithering less than usual. After years and years of looking up to Jane, after years of hearing about her tremendous earning power and her efficiency and industry, about her ability to rise at five o'clock in the morning and to be at her desk by seven-thirty *after* a trip to the gym, it seemed that her pregnancy had put them, at last, on something resembling equal footing.

"She looks *miserable*," Ginny had whispered fiercely to Lillian the previous night, after Stephen and Jane had gone to bed. Lillian, sitting at the kitchen table with Philip, about to hitch up her shirt and give him a final feeding before putting him down, had agreed.

"Swollen ankles don't discriminate," she observed.

"Yes," said her mother, and they'd sat there companionably for some minutes while Philip worked his way onto the breast and settled down contentedly to nurse.

As for discriminating, the same was true for heartburn and overworked veins and all of the other maladies visited upon mothers-to-be in their third trimester. No matter how fancy your business degree, no matter by how much you outearned your husband, no matter how your presence in your sleek and quiet office contributed to the mysterious workings of the international economy, the fact of another being growing inside of your body was simply not comfortable.

The phone rang. William, blithely attacking the mulch with his shovel, didn't hear. Lillian rose, then stood for several seconds, regarding the scene before her. It was no longer *her* telephone that was ringing; it was her parents' phone, and the likelihood that it would be for her was relatively small. Should she answer it? Or should she let it go, let her parents' ancient, creaking answering machine to pick it up?

"Dad," she called into the garden. "Dad, phone's ringing. You want me to get it?"

William did not look up from his work.

"Right back," she said to Olivia, who had stretched herself out on the bench, eyes closed, little pointed chin lifted to the sky, and who was uncommonly, exceptionally, blissfully, quiet and immobile.

She returned to the deck holding the cordless phone, and it must have been something in her tone of voice that caused both Olivia and William to look at her with identical expressions of concern and attention.

"It's Stephen," she said sharply, holding the phone out to her father, watching him put down the shovel, peel off his gardening gloves, and make his way over to the deck before she'd completed the sentence. "He wants to talk to you, Daddy. He's calling from the hospital. I think something's wrong."

From inside the house, from the depths of his car seat, loudly, boldly, announcing his disinclination to be ignored, and his awareness, perhaps, that he would be ignored anyway, Philip began to cry.

Ginny's face went pale. She was holding a paper sack of groceries, which she set down on the counter. William began to unload them, laying out the food carefully on the counter.

"Jesus Christ," Ginny said, and Olivia, thrilling to the words that she knew, perhaps from Ginny's tone and perhaps from the way Lillian looked at her warningly after Ginny had spoken, to be forbidden, looked down and repeated it softly, to her sandals: *Jesus Christ.*

"Bed rest," said Lillian. "Can you believe it?"

"We'll have to move them upstairs," Ginny said. "To your room, Lillian."

"*My* room?" Lillian had Philip pressed up against a burp cloth on her shoulder. His eyes were open and he was breathing deeply, contentedly; he had just eaten.

"Well, we can't have her lying down all day in the den, can we?"

"Why not?" said Lillian. "The den's more comfortable."

"Because that bed isn't as good," said Ginny. "You can't be on bed rest on a pullout couch. The springs jab you in the back."

"Then we shouldn't have had a pregnant woman sleeping there in the first place," suggested William.

"There's a television—" said Lillian.

William watched his daughter and his wife. He had so far remained out of the conversation; he had left it to Lillian to relate the situation to Ginny, and he had begun putting the food away. He had filled the sink and was dunking the plums into the water. "Doesn't matter about the television. The bedroom's better," he said firmly. He peeled a tiny orange sticker off one plum and a bit of the skin came off too, exposing the tender flesh beneath.

"Can I have a plum?" said Olivia, and wordlessly William handed her the one he was holding.

"This one's broken," she announced, looking at the peeled-away section of skin.

"It's not *broken*," said Lillian.

"Broken," said Olivia. "I want a different one."

William chose another from the sink and held it out.

"Be careful of the pit," said Ginny and Lillian at the same time, looking at Olivia before turning again to face each other.

"But I can't sleep in the den." Lillian's voice rose. "I've got the baby. The den's too…public. People walking in and out."

"Exactly," said William. "That's why Jane can't have the den."

"But I've got to nurse!" said Lillian plaintively.

"You can go into Stephen's room for that," suggested Ginny.

"And in the middle of the night—"

"In the middle of the night," said Ginny, "there will be no need to worry about privacy."

"There's no *room* in Stephen's room! It's full of junk."

"Hey," said William.

"Well, it *is*." Lillian chewed vengefully on a thumbnail.

"We can move some of it."

"Now?" said Lillian. "After ten years of piling crap in there?"

"Crap," said Olivia delightedly.

"*Lillian*," said William. "We can move some things out of there—not all, but some—and you can sleep in there, if you like."

"No," said Lillian. "I don't like."

William was beginning to feel a trickle of annoyance with his oldest daughter—no, more than a trickle. More like a stream. "Lillian," he said. "You're being uncharitable. You're being ridiculous."

Lillian colored. "*I* am?" She turned to Ginny. "*I* am?"

"Well, *sweetheart*," said Ginny. "Just listen to yourself."

"Yes," said William. "You are. And I've had enough. Here's

what we'll do. Jane will take over the bedroom, and that's that. You can move in with Olivia, Lillian, or you can sleep in Stephen's old room, or you can move down here to the den. Whichever you prefer."

"Fine," said Lillian. "Den." And then, reluctantly, "I'll move my things."

"Wonderful," said Ginny.

"Wonderful," said Olivia, who had plum juice running from the corner of her mouth and onto her white T-shirt. The T-shirt said, *"Princess in Training"* in pink sparkly cursive, but too many journeys through the washing machine had caused the first *r* to rub mostly off so it actually said, *"Pincess in Training."*

"I'll go change the sheets, get it all sorted out for her," said Ginny. She rubbed her temples in a gesture that William recognized as a sign of stress and anxiety. "And then, let's see—what else should we do? To get ready? Lillian, what would you need, if you had to go on bed rest? Books, magazines?"

"Straitjacket," said Lillian. She was still put out, anyone could see that. Her eyes narrowed.

"Oh, come now," said William. He folded the paper bag from the grocery store and put it in the pantry closet with the others.

"I mean it. She's not going to be able to keep still. For *weeks? Jane?* It's not going to happen."

"Well, it has to happen," said William. "My understanding, from Stephen, is that it has to happen, or the baby will be at risk."

"Well, yes, but."

"There is no 'yes, but' is the way I took it," said William.

One thing he had not yet related to Ginny was the current of panic he had heard running underneath Stephen's words during his conversation with him. He thought of Jane earlier that day, drinking orange juice in the kitchen, checking in with work. He thought of the authority with which she'd ended her phone call, and the certainty and confidence with which she talked about work. Here, in this house, in Vermont, perhaps she was a little bit of a fish out of water. But he knew from Stephen, and he knew from Lillian, and he knew from observing her himself, that she was steely.

He remembered Stephen in high school, and the anxiety—no, not just anxiety, the *terror*—he had exhibited before each cross-country race. Even though he was the best on the team, even though he never came in lower than third for his school, he threw up in the bathroom before each race—and once, ominously, in the woods partway through the course. He suspected that of the two of them, Stephen and Jane, it might be Stephen who would have a more difficult time with this.

"She's going to go crazy," said Lillian. "She's going to go absolutely nuts." She moved Philip to her opposite shoulder and rubbed his back vigorously until a burp, as small and unobtrusive as an afterthought, emerged. "Attaboy," she said, and Philip closed his eyes.

"Lillian!" said Ginny. "Never mind about what you think she will or won't do. Come upstairs and help me get the room ready. I've got something I need to run over to the rectory right after."

"What?" said Lillian quickly.

Ginny gave her a look. "An announcement for the bake sale that needs to go into the bulletin. Why's that matter to you?"

"I'll do it. I'll run it over."

"Okay," said Ginny. She was writing something on a new grocery list. "If you don't mind."

"I don't mind at all."

William drained the water from the sink and wrapped the plums in a dishcloth. "Bowl, or fridge?" he said to Ginny.

She felt one. "Bowl," she said. "No, fridge."

Lillian shifted Philip again and looked about for somewhere to put him.

"Give him to me," said William. "Just let me wash my hands first." After he dried his hands he held them out for the baby, and Lillian, handing Philip over, said, "Just watch his head there, Dad. It still needs some support."

"*I* know," said William, smiling, softening as he felt Philip's weight give in to his hands. "I happen to have done this before."

"I suppose you have," said Lillian. "Sorry." She reached out to wipe the plum juice from Olivia's mouth with a paper towel she tore from the kitchen roll. "You're not worried, are you, Dad?" asked Lillian.

William shrugged and sat in a kitchen chair. He moved Philip so that he lay in William's lap with William's hands behind his head. Philip squinted up at him. He curled his legs up like a frog and then straightened them, sighing.

"She going to be fine," said Lillian. "It's just bed rest. It's just a precaution. It happens all the time, tons of people get put on bed rest." And then, more softly, "Dad? It's just a precaution."

"I know," he said, and he noticed how old and sinewy, how spotted and veined, his hand looked next to Philip's smooth white head.

"I'm going up to get my stuff," said Lillian. She leaned down. William thought it was to kiss the baby but instead she kissed him, a cool, unexpected whisper on his cheek that was over so quickly he barely had time to register it. He didn't acknowledge it—he looked steadily down at Philip's unblinking gaze—but he felt his heart lift slightly. It was funny, the way your adult children could both delight and annoy you in the very same ways that they had when they had been actual children. He wouldn't have predicted that particular truth of parenting, thirty years ago.

"You," he said sternly to the baby. "*You* keep getting passed around like a hot potato." Beside him, Olivia, quivering with anticipation or excess energy, said, "Grandpa? What's a straitjacket?"

To Philip, who was regarding him thoughtfully, fluttering his eyelids, William said, "Listen to that one. You're going to be in for it, with her as a sister."

Philip said, "Bah" and raised a fist toward William.

To Olivia he said, "I'm not sure what a straitjacket is. You should go ask your mother."

"Why don't you know?"

William shrugged. "Don't know everything. I know a lot, but not everything. Go ask your mother. She's upstairs with Grandma."

"Okay," said Olivia, and she left him, dancing lightly up the stairs, with all the verve and brio of a three-year-old on a summer afternoon.

Lillian knocked softly at the door of the rectory. She expected that someone other than Father Colin would answer, but it was the priest himself.

"Lillian Owen!" he said, smiling. "This is a nice surprise."

Why was she flushing? "Here," she said, thrusting the paper at him. "I told my mother I'd bring this by. Something about a bulletin and a bake sale."

"Ah." He took it from her. "Thank you. Come on back to the office, and I'll make sure to put it in the right spot before I lose it."

Lillian had never been in the rectory. She followed Father Colin down a long dark hallway, past a living room with old-lady furniture, past a dated kitchen with green Formica countertops, and into the office. "Not my choice of décor," Father Colin said over his shoulder. (Could he read her mind?) "But it is what it is."

Was he always smiling? Lillian couldn't say for sure, but if she thought back again to those boys in college it seemed possible that he was. Things seemed to roll off their backs, those boys.

"Come, come," he said. "This is the parish office here, but this little nook back here is all mine. I mean, Father Michael's, of course. But temporarily mine."

"It's nice," she said insincerely.

"Well, it doesn't feel like home," he admitted. "I got a lot of visitors in Boston. Baked goods, kids coloring pictures for me, the whole nine yards. But here...it's been rather quiet."

"I guess maybe it's confusing to people," she said, "not knowing how long you'll be here. And Father Michael was such an institution."

"That's right," he said. "Hard shoes to step into."

She felt her cheeks grow even warmer. "Oh, no! That's not what I meant."

He waved a hand at her. "That's okay, really. I know what I'm up against. People get accustomed to doing something one way, and it's hard to change."

To shield her awkwardness, Lillian looked around the room. It was rather cluttered, with piles of books and papers stacked against the wall, and a few cardboard boxes in the corner. The desk was neater, with a computer, a black office telephone, one stack of papers, and a framed photograph of three young boys.

"Nephews," Father Colin said when he saw her looking. "My brother Seamus's kids. They live in Southie, three blocks away from where I grew up." She picked up the photo and looked at it. The boys were all wearing baseball mitts and caps. They were freckled and shorn, with open, honest smiles like Father Colin's.

Behind Father Michael's desk was a print of the Crucifixion. Lillian stared at it, at the grotesque angle of Christ's arms, the way his right foot crossed over his left, the sinewy muscles of his calves and thighs.

"Grünewald," said Father Colin. "One of the bleaker perspectives on things."

"I guess so," said Lillian. "But I guess there isn't really a cheerful perspective on that, is there?"

Father Colin looked for several seconds at the print. "No," he said. "No, I suppose there isn't." He smiled and rustled the papers on his desk. "There," he said. "I think I've got it in the right place. Though the bulletin, I'm happy to say, is not my responsibility. Thank you for bringing it by."

"No problem," said Lillian. She turned toward the door but found that she was casting about in her mind for something to say, for a reason not to leave. Why was that? She couldn't articulate it. But later, driving home, and still later that night, lying on the pull-out couch in the den, moving slightly back and forth to settle her back between the springs, listening to Philip's little snorting noises as he slept, she thought that there was something about the office in the rectory that made her feel sheltered and safe.

⁂

The light was coming into the apartment at a peculiar and arresting angle; it made the apartment, and, indeed, the entire city appear to be lit from within. Rachel was trying to read through the script for the film she was going to cast. Tess wanted to see her list of actors to call soon. Rachel had a pad of paper and a pen next to her to make notes. She shook a page of the script, then began to read it out loud. Her voice sounded odd in the empty apartment, as though it were not part of her but rather had come floating in the window on the back of a cloud.

She gave up and dialed Lillian's cell phone number.

She did not allow herself to think about the test she had taken the day before. She concentrated on the script, in which two brothers were arguing about what to do with their alcoholic father. All the scripts she read lately, it seemed, featured two brothers and an alcoholic father.

"It took me a while to find you," said Rachel. "What are you, in hiding?"

"No," said Lillian. "Don't be ridiculous."

"I left three messages on your home machine, and then finally Tom called me back."

"Tom?" said Lillian quickly. "What did he say?"

"He said you went up there—"

"Well," said Lillian. "I did come up here. So what?"

Rachel looked out the window. In the building across from hers she could see three people sitting on a roof deck next to a giant red pot of flowers. They were drinking something out of tall frosty glasses. The trio, and the air of festivity that surrounded them, seemed to underscore her own solitude.

She would never sit on a roof deck with other people drinking frosty beverages.

She would never own a red pot.

If she did happen to come into ownership of a red pot she would never have the initiative or the resources to make her way to a garden center and purchase flowers to plant in it.

Did they even have garden centers in New York City? Surely they did—they had everything in New York City—but she hadn't the faintest idea of where they were or how to shop at them. She thought of her father, and the way he got excited if he found a particularly exotic plant to buy.

She had bought the test during her lunch hour, walking an extra six blocks to visit a pharmacy where she was unlikely to run into anyone she knew, and she had carried it into the bathroom in the lobby of her office building.

"What else did Tom say?" demanded Lillian. "About why I came up?"

"Nothing. Why?"

"No reason." There was a pause, and then she continued. "What's going on?" said Lillian. "How's work? And...other stuff?"

"I don't know," said Rachel. "Okay, I guess."

"Oh, come on. Don't be a sourpuss. Just tell."

Then in a rush Rachel was telling Lillian about the independent film she was going to cast, and about Whitney's wedding plans, and even about the money William had sent her after she called him the previous week, and which she had deposited, and which she had then promptly spent on the past month's rent and on the shoes to go with the bridesmaid dress for Whitney's wedding, and which was now gone.

"Jesus, Rach," said Lillian. "It's good about the film, that's fantastic. But otherwise...you're kind of a mess."

"Not how I like to think of myself," said Rachel stiffly. "But I guess you could say that."

"So..."

"So the problem," Rachel said, "is that the money Dad sent was sort of like a Band-Aid. When really I need—"

"Really you need major surgery."

"Exactly," said Rachel, relieved that her sister understood and would, perhaps, advise her on what to do next. "I need major surgery. And I don't know what to do."

"Move?" suggested Lillian. The three people on the roof deck stood in unison—Rachel half expected them to bow—and disappeared one by one down a hole in the center of the roof. They left the glasses. How was it, Rachel wondered, that they left the glasses? Who were they expecting to come up and clear them away?

"Way, *way* easier said than done," she said to Lillian. "This is Manhattan. I'd need a security deposit, and the Realtor's fee, and moving costs. Well, it's just impossible. It would cost me more to move to a cheaper apartment than to stay here."

"So you'll stay there, then."

"But I can't. I can't pay the rent, not on my salary."

She opened the door to the refrigerator. It was, as she had suspected, completely empty, save for the ancient box of Arm & Hammer that had been there when she and Marcus had moved in and which she had bothered neither to replace nor to dispose of. The box reminded her of her mother, who always kept baking soda in the refrigerator, and she felt a sudden, intense flash of nostalgia for the order that resided in the house in which she had grown up: for the washcloths and towels folded in neat stacks in the linen closet, for the spices organized in the cupboard to the right of the stove, for the oversized Rubbermaid containers, labeled in her mother's tidy hand, which held outgrown or off-season clothes in the attic and which had done so for as long as Rachel could remember and which, she was certain, were still doing so.

"So what will you do?"

"I don't know." Rachel fingered the yellowing leaves of her only houseplant, a pothos Marcus's mother had given them when they'd moved in together. Marcus's mother had promised Rachel that it was impossible to kill, but Rachel seemed to be doing an alarmingly efficient job of killing it anyway. She turned the tap on and filled a juice glass full of water, then poured it into the pot.

※

Rachel had tried to hold the stick straight under the urine stream, the way the directions had said, but even so she ended up with urine on her hand and she sat there uncomfortably for the requisite three minutes while two girls from another casting agency on the third floor (not Rachel's) had come in and talked in quiet, bitter voices about the meeting they had just come out of.

One of them was saying, "Well, if that's the way he's going to play it—" when the second pink line emerged, faint at first, then darker, then darker still, until there was no denying it.

She wrapped toilet paper around the stick, and put it back inside the box, and waited until the girls from the third floor had gone; she could smell their perfume, and also a hint of cigarette smoke. She stuffed the box in the bottom of the garbage can, underneath a clump of wet paper towels, and after a moment's consideration she unearthed it and wrapped the whole thing in more paper towels and put it inside her handbag. She washed her hands and washed them again and considered her face in the mirror.

Pregnant, she said to her reflection, and she watched her lips move and watched them settle themselves into an angry knot in the center of her face. You stupid thing. You *idiot.*

"I think," she said slowly, "I think I need to ask Mom and Dad for more money."

In the background Rachel heard a little infant noise. "Aw," she said. "Philip." Her heart lurched.

"Rachel! *Don't* ask them to give you more money."

"Not a *gift,*" said Rachel. "More like a long-term loan. To get me back on my feet again."

"You can't ask them for more."

"Why not? If they have it to give."

"Who says they have it?"

"I don't know. Don't they? They're *parents,* for God's sake. They're supposed to have it all together."

"Rachel. You're nearly thirty. You have to be on your own."

"*You're* thirty-six," said Rachel.

"And?"

"And you ask them for stuff all the time."

"Like what?"

"Like everything! You're hiding out there!"

"Not hiding out. Visiting." There was a clattering in the background, then Lillian said, "Shit," softly.

"That's not the picture Tom painted." Rachel wandered into the tiny square of bathroom and rummaged in her makeup drawer for a pair of tweezers.

"That's none of your business."

"Isn't it?"

"No! It isn't. Anyway, it's a different situation entirely."

"How's it different?"

"I have children. I need more help. Different help. It's a whole different world, once you have children."

"You have a husband, too. You should need less help, not more," said Rachel. She knew as she said it that they were beginning to tread on dangerous ground. With the tweezers she plucked at an errant hair just above her right eyebrow, and she was looking at the droplet of blood that formed there when Lillian said what she said next.

"But you've never been a parent," Lillian said gently, almost tenderly, and Rachel could tell that her older sister knew that it was the difference between the softness of her tone and the austerity of her words that would wound Rachel the most. "You don't know what you're talking about."

"Lillian," she said. "I'm—"

"You're what?"

"I'm." She couldn't say it, she couldn't say the words: I'm pregnant. Instead she said, "I'm in the middle of something. I have to go."

※

Before Nina, before Lillian left for Vermont, before Tom began to fear that he might actually forget the particular scent of his daughter, Olivia, after she'd been playing outside in the yard—the pungent clothing, the innocent three-year-old sweat in her hair—

there was a night that Tom went back to again and again over the summer, etching the details in his mind.

Lillian had been for her six-week postpartum checkup that morning, and Tom, finding himself in an ebullient, celebratory mood, picked up take-out Thai food on the way home and a bottle of white wine to go along with it.

Tom entered the house whistling, not minding, for once, the sight of the overgrown lawn (he had to get the mower serviced) and the crabgrass growing angrily through the cracks in the driveway (he had to get the driveway repaved). He even, after one quick glance, averted his eyes from the inside of Lillian's car, which was littered with empty Dunkin' Donuts plastic cups, the melted ice and leftover coffee forming a shallow brown lake in the bottom of each.

Lillian was sitting on the cluttered sofa in the living room with Philip attached, as ever, to her breast. Tom could see four or five of Olivia's books scattered around her and a giant jigsaw puzzle upended on the coffee table. On the carpet, in various stages of undress, lay several of Olivia's dolls. It looked like the site of some sort of catastrophe, not the scene of domestic calm and tranquility he had been imagining when he ordered the food, when he chose the wine. Olivia was nowhere to be found.

Tom took a deep breath and presented the food and wine to Lillian. She looked up briefly, then returned her gaze to the top of Philip's head.

"Oh, Tom," she said reproachfully. "That's sweet. But you know I can't drink that. I'm *nursing*. And the food…well, isn't it spicy? And it will only get cold. Olivia hasn't eaten yet. Then she needs a bath. We won't sit down for hours. And then"—this part she said to Philip, addressing him in a flimsy, cutesy voice Tom had rarely, if ever, heard issuing from her—"and then *you'll* be ready to eat again, mister. Won't you? *Won't* you?"

Olivia appeared then. She was shirtless and without pants but wore a pair of pink ballet tights with a hole in the knee, a tiara, and a pair of Lillian's old heels that she had recently seized for her dress-up box.

"Daddy!" she said. "Can we have mac and cheese for dinner?"

Lillian closed her eyes and leaned back into the sofa cushions. She waved her hand in Tom's general direction and rubbed the other hand on Philip's head. "Go ahead," she whispered. "Make her mac and cheese. We'll nuke ours later."

He put the wine in the refrigerator and abandoned the Thai food on the crowded table among newspapers, moderately organized piles of mail, an incongruous packet of cucumber seeds and a child's orange shovel crusted with dirt. While he waited for the shells to boil, and after he had opened the little packet of orange cheese powder and mixed it with the milk, and after he had answered a half dozen of Olivia's questions (yes, when she was seven years old she could spend the night at Stephanie's house; no, he didn't think they had any bats in their attic like the MacAllisters across the street; yes, she would one day have the chance to ride in an airplane; no, they weren't going to go to Disney World next week; no, one did not pick pumpkins from trees; yes, all the dinosaurs were gone from the earth, and no, they weren't coming back), he retrieved the bottle of wine from the refrigerator, poured Lillian a glass, and brought it to her in the living room.

Surely one glass was permitted; he did not recall any no-alcohol policies when she was nursing Olivia. Philip had finished his meal and was reclining on the burp cloth on Lillian's shoulder; his eyes were closed and his tiny shoulders were pulled toward his ears. Lillian's eyes were closed too, her mouth was open, and her chin was tipped back. She was deeply asleep. He placed the glass on the table on a coaster and stood for a minute, considering them: mother and child. He felt a surge of emotion that later, when he examined it in the darkness of their bedroom, with Lillian asleep beside him, he could identify only as loneliness.

After the children were down (though down, as far as Philip was concerned, was a relative term; he slept fitfully at this time of night, waking without provocation, yelling out, then settling himself back down for a few minutes before beginning the routine again), they nuked the Thai food and watched an episode of *Lost* they had recorded on the DVR. Partway through the show Tom sensed that he was alone in the living room so he glanced over at Lillian: sleeping again. Nobly, he attempted to wake her by shaking her gently—one could not, after all, easily recover the story line after missing part of *Lost*—but she didn't respond. Eventually he turned off the television and woke her enough to get her upstairs and into her pajamas and then into bed, where she slept soundly until Philip cried at eleven for his feeding.

When Lillian had disappeared into Philip's room—Tom watched her stumbling progress down the hallway with a mixture of pity and irritation, because how could it not be forced for his benefit?—he lay there, blinking at the darkness, watching the shadows from a passing car move across the ceiling.

When Olivia was a baby, it had not taken so long to get back to something resembling normalcy, to the core of themselves, and to the sex. Had it? No, surely it hadn't. And it wasn't even the sex he was thinking of (well, okay, partly it was) but the physical contact that preceded the sex—the hint, at least, that the desire for sex was in there somewhere. Where had that gone, this time? Was it over between them? Was what he was witnessing here the slow, silent disintegration of his marriage, the inevitable march toward conventionality?

He was thinking about all of this the next morning, when he emerged from the shower and Lillian, standing there in the middle of the bedroom, said, "Sorry. For falling asleep last night."

"That's okay." He looked at her, and found that if he looked past her stained T-shirt and sweatpants, past her uncombed hair, past the white-knuckled hand clutching the coffee mug, he could still find the woman he had fallen in love with. She was hidden, perhaps, underneath the fatigue and the mood swings and the concentration on nursing the baby. But she was there.

Walking through the empty rooms of the house now, with the outlines of the furniture rendered ghostly in the moonlight, he would have given anything to be back in the middle of the mess he found that night when he came home with the Thai food, the warm, chaotic center of his family, and he couldn't stop thinking about it, how that was what he had, until he didn't.

※

Lillian was calmer the next time Tom called, and better rested. It was late at night, and she always got a burst of energy after Philip's eleven o'clock feeding.

She thought when she first heard Tom's voice that she was capable of a reasonable conversation. She thought they could discuss the children, at least, and that she could tell him about Jane. But after she'd mentioned the sniffle Philip had picked up, and told him grudgingly about how Olivia had made friends with a little girl down the street, and filled him in about Jane's bed rest...well, after that there was a space in the conversation, and into it bubbled all the rage that she thought she'd been pushing down.

"I'm sorry, Tom," she said. "But I'm just not ready to talk to you. I'm still mad—I'm still so, so mad."

"Really?" said Tom. She imagined him walking through the rooms of their empty home. She imagined him making the rounds: Philip's room, Olivia's room, their room. "Well, it's not all up to you, Lillian, whether you interact with me or not."

"Isn't it?" She sat carefully in her father's recliner. Philip, in the Pack 'n Play, had gone to sleep.

"They're my children too. I get to talk to them, see them."

She laughed bitterly. "Oh yeah? I think you gave up the right to make rules about that when you slept with your assistant." She pulled the handle to release the recliner's stool and stretched out her legs.

"Jesus, Lillian."

"Well? Didn't you? Isn't that why I'm here?"

"It was an *isolated* incident. I was *drunk*. I made a mistake."

"Pretty big mistake."

"It's not like you've been perfect throughout everything."

She said, very carefully, very evenly, "What do you mean by that?"

"You can't guess what I mean?"

"I can't." She thought, though, that maybe she could. She thought about the night after her six-week checkup when Tom brought home Thai food, a bottle of wine. And what had she done? Told him the food was too spicy for the breast milk, told him that she couldn't drink wine. Retreated into her own little cocoon. Had she even thanked him? She didn't think so.

"You've been mad at me ever since Philip was born!"

"I've been *tired* ever since Philip was born."

"Tired is one thing. Taking it out on me is another."

"You have no idea," she said, "what it's like to be this tired. You have no idea what this takes out of you, Tom. You can't possibly imagine. I am sick of thinking about you. I am exhausted. I am feeding the baby eight times a day, plus taking care of Olivia. You have no idea what goes into this, or you would have been there for me."

"There for you! I tried to be. You didn't want me. You were grouchy and unpredictable—"

She felt her heartbeat quicken; her cheeks grew warm. He continued: "Impatient. Half the time you act like you don't even *like* me!"

"So," she said. "Your wife has a baby and is too tired for sex and *that* gives you an excuse to sleep with someone else? Let me tell you, if that were the case there would be a lot of affairs going on!"

"Oh, come on."

"Every single husband you know would be sleeping around." She thought of the time she'd met Nina in the office. She barely looked up from the cell phone on which she was madly texting. She chewed gum like a teenager. She drank those frozen coffee drinks. Worse, she was actually pretty. Her legs were lean and tanned: no freckles, no sunburn. She looked like she might be fun. She looked well rested, up for anything. She looked, in short, like everything Lillian was not. "Whatever happened to 'for better or worse'? This part right now that I'm going through? This is part of the worse."

"Nothing happened to that, Lillian. I'm here. I'm waiting." He paused. "I'm sorry. Come home."

"They need me here. With Jane—" This wasn't strictly true, of course. If anything, they needed her gone. The house was beginning to feel crowded.

"I need you more."

"It's nice here. They're taking care of me, Tom. You can't imagine what a relief that is to me, to be taken care of instead of doing all the taking care."

"Oh, come on, Lillian. I take care of you. That night I brought home the Thai food—"

"That," she said, "was just because you knew I was cleared for sex. That wasn't taking care of. That was about the sex."

"It wasn't about the sex! The sex is an *expression* of something, that's all."

"Oh really? So what were you expressing with Nina?"

"Jesus, Lillian, nothing."

"Tom, at home I feel like I'm *drowning* in other people's needs."

"Needs? That's what I am to you, another need?"

She paused. She thought, *Here we go.* She said, "Yes, actually. Sometimes."

"That's harsh. You think I don't get it—"

"But you don't, not really. You *don't* get what it's like. I'm with them *all the time.* All day long. Every day! Not a moment to myself."

"I know you are."

"You don't know!" Her voice rose desperately. "I eat every meal standing at the counter. If I eat at all. I can't complete a thought. Every breakfast, every lunch! Hopping around like a waitress. You know I do. You get to eat with grown-ups any time you like. You go to restaurants. Even if you don't go to a restaurant, you get to have a quiet sandwich at your desk. And then you go and do something like this—it's like you're getting *all* the good stuff, all to yourself."

"How can you say that? I haven't seen my children in a week."

"You should have thought of that before," she said, and then she clicked the phone shut.

☀

Stephen stood outside Jane's bedroom door. It was *his* room, too, for the time being, and he had as much right to be in there as anyone else, but something was stopping him from opening the door and entering. He had been in earlier in the morning, bringing Jane a tray with her breakfast on it, and he had sat in the chair next to the bed and watched her eat. She chewed slowly and carefully, as though any movement she made in haste or without thought was likely to be detrimental to the baby. He wouldn't leave the room until she had eaten every bite: a bowl of oatmeal, three sizable strawberries, a small glass of milk.

"You don't have to *stare* at me," she'd said. "I'm not going to hide the food under the pillow when you're not looking, like an anorexic."

"I know. But I like being in here with you anyway."

It had been two weeks since they'd come home from the hospital and settled Jane into this bed. She was allowed to get up to use the bathroom, but she was not allowed to go up or down the stairs, except to go to her checkups at the hospital.

"Could be much worse," the nurse had said cheerfully, packing them up to go home.

"How?" asked Stephen. "Out of curiosity."

"Could be bed rest in the hospital. Could have been that the bleeding didn't stop and the baby came early." She handed Stephen a xeroxed list of dos and don'ts for bed rest. (Do: Keep up your fluid intake to avoid constipation. Don't: Try to do more than your doctor recommends. Do: Expect to feel helpless and frustrated, even angry.)

Yesterday a heat wave had settled on the region, locking the humid air so tightly over the lake that you could almost see it there in front of the Adirondacks, smoky and seditious. Stephen had ventured into the basement to retrieve an ancient black oscillating fan, which he set up on the dresser, pointing toward Jane. The fan was on now, and each time its oscillation sent the air in their direction it lifted Jane's napkin and settled it back down onto the tray.

Placenta previa, the doctor had said. *Partial* placenta previa. But to Stephen it didn't feel partial at all. It felt completely and utterly terrifying.

She was allowed one shower every other day, and, helping her into the bathroom, undressing her, sitting on the toilet while she showered and washed her hair, Stephen held his breath, willing the baby to stay inside her for at least a little bit longer. He had to stop himself from climbing in the shower with her; he couldn't help but think that the farther he let himself go from her, the more danger she would be in.

And sex: well. Perhaps some time in the future, if the doctors documented that the placenta had moved away from the cervix, and if the bed rest restrictions eased, then maybe. But he had seen the look of horror on Jane's face when the doctor said that, and he had to admit that he, too, felt terrified at the prospect.

He had borrowed Jane's laptop to visit a variety of websites about bed rest. He had learned that frustration and anger were normal responses on the part of the patient. He had learned that he, as the caregiver, must not take any manifestations of that frustration and anger personally.

He had learned that Jane might find her cross easier to bear if she brushed her hair each morning and dressed in a pretty nightgown. He had presented her with that piece of advice, and she had shouted with laughter. He had learned that an astonishing number of mothers in Jane's situation posted daily blog updates about their experiences with bed rest, and he had bookmarked the ones he decided were the most compelling, the least annoying and pity-seeking. He had offered these to Jane as reading material. She had declined.

Most difficult for her, he knew, was the knowledge that back in Manhattan, without her, the wheels were still turning in her company; the financial world had not, in her absence, come to a complete standstill.

She had joined two conference calls so far and had spent a significant amount of time on e-mail.

"Really?" Ginny, who had been dusting in the dining room, had said when he'd gone to fetch the cordless phone. "A conference call? Isn't she supposed to be resting?"

"Well, she *is*. This is more restful to her than worrying about missing it would be."

Ginny told him with a flick of her dustcloth that she disagreed.

Now he did his best to see into the bedroom without pushing open the door; if she was sleeping, he didn't want to disturb her. He knew she didn't sleep well at night; he could hear, from the spare mattress he'd laid down for himself on the floor by the bed, tiny, muffled movements and sighs all through the night. He wasn't sleeping well either: with the darkness came the fears that something might happen to the baby.

"I can see you out there, peeking through the crack," said Jane. "Just come in already."

"I was just—"

"I know. But come in, why don't you. No need to stand out there."

He entered the room and stood by the bed.

She was tapping away at an e-mail. "You can sit, you know."

He lowered himself onto the edge of the bed slowly, gingerly.

"You look good," he ventured.

"God, no. I look like crap." She wore maternity shorts and a giant gray T-shirt that had once been his. Her hair stuck to her forehead.

Be supportive and agreeable, one of the websites for caregivers had told him. *No matter what.*

"You look like crap!" he said cheerfully. "But so what. Embrace it."

She rolled her eyes and kept on with the e-mail.

"What are you working on?"

She waved her hand at him and continued to look down.

"Just a thing. For my boss."

He looked at the mound of belly. He thought if he could see some movement, if he could *see,* with his own eyes, a flicker of motion, he would feel better about the world, better enough to leave Jane alone. "Important?"

She met his eyes briefly, then looked back down. "Honestly? You have no idea how important."

"Really? More so than usual?"

This time she didn't look up. "Much more so. It's crisis mode."

"What's the crisis?"

"It's a lot of crises, all mixed up together. It's … it's too much to go into right now."

"Anything you can't handle?"

"Truthfully?"

He nodded.

"Truthfully, I'm not sure."

"I don't think I've ever heard you say that before. About anything."

"Well." She continued typing.

"Everything OK in there?" he said, nodding his head toward the mound.

She looked up and sighed, irritated. "It's okay. It's fine. Same as yesterday, same as tomorrow, blah blah."

"Have you felt it moving?"

"Yes."

"How many times?"

"I don't know. One? Seven? I didn't count."

"But you definitely felt something."

"I definitely felt something."

"Well … that's great! I should let you get back to work." He continued to sit on the bed. Studiously, she ignored him.

He sat there for another moment until she said, "Stephen. You don't need to babysit me. I'm okay."

"I like being here with you."

"But maybe I don't like it." She turned slightly away from him, bringing the laptop with her.

"Oh—"

"Maybe I want to be left alone." She said this softly.

You'll need all of your patience, one of the websites had said. *You'll need more patience than you've ever needed before.*

So summoning that patience, and summoning all the good will and good cheer he could locate in every corner of his body, he got carefully up from the bed, leaned slowly over her, and ever so tenderly, ever so delicately, planted a kiss in the center of her sweaty forehead. Then he left the room and closed the door, as quietly as he imagined you would close the door in a house where a baby was sleeping.

JULY

The phone rang: Rachel's mother. Rachel considered not answering, then she did, then just as quickly she wished she hadn't. Her mother's energy frightened her. She ran her fingers over the dusty top of her bookcase and let her mother talk: Olivia was keeping them all hopping. The other day she had brought home the neighbor's cat and tried to dress it in one of her doll's dresses.

"Really?" said Rachel. "That sounds like something out of a sitcom."

"It was," said Ginny. "Except for the scratches all up and down her arm. The cat didn't care for it." Jane was settled into Lillian's old bedroom, poor thing. Hanging in there.

"That's awful," said Rachel. "That's completely awful. I hope everyone is being nice to her. Mom? Are they?"

"Of *course*," said Ginny. "Of course, we're all being very nice. And the bed rest may not last for the entire pregnancy. It's a wait-and-see, for now. I can't remember all the details."

"Are you sure you're being extra nice? Because with Jane you aren't always —"

"Oh, stop it, Rachel. That's unfair." Ginny continued her litany. Philip was still up several times a night. Father Michael, their parish priest, had taken ill. The flu, they thought it was at first, but it turned into pneumonia, and there was someone new there to fill in for him, a wonderful young priest from Boston, just full of energy. So refreshing! Youth behind the pulpit! And how was Rachel?

"Fine," she said. "I'm doing some reading for work." She was at it again: the brothers with the alcoholic father. Casting was due to start within the month. She rose from the bed and crossed the room to the window. She could see, on the sidewalk beneath, a young boy, maybe eleven or twelve, zipping along the sidewalk in those sneakers with wheels on the bottom. Rachel found it disconcerting, this boy's ability to go from walking to rolling to walking again. She didn't know how he transitioned so easily without falling on his face. She supposed that with the shoes, as with many things, there was not as much to it as it seemed to an observer.

"I thought I had something else," said Ginny. "Now, let's see, what could I have forgotten?"

"Mom?"

"No," said her mother. "I've lost it again. Let's see, I was standing right here when I thought of it earlier—"

"Mom?" Rachel said. "Mom? It's okay. You can call me back if you think of it."

"But I think it's right—"

"No," said Rachel firmly. "I have to go. You can call me later. Or I'll call you."

Since taking the pregnancy test she'd allowed herself to sustain a little fantasy life. In this fantasy, she told Marcus about the pregnancy, he moved back in, they prepared for a life of domestic bliss. Meanwhile, Tess would fall gravely ill and ask Rachel to take over the majority of the agency's work, a task that Rachel, in her glowing, pregnant state, would perform fabulously and that would catapult her to the very zenith of the casting world.

She crossed the apartment to the kitchen, and then opened one cupboard after another until she found a chocolate bar she had hidden from herself several weeks ago.

She took out the chocolate. She would have just a tiny piece, just a square or two. She opened it carefully, avoiding a peek at the food label. White chocolate, she reasoned, must be slightly lower in sugar and calories than dark. Right? But, just in case, she wouldn't confirm it by looking.

Her stomach felt strange, a not-quite-right sensation that could have been nerves or indigestion.

She left the chocolate on the counter, grabbed her purse, and stepped out of the apartment. She walked down the stairs and out of the building. She looked up and down. The kid with the wheel shoes had gone.

She realized that she did not, after all, have anywhere to go. The entire city was at her disposal, and she had nowhere to go. She was reminded of the feeling that came upon her sometimes in a store, where all the clothes were arranged so meticulously and lavishly that she became too paralyzed to buy anything.

She would not think about the test. Or maybe she would! Maybe she would call Marcus now and tell him about it. Maybe she could turn the fantasy into reality at that moment.

But she couldn't. If he rejected her, if he rejected the fantasy, she didn't think she could bear it. Instead she called Whitney, who answered on the first ring.

"Rach?" said Whitney.

"Yes."

"Rach, you okay?" Rachel's position in the center of the sidewalk, where people were passing her on both sides, gave her the unmistakable sensation of the rest of the world moving ahead of her while she stayed immobile.

"I'm fine."

"Something wrong?"

"No."

"Something about work?"

She thought about that. "No," she said. "I'm fine." But there was something, of course. She tried to say the words. She tried to say, *I'm pregnant,* but she couldn't.

"Okay," said Whitney doubtfully. "What are you doing now?"

"Going for a walk."

"A walk? Where?"

"Nowhere. Just a walk."

"Want me to come?"

"No."

"Sure?"

"Sure. Well, I don't know. What are you doing?"

"Nothing. Just—" Rachel heard a snippet of conversation, then Whitney's voice returned in full force. "Just sorting out something with this registry. Rob's off today, so it's our only chance. He's working nights all next week."

"Oh."

"But, Rach? It doesn't matter. I can totally blow this off. If you want me to come with you."

"No," said Rachel. "Really, no. I'm not going far. I'm practically done already. I'm heading back."

"Okay. But call if you need me."

"I will."

But Rachel was not done. She was just beginning. She walked. She walked all the way to the park but did not enter; instead, she turned and walked the fifteen blocks back home. She didn't look in any shop windows. She didn't meet the eyes of anybody she passed. She just walked. And while she walked she thought of something her mother had said to her the day she'd graduated from college.

"You lucky thing, you," Ginny had said. "Your whole life ahead of you. You have no idea what a gift that is."

She would have walked more, but she needed the bathroom so she turned into her building.

"There is so much ahead of me," she said to her empty apartment when she got home. "There is *so much* ahead of me."

She wouldn't think about the pregnancy, not now.

It wasn't until she was wiping herself in the bathroom that she realized something was wrong, and then she saw all the blood on the toilet paper, and then she looked into the toilet, and she saw more blood there, and also something that wasn't blood, exactly, something small and thick and clotted. She pulled herself from the toilet to the floor, the corner where the tub met the wall, not caring about the mess, and when she heard the phone ringing from the other room she turned her body carefully away and thought about the pool in her friend Jennifer's yard in Burlington, and about the summer when they were ten, when they swam every single day. She thought about the pink bathing suit with crisscross straps she'd had that summer.

She sat there for some time and eventually she got up and cleaned herself off and cleaned the bathroom too, and then she put on her pajamas, the ones that Marcus made fun of because they were a long-sleeved matching set with flowers on them, like something a child or an old lady would wear, and she got in bed and cried and cried, for what she didn't have yet and also for what she'd lost.

⁎

The heat was here to stay. Lillian, walking by the lake, could feel it. She felt as if everyone — and everything, even the expanse of water before her — was trapped inside a giant bubble of humidity, pulled ever closer to the center of the earth. Philip, asleep in the Björn, was stuck to her chest; his back, when she put her hand on it, emanated heat. Olivia sat limply in the stroller. Every now and then she lifted her sippy cup of water to her lips and drank listlessly, more out of necessity than pleasure, the way a jaded drunk in a dark bar in the midafternoon might drink.

She stopped for a moment and adjusted Philip's sun hat. They were nearly to the little wooden bridge that covered a rushing stream feeding into the lake. As a child she had stood with Stephen and Rachel tossing sticks into that stream, watching them get trapped in the nest of leaves and rocks just under the surface. Perhaps Olivia would enjoy doing the same thing.

She was about to bend down to release Olivia from the stroller when she heard footsteps behind her, then felt a tap on her shoulder. She turned, expecting, as ever, that Tom had come to find her. But no. Father Colin. In running clothes.

Her heartbeat quickened. She felt her cheeks warm, her transparent, cursed cheeks, and she had to look down. What to say? She couldn't very well say that she'd been thinking about her visit to the church, that she had found herself, at odd moments, trying to capture the feeling of serenity there in the same way the rocks under the water captured the sticks and the leaves. She said, "Father Colin! Running? In this weather? You must be crazy."

He said, breathing heavily, "In my own way, I guess. But I've never minded the heat." This was surprising, she thought, given the Irish tone to his skin, and the way the blood vessels had risen to prominence in his cheeks. Like hers. Like Tom's too! She tried not to look at his long, nearly hairless legs, at the circles of sweat underneath his arms. It seemed bizarre and inappropriate to see a priest this way. Like walking in on your grandmother in the bathroom! He leaned over, hands on his knees, and when he looked up, he said, "These must be your children."

"Yes. Philip, here, sleeping. And this is Olivia." She motioned toward the stroller. "She's three."

"Three and five-eighths," said Olivia, dislodging herself from the straps.

"Olivia, please say hello to Father Colin. But I don't want to interrupt your run, Father. My brother was a runner. I know how these things go."

Father Colin crouched down beside Olivia. "I'm just about done anyway," he said. Then, "Olivia. It's very nice to meet you. What beautiful blue eyes you have."

Olivia stared. She scratched at a mosquito bite on her arm.

"'Hello, Father,'" said Lillian in a high voice. "'How nice to meet you.'"

Father Colin laughed. Olivia said nothing.

"Olivia!"

"No worries," said Father Colin. "I know how it is. Kids talk when they want to talk." He stood, then pulled his heel up to his seat, stretching.

"Aren't you going to ask me when I'm coming to church?" Lillian heard the teasing note in her own voice: how embarrassing. She looked down again.

"No," he said. "I never ask that of anyone. But it would be a pleasure. We welcome people back to the flock at any time, no questions asked."

"Well," she said, looking down at her sandals, and noticing that her toenails could use a fresh coat of polish. She looked up and squinted, and what was that sensation inside her, that brief unsettled flutter? "Well," she said again. "You look miserable. You had better go and get yourself some water. There's a fountain just up ahead—"

"I should," he said, wiping his face with the sleeve of his shirt. "And you know what, I think I will. So I'll see you soon, I hope. Lillian. Olivia. Philip."

Lillian continued toward the bridge with her children. She said to Olivia, "Liv, next time someone gives you a compliment, you say thank you. You don't just look at them."

"He was sweaty," said Olivia.

"I know," said Lillian. "It's very hot out. But still."

Later that day, at home, she heard Olivia telling her pink elephant, "What beautiful blue eyes you have."

The elephant, whose eyes were little black buttons, stared back at her, saying nothing.

※

When Rachel received the Sacrament of Reconciliation as a child, she had nothing, really, to confess. She remembered lowering herself onto the small kneeler in front of the brown divider, searching her mind for sins to report to Father Michael. *I was rude to my mother,* she said finally. *I said a bad word.*

Now, the phone in her hand, she tried to recall that feeling: the sensation of being so free from real sins that she had to make them up.

It was early in the morning. She hoped to get Tess's voice mail, but Tess answered the phone breathlessly. Really, the woman seemed to work nonstop. No wonder Rachel couldn't measure up.

Rachel took a deep breath. "Tess?" she said. "It's Rachel. Listen. I have to go home for a while. My father—my father is very sick."

I have committed the sin of lying. I have committed the sin of sleeping with my ex-boyfriend. No punishment necessary, Father, for my body has punished me enough already. And now, Father, hear what I'm saying about my dad.

"Oh, Rachel," said Tess. "I'm very sorry to hear that. What happened?"

"He's just…well, I can't really talk about it," said Rachel. "It's too upsetting. But thank you."

"Well," said Tess. "Family comes first, you know I believe that." Rachel had seen Tess with her children exactly once. "So take all the time you need, pet."

"Really?" Rachel felt her heart lift. She experienced a sudden and unfamiliar feeling of fondness for Tess.

"Of course. You have…let me see. It looks like you have five days of vacation here. So once you go over that, it will be without pay, of course. But please. Take all the time you need."

Rachel's feeling of good will evaporated. She could almost see it there in the air before her, a white cloud quickly gone. "Okay," whispered Rachel. "Thank you." She closed the phone and began to pack quickly. How easy it was, sometimes, to set a lie in motion.

Forgive me, Father, for I have sinned.

❋

Ginny was on her way up the stairs with a laundry basket. "Towels," she said cheerfully. "It's amazing how many you go through with houseguests." She began unloading the towels into the linen closet, then stopped and looked at Stephen. "Everything all right with the patient?"

"Sure," he said.

Ginny removed an untidy stack of washcloths from the closet and refolded them quickly, then put them back in. On the floor of the closet, where Ginny kept extra tissues and toilet paper for the upstairs bathrooms, lay one of Olivia's princess dolls, half dressed, hair disheveled.

"She looks like she stayed out too late last night," observed Stephen. Ginny picked up the doll, smoothed her skirt (it was the top she was missing), and placed her on the straight-backed wicker chair that had sat in the corner of the hall for as long as Stephen could remember.

"Now, how on earth did that get in the closet?" Ginny peered at Stephen. "Are you sure everything is okay? You look a bit—I don't know."

"A bit what?"

"Overwhelmed."

"I'm not," he said shortly. He suddenly felt very, very tired.

Ginny regarded him from a crouched position near the bottom of the closet, where she had also found a large dust bunny, which she swept up with her fingers.

"I mean, I am. Of course I am."

Ginny straightened. "It's a lot."

"It's a lot," he agreed. "But it's . . . manageable."

"Well," said Ginny. She moved a pile of pillowcases from the second shelf to the top. "I suppose that's what you hope for, at this point. Managing."

"Mom," he said, his voice in a whisper, "I'm sorry about all of this—"

"About what?"

He waved his arm to take in the hallway, Jane's doorway.

"Sorry? You've got nothing to be sorry about, mister."

"Well, for the disruption and all. It's *crowded* here, all of a sudden. We only meant to be here a couple of days—"

Ginny closed the door to the linen closet firmly. "I've dealt with crowded before. You didn't do it on purpose, did you?"

He looked startled. "Do what?"

"Give Jane a pregnancy complication."

"No. Of course not—"

"Well, then. There's no need to apologize."

"But—"

"But nothing," Ginny said. She set the empty basket by the stairs. "Now, your father's got to go to the store to pick up some tape for the sprinkler system hose. Why don't you go with him?"

"What about—" He nodded toward the bedroom.

"I'll keep an ear out. Nothing's going to happen if you're gone for fifteen minutes."

Stephen studied the pictures on the wall. "Out of all the pictures of me you have in your possession," he said, "why hang this one on the wall?"

"I *love* that one."

"The braces! Don't you have one without the braces?"

"I loved you in braces."

"Ugh. It was so painful, getting them tightened. I remember that."

"They gave you a lisp. It was very sweet."

"God, Mom. There's nothing sweet about a lisp in a teen-aged boy."

"You weren't a teenager, quite. You were twelve."

"Even worse. On the *cusp* of being a teenager."

"In you, there was something sweet, somehow. I know, I know, you didn't think so. But it made you seem so —"

"So what?"

"So innocent. Or something."

"Right," he said.

"Stephen?"

"What?" He had discovered a spot on the hardwood and bent down to examine it.

"Nothing is going to happen in fifteen minutes."

"I know."

"So go, already," she said. "Go to the hardware store with your father. He could use some male company, God knows. Just *go*."

⁕

After they got the tape William said he wanted a Creemee.

"Really?" Stephen thought of Jane at the house. She would call Ginny if she needed anything, of course. Lillian was around

141

somewhere too, and Olivia and Philip. Jane was not alone; Jane would not succumb to any sort of tragedy if he, Stephen, decided to eat ice cream with his father. "A Creemee sounds good," he said reluctantly, untruthfully. "Let's do it."

They drove down to the Creemee stand between the waterfront and the bike path, where a teenager with a long flop of hair served them each a cone. Stephen took a stack of the thin, barely useful napkins from the holder and they settled themselves on a bench overlooking the lake. Not far from them a line of tourists waited to board a cruise ship. Two boys — ten, maybe, legs skinny and brown and scabbed, shaggy haircuts and baggy clothes — went by them on skateboards.

"Sometimes I do this," William said, licking the sprinkles off the tip of the cone.

"Do what?"

"Sneak out on your mother in the middle of the day and have an ice cream."

"Geez, Dad," said Stephen. This knowledge, delivered though it was in a genial, conspiratorial tone, made him sad. "Do you have to sneak out to get an ice cream, at your age?"

"Sixty-five next month," William said cheerfully.

"Aren't you supposed to be sneaking out for a beer, if anything?"

"Ah." William licked at his ice cream. "That's the thing. A beer tastes better at home in the summer, in front of the Red Sox, after a hard day of work. A Creemee: that's better away from home."

"But you have to sneak it." Stephen watched an elderly couple toddle down to the edge of the water. The man held a cane; the woman held onto his elbow and guided him.

"No, I don't *have* to sneak it."

"But you like to sneak it."

"Well, it's easier, sometimes."

"Easier why?"

"Because then I don't have to see if your mother wants to go, or arrange to bring something back for her if she doesn't, or explain *why* I want an ice cream, or feel guilty for having it, or wonder if she's thinking about my cholesterol. Which makes *me* think about my cholesterol. It's just easier, sometimes, to go out on my own."

Stephen surveyed the scrappy grass under his feet. There was a group of ants moving about. He envied them suddenly, their ignorance and industry, their incapacity for self-doubt. "Jesus," said Stephen. It was depressing to him, to think of his father and his surreptitious ice-cream cones. "Is that what marriage becomes, in the end?" Guilt over an ice cream? Hiding on a picnic bench somewhere by yourself? And yet there was William, licking away, as happy as a little boy, so who was Stephen to begrudge him his small pleasures?

"That's not *all* marriage becomes," said William. "And I don't consider this the end."

Stephen squinted at the ants. He searched his mind for scraps of memory about his parents. He could remember his mother in a bathing suit, wading out into the lake on a humid August afternoon. He could remember his father teaching him to ride a bike without training wheels; he remembered the feel of his father's hand on the bicycle seat and then the terror and the exhilaration when he let go. He could remember Lillian running up the stairs and slamming the door to her room, and his mother standing at the bottom of the stairs, her face red and pinched. But everything was filtered through the lens of his own experience, and nothing gave him any clues to what his parents' actual marriage was like. "So what does it become?" asked Stephen.

"A lot of things."

"Good things?"

"Mostly." William popped the remainder of his cone into his mouth and leaned back, lifting his face to the sky. "This weather is *perfect.*"

"Ugh," said Stephen. "Too humid."

"You New Yorkers. With your air-conditioning."

"I worry that Jane's going to melt up there in the bedroom."

"She may," said William mildly. "But she seems to be handling it well."

"We're only two weeks into it." The elderly couple had seated themselves on a bench. He saw the woman point to something out on the lake. "There's so much left to go."

William nodded, and crumpled his napkin into a ball. "True," he said. "But she's made of steel, that one. She'll persevere."

"Yeah," said Stephen.

"You will too."

"Yeah."

William reached over and clapped him on the back; it was a gesture so familiar, so reminiscent of his childhood, that he was suddenly grateful for his father, and for the Creemee, which he had eaten too fast and which was already giving him a bellyache, but a pleasant sort of bellyache, like the sort you got as a child on Halloween just before bedtime when your parents finally took away your bag of candy.

"I guess it will be a whole different world for Jane anyway, after the baby is born." William lobbed his napkin into the trash bin and stood, jangling his keys in his pocket.

Stephen took a deep breath. *Here we go,* he thought. He rose. "Actually not all that different," he said.

"Oh?" William had his wallet open and was arranging the change from the ice-cream cones with the other bills.

"She's going straight back to work."

"Straight back, as in?" William closed the wallet and returned it to his pocket.

"As in after three weeks or so. Maybe four."

"And then?" William had begun walking back toward the car and Stephen followed one step behind him; he felt like a child again, hurrying to keep up with a parent.

"And then I'm going to take care of the baby," he said to his father's back.

His father stopped, and turned slowly around. "Really?"

"Really."

William opened his mouth and then closed it again. "Full-time?"

"That's the idea."

"And your work? The editing?"

"I'll take a break from it. I'm not all that crazy about it at the moment anyway."

"I see." William looked briefly to the sky, then turned his eyes back to meet Stephen's gaze.

"You see, you really see, or you see, you don't know what else to say?"

"Not sure," said William. "I see…well."

"What?"

"I guess what I *don't* see is why—"

"Why *what?*"

"Nothing."

"Why what? Why you spent all that money sending me to Middlebury?"

"Stephen. I didn't say that."

"But you thought it."

"Perhaps."

They began walking again, together, and William pointed his keys toward the car and pressed the unlock button. The car beeped its response.

"But. Did you ever ask *Lillian* the same question, why you spent so much to send her to college?"

"Well, no. But. It's different."

"Is it?"

"I don't know. Isn't it?"

"It shouldn't be." Stephen slid into the passenger seat and looked steadily out the window. The elderly man and woman were making their way back across the parking lot, pausing every so often.

"Does your mother know?"

"No. Not yet."

"If I were you, I'd hold off on telling her just now."

"Yeah," said Stephen. "I figured."

"She's apt to blame Jane for it."

"I figured that too."

"She's apt to think it's a bad decision."

"I *know* that."

"She's—"

"Dad, I know."

They drove in silence away from the waterfront and back toward home. Stephen looked out the window, at the old mill buildings turned into trendy shops or funky eateries. Every time he came home, it seemed, the city he had grown up in had changed more and more. Revitalization was what they called it. Giving new life to. And wasn't that what he and Jane were doing, in a way? Giving life to. Not new life, but life. Giving life to something that had not had life before. Not revitalizing. Vitalizing.

"What does Jane's mother think?"

"Robin?"

"Does she have another mother?"

"*No,* Dad. Of course she doesn't."

They passed a long low building advertising hot yoga. On the other side of it was a building materials shop and a computer repair shop. It seemed incongruous to Stephen, these three vastly different businesses all in the same place, but then again perhaps that was the point of the revitalization.

BIKRAM YOGA, the sign said, with flames leaping out over the *B* on the sign.

"There's no place I'd rather be *less* than a hot yoga studio," said Stephen.

"Now, or always?"

"Well, *always,*" said Stephen. "But now especially. I mean, on a day like today."

"I think the idea is that you get so hot in *there* that when you come out *here* it doesn't seem like any big deal."

"Oh. Is that the point?"

"I don't know for sure. So, what's this about Jane's mother? And your arrangement?"

"She thinks that it's wonderful."

"She does?"

"She does," said Stephen. "She thinks this is the way it should be. She thinks men should step up, do their part."

"Their part?"

"Yes," said Stephen. He let his hand fall cautiously in the breeze outside car, and then he fully extended his arm, watching the wind work at the fine, soft hairs between his wrist and his elbow. ("Not fair," Rachel had told him when they were in high school. "Your arms are more like girl arms than mine are." He could see her now, scrunching up her nose in the bathroom, a bottle of bleach cream spilling onto the countertop.)

"She thinks," he continued, "that an arrangement like this might have saved her marriage, back when Jane was a baby."

Now he was embellishing, though embellishing was rather a kind phrase for what he was doing, and lying outright was perhaps more appropriate; Robin, though supportive of his and Jane's decision, had never said anything of the sort.

In fact, he knew very little about Robin's marriage to Jane's father, and neither of them mentioned him often. It was as though he had vanished completely into the mist, leaving Robin and Jane to fend for themselves.

"I see," said William. They had come to a four-way stop. William waited patiently for the other three cars to progress—only in Vermont, thought Stephen, was such forbearance possible—and guided the car into the intersection.

"Yes," continued Stephen, figuring that he was in for a penny and might as well be in for a pound. "You see, they were so ambitious, both of them, both her and Jane's dad, and there wasn't enough room for all that ambition and a baby. Something had to give."

"And Jane's father gave."

"And Jane's father gave," agreed Stephen.

"I see." They drove on in silence, and after a few minutes they turned down the road that led to their neighborhood. Most of the summer gardens were coming into full bloom now; the window boxes on the little Cape around the corner were full to bursting; in one yard, in defiance of Burlington's earth-friendly attitude, a sprinkler had been casting an arc of water since William and Stephen passed the house on their way to the hardware store.

"Dad?" said Stephen.

"Yup." William had turned the radio to a jazz station; he was tapping his fingers steadily on the steering wheel.

It was difficult for Stephen to know what his father was thinking. It occurred to him that it had always been difficult to know what his father was thinking, but for the most part that hadn't mattered. When it had, the three of them had had Ginny to act as translator. Now, suddenly, it seemed very important that he understand his father's point of view; it seemed important that he garner his father's approval and acceptance.

"I know what Mom would say. I mean, I think I can guess—"

William snorted. "And you'd probably be right."

"But the thing is, this feels right. It feels like the *most* right thing I could be doing right now."

"Good," said William, nodding. "That's all you can ask of yourself."

"But I get nervous."

"About what?"

"About something happening, to the baby."

"It won't."

"It could."

"But it won't."

"If anything happens—" said Stephen.

"Then what?"

"Then I'm not sure our marriage would survive it." It was the first time he'd admitted this, to himself or to anyone else. He thought of Jane sweating in the bedroom, wearing his gray T-shirt. He thought of her small upturned face, her plaintive eyes, her protruding belly. He thought of how she looked at home, in New York, when he interrupted her at work: like an animal cornered.

"Oh, now," said William. "Your marriage can survive plenty."

"Maybe so," said Stephen.

"You'd be surprised by its resilience. Most people are, once they put things to the test. You think you're there now, you think you're all the way in it, but you're only in the middle of one stage."

"I guess so," said Stephen, but he wasn't at all sure that his father was right. It seemed that since Jane had become pregnant their marriage had undergone a subtle but unmistakable shift, and he was sure that if she were to become *un*pregnant they would be unable to go back to being the way they had been before.

"Why, your mother and I—"

"Stop!" said Stephen, holding up a hand. "That's enough. I get what you're saying."

"Stephen?"

"Yeah."

"I'm sorry about that, back there. My reaction."

"Yeah."

"You'll be a great father."

"Yeah? I think it will be hard."

"It's all hard, you know. All of it. Any way you slice it. There's no point looking for the easy way out because...well, there isn't one."

"Yeah. I guess that's it."

William turned into their driveway. Olivia was drawing in chalk on the porch steps. A container of bubbles had overturned on the grass in front of her, and an assortment of stuffed animals was seated on a plaid blanket in the center of the yard, with paper plates and sippy cups set out in front of them. A purple pig wore Olivia's sun hat low over its eyes.

"Can you believe you're going to have one of *those* someday?" said William, nodding his head toward Olivia.

"God help us all," said Stephen.

William stopped the car and pressed the buttons to raise the windows before he turned the engine off.

Olivia danced an approximation of a jig toward the car. She wore a blue sparkly tutu with the top part of a green two-piece bathing suit. Her hair was done up elaborately in many pigtails, with all manner of barrettes and ribbons attached to them. "Grandpa!" she said.

"Olivia," said William. "Where has your grandmother gone?"

"She went to the bus station. For Aunt Rachel."

"Who?" said Stephen.

"*What?*" said William.

"Aunt Rachel! Aunt Rachel is coming."

Ginny drove too fast to the bus station. *If they stop me,* she thought, *I will tell them my little girl is in crisis and I'm going to get her.*

How she worried about Rachel sometimes: how her heart ached for her. Ginny's youngest daughter had grown up so happy and optimistic, trusting in the world and its basic goodness, that the prospect of watching her suffer from life's little cruelties was too much for Ginny. There was a time, in Rachel's youth, when she didn't want to let the little girl out of her sight, when she didn't even want to drop Rachel off at a birthday party or the shopping mall with her friends. She couldn't trust that the world's unkindness would not bring her to despair.

And if they stop me and then they get in my way, I will run them over.

She *did* drop her off, of course, she tried her best to peel back the layers of concern and to allow Rachel to navigate the world on her own. Which it seemed for a while she had finally learned to do: she had secured a job, and then a boyfriend, a live-in arrangement that didn't exactly mesh with Ginny's own sense of propriety but had allowed her to believe that Rachel was heading in the right direction. Was well taken care of. And then he had broken her heart, Marcus, and he had left. And now this.

Perhaps it was the way she was standing, with her shoulders sagging forward, or perhaps it was the size of the Greyhound bus behind her that dwarfed her, but Rachel looked small, vulnerable. Shrunken down and defeated.

"Oh, *sweetheart,*" said Ginny. She had barely parked the car before she was out of it and running toward Rachel. "Oh, sweetheart, you poor thing." She led her toward the car and, when she was safely inside, closed the car door carefully, the way she would with a child who might not know enough to keep her fingers out of the way.

When they were on their way back to the house she said, "How long are you staying?"

"I'm not sure."

"What about your job?"

"Mom! I don't know. I don't know. I just want to go home and go to sleep."

"Do you want me to make you an appointment with Dr. Green?"

"No! No. There's nothing to do, really. There's nothing to check. I looked online."

"Online!"

"It's just…gone. Over." Rachel's face crumpled.

"I could kill him, you know," said Ginny.

"Marcus?"

"Yes."

Rachel looked out the window. "Don't, Mom. He didn't even know."

"Oh, honey. Why didn't you tell him?"

"I just thought," said Rachel, staring into her lap, "I thought, I can call Marcus about this, or I can go home." She shrugged, and Ginny was reminded of her slender six-year-old shoulders, shrugging as she told some story about first grade. "And given those two options, well…I just wanted to come home."

"I'm glad you did," said Ginny. "We'll have to put you in with Olivia, in your room. That's the only space that's left. Unless you want Stephen's room. But that's full of junk."

"I'll go in with Olivia. Wait, she doesn't wet the bed or anything?"

"Not that I know of."

"Okay, then. Put me there. But I don't want to tell anyone, okay? Not Dad or Lillian or anyone. Let's just call this a visit. Okay?"

"Okay," said Ginny. Later that summer a feeling of gratitude and appreciation would come upon Ginny in swells when she thought about that ride home with Rachel, because Rachel needed somebody, and she chose *her*.

"Let's get you home," she said. "You poor thing. Let's just get you home."

William, just back from an early round of golf, came in the door holding a bouquet of red roses in a tall glass vase. "Lillian!" he called. "I have something for you!"

"In here," said Lillian softly. "Philip is asleep."

William held the flowers out to her. Lillian flushed. "There's a card," he said. "Do you want me to read it?"

"*No,*" she said. "Give the card to me. Please." She lay Philip down on the sofa and scanned the card quickly. "I don't want them," she said. "Why don't you bring them up to Jane?"

Olivia appeared then.

"Oooooh," said Olivia. "Who are *those* from?"

"Daddy," said Lillian.

"Wow," said Olivia.

"Do me a favor, Dad? Please? Bring them up to Jane. I really don't want them."

"Grandpa?" said Olivia. "Will you make me a PB and J?"

"If you don't mind," said Lillian, "that would be fantastic. And one for me, if you can stand it. I'm starving."

After William had made the sandwiches, and after he had poured a cup of milk for Olivia, and after he had folded a napkin for her in the shape of a bird, and after he had brought Lillian her lunch, he carried the flowers up the stairs and knocked softly on Jane's door.

"Yes," she said.

"It's William."

"Oh! Come in."

He pushed open the door. "I've brought you something," he said.

"Roses!"

"Admittedly, they're castoffs from Lillian, but still. I thought it might brighten things up a bit."

She smiled. "Thank you," she said. "I think they will."

William shrugged. "I'm not sure why they're castoffs." Jane nodded. "It seemed like a delicate subject, so I didn't ask." He put the vase on the dresser and stood uncertainly in the center of the room. "Is there anything else...is there anything I can get you? I'm whipping up peanut butter and jelly sandwiches downstairs. I'm folding paper napkins to look like birds."

"No. Thank you, William, but no."

"Are you comfortable? Are you miserable?"

"As comfortable as I can be," she said. "And as miserable as you'd expect."

⁂

"Olivia," whispered Rachel. "Stop tossing around and go to sleep."

"I can't," said Olivia.

Rachel thought Olivia should be able to, because Olivia had the bed—Rachel's old bed—while Rachel had been relegated to the extra air mattress on the floor beside the bed. It wasn't even a good air mattress. She could tell that it would probably once again lose a large percentage of its air before dawn.

That wasn't strictly true, the relegating. Her current position on the floor was her own doing. When Rachel saw the host of stuffed animals Olivia kept in the bed with her, and realized that those animals wouldn't fit on the air mattress, or would slide off in the middle of the night, as if from an ark rapidly sinking into the carpet, she told Olivia she could keep the bed. She thought perhaps Olivia would protest and insist on Rachel taking the bed, but of course she didn't: she was three, and oblivious to other people's feelings, and Rachel had been silly to expect otherwise.

Anyway, it was interesting to study her old room from this vantage point. Before turning off the lights she had a direct view under her bed, where she could see a stack of old magazines — *Seventeen,* most likely — and a clear square bin full of scrunchies. On the door, an old Nirvana poster. On the wall — still! — was a giant poster from *The English Patient,* the two lovers locked forever in that forbidden kiss. (How she had cried at that movie, how she had vowed never to let her true love escape.) Earlier that day in the very back of the closet she had located an old prom dress and the dyed sandals that matched it, and alongside them a row of Halloween costumes on wire hangers: a giant puppy suit, a race-car driver outfit, a Michael Jackson moonwalk jacket. She couldn't remember having worn any of those costumes. Had she?

"Olivia!" she said again. "If you stop moving around you'll be able to go to sleep." She had a moment of longing for her New York City apartment, its solitude and order. Here at the house, she was discovering, everything was slowly descending into chaos. Her mother's normally orderly kitchen was orderly no longer; you could hardly find anything decent in the refrigerator with the bottles of breast milk and juice boxes and plastic-wrapped bowls of leftovers clogging it, and every time you reached for a glass you found that the dishwasher was either full and waiting to be run or full and clean and waiting to be unloaded. In the den you could not sit down to watch TV because the den was now Lillian's room and had been given over to stacks of children's laundry and a diaper pail giving off a stale and offending odor. You could not even consider putting in a load of laundry without first interviewing the entire household to find out who had left a load of whites squatting in the washing machine. It was like living in a college dorm again, without the camaraderie and the meal plan.

Still, given the choice between this and staying in the city, constantly reminded of the pregnancy and the miscarriage and her inadequate job performance and of how far behind Whitney she was on the path of life—indeed, how far behind everybody she was!—given that choice again and again, she would choose this every time.

"I *can't* sleep," said Olivia. "I can't go to sleep!"

Rachel sighed. "Well, Olivia, you just have to."

"But I can't."

"Do you want to go downstairs and sleep with your mother?"

"No."

"Well. What then?" Someone had installed a night-light in the room, and in its glow Rachel could make out just the contours of Olivia's body in the bed.

"You could read to me," said Olivia.

"I could?"

"Yes. If you read me one book, then I promise I'll go to sleep."

"Promise?"

"Promise."

So Rachel rose from the air mattress, turned on the light, and stood before a pile of library books stacked by Olivia's bed. Library books! She found that quaint and surprising. She hadn't taken Lillian for a library user. She supposed that was her mother's influence. She chose the first book in the stack.

"Frances!" she said. "I remember Frances. That little badger. Slide over."

Olivia moved over in the bed and Rachel climbed in beside her. It was awkward with all the stuffed animals, and the pillow Olivia was using was thin and inadequate for the two of them, but with a little maneuvering, and a little rearranging of the animals, Rachel was able to get comfortable. Olivia put her thumb in her mouth and began working at it, and Rachel, after peeking at the date-due card (the book was already overdue, but who was she to judge?) and fingering the plastic library sleeve, which held the odors and sensations of her childhood, began to read.

"'It was breakfast time,'" she began, "'and everyone was at the table.'"

She glanced at Olivia, whose eyelids had fallen already to half-mast.

She kept reading. By the time she got to the part where Frances was waiting at the bus stop, skipping rope and singing her signature song, she sensed a change in Olivia's breathing. She extricated herself carefully and smoothed the hair back from Olivia's face. The little girl was deeply asleep.

⁓⁂⁓

"Come with me," said Ginny to Stephen. "I need help picking out your father's birthday cake."

Stephen was bent over the newspaper at the kitchen table.

"Really?" he said doubtfully. "His birthday isn't until next month, right?"

"I know. But I don't want to forget."

"You can't do it without me?"

Ginny had her purse hooked over one arm, her sunglasses on, her car keys in her hand. "I can't do it without you," she said.

They drove to Mirabelles on Main Street. The girl behind the counter was waifish and had a spider tattoo above her wrist. Why, thought Stephen, looking at her, would anyone tattoo a spider on her wrist? How could you possibly think that a spider tattoo was something you wanted to live with for the rest of your life?

"I need a cake," Ginny told her. "For the twenty-third of August. For...let's see." She looked at Stephen. "How many are we now?"

Stephen shrugged. Ginny began counting on her fingers. "You, and Jane, and Lilly…well, let's just say ten. Nothing wrong with leftovers. The most chocolatey chocolate cake you make."

"Gotcha," said the girl. "You want the Old-Fashioned Chocolate Cake."

"Old-fashioned sounds exactly right," said Ginny. "And two lattes," she added. "For here."

"Mom—" When Stephen was away from Jane he felt anxious.

"For *here,*" she said again, firmly, and the waif looked from one of them to the other, her eyes big and round in her face, like those of a baby.

When they had their lattes Ginny found them two seats at a small round table and they sat. Stephen was facing the street. He watched a mother push a baby carriage. He wondered about the baby inside the carriage, and he wondered about the mother too. What had she been like at the end of her pregnancy? Had she yelled at her husband? Had her husband been more understanding than he? This was unexpected, the distance he felt suddenly from Jane.

Ginny turned to see what Stephen was looking at, then turned back. She took a sip of her drink and said, in one breath, "I hear you're going to be a stay-at-home dad."

Stephen lifted his chin. Hadn't William told him not to bring it up? And clearly he had brought it up himself. "For now," he said.

She laughed.

"What? What's funny?"

Ginny stirred sugar into her drink. "Nothing. I just…it's just, it's a big leap you're making."

"Why? I'm home all day anyway. It's less of a leap for me than it would be for Jane."

Ginny frowned. "I don't know."

He leaned toward her. "Mom. She earns all the money! She's *already* the breadwinner. Without those bonuses we'd never in a million *years* be able to pay the mortgage. Why do you have a problem with my taking on the other role, if I don't?"

She looked briefly to the ceiling. "I don't have a *problem* with it."

"Clearly, you do. Or you wouldn't have brought it up."

"I just don't know if you realize what you're in for."

"Does anyone, though? Does any new parent? Did you, when you had Lillian?"

"I suppose not. But I was—"

"What? Younger? Less prepared?"

"I guess."

"Female?"

"Well, yes, of course. That too. But also, I had no expectations about any of it! About keeping my life, and so forth. I had no life to keep. I was a young bride, and that was that. Parents these days—"

"What?" Stephen said. He pushed his cup away from him, as though by disowning the drink he could find his way out of the conversation.

"It's different, that's all. I mean, Lillian—"

"I am not Lillian," Stephen said savagely. "*We* are not Lillian. I'm not looking to be Lillian."

"I know that. I know you're not." Ginny made a tiny gesture of supplication toward him. "But parents these days, it is different, I know it is. There's a certain level of... *dissatisfaction* that wasn't there when I was first a mother."

"How do you know? How do you know it wasn't there?"

"Because! Nobody talked about it. Nobody worried about living up to some absurd ideal. There was no ideal. But now, I don't know. It just seems like you're all laboring under this belief that you can have it all. I know that sounds like a cliché, but really that's what it is."

"But I'm not! We're not trying to have it all. We're each trying to have a piece of it, and we're trying to make it all come out right for the baby."

Ginny was silent for a moment. She studied the pastry case. "Maybe so. But that baby is going to need its mother."

"But that baby will have its mother! Nights and weekends. And the rest of the time, it will have its father. It will have *me*."

"Yes," she said. "I concede that. But that time is so precious, and it goes so quickly. I mean, already Philip—" She paused. "And Jane's going to miss so much of it. And I don't think she's going to realize it, until that time has passed."

"But that's such—that's such an *old-fashioned* way to look at it."

Ginny sighed, then sat up straighter. "I know. But why is old-fashioned bad? That way worked for so long."

"It worked, until it didn't work. So people found other ways around it."

"No. It worked until people decided it *shouldn't* work that way, and then it stopped working. People started messing with it."

"But there are plenty of happy stay-at-home mothers. And plenty of happy stay-at-home fathers. It's just more *flexible* now. It can work a bunch of different ways."

"Maybe." Ginny lifted her cup and drank the last of the latte. When she put the cup on the table Stephen put his hand over hers. It was the same hand it had always been, the same hand that had held his, had steered him and guided him across countless streets. "Mom," he said.

"What?" She nearly whispered it.

"You worry entirely too much. I can do this."

"I know. I know you can. But it's hard," she said seriously. "It will change everything. *Everything*."

"Hard doesn't scare me. So let me do it. Okay? Let me show everyone I can do it."

"Okay," she said. "Okay, I will." And together they rose and threaded their way through the tables and exited the cafe for the humid July air.

❋

"What's the news from Tom?" Ginny said to Lillian later that day. Despite the heat, they were making dough for cookies for the church bake sale. Olivia was standing on a footstool at the counter, wearing a gigantic apron that said "Kiss the Cook."

"Don't touch your nose," said Lillian, ignoring her mother's question. "If you touch your nose you have to march right back in the bathroom and wash your hands all over again."

"I didn't," said Olivia.

"In the bowl," said Ginny, handing Olivia a measuring cup full of sugar. Olivia dumped it in. "Good," said Ginny. She had a speck of flour on her chin.

Ginny peered at Lillian. "Is everything all right?"

"Of course," said Lillian. "What wouldn't be all right?"

"It just seems odd," said Ginny, "that Tom hasn't called much. You've been here for weeks."

"He calls on the cell phone," says Lillian. She checked to see how carefully Olivia was listening. "Late at night."

"Aren't you sleeping late at night?"

"Not always."

When she went for drinks with Heather two nights prior, her friend had said, "Don't you think he deserves to talk to Olivia, at least?" They had sat outside the restaurant on Church Street where Heather used to work and ordered drinks with tropical names that came with patterned paper umbrellas.

"No," said Lillian shortly. "He deserves nothing."

"But—"

"*Nothing,*" said Lillian.

Now Olivia dipped her hand into the batter and extracted a chocolate chip.

"*Don't,*" said Lillian and Ginny in chorus.

"I didn't," said Olivia.

"You *did,* though," said Lillian.

"But I didn't *mean* to." She worked her mouth into a pout and her lips began to tremble.

"Oh, eat the chip," said Lillian. "I guess the world won't end." She held the electric mixer in one hand and searched with the other hand for the beaters.

"Wrong drawer," said Ginny. "Top left."

"Got it," said Lillian.

"*Grand*ma," said Olivia. "When can I *eat* a cookie?"

"You have to bake them first, my love," said Ginny. "Do you think he'll come up?"

"Who?"

Ginny sighed. "*Tom.*"

"Oh. I don't know. Sometime, I guess. He's *very* busy at work."

"Who?" said Olivia.

"Daddy. He's got a huge project going on. He can't afford the time."

"Beat, Lillian," said Ginny.

Lillian turned on the mixer and they all peered into the bowl.

"Now we roll the balls," said Ginny. She held out a spoon to Olivia and laid three baking sheets on the counter. "That's the best part! Like Play-Doh."

"Can I eat a ball?" said Olivia.

"Not until they're cooked."

"*Then* can I eat a ball?"

"Then they won't be balls anymore," said Lillian. "They'll be cookies."

"I want them to be *balls*," said Olivia.

"Either way," said Ginny. "Let's get them in the oven." She dipped her hands into the bowl, rolled, dipped again. After she put the first batch in she closed the oven door triumphantly, then turned around. "You," she said to Olivia. "Off the stool, and into the bathroom to wash up. The apron stays here."

After Olivia had gone Ginny turned to face Lillian and said, "Lillian. If there's something—"

"There's nothing," said Lillian shortly.

"But *if* there's something."

"*Mom!* There's nothing," said Lillian. "It's summer. You live by a lake. I live in the middle of a suburban development. Tom's working all the time. It's *better* here, that's all there is to it. Okay?"

"Okay," said Ginny. "Okay."

"But if you want us to go—"

"No!" said Ginny. "Of course I don't want that."

Quickly, industriously, Lillian began stacking the dishes and spoons and measuring cups and beaters in the sink, and then she ran the water very, very hot, and stood over the sink as it was filling up.

For a long moment she could feel Ginny's eyes on her, watching her, but she just kept scrubbing at the sticky dough in the big metal mixing bowl, and she didn't look up.

※

Olivia wanted to go with Lillian to deliver the cookies to the rectory for the bake sale, but Lillian preferred to go alone.

"To the side door," said Ginny. "If nobody is there, leave them. But write a note." To Olivia she said, "You stay with me. We'll watch *Dora* together while your brother sleeps."

"I don't like *Dora* anymore," said Olivia.

Ginny opened a drawer in the kitchen and pulled out a pad of paper and a pencil, which she presented to Lillian. Lillian balanced the pen and paper on the container of cookies.

As it turned out she didn't need the paper. The lady who kept house at the rectory opened the door. Lois Tolland. Lillian had gone to high school with her son, Tyler. Lillian tried to peer around her, into the rectory, looking for Father Colin. She asked after Tyler Tolland. He had moved to California with his wife and daughter, Lois's only grandchild.

"Sort of takes your breath away," said Lois. "When they leave you like that."

"I'm sorry," said Lillian. And she was: you could see the disappointment scratched across Lois's face. Lillian remembered Tyler only vaguely; he had been one of the quiet ones, not really tied to any group that she could remember. Once, in the cafeteria, he had tripped on a table leg and dropped his tray. That's what she remembered most about him: mashed potatoes on his shoes, canned corn dripping down the front of his shirt.

"She's ten now," said Lois. "In a blink, she'll be a teenager. And then what? Then I'll never know her."

"I'm sorry," said Lillian again.

"Anyway, I'll bring these back and put them with the others," said Lois Tolland. "Tell your mother I said thank you."

Father Colin appeared behind Mrs. Tolland then. "Lillian!" he said.

"Cookies." She gestured toward the container.

"Ah," he said. "This bake sale is turning into quite the extravaganza, with Lois here at the helm."

Lillian squinted at him. She had noticed that it was difficult to tell when he was being sarcastic or ironic and when he was just being nice. She supposed that was the Southie in him; she liked that.

He clapped his hand on Lois Tolland's shoulder, and Lillian saw the way that made Lois smile. Nice, she thought. Not sarcastic. That was the power a good priest had, to dispense comfort with a small gesture like that. She thought that must be a wonderful talent to have. Why didn't she have that talent? Did she have any talents at all? She couldn't think of any.

Father Colin was on his way to run an errand, he told Lillian. Perhaps she wanted to go with him?

"What sort of errand?" asked Lillian.

He had to buy something for his nephews. He had to go downtown, to the bookstore. He wouldn't mind the company.

"I'm not sure," said Lillian. But then she considered it. She had fed Philip recently. Olivia was happy with Ginny. Rachel, once she got out of bed, would be around too. And wouldn't it be nice to get out for a while? "Okay," she said finally. "The bookstore. Why not?"

She thought she saw Lois Tolland's shoulders twitch.

Lillian thought that a priest would not carry a wallet, sort of the same way you figured the president of the United States would not carry a wallet. But Father Colin did; he placed his near the gearshift when they were in his car. The car was a tomato-colored Corolla of indeterminate age, and the seats were black and hot. Lillian had also not thought about a priest having a car, or going shopping. She told him that, on the way to town. "It's just because all the priests I've known have been old," she said. "I guess I thought you were all—"

"What? Free from earthly cares?"

"Something like that."

He laughed. He had a nice laugh, louder than you would expect: brasher. "Not at all," he said. "Not at all. Though that would be nice." She watched his freckled hands on the steering wheel. His skin was like hers; she could see that it would not take kindly to too much sun. Rachel tanned easily, and Lillian had always envied her that. She thought about the day she'd seen Father Colin running on the bike path without a hat. She thought he ought not to do that too often, with that skin. She said, "Do you run a lot?"

Father Colin pulled up to a stop sign, looked both ways, eased ahead. "Most days," he said. "The other day was unusual for me, though. Normally I go in the morning. Very early. Dawn, usually."

They reached the downtown. "Go straight," she said. "Then turn right in two streets. These one-ways will drive you crazy if you don't know them." Then she said, *"Dawn?"*

"I'm a terrible sleeper," he said. "A complete insomniac. I'm always awake with the birds."

She saw a pile of tourists heading toward a minivan. "There," she said, pointing. "They're leaving."

Father Colin parked the car and turned off the ignition. They were out of the car now and walking toward the bookstore. "Dawn," she said again. "Geez." She had been about to say *Jesus,* but she amended it at the last minute. She followed him through the door, which he held open for her. Did Tom hold doors open for her? Truly, she couldn't remember.

He bought three books: one about dinosaurs, one about fire trucks, one about spaceships. Three nephews, three books. That's how he explained it. There was a coffee shop in the bookstore, and after he had paid for the books he headed toward it without asking her. It wasn't until he had taken a place in line that he looked at her expectantly, and she said, "Iced coffee, I guess. Please." She thought of Philip and calculated when she would next need to nurse him. "Half decaf," she said. "Please." She thought some more. "No, all decaf. Thank you."

They sat. And how strange it was to be sitting across from this man she hardly knew, this man in the clerical collar. But at the same time how not strange it was, and that in itself was strange. She worried at first that she would have to cast about for something to say, but never mind about that: it turned out Father Colin was a talker. He told her about his brother, and his brother's wife, Theresa. "She's one of my favorite people," he said. "She was a champion soccer player, a real star. Now she's a nurse. But she's still got this athletic way of moving: quick and dirty. She keeps those boys in line, let me tell you. Plus Seamus. She's around death all day, and yet she's got this vibrancy. Pure joy."

Lillian couldn't imagine keeping anything in line. She couldn't imagine ever being described as vibrant or joyful. She felt a spark of envy for a woman she would never meet.

"I remember the nephews from the picture," she said. "In your office." She noticed the way his face shone when he talked about them, lit up from within. He said they reminded him of himself when he was their age, growing up in South Boston. He said in those days you played ball in the streets, and if you misbehaved you were as likely to be spanked by someone else's mother as your own.

"Really?" she said. "I don't think people spanked each other's children in Vermont. I don't think they spanked their *own* children."

"Peace lovers," he said, smiling. "In Southie, people did what it took. And we were no worse for it." He remembered women standing outside their apartments in their nightclothes; he remembered thinking that was normal. That *was* normal, then, to them.

"I've never really talked to a priest," she said. "One on one, like this. Except for confession. And that was a *really* long time ago."

He smiled at that. "It's not so different from talking to a regular person, is it?"

She considered that question. "No," she said. "But I guess I can imagine you before you were a priest, maybe that's why." She looked down at the books he bought for his nephews. She could picture them running to the door to meet him, their uncle the priest. She could picture him taking the steps two at a time, opening his arms wide. Would they jump on him, wrestle him to the ground? Yes, she decided. Yes they would. And he would wrestle back.

She narrowed her eyes at Father Colin. "How'd you know, anyway? That you wanted to be a priest." He raised his eyebrows and leaned back in his chair, and Lillian said, "You probably get asked that all the time."

"You know what? Hardly at all." He paused. "I remember the first time I realized I was meant for this."

"Yeah?"

"I got beat up one day outside of school for being nice to this black kid. There was lots of racial tension then in Southie, lots." He paused again and Lillian didn't say anything, just let him talk. "So the next Sunday, I was kneeling at Mass next to Seamus, and I suddenly understood that I had something few people have."

"What was that?"

"A capacity for forgiveness, I guess you could call it. Seamus didn't have it, that's for sure. He tracked down the boy who hit me and punched him square in the face. Two teeth came out."

"Geez."

"My mother didn't have it. My father didn't have it. They couldn't forgive each other half the time."

"But you could."

"I could! Kneeling in the pew there, thinking about the boy who beat me up, I was filled with this—this is going to sound corny, I know, but it's true—this sort of *sensation*. A warmth. A feeling that there was something bigger at work that I could be part of. And the rest, as they say, is history."

"Wow," said Lillian. She drank her coffee. His eyes were really very kind. They were so clear, such a light, pale blue, that she felt as though she could see right through them. Here was a man, it was possible, with no secrets, nothing to hide. "I didn't know it happened like that," she said.

"I don't know if it does for everyone," Father Colin said. "I can only speak for myself. But it did for me."

"That's fascinating."

"Is it?"

"It is. I'm jealous of the certainty you feel. I don't feel that certain about anything."

"Now," he said. He moved the ice around in his cup. "I've told you lots. You tell me something."

"Like what?"

"Anything. Something about yourself. Or your family. You have a lovely family. What does your husband do?"

As she told Heather later, the answer came unbidden. "My husband," she said. "He betrayed me." (And looking back on it, she thought it was a little too dramatic, the way she said it, a little embarrassing, but also there was some relief in it, in having the words out there.)

At that Father Colin sat back and made an awkward gesture toward her. "Sort of like he wanted to take my hand," she told Heather. "Or pat me on the shoulder or something. But he didn't, of course."

"So *then* what?" said Heather.

Father Colin's face took on an expression of gentleness and compassion. He said calmly, "I'm sorry to hear that."

Then, to lighten the moment, Lillian said, "But he's also a software engineer. If that's what you meant."

"Ah," said Father Colin. "It was, actually." Then, after a pause, he said, "I've counseled many couples. And it's amazing, the capacity for forgiveness people find—"

"Not me," said Lillian shortly. She didn't look at him when she said that; she fixed her eyes on the glass case with its rows of blueberry muffins and cranberry scones. She blinked hard. "I can't forgive," she said quietly. "I won't. That's why I'm here. I've escaped."

"Perhaps not yet," said Father Colin. "But after some time has passed—"

"No."

After a moment Father Colin said, "Forgiveness is a very powerful tool, you know, Lillian."

"I don't really intend to find out."

The moment seemed suspended in time and space, hanging like a bubble, and around her sounds became magnified. There was a clatter behind her as somebody dropped a spoon. Far away, a baby cried. She felt her breasts begin to fill. It wasn't Philip's cry, but sometimes her body didn't know that. Eventually she said, "Have you?"

"Have I what?" He bent toward her.

"Ever had to forgive anyone? I mean as an adult, not the boy who beat you up."

He was taken aback, she could see that. "Sure," he said slowly. "Sure, I have. Everyone does, at some point, I think. I think it's the way of the world." His voice sounded odd. He was looking in her direction, but for the first time since she'd met him she had the feeling that he wasn't really looking at her at all.

"Who?"

"What?"

"Who? Have you had to forgive. As long as we're sharing. And how'd you do it?"

Father Colin paused and stared at his cup. "It's a long story."

"I have time."

He sat back. His face looked different. He began to talk. "There was a woman in my parish," he said. "She lost a child."

Lillian let him talk. She didn't interrupt. Around them, the customers in the coffee shop came and went: women pushing baby strollers, tourists looking to get out of the sun, solitary people with books they'd just purchased. And Lillian and Father Colin sat. The woman, he said, had lost a child in an accident: an unspeakable tragedy. He, who had seen a lot of grief, had never seen grief like this woman's. He counseled her. Week after week, she came to him, and she talked and he listened. It was work, he sometimes thought, that would have been more appropriate for a therapist than for a priest. And yet he continued. He thought that if he kept talking to her, if he kept listening, he would eventually be able to help her.

"And could you?" she said. "Did you?"

He shook his head. "Never. I couldn't, because I didn't know the answers myself. In the end, I believe I failed her."

She had to resist the urge to put her hand over his. "I'm sure you didn't," she said. "What that must have meant to her, to have someone like you to talk to."

He shifted. "Maybe. But still, I couldn't answer her question."

"What question?"

"About why things like this happen. How the death of a child... how that could possibly fit into God's plan. I didn't know then, and I don't know now. And yet I felt like I owed her an explanation."

She absorbed all of this. There was nothing, she thought, that could be worse than the death of a child. Her own troubles seemed tiny and insignificant in the face of this story; she felt herself grow smaller, like Alice in Wonderland shrinking. Finally she said, "That's a terrible story. But that doesn't explain who you had to forgive."

He looked surprised. He crumpled his napkin and put it inside his cup, then secured the plastic top. He smiled at her, but his smile seemed different now, more cloudy and impenetrable. He looked at his watch. "I think I should be getting you back," he said. "I didn't realize how late it was."

"Okay," said Lillian. She drank the last of her coffee. So he did have secrets, then. They wound their way through the tables and out the door. She supposed that everyone had secrets, no matter the open facade they might present to the world.

What a relief it was to be outside, even though they had given up the store's air-conditioning for the heavy summer heat, and the relative quiet of their spot there for the mass of people on Church Street, with their ice cream and Kettle Korn and mammoth shopping bags.

When Father Colin pulled into the parking lot at the church Lillian was almost surprised to see her own car sitting there in the sun. It was as though she had been on a long journey to a foreign country, and she hadn't expected to be back in familiar territory so soon.

*

"Really?" said Ginny the following Sunday. "Church? And to what do we owe the pleasure?"

"Nothing," said Lillian. "Just thought I would go, that's all."

"There's doughnuts after," said Olivia helpfully.

"Good," said Lillian. She was looking into the hall mirror, putting lipstick on with one hand and holding Philip with the other.

"Well," said Ginny. "I don't suppose Rachel—"

"No. But Stephen, maybe."

"Maybe," said Ginny. She sighed, then brightened. "I suppose it's better not to question it, and just to enjoy the company."

"Exactly right," said Lillian. She put the cover on the lipstick with her teeth and snapped it closed, hard.

*

Rachel lay on the air mattress, listening to the sounds of everyone departing for church. She ignored the rustlings of Olivia's waking up, her search for the pink T-shirt with the purple flowers, her return to the room to retrieve her orphaned sandal. With the exception of Jane, whose presence was so unobtrusive that Rachel had gotten out of the habit of counting her, Rachel was alone in the house. She ate a leisurely breakfast on the deck and then repaired to the den to read the paper in her father's recliner. Before she started reading she turned on her phone, which she had purposefully kept off since Friday.

Two messages waited. The first one: Tess. "Rachel. Rachel, pet, I hope your father is doing okay. But you've got to check in with me. You can't just disappear. We've got submissions backing up here. I'm looking at a stack of head shots. I can't possibly find the time to do this myself. Call me back."

The second one was Tess also. She wandered into the kitchen as she listened to it. "Rachel," said Tess. "I'm confused about why you won't call me back." Rachel put the phone down for a second and when she returned it to her ear the voice was still going. "Listen, we've got to talk about this film. If you're not in touch with me soon I'm going to hand the project over to Stacy." Stacy was four years younger than Rachel, officious, fussy, supremely organized. There was a rumor in the office that she had once delivered a box of homemade muffins to Tess's apartment on a Sunday morning. "Do you hear me, Rachel? You've got to talk to me about your time frame here. I'm scheduling a producer session for the first of August. I need you here. Pet. I mean, I wish your father the best and all, but you have got to: Call. Me. Back."

She listened to Tess's message again. Then she turned her phone off, closed it, and put it into one of the bottom kitchen drawers, beneath a Ben & Jerry's ice-cream pint sleeve and a bunch of grill skewers. She was poking through the drawer to see what else was in there (a ginger grater, a collection of wooden salad spoons, one of those flat rubber things you use to open jars, and Olivia's pink stuffed elephant) when she heard footsteps on the stairs. Her mind jumped instantly to a worst-case scenario—an intruder! a rapist!— and she was allowing herself to run down a list of horrors when Jane appeared in the kitchen. She was walking gingerly, bent over, like an old lady, her shoulders pulling together in front of her body, one hand on her stomach. She started when she saw Rachel, but she didn't straighten, so the effect was not just of a deer caught in headlights but of an aging, crippled deer.

"Jane! What are you doing up?"

Jane lowered herself carefully into a chair and Rachel made an awkward motion toward her, as though to catch her. "Shhh," Jane said. "You can't tell anyone, Rachel. I didn't think anyone was home. I just had to get up. I had to get out of that room."

"But you're not supposed to—"

"I know," said Jane. "I know I'm not supposed to. But sometimes I do anyway. It keeps me sane, to see a little bit of the outside world."

"*Keeps* you sane? You do this *often?* This isn't your first time?" Rachel felt her mouth hang open like a cartoon character: big thick lips dragging toward the floor.

"When I can," said Jane. "When everyone leaves at one time. Which isn't often."

"But what do you do?"

"Nothing much. Wander the house." Jane looked sheepishly up at Rachel.

"Wander! You shouldn't be wandering."

"Sometimes," said Jane, "I sit in your father's recliner and look out at the garden. It's a beautiful garden, and I can't see it from my bed." They both looked toward the window. It was a beautiful garden. It had come into full bloom, and every color was represented in exactly the right proportion.

"But the baby!"

"I know," said Jane. "I know all about the baby. All I *think about* is the baby. Work, or the baby. The baby, or work. My placenta!"

Rachel pulled out the chair next to Jane's and sat. Truly, she wasn't exactly sure what a placenta was. Was she supposed to know that? "But you go to your appointments, right? You leave then."

Jane sighed. "Yes. But that's only every two weeks. And I feel so...so chaperoned during those."

"Like at a school dance," said Rachel, nodding. "In junior high."

"Right," said Jane. "Or like a prisoner. I mean, I know Stephen's helping the best way he can, but if I breathe wrong or lean over too far to pick something up he flips out. He's so nervous that it makes me feel nervous. Walking downstairs to look out at the garden feels much more reasonable all around."

"The whole thing sounds terrible," said Rachel. She looked at the mound underneath Jane's robe. If things had gone in a different direction for her, she would have had a mound like that several months hence. She couldn't imagine that, not really, a mound belonging to her and Marcus. Still, a seed of resentment sprouted somewhere deep inside her.

"It is terrible," said Jane. "Temporary, but terrible. I mean, really the end could be in sight. If the bleeding stops, if the placenta moves away...well, this could turn out very normally in the end. I forget that sometimes."

"Yeah?" Again with the placenta. (Moves away from what?) Rachel must have revealed some bewilderment in her expression, because Jane said, "I'm sorry, I'm probably boring the hell out of you. It's just I think about the placenta all the time! I can't help talking about it. It's like I'm willing it to move."

"Um," said Rachel. "Pardon my ignorance. But move *where?*"

"Oh! I'm sorry. Of course you wouldn't know anything about that. I didn't, until I ended up here." Jane smiled and motioned in the general area of her stomach. "Stop me if I'm giving you too many details." She went on in a brisk, businesslike manner. Rachel could imagine her at some high-level business meeting, explaining complex financial topics to a roomful of people in suits. "The placenta is the thing—it's an organ, actually—that nourishes the fetus as it's growing. It's supposed to move toward the top of the womb as the baby grows. But sometimes it doesn't; mine didn't. Mine's lying too close to the cervix." Rachel noticed that when Jane really got going she used her hands a lot. The word *cervix* seemed a little too personal and intimate, but Rachel continued to listen. "So. That's why I started bleeding. And if I move around too much, I might start bleeding again. It's called *placenta previa*. I'm lucky, because in my case the placenta is only partially covering the cervix, and there's a decent-sized chance it will move away before it's time to deliver. But on the other hand, most people with partial previa don't have much bleeding. So mine's—how'd the doctor put it?—mine's a dramatic case."

"Lucky you," said Rachel.

"I know. I never was one for drama, so it's ironic." She looked at Rachel. "But I'm boring you! I'm sorry. See what I've become? God! I don't even recognize myself."

"You're not boring me at all." Rachel studied Jane. She hadn't really thought much about why her sister-in-law was up in that bedroom; wrapped up in her own troubles, she had sort of forgotten that there was a whole story there. *Understand the backstory,* Tess always told her. *Even if you're casting the smallest part in a tiny production you don't think anyone will ever see, understand the backstory. That's what makes a casting agent better than good.* And Rachel had lost sight of the backstory.

"It's terrifying, how many things can go wrong in a pregnancy," said Jane. "When you really think about it, the amazing thing is that any babies are born normally."

Rachel pushed the seed of resentment down, down, until it all but disappeared. It wasn't Jane's fault Rachel had once been pregnant and now was not. It wasn't Tess's fault either. And here was a chance to forge a connection with Jane, a connection that went beyond pregnancies. Why not seize it?

"Do you think it's possible," Rachel asked carefully, "to mess up at your job and then make things right again? Or once you mess up, once you really mess up, is it all over?"

Jane looked at Rachel. She pushed a piece of hair out of her face. "Why do you ask?"

"Oh, I don't know," said Rachel. "I was just thinking about a work situation. That I find myself in."

Jane leaned toward her. "Do you want to talk about it?"

Rachel thought about that. "No. Not really, I don't think so. I'm just wondering if—well, I guess what I'm wondering is this. Would I already know by now if I was going to be good at what I do? Would I already be a star?"

"Well," said Jane slowly. "I think there's always room for a fresh start."

"You do?"

"At least I hope so."

"You!" said Rachel. "Why do you hope that? You already are a star. A rock star."

"Noooo," said Jane. "No, no. I just work hard. That's it. I just work really hard, harder than anyone else in the room. But that doesn't mean I don't make mistakes."

"But you make so much money," said Rachel. She lowered her voice as though the very appliances were listening. "Right? I mean you do, right?"

"Sure, I guess," said Jane. "I mean, yes. I make a lot of money. In a good year, there are bonuses. Yes, I make a lot of money."

"If I made the kind of money you must make—God, I don't think I'd have any problems at all," said Rachel. "I would feel like I had arrived."

Jane laughed.

"Why are you laughing?"

"Because it's funny that anyone would think that."

"Why funny?" Rachel felt a little embarrassed, so she rose from the table and made herself busy in the kitchen. She found a package of paper napkins and refilled the empty dispenser. She sprayed cleaner on the refrigerator doors and wiped them down — everywhere on them, it seemed, was evidence of Olivia's fingerprints. Jane watched her.

Finally she said, "It's funny because there is no point to get to, no amount of money that makes you say, *There, I'm done.* There is no arriving. There's just doing. And doing, and doing."

Rachel considered this. She sat back down at the table and faced Jane squarely. "No arriving," she said. "That's depressing. So you can't arrive. But I guess...I guess you can depart. You can disappear?"

"Yes," said Jane. "By all means, I think you can disappear."

They were silent for a moment. Rachel considered the garden again.

"Jane? Can I touch your stomach?"

Jane looked startled.

"I'm sorry," said Rachel. "Is that too personal a request? Is that weird?"

"Not at all," said Jane, turning in her chair so that her stomach was within Rachel's reach. "It's just that—"

"What? I don't have to. I really don't have to."

"No! Do. *Do.* It's just funny to me that I've been living here for *weeks,* and with the exception of Stephen you're the first person who's asked me that."

Rachel wasn't sure she'd ever touched a stomach in such a late stage of pregnancy. She hadn't seen Lillian right before the children were born, and her friends in New York did not yet have children. She placed her hand on the swell. She saw now why strangers wanted to do this, why they were drawn to it, to the pulse of life underneath that surface. Jane's stomach was harder than Rachel expected it to be, and more unforgiving.

"It's okay," said Jane. "Really, you can press harder. It's not made of glass."

"God," said Rachel. "I thought it would be softer. I didn't realize. How protected that baby is in there. So insulated! I'm jealous, in a way. You know what I mean?"

"I do," said Jane, and she placed her hand on top of Rachel's. "I really, really do."

✳

Lillian set the car seat heavily on the kitchen counter.

"Oh, *Lilly*," said Ginny. "Not there. It could topple over, for God's sake! And I'm using this space." She was making a blueberry pie; she and Olivia had gone together to Charlotte to pick the berries the day before. Olivia was watching *The Little Mermaid* on the television in the den.

"Sorry," said Lillian. "I'll put him on the ground, then."

"Why are you putting him anywhere?"

"Because I'm going to lunch with Heather. She got a sitter."

Ginny flipped rapidly through the pages of her old recipe book. "Let's see... one and a quarter cups of sugar." She stopped and looked up at Lillian. "And I suppose you got a sitter too?"

Lillian smiled at the counter. She put her finger on a sticky spot left from breakfast. Then she met Ginny's gaze squarely. "No..."

"But I'm here."

"But you're here. And I thought, well, you don't mind, do you?"

"I'm here," said Ginny. "And I wouldn't mind. But I am making a *pie*. With a crust from scratch."

"Philip will just sit here and watch." And then, to the car seat, "Won't you, prince?"

"And what if he needs to be held?" demanded Ginny. "And I've got blueberry all over my hands?"

"He won't," said Lillian, squinting to see the digital clock on the microwave. "He's practically asleep. Look at his eyelids!"

They both looked. "See?" said Lillian. "He'll be out before I'm down the driveway." Philip opened his mouth and let out a small unhappy sound.

Ginny sighed.

"Rachel's around, right?" asked Lillian. "I can ask her to keep an eye."

"Don't," said Ginny. "Don't ask Rachel. She's resting in my room."

"Resting? What does she have to rest from?"

Ginny said nothing.

"Oh, honey," Lillian said to the baby, leaning into the car seat and distributing little kisses all over his face. "Isn't it awful? Nobody loves you."

"Nonsense," said Ginny. "Leave him, then."

"Really?" Lillian smiled. "Really, you don't mind? It's just lunch. I'll be back in an hour—"

"One hour, to pick up Heather, eat, and get back here?"

"Give or take." Lillian jingled her car keys and leaned into the den. "But if you don't want me to go, I won't." Ginny searched Lillian's face carefully for signs of sarcasm or malice, but she found none. It was lovely, after all, to see her looking so happy. It was lovely to see her smile.

"Go," she said. "Really, go. Have a good time. I mean it."

"Bye, sweetie," Lillian said to Olivia, who had her thumb in her mouth and did not look away from the television screen. To Ginny she said, "He'll sleep the whole time, I'm sure of it." She leaned into Ginny and hugged her, and Ginny had to work at not holding onto her too long, because after all it was delicious to have her daughter, however briefly, in her grasp.

~⋇

"I don't have an opinion at all," announced Ginny at her book club meeting the following week. "I could barely concentrate on it. My house is completely full. I can hardly complete a thought, never mind a book."

"I'm sorry," said Myrna kindly. "But I can't sympathize with you at all."

"No?"

"No. I *beg* my children to bring the grandkids, but all I get is excuses. Buffalo's so *far,* they say. Or they have *swimming lessons.* Or this and that. I'd give anything for a full house—" She picked up the book and put it back down again.

They were meeting at Myrna's house in South Burlington. It was magnificent new construction with stunning views of the lake. She had moved into it two years ago, six months before Myrna's husband, Hank, went to the gym to use the elliptical machine, suffered a heart attack, and never came home. Now Myrna had three bedrooms and a hot tub on the deck all to herself.

"And you, a widow," said Hedy. "They should be here all the time, looking after you."

"*I* don't need looking after," said Myrna. "I do very well looking after myself, thank you very much. But the company I could use." She disappeared into the kitchen and returned with a cheese-and-cracker platter as big as a bicycle wheel. "The companionship would be nice," she added. "I'm not saying all the time. But occasionally."

"It's the daughter-in-law," said Alice. "It's *always* the daughter-in-law."

"I don't know—" said Myrna, spreading cocktail napkins in the shape of a fan on the table.

"Well," said Hedy. "My grandchildren live around the corner, and believe me, there are times when Buffalo doesn't sound like such a bad thing."

"Hedy," said Alice. "What a thing to say." She uncorked a bottle of white wine and tipped it toward Ginny, who pushed her glass closer.

"Not if you heard the *noise,"* said Hedy. "My God, but they're *loud!"*

"That's because they're boys," said Myrna. "My little grand-babies are perfect angels."

Hedy snorted.

"What? They are."

"That's the distance talking," said Hedy. She adjusted her skirt across her lap and reached for a cracker. "And it's not just the noise. It's something more."

"What?" said Ginny eagerly.

"It's my daughter! It's the way she assumes that I'm available for babysitting. It's 'I have a doctor's appointment, I'm just going to drop them off.' Or 'Just a quick hair color, can you come over for an hour?'"

"Did we do that?" asked Alice. She poured wine for Myrna and Hedy. "To our parents?"

"We didn't," said Myrna. *"I* didn't. We grew up faster. We were on our own sooner. College, married, babies, *boom.* We didn't have time to get dependent on anyone. We were right in the thick of it, still babies ourselves."

"My parents wouldn't have taken it," said Hedy. "They would have had me married off at sixteen if they could have."

"It was a different world back then," said Ginny. "Don't you think? All this hemming and hawing over what everyone should do with their lives. We didn't do all that, right? We just *lived*."

"I'm with Ginny," said Alice. "They over*think* things, these kids. They want everything to be perfect, so they spend all this time figuring things out—"

"When really," said Hedy, "it'll never be perfect. It will just be life." She drained her glass and reached for the bottle. "Messy."

From a faraway room a telephone rang and Myrna waved her hand dismissively. "It's nothing," she said. "Telemarketer."

The last vestiges of the sunset were settling over the lake, and Myrna got up to switch on a lamp. "We haven't discussed the book."

"Well, I didn't care for it," said Hedy.

"Didn't you?" said Alice.

"Such a dreary premise. I couldn't get past it—"

"I liked it well enough," said Myrna. "But other people said they couldn't put it down. I put it down plenty."

While they talked, Ginny looked out at the lake and let her thoughts float and settle, trying to put her finger on what it was she was feeling, where this sense of peace and fulfillment was coming from. And while she couldn't articulate it exactly, she thought that probably the presence of all of the people in her house—all these different creatures, with their hungers and their desires and their moods and their love—was allowing her to feel necessary, to feel loved and embraced again, in a way that she hadn't realized she'd stopped feeling. Hadn't realized she'd been missing.

Now suddenly it didn't matter much to her why Lillian and Philip and Olivia and Stephen and Jane and Rachel were there. It didn't matter how long they were going to stay. It only mattered *that* they were there.

"Ginny?" Alice was saying. She bit a cracker in half. "You go first. Anything to say, on or off the record?"

"Nothing," said Ginny dreamily, taking a sip of wine. "Nothing at all. You go ahead."

"Well," said Alice. "Let me at it, then. I've got lots to say."

Driving home two hours later, her car alone on Spear Street, the farmland to her right shadowy and mysterious in the summer darkness, Ginny thought of all of them in their myriad beds: Lillian and Olivia and Stephen and Jane and Rachel and even sweet little Philip in the Pack 'n Play, on his back, with his frog legs pulled up to his hips. *This,* she thought happily. *This.*

William was not in bed. William was at the kitchen table, doing a crossword.

"How was your thing?" he asked, not looking up.

"Not bad," she said. "Good, actually. Wine, conversation. The usual."

"Hmph."

"I haven't seen you do a crossword since we were newlyweds," Ginny observed. She hung her car keys on the hook by the kitchen and picked up a baby rattle from underneath the table. William grunted. Ginny began to put away the dinner dishes from the drainer. Somebody had washed them, which was nice, but nobody but her ever put them away after. Washing was satisfying. This was just annoying. "Baseball not on tonight?"

He nodded his head toward the den. "Lilly turned in early," he said. "Had to shut off the television."

"Where's Stephen?"

"Upstairs already, I guess."

"It's only nine forty-five!" Stephen was a notorious night owl, always had been.

"Don't know," said William. "Didn't ask him to punch a time card."

"Rachel?"

"Went downtown to the movies. Now she's back."

"Alone? Whose car?"

"Mine."

"William! You should have gone with her."

William looked up and considered Ginny. "How do you know I didn't offer?"

"Did you?"

"No. I thought I was going to watch the game."

"So go upstairs and watch the game," Ginny said. "There's a perfectly good television in the bedroom."

"Not perfectly good," William said, applying the eraser to the crossword in what Ginny thought was a rather aggressive manner. "Too small, too far from the bed. Not good for baseball."

"Ah," she said. "And so he crossly does the crossword."

"Funny."

"You're in a mood." She dried a water glass with the dish towel.

"I am just," he said, "trying to do a *crossword*. In *silence*."

"And who's stopping you?"

"You are! Everyone is!" He stood, and drew himself up to his full height, which was considerable. He shook out the paper and folded it carefully, then placed it on the table. "There doesn't seem to be any *silence* in this house."

"Nobody's down here! Just me."

"Exactly," he said.

After he had gone Ginny sat down and opened the crossword. William had filled in only two words. There was a little rubbed-out spot where he had erased too hard. She looked at the puzzle for a long time, but she wasn't trying to complete it, not really, and after a while she put the paper into the recycling bin, locked all the doors, and climbed the stairs slowly.

She heard no sounds coming from Olivia in Rachel's old room, and it was also silent in Lillian's room, where (she hoped) Jane and

Stephen were sleeping. Only the door to Stephen's old room stood ajar; the rest were closed tightly against the night.

Standing there, she was reminded of nights just like this — summer, warm, the humidity still trapped cozily around them — when the children were young and she stood in this very spot after closing up the house for the night. Listening. Feeling all the life on the other side of the doors.

She knew she'd been tired so many of those nights; she knew her mind, cluttered with an ever-expanding to-do list, had already been leaping ahead to the next day and the day after that, sorting out meals and activities and carpools and all the rest of it.

And yet! Standing there, hearing only one or two lonely crickets outside in the yard, she felt a certain fondness and longing for that younger incarnation of herself, and also for the children she and William had ushered into the world from the cocoon of this old house.

Quietly she opened Olivia's door. The little girl stirred but did not waken. She slept on her back, in a pose very like the one in which Ginny used to find Rachel or Lillian: arms above her head, as though in her sleep she had recently been reaching for something. And Rachel, on the air mattress, looking childlike herself, her long dark hair spread out behind her.

The shade was partly open, and so was the window, and as Ginny stood there a light breeze moved the shade against the window. She backed out and closed the door again and moved silently down the hallway.

William might not think it was quiet in their house, but Ginny did; she thought it was not merely quiet but was sheathed in a deep, heavy, satisfied silence, and she relished every ounce of it, drinking it in like a nectar.

Was this happiness? Ginny wasn't sure. As she moved closer to her own bedroom she could hear the sounds of the baseball game, the gentle lull of the announcer's voice, the occasional burst of applause. Perhaps it wasn't happiness, not exactly. But surely it was close.

꽃

Something awoke Lillian, but she didn't know what it was. She lay on her bed in the den, careful not to stir too much. She didn't want to disturb Philip, who had been sleeping for four hours straight. She thought she heard a sound above so she walked softly up the stairs and in the direction of Olivia's room. She stood outside the door.

She heard crying. But it was not Olivia's brand of crying. Olivia, when awoken in the middle of the night, made no secret of her unhappiness. Her cries had, in the past, been strong enough to draw comments from Lillian's neighbors in Massachusetts. No, this crying was muffled and clandestine. This was the crying of someone who didn't want to be found out. This was Rachel crying.

Lillian pushed open the door. There was enough of a moon to allow her to see that Rachel was lying on her stomach on the air mattress with her face pressed into the pillow. Her shoulders were shaking, and even her legs, as though borne along by the inflation and deflation of her lungs, were moving.

She reached out and touched Rachel on the back and Rachel flipped around like a startled animal. "Jesus," she said. "What the hell?"

"Hey," said Lillian softly, crouching down next to the air mattress. "Hey, hey." She gestured toward Olivia's bed, where Olivia slept on, undaunted. "Come downstairs." And Rachel, chagrined, obedient, and looking, somehow, in the dim light of the hallway, exactly like a child, allowed herself to be led.

By the brighter, accusatory lights of the kitchen Lillian could see that Rachel had been crying for some time. Her eyes were red and swollen; her face was splotchy; her hair was wet and matted to her cheeks. Lillian felt a flutter of nervousness and embarrassment at this unabashed display of emotion. She could not, though she scoured her memory, think of the last time she had seen her little sister cry like this. She busied herself with the teakettle and tea bags while Rachel mopped her face with the wet paper towel Lillian gave her. When she had poured the water into the mugs and brought them, steaming, to the table, she pulled out a chair and faced Rachel squarely.

"Sit," she said firmly, as though she were talking to Olivia. "Tell."

So Rachel told. She told all of it: the post-relationship sex with Marcus, the pregnancy, the miscarriage, the apartment, the terrible financial strain, the fact that, despite this strain, she seemed to have walked away from a perfectly good job, and a good opportunity for advancement within that job, thus sullying her reputation in what was a very small, very close-knit industry.

"I wondered about that," said Lillian. "Mom said you had a lot of vacation saved, but that just didn't seem possible."

"I know. I asked her not to tell," said Rachel. "I just couldn't stomach the possibility of going back to work, sitting in that office, working on casting this film without my heart in it. I don't have the energy. I don't have any energy!"

Lillian nodded. Privately she thought anyone without an infant to care for should have an abundance of energy, but she could see that now was not the time to bring that up.

Rachel went on: "I just figured... everyone here is so wrapped up in their own stuff, nobody would notice."

Lillian accepted that dig, swallowed it down. "Does Dad know?"

"Oh, *God* no! I hope not. I asked her not to tell."

Lillian felt the practical side of her come into focus, the list-making, organized side that had carried her through college and her long-dead career. "It's all not what you wanted, I can see that, but what about it can we fix? Where can we start?"

"I don't know," said Rachel morosely. She had finished her tea and she folded her hands and laid her chin on top of them, looking up at Lillian like a puppy. "I just can't believe I did this. I can't believe I scared Marcus away, and I thought I would still have a career, and then I screwed that up too."

Lillian cast about for a paper and pen. Then, finding neither, she tore off a piece of that day's *Free Press* and took up a purple crayon that Olivia had abandoned on the table. At the top she wrote: Apartment. Job. Boyfriend. She formed each word into a column and looked expectantly at Rachel, crayon at the ready.

"Lillian," said Rachel. "Lilly."

Lillian waved a hand at Rachel. "Just start spouting things out. I'll categorize them. We'll figure out what the most pressing situation is, and we'll tackle that first."

"Lillian," said Rachel again. "I appreciate this, but this isn't what I need."

"Really? What do you need, then?" In Lillian's PR days she had learned all of this, how to talk to clients, how to get them to figure out what they wanted so she could give it to them. She made another, blank, column, and waited.

"I don't know," said Rachel. "But not this. Not charts! Not you, even. I'm not sure I need you."

That stung. "Okay," said Lillian. She put the crayon down, folded the paper.

"In fact," said Rachel, "sometimes being around you makes it worse."

"Worse? Why?"

"Because here I am, around you all the time, reminded of your stupid happy family, your ability to procreate. I'm sleeping in the same room as your daughter, for Christ's sake! In *my* old room. But she has the bed. It's like you're trying to throw it in my face—"

"Throw what in your face?" said Lillian evenly.

"That you have *all* of it. Everything I don't have. And sometimes—"

"What?"

"Sometimes I hate you for it." Rachel started crying again.

"Oh, Rachel." Lillian, torn between offense and pity, began to allow the latter to overtake the former. She felt herself beginning to soften. "Oh, *Rachel.* You have no idea."

"About what?"

"About any of it. It's so different from the inside."

"What do you mean?" asked Rachel. She blew her nose.

Lillian thought of Tom. She thought of Father Colin, and their conversation in the bookstore. She thought of the woman he'd told her about, the woman who'd lost a child. She thought of their father, and his steady, unwavering loyalty toward their mother; she thought of all the days and nights and family vacations and first days of school and sick children and broken-down cars and picnics at the lake that had built that loyalty, brick by brick.

"What do you mean?" said Rachel again. "Tell me."

Lillian wondered why she didn't tell. There was real intimacy between them that night, under the fluorescent lights, surrounded by the noises of the old house lifting and settling. Partly, selfishly, she didn't want to ruin the image of herself as a wise elder, someone who knew more than her sister knew about the ways of the world. Partly she was suddenly too tired to get into it. But partly—perhaps this was the most compelling reason of all—she wanted her sister to continue to believe in all of the things she wasn't sure she believed in anymore, the fairy-tale magic of marriage, the bolstering power of children and family.

Philip began to cry and Lillian looked toward the den. She had forgotten, for a few minutes, that he was in there, that he existed at all.

"I'm sorry," whispered Rachel. "You haven't slept. You must be exhausted."

Lillian pointed out the window, where faint threads of light were visible crossing the sky above the garden. "Look!" she said triumphantly. "Daylight."

"Sorry," whispered Rachel again.

"Don't be," said Lillian. "I couldn't be happier. This is a new world record. This is the longest stretch of time he has ever, ever slept."

✳

Jane's eyes were bright and wet and she was looking at Stephen intently. Stephen, recently pulled out of a deep and satisfying sleep, tried to focus on her. She had turned on the bedside light and was sitting up against the pillows.

"Stephen?"

"What is it? The baby?" He reached toward her stomach.

"No, not the baby."

"Oh. Thank God." He fell back against the pillows. His mouth was dry; he wanted very badly to brush his teeth.

"What is it, then?"

"I'm going to lose my job."

"Janey! Of course you're not. *Why* would you say that?"

"Because." She lowered her voice and looked surreptitiously around. "Because, there's a very big mess going on over there right now—"

"So?"

"No, you don't understand. A very big mess. Bigger than you can imagine, bigger than I can explain to you."

Stephen sat up again. In the glow the bedside light cast, Jane's face looked drawn and strange, like an older version of its regular self. She rubbed her eyes. She said, "And a lot of people are going to lose their jobs. High and low, a lot of people."

"How do you know?"

"I know, Stephen. Trust me, I know."

"But *you?*"

"It's a possibility. It's a real, true possibility." She made a move like she was going to get out of bed and instinctively he reached out to stop her.

"Jesus Christ. Really?"

"Really." She drew in a deep breath and looked up to the ceiling, then met his gaze again. "And if that happens, I don't know what we're going to do."

He put his hand over hers. Her hand felt chilly, and he picked it up and placed it between his two hands, rubbing it. "We don't have to figure all of that out now." He reminded himself of his father as he said that. All Stephen's life, it seemed, William had been able to diffuse the urgency of a situation simply by denying that it was urgent.

"But we *do*. We do have to figure it out now."

"Right now, in the middle of the night?"

"Yes. We have to be ready for it."

"But," he said. "Won't you be able to get another job? *If* you lose this one."

He felt her hand stiffen. "I don't know. It's possible that I won't."

"Then I'll get a job."

She snorted. *"You?"*

He thought back to the bed-rest blogs. Patience. Patience and understanding. Still, he was wounded. "Yes, me," he said. "I had plenty of full-time jobs, before I started freelancing. I can get a full-time job, and you can stay with the baby."

"But you," she said, "wouldn't make as much money! Nowhere near as much. I mean, our mortgage alone. We live off the bonuses!"

She was right, he knew she was, but he was insulted and hurt to have it pointed out.

"How do you know?"

She laughed. "Well, *would* you? I mean, come on. Would you?"

"I don't know. No."

"Exactly."

He thought maybe he hated her for a moment. He said, "We're not going to figure it out right here, tonight. We don't even know if it's going to happen."

"You are burying your head in the sand," she said.

"So what if I am. It's the middle of the night. You need to sleep. The baby needs you to sleep. That's the most important thing."

She said, "The baby!"

"Jane," he said, and he surprised himself by how sharp he sounded, how severe. But hadn't he been the epitome of patience and understanding all summer? Did he deserve to have all *that* piled on him, and now *this?* "Stop it. Stop talking right now, and go to sleep."

She turned away from him and positioned herself on her side, and he turned off the light and lay there for a long time in the darkness, marveling at his capacity to hurt, and to be hurt.

※

"Fighting?" said Lillian, sitting up straighter in the deck chair in which she was sunbathing. "How do you know?"

"Well, I don't know," said Ginny. "Not for certain. But last night, I thought I heard something from their room. Raised voices."

"Raised?"

"Semi-raised. Raised, as far as Stephen is concerned."

"God," said Lillian. "What about, do you think?"

"Who's fighting?" said Olivia. William had bought her a small plastic sandbox in the shape of a frog, and she was sitting cross-legged inside it, pouring sand from a hot pink pail to a yellow pail and then back again.

"Nobody," said Ginny and Lillian together.

With one hand on the screen door Ginny turned and looked back. "Lillian?"

"Sleeping," said Lillian. "I'm fast asleep."

"You should go talk to her, Lillian."

"To whom?" Lillian adjusted her sunglasses.

"To Jane."

"Jane? I do talk to her! I talk to her all the time."

"It just seems like she must be lonely, poor thing."

"That," said Lillian, "is the most sympathy I've ever seen you show toward Jane."

Ginny sighed and picked at a small hole in the screen. "It can't be easy."

"No," said Lillian. "No, it can't."

"So you'll talk to her?"

"I'll talk to her," said Lillian. "I don't know what I'll *say*. But I'll talk."

※

"We're going to the Ben and Jerry's factory," said William. "Come with us."

Rachel looked up from her book. "Me? Who else is going?"

"Just Olivia and me. And now you."

Rachel turned the corner down on the page to save her place in the book. She felt a ripple of guilt for doing this in her father's presence, because theirs was a house in which you were always supposed to have a bookmark at the ready. She said, "Why not Lillian?"

William shrugged. "She said she wasn't interested. But Olivia is over the moon." He tipped his head to the ceiling; they could hear little feet running rapidly up and down the upstairs hallway. "That's her getting her shoes on."

"I take it you told her about the free sample at the end?"

"Bingo. And she's fascinated by the idea of the Flavor Graveyard."

"Who wouldn't be," said Rachel. "I wonder how many flavors have died since I was last there? When was I last there, anyway? Can't remember." She stretched her arms above her head and yawned. "And what about Mom?"

"Not interested either. She's got things to do."

"Stephen?"

"Errands for Jane."

"What kind of errands? And what if I'm not interested either?"

"Don't know what kind of errands. And not interested is not an acceptable answer from you."

"I don't have a lot of choice, do I? When you put it that way," said Rachel.

"Exactly," said William. "Get your things. We're aiming for the eleven thirty tour."

Though she'd been sleeping more than usual since arriving home, Rachel found that as soon as they pulled onto the highway she was overcome with a dense, stubborn sleepiness. No matter how she tried she could not force her eyes to remain entirely open. The heat from the sun coming in the window, the gentle motion of the car, the serene NPR voices emanating from the radio: all these combined to give her a sense of safety and well-being, a feeling like being rocked gently back and forth in a cradle. She was somewhat embarrassed about this, for it seemed like a childish and vulnerable thing to do, at age twenty-nine, to fall asleep in a car your father was driving, on the way to what amounted to a field trip, so she turned her head toward the window and arranged her sunglasses in such a way that her father, were he to look over, might assume she was enjoying the view. She guessed from the silence in the car that Olivia was asleep. Rachel was in that odd, rosy stage, the waiting room between full sleep and wakefulness, when her father spoke, loudly, abruptly.

"I never liked him, you know."

"What? Who?" She sat up and lifted her sunglasses.

William glanced over at her. His hands were tight on the steering wheel, and his mouth was set in a straight line.

"Marcus," he said. "*Marcus.* I always thought you were too good for him."

"Oh, *Dad.*" Rachel sighed. "That's such a . . . such a parent thing to say. I mean, I appreciate it and everything, but you really don't have to—"

"I'm not," said William. "I'm not doing anything except speaking the truth. Marcus is a jerk, and you're too good for him, and I'm glad that you're done with him. And that's that." He spoke with an uncharacteristic vehemence. Almost a venom. How much did he know? Had her mother told? Rachel felt some color rise to her cheeks at that possibility. She looked down at her hands, then out the window. The trees against the summer sky, the sun now almost directly above, the day so bright it almost hurt to think of getting out of the car.

A stirring from the back seat then, and Rachel turned around to see that Olivia's eyes were open, and that she was watching and listening. How long had she been awake?

"Marcus is a jerk," said Olivia softly, somberly. "Marcus is a jerk." And then louder, with more glee: "A *jerk.*"

"Olivia!" said Rachel. "That's not a nice word. Don't use that word."

"Grandpa said it."

"I know. But he shouldn't have. He didn't mean it. Right, Grandpa? You shouldn't have. You didn't mean it."

They were off the highway then, on the winding two-way road that led to the factory.

"Cows!" said Olivia, pointing at the sign.

"I shouldn't have, in present company," said William. "And I'm sorry for that." Then, more softly, "But I did mean it."

They pulled into the crowded parking lot, and Rachel felt some heaviness in her beginning to lift or ease. Perhaps she should have been torn between leftover loyalty to Marcus and finding comfort in what her father had said. But she allowed herself to veer almost entirely toward the comfort. She took Olivia's hand and led her across the parking lot and toward the entrance.

After the tour, and after they emptied their pockets of change for Olivia to use in the penny-squashing machine, and after they explored the Flavor Graveyard, and after they admitted that the end-of-tour samples whetted their appetites without satisfying them, they ordered cones from the counter and sat outside at the picnic tables.

"This is nice," said Rachel after a while.

"I know," said William. "It is. I'm glad you came." He put his hand on hers, but only very briefly: truly, they were not a physically demonstrative family. But to her surprise he went on, even after he had returned his hand to his cone. "We used to do things a lot together, do you remember?"

"Like what?"

"Oh, I don't know. Things like this. When your brother and sister had grown out of doing things with their parents and you hadn't yet."

She thought, but didn't say, Go on.

"You were always the easiest to be with."

"I was?" She was pleased. "I would have thought that was Stephen."

"Nope, you were. It took less to make you happy." He must have seen some disappointment or sense of slight in her face because he held his hand up. " I don't mean that in a bad way. It's a compliment, really. I don't mean that your standards were low. I suppose it was something that came from being the youngest. You had an ease with the world. A joy. Anyone who came near you, you could make them smile."

"Dad!" said Rachel, flushing. "Not really!"

"What? It's true. But don't you dare tell Lillian or Stephen that I said so. Lillian will get herself in a snit about it."

She was absorbing this when Olivia said, "I need the bathroom."

"Really?" Rachel looked at her father, panicked.

"You're up," he said, shrugging. "I can't very well take her into the men's room."

Rachel had never taken a child to a public bathroom. She had never, in fact, taken any child of any sort to any kind of bathroom. What rituals and etiquette were required? What complications might arise?

Olivia handed her dripping cone to William. "Save this," she instructed.

It was not so bad. Rachel managed to squeeze into the stall with Olivia and helped her navigate the tie on her shorts. "Mommy always wipes the seat first," said Olivia, and dutifully Rachel took several squares of toilet paper and did as she was told. The only tricky part was after, lifting Olivia to the sink to wash her hands; Rachel's hands were damp from her own washing, and there was no way to support Olivia and dispense the soap at the same time, but Olivia was a good sport about it, and they worked their way through it.

When they were nearly done an older woman who had just come out of a stall and stood washing her own hands said to Rachel, "Your daughter is adorable."

"Oh," said Rachel. There was a beat when she could have corrected the woman, but she didn't. And Olivia, generally an ardent and enthusiastic calibrator of adult mistakes, didn't say anything either. "Thank you," Rachel said. She tightened her hold on Olivia's damp hand and they looked at each other, aunt and niece, in the fluorescent light of the bathroom, this secret—all secrets— safe between them.

※

Lillian knocked cautiously on the door to Jane's bedroom and when Jane said, "Come in," she entered.

"Sorry," said Lillian. "I didn't know if you were sleeping. So I knocked really quietly, just in case—"

"Ha," said Jane. "Sleeping. That's an optimistic thought."

"Really?"

"Really. I'm never sleeping."

"Never?"

"Feels that way."

"So what are you doing, then?"

Jane nodded her head toward a small color television balanced rather precariously on the dresser. Stephen had dug it out of the basement and had somehow figured out, with William's help, how to splice the cable to share the signal from the downstairs television. "Sit, why don't you," said Jane.

Lillian sat on the straight-backed chair from the hallway that someone had pulled into the room. "I never took you for an *Oprah* watcher," she said, rubbing a finger on the arm of the chair, where there was a scratch as thin as a thread. Why hadn't she thought of putting the chair in here when she was using the room, for when she was nursing the baby? Instead she had propped herself up in bed with a stack of pillows, but one of them—the baby, the pillows, or she herself—was always sliding around inopportunely.

"I'm not, usually. But I'm...well, I'm a bit low on options." Jane's computer was closed on the bed beside her. The sheet was pulled up over her stomach. On the floor beside her was a pair of pink slippers, and on the nightstand a glass of water with tiny bubbles floating on the top.

"It's hard to sleep at the end of a pregnancy," said Lillian. "Awful, really, that your body is expected to carry on more or less normally when you have all *that* going on inside it."

"I *know,*" said Jane. "I mean, I doze sometimes. But the real sleep, that's pretty rare. And Stephen—"

"What?" Lillian leaned forward toward the bed.

"Well, he doesn't get it."

"Of course he doesn't. No man does."

"Is that right?"

"Yes," said Lillian emphatically. "It's a simple matter of biology. They will never get it."

"I mean, he's wonderful, don't get the wrong idea."

"I'm not," said Lillian. "I promise you that. But you're pregnant and you're miserable and he's the one who put you in this position and whether it's logical or not there are times when you hate him."

"*Exactly,*" said Jane, smiling. "That's exactly right."

"God," said Lillian. "I can't believe you're surviving this at all, to tell you the truth. I'd lose my mind."

"I did, I think. Last week. Completely lost it. Thought they might have to put padded walls in here for me."

"Ha," said Lillian. "Could raise the value of the house."

They sat for a moment, contemplating the television.

"Miracle sextuplets," said Jane, nodding toward the screen. "Plus twins, separated at birth."

"In the same episode? You got lucky."

Jane laughed. "I guess so."

"Sextuplets is ... six, right?"

"Right. They thought there were five, but one was hidden in the afterbirth."

"Gross," said Lillian. "Really?"

"Truly."

"*Hidden?* In the *afterbirth?*"

"Right."

"Imagine *that* being your legacy."

"All of their names start with the letter K. Kieren, Kaleb ... I can't remember the rest."

"Jesus," said Lillian. "That seems like a poor choice." She placed her palms flat on her thighs and leaned back. The chair, after all these years, had really held up quite well.

"And now I know what I've been missing all this time," said Jane. "I'd never watched *Oprah* before, until last week."

"Never?"

"Not once. Didn't know what all the fuss was about."

"Not even in college? Killing time in the afternoons?"

Jane blinked and looked startled. "Killing time? In college? No."

Lillian yawned and stretched her arms above her head. "Really? What did you do in the afternoons, then? In that blissful time between your last afternoon class and dinner? We used to sit around the common room in the dorm and watch *Oprah*. Which dates me, I guess, because now college students have everything in their dorm rooms: computers, flat-screens, all the rest of it. But not us. We had one TV in the common room, and we crowded around it, elbow to elbow. God, I used to love that four o'clock time. Nothing to do. Nothing expected of you."

"In the afternoons?" said Jane. "In college? I don't remember having any free time. In the afternoons, or any other time."

"*Really?*"

"Really. I was studying."

"All the time?"

"All the time. When I wasn't in class, I was at the library. Same with business school. I studied for seven years without taking a breath."

"God," said Lillian. "How dreary."

Jane looked down. "Not to me. I was…pretty intense, in college. I guess I still am. When it comes to work."

Lillian inspected a freckle on the back of her hand. Funny, the way people said "know it like the back of your hand," when really she thought she spent very little time contemplating hers. She hadn't really known about this freckle, until now. Perhaps it was new. She wondered idly if she should make a note of it, in case it turned into something suspicious. Cancer. Weren't you supposed to do that? Maybe she would take a digital photo of it, and store it on her computer, along with all the other digital photos she would never get around to dealing with.

Thinking of her digital photos, and her computer, caused her to think about the unorganized piles in the basement and the garage that she had meant to go through before Philip's birth, which then led her to think about Tom living alone in their house, which then led her to think about her marriage, crumbling like a pile of old bricks, and all this caused her heartbeat to quicken uncomfortably, so she turned her mind firmly away and forced herself to study Oprah's beautiful glossy black curls and made her voice sound casual and nonchalant. "Better late than never, to become a member of the Oprah club," said Lillian. "I should think it would be hard to rejoin regular life, after all *this* luxury."

"Right," said Jane, snorting.

Lillian stretched out her legs in front of her and examined her toenails, which were crying for attention. Perhaps later that afternoon she'd leave the children with her mother and run out for a pedicure. It wouldn't take more than an hour, round trip, maybe an hour and a half. She could go during Olivia's naptime. If Olivia decided to succumb to naptime. She looked back at the television screen. "Is it just me, or has Oprah looked the same age forever?"

"I don't know," said Jane, shifting in the bed. "You know, they say no single person has had as much of an effect on the average American."

"As Oprah? Is that right?"

"I believe it, kind of. Day after tomorrow, by the way, is 'The Day I Found Out My Husband Was a Child Molester.'"

"You're kidding."

"I'm not."

"You know, if I were as rich as Oprah, I'd quit my job." Lillian stood and walked toward the dresser. The music box she'd had as a little girl was still there, placed incongruously next to the glass vase of marbles. From the window she could see William watering the container plants on the deck.

"Would you?" said Jane eagerly, casting a glance toward her computer. "I wouldn't. I *couldn't*." She flushed briefly. "In fact, I can't wait to get back to work. To feel useful again!" She looked at Lillian. "Sorry, I didn't mean —"

"No," said Lillian. "It's okay."

They both turned their attention back to the television. When a commercial for yogurt came on, Lillian leaned toward Jane and said, "I *never* felt that way, about work. Back when I worked."

"Really?"

"Really. I always thought—I mean *always*—that once the first baby came along I'd quit."

Jane's BlackBerry, on the nightstand, buzzed. She looked at it and then looked away.

"You can get that," said Lillian.

"No, that's okay."

"Do you want me to hand it to you? You look like you want to get it."

Jane shook her head. "I'm trying to sever the ties a little bit. Once this baby's out...well, they'll have to do without me for a little while. A few weeks, anyway. But things are really nutty at the moment, so it keeps going off."

"Nuttier than usual?"

Jane studied Lillian. "Much. Much more than usual. I can't even begin to say—"

"That's okay," said Lillian. "I doubt I'd understand anyway. But *weeks?* Weeks is nothing. You'll want months, won't you?"

"I don't know," said Jane. "But I think I'll only have weeks. I mean, after this unintended vacation—"

"This," said Lillian, "is not a vacation."

"No," agreed Jane. "No, it certainly isn't."

"You know," said Lillian slowly. "I read an article that said that women *preselect* careers that will allow them flexibility to care for their children. They don't realize they're doing it, but they do. So that when they eventually give up the jobs it's no big deal."

"I read that article too," said Jane. "But not all women. Not me."

"Of course not all women," said Lillian. "Lots of doctors don't. And lawyers. And politicians. And not you. But lots do."

"Did you?"

"I did, I think. Without knowing it. Isn't that strange? I wasn't even thinking about children at the time, when I went into PR, but in a way, subconsciously or something, maybe I was. Or society was, on my behalf."

"Society?"

"Yeah. I think maybe I was *steered* in a direction where I'd be earning less than my husband so that it would be no question that if one of us were to give up a job it would be me."

"Really?"

"Really. I think so. And the thing is."

"What?" Jane sat up straighter, and shifted the pillows behind her back.

"I was *good* at my job."

"I'm sure you were."

"No, really. I was *good* at it. I was organized, and I never missed a deadline, and I wrote really good press releases, and I could talk to journalists —"

"And did you love it?"

"Love it? No. I wouldn't say that."

"I love mine," said Jane.

"Do you?"

"I do. I'm happiest when I'm there."

Lillian was silent, contemplating this.

"I mean, usually. And now, there's a lot of crap going on, and I *hate* not being there. I'm in such a panic, stuck here. I can't stand it." Jane stirred in the bed. She took a sip from the water glass.

"I know," said Lillian. "But you have to be here. There's no other option."

"I know," said Jane. "But the people I work with...I mean there's some very heavy stuff going on, very heavy. It's a big deal. And I need to be there."

"But you're here."

"I'm here."

"And the minute that baby comes out, that's all that will matter."

"Maybe," whispered Jane, looking down. "But maybe not. Who can say?"

They were silent for a moment. Then Jane spoke. "And now? Do you miss it?"

Lillian sighed. "I don't know. Yes, some of it. I miss the order of it, and the satisfaction of completing something, and having someone tell me I did a good job. I miss having deadlines. But missing it doesn't seem...it doesn't seem to be the point anymore."

"You could go back." Jane set the water glass carefully on the coaster.

"Could I?"

"Of course. Why couldn't you?"

"I don't know. I'm...rusty. I'm out of practice. And if I were to go back, someone else would have to take care of the things I take care of now. The children and the shopping and the laundry—"

"You could hire someone. Tom could help. If you go back to him."

"I thought you think I shouldn't."

Jane shrugged. "I do think you shouldn't. But I think you will."

"You think so? I don't know. And if I do, well. *That's* not what Tom signed up for."

"But is it what *you* signed up for?"

"I don't know. I'm not sure what I signed up for. I just know where I am."

Jane said abruptly, as though she'd been holding onto the thought for a long time and had finally decided to set it loose into the atmosphere, "Stephen's going to stay home with the baby."

"*Stephen?*" Lillian laughed. "Our Stephen? A stay-at-home dad?"

"Yes," said Jane stiffly. "Is that a surprise?"

"It is," said Lillian. "I just can't picture it. The diapers and the bottles and the wrestling with the stroller—"

"But *why?*" persisted Jane. "Why can't you picture it?"

"Because, well...because it's *Stephen*."

Jane said, with a pained look, "Why is it, in this day and age, that you would react like that? When if I said I was quitting my job you'd hardly blink? I'm the one who got an advanced degree. I'm the one who makes all the money. I'm the one who's up at two in the morning, answering e-mails from Asia. Not Stephen. He sleeps like a goddamn baby himself. But I'm awake, working. *Me.*"

"I don't know," said Lillian slowly. "It's just so hard to imagine. Stephen, and a tiny baby, alone all day."

"But me and a tiny baby alone all day, you can imagine that?"

"I don't know," said Lillian. "Better, I guess." She looked at Jane. "Well, I don't know."

"But it's ridiculous even to question it! My salary is four times his."

Lillian considered this. "When you put it that way—"

"Right," said Jane. "When you put it into *monetary* terms it becomes a whole lot more clear."

They were both silent for a moment. Finally Lillian said, "Jane? I'm sorry. I didn't mean—"

"No," said Jane. "I know you didn't. But that's just the thing. Nobody *means* to judge like that. But they do."

"I know."

"*Why?* It's 2008, for Christ's sake."

"I know," said Lillian. "I don't know. It isn't how it should be, but—"

"But it's how it is."

Lillian shrugged. "Sort of, yes. Sort of, it's how it is." She put her hands to the top of her chest and said, reluctantly, "I've got to go down. The little prince is going to need to eat soon. I'm filling up."

"Okay," said Jane. "Thanks for the company."

"Sure."

"No, really," said Jane. "I mean it. Thanks." Her head dipped down. Lillian could see that her hair color needed to be redone. This tiny revelation made her feel suddenly tender toward Jane. It seemed to reveal a chink in the other woman's armor; it represented a new set of vulnerabilities that it had never occurred to Lillian that Jane might have. But here Jane was, stuck in bed in the room where Lillian had grown up, subject, like all women in late stages of pregnancy, to the whims of nature and biology.

"Lillian?"

Lillian turned from the doorway. "Yes."

"I'm—"

"What?"

"Never mind—"

"*What?*"

"You've got to feed the baby."

"No, go ahead." Lillian paused in the doorway. "He's not even crying yet. Believe me, if he needed to be fed right this second I'd know it. We'd all know it. He doesn't hold anything back."

"That must be strange," said Jane. "Is it?"

"Nursing?"

Jane nodded.

Lillian looked briefly to the ceiling. "It is, at first. It's *horrible,* at first, and don't let anyone tell you it's easy because they're lying. It's not easy for anyone the first time. But after—"

"After *what?*" said Jane eagerly.

"After you get used to it, well." Lillian paused, and in the mirror over the dresser she could see herself beginning to smile. "There's something amazing about it. Something indescribable."

"Try. Try to describe it."

"I can't, that's the thing. But it's…it's very natural, and satisfying."

"Satisfying, how?"

"Well. You've got this little helpless creature in front of you, and *you're* the reason it's alive, and if the whole world went away and if it was just you and him you'd be able to *keep* him alive. Only you. It's ridiculously powerful."

On the television, the closing credits were rolling. Oprah was sitting on the beige couch next to the parents of the sextuplets, leaning so far forward toward them that she was practically in a crouch. "Wow," Jane said soberly. "That sounds like something."

"It is," said Lillian dreamily. "It's otherworldly."

"God, I'm unprepared!" Jane beat the sheet lightly with her open palm. "And I really don't like to be unprepared. Preparation is my thing, I'm always prepared. I thought I'd have all this time at home, to get ready."

"Jane," said Lillian fiercely, sitting back down on the bed. She felt she needed to make things right with Jane. From downstairs, she heard the baby wail.

"Go," said Jane, nodding toward the door.

"Mom'll get him, for a minute. Listen, Jane, you're as prepared as anyone, you and Stephen."

"But—"

"But nothing."

"But you must have been more prepared than I am. Look at you! You're so good at it. At being a mother."

Lillian grunted. "You *must* be losing your mind, shut up here all day long like a prisoner."

Jane pointed the remote control toward the television, and the screen went black. "You are, though. You're really good. So…I don't know. Together."

"Together?"

"Absolutely. You know what you're doing." Jane was looking down at her lap. Impulsively, Lillian took one of Jane's hands. It was small and pale, and the nails were filed neatly—short, the way Lillian imagined the nails of a pianist or a doctor would look. She expected Jane to pull away, but she didn't, and they sat there companionably for several seconds.

"I don't," Lillian said finally. "I don't have the faintest idea what I'm doing."

"But—"

"No, not the faintest idea. I'm making it up as I go along. Sometimes I get so angry—"

"Everyone gets angry."

"I don't know," said Lillian. She squeezed Jane's hand once and let it go. "Do they?"

Jane nodded, and looked at her computer. "I get angry, at work, when things don't go the way I want them to."

"You do?"

"*So* angry. When people don't do what's expected of them. Nothing makes me more angry than that. You can't imagine the reputation I have, with some people."

"And does that bother you?"

"Not really." Jane shrugged. "Not at all, actually. I think it's a necessary part of doing business, of being as exacting as you need to be."

Lillian sighed. "I don't know. It's an awful feeling, to lose your temper with your own children. You'll see one day, I guess. Everyone does. I mean just the sensory overload. Sometimes it's too much. You can't keep your sanity."

Jane smiled. "You make it look easy."

"I've got you fooled, that's all. That's what most parents do.

We're all fooling, most of the time. You'll see. But I'm scaring you. I don't mean to scare you."

Jane sat up and cleared her throat. "That's okay. Not much scares me, usually."

"Yeah."

"But this does."

The wail rose.

"Lillian!" called Ginny.

"Upstairs!"

"You come down right now and feed this poor baby! He's chewing his fist off."

Lillian rolled her eyes at Jane. "Gotta go," she said.

"Okay," said Jane. "Maybe I'll try to take a little nap." She leaned back on the pillow and closed her eyes.

"Jane," said Lillian. "It's going to be fine, you know it's all going to be fine."

Lillian closed the door behind her and stood outside for a moment, listening to the *ding ding* of the laptop coming to life and then to the furious tapping on the keyboard. This was no nap, and she could almost see Jane's brain turning on, the synapses lighting up, carrying all that important, impenetrable information from one place to the next. She felt a little bit of envy at that, but it didn't last long, because Philip's cry had gone from needy to hysterical, and, like most of her thoughts these days, the envy, and the conversation that precipitated it, vanished quickly, until, by the time she had relieved Ginny of Philip—who was red in the face, eyes squeezed shut, mouth open—it was entirely gone.

AUGUST

William did not typically do laundry on his own, but he was down to his final pair of underwear, and Ginny had gone to the Essex outlets with Lillian and Rachel and the kids. Instead of waiting to ask her about it he decided to gather up a lump of clothes from the dirty clothes hamper.

He put the clothes in, mixing lights and darks in a haphazard manner that was somehow satisfying. He added what he thought was the correct amount of detergent. He was on his way up the basement stairs when the strange noise began. It sounded, to William, rather like the noise a man would make dying on the battlefield in some ancient war before modern weaponry was invented: all hisses and gurgles.

He returned to the basement and stood in front of the machine, watching it. As he watched, it seemed to give a shudder of resignation or despair and then stopped working altogether.

"Jesus Christ," he said aloud. He kicked the machine tentatively, the way one might kick the fender of a car one was considering buying, and stepped back for a moment. Nothing. He crouched as low as his protesting quadriceps would allow him to crouch and inspected the cement floor for signs of water damage. Nothing. He unplugged the machine from the wall, plugged it back in, and pressed all the buttons he had pressed already. Nothing, nothing, nothing. "For*get* it," he told the washing machine. "Just forget the whole thing."

Going up the stairs, he took a childish pleasure in stomping his feet as loudly as he could. Standing in the center of the kitchen, he looked around. The kitchen was not up to Ginny's usual standards. It was not, he thought, even close. In the sink sat a haphazard pile of cereal bowls, some with errant Cheerios floating in watery milk.

He opened the dishwasher to put them in, but the dishwasher had been run but not unloaded. He thought about unloading it, but to do that he would first need to clean off the counter above the dishwasher, which was sticky with a hexagon of something that was possibly, but not definitely, orange juice.

He looked in the sink for the sponge and found it crushed under the cereal bowls, like the victim of a terrible car wreck. The sponge was cold, and suspiciously sticky itself, and he decided to look on the shelves in the basement where Ginny kept cleaning supplies to see if an extra sponge might be found there.

Walking across the room from the sink to the table, his foot kicked a princess-themed sippy cup and sent it skittering under the counter. He bent to pick it up and knocked his head on the edge of the counter.

"This," he said to nobody, "is absolutely absurd."

He left the kitchen mess and went in search of the paper, then discovered that it had never been collected from the driveway. He retrieved it and moved toward the den to sit and read.

In the den he found the pullout couch unmade, sheets and a white blanket sitting in a hump in the middle of it. There was a pile of Olivia's toys in each corner of the room, as though they had been dispersed north, south, east, and west on purpose, and as he crossed the room to reach his recliner one of the toys—which he had not touched, he could swear to that with utter certainty—began to sing an overly cheery rendition of "Head, Shoulders, Knees, and Toes."

He moved again to the kitchen and opened the refrigerator door. He had forgotten to eat breakfast. That, perhaps, was contributing to his foul mood. Eventually he located a container of yogurt, and he had set it on the sticky counter and was rooting around in the dishwasher for a spoon when Stephen, coming around the corner, shouted, "Stop!"

William turned. *"What?"*

"That's Jane's. That yogurt, it's Jane's."

"Oh," said William. "I didn't realize we were shopping individually these days."

Stephen was wearing boxer shorts with little coffee cups all over them, and a black T-shirt faded to gray. "No, we're not. I mean, not for everything. It's just the yogurt. It's just that that's the only thing Jane will eat before noon, and I really want her to keep her strength up."

"No worries," said William. "I'm putting it back. See?"

"Dad, I'm sorry—"

"Not a big deal," said William crossly. "I can eat something else. I can eat anything. *I'm* not pregnant."

"No," said Stephen. "No, you're certainly not." He cast his eyes around the room.

"Geez," he said. "Bit of a mess, isn't it?"

"I'll say," said William. "I was just about to tackle it."

"I'll help," said Stephen. "Jane went back to sleep. I'm letting her sleep as much as possible." He peered at the clock over the microwave. "Geez, is that the time? Already?"

William found a paper towel and some spray to clean the counters, and together he and Stephen worked to stack the clean dishes on the counter. Then they developed a system whereby William took care of everything to the right of the dishwasher while Stephen put away everything on the left. When the dishwasher was empty William loaded the cereal bowls into it and swept the toast crumbs from the table into his hand and shook them into the sink. He was contemplating unearthing the vacuum cleaner when Stephen said, "Dad?"

"Yes?"

"How much do you know about these—what are they again—mortgage securities? No, wait, mortgage-*backed* securities."

William could not, after all, locate the vacuum cleaner. Its usual spot in the kitchen pantry was empty. He said, "I'm sorry. I wasn't listening. Say again?"

"Mortgage-backed securities. I think that's it."

"Sounds familiar. But where the *hell* is the vacuum?"

"I hadn't heard of them. Until the other day. From Jane. But I haven't really been paying attention to much these days, outside of what's going on here."

"Oh. Well. If it's Jane's world you're talking about, that's all completely foreign to me."

"Yeah. Me too. But she—"

Just then the front door opened and in walked Ginny and Lillian and Rachel. Lillian was carrying the car seat, from which a tiny fist was waving, as if for emphasis. Olivia formed the rear of the parade. She was struggling with a massive bag that said "Carter's" on the side.

"Washing machine is broken," William said to Ginny. Stephen took a coffee cup from the cupboard and tipped the carafe from the coffeemaker hopefully, but nothing came out.

"All gone," said Ginny. "Give me a minute, I'll make more." To William she said, "Good Lord. That washing machine is brand-new! That's not possible."

"I know. But it is possible, because it's happening."

"Overuse, probably," said Lillian cheerfully. William took the coffee carafe from Stephen, rinsed it, and began to measure grounds into the machine.

Rachel said, "Don't look at me. I haven't done laundry in years."

"I'll have a cup," said Lillian, "as long as you're making it."

Rachel said, "Me too. Or two cups."

Olivia went into the den and returned with the toy that had been singing. William saw now that it was a brightly colored dog with the names of the various colors written all over it.

"Did you call anyone?" Ginny moved the Carter's bag from the middle of the kitchen floor, where Olivia had dropped it, to the foyer.

"Who," William said deliberately, "would I call?"

"I don't know," said Ginny. "The number on the sticker. There's usually a sticker."

"Terrible timing," said Lillian. "I've got buckets of clothes to do."

Olivia discarded the dog, who was still singing—he had moved onto "The Wheels on the Bus"—and stood in front of the refrigerator, rearranging all of the magnets she could reach.

"Olivia," said William sharply. "Stop fiddling with those."

She turned, sensing something unfamiliar in William's tone.

"Sorry," he said. "But it's noisy. I can't think."

"It's not noisy," Olivia said. "It's quiet."

In the car seat, Philip began to whimper. Lillian looked quickly at him but didn't do anything. The whimper morphed into a cry. Ginny bent to unbuckle the straps and lifted him out. He regarded them, sucking on his fist.

"*That's* noisy," said Olivia. "Not magnets."

"I didn't check for a sticker," said William to Ginny.

"You didn't?" said Ginny. "Shall I?" She was still holding Philip; she looked around for where to put him.

"Here," said Lillian, who had unpeeled a banana and broken a piece off for Olivia, leaving the peel on William's clean counter. "Give him to me while you go look."

"*I'll* look for the sticker," said Stephen. He disappeared down the basement steps.

Lillian kissed Philip on the nose. "You can't be *hungry*," she said. "Not already! I just fed you."

"Couple of hours ago," said Ginny. "Wasn't it?"

"I guess. But he should be going longer stretches, don't you think?"

"*I* don't know," said Ginny.

"Can I color?" asked Olivia.

"In a minute," said Ginny and Lillian together.

"We've got to sort out this washing machine situation," said William.

"Pun intended? Or not?" asked Lillian, smiling at Philip.

"Not," said William sternly.

"*You*," Lillian said to the baby, "are getting cute. Finally."

Stephen returned with a paper towel on which he had written a series of numbers. "Here," he said. "Serial number. One-eight-hundred number. Warranty number, whatever *that* is." He held it in front of him like a banner. "Here," he said again. "Who wants it?"

"I'll take it," said William. He stalked out of the room and up the stairs to the bedroom. He looked for the bedroom phone, but it was not in its usual place on the bedside table. "Ginny!" he bellowed. No answer came from downstairs. "*Ginny!*"

She came upstairs—not as quickly, he noted, as she might have, but still she came. She stood in the doorway. "What, for heaven's sake?"

"Where's the phone?"

"How should I know? *I* didn't move it."

"Then who did?"

"I don't know! But we've got three other extensions in the house. It isn't the end of the world. What are you in such a *mood* about?"

He lowered his voice. "I am not," he said. "In a *mood*." He sat on the armchair and bent to put on his shoes. He tied one, then looked at Ginny. "I'm just tired of—" He paused, and looked down at his shoes. He began to tie the other shoe, and he said, to the laces, "Tired of the mess."

"You! When were you ever bothered by a mess? In nearly forty years of marriage, I've never known you to comment on a mess."

"I'm bothered now," he said. "Nothing is where it's supposed to be. It's—" He searched for the word. "It's disconcerting. I'm disconcerted."

She sat on the arm of his chair and regarded him. Her voice softened, and her face softened too. He could almost see the creases above her forehead and around her mouth relax. "But you were all for helping them. You said it was nice to have the house full up with life!"

"Did I say that?"

"Exact words. Full up with life. You said that to me when I was thinking what you are now!"

"Maybe I did," he said. "But I didn't really think it through, I guess. I didn't really think that all that life would be so—"

"Messy?" Ginny offered.

"That's right. So messy. So...intrusive."

As if to punctuate the point, from the floor below came the sound of shattering glass. Then they heard Lillian screech, "Olivia! Stay where you are. Don't move an inch. I'll get a broom." William stood halfway up, and Ginny said, *"Don't,"* and pushed him gently back down onto the chair. "They can handle it themselves, whatever it is."

He studied her. "When did you become so reasonable?"

She shrugged. "I don't know. Somewhere along the line I decided I didn't have a choice." She met his gaze squarely and then lifted her chin in a small gesture of courage or defiance. "I mean, William. They are our *children*. They need us. We should help them. Why wouldn't we help them, if we can?"

William thought of the check he had written and mailed to Rachel before she had appeared at the bus station. He hadn't meant it to be in secret, exactly, but he noticed he hadn't rushed to tell Ginny about it either. He thought of Rachel's voice on the other end of the phone—thin, disembodied, nearly unrecognizable; emblematic, in many ways, of New York City as a whole.

He opened his mouth to tell Ginny about it. It would be a relief, in some unnamable, mysterious way, to have her know about that.

Then, from the kitchen, they heard Olivia begin to cry.

"*Oliv*ia!" shouted Lillian. "I *told* you not to move!"

"Heavens," said Ginny. "That doesn't sound promising." She rapped William gently on the arm. "We should go," she said. "They might need a hand after all. Or, you know what? I'll go. You stay here. Enjoy the quiet. We'll take care of the washing machine after."

William closed his mouth. He wouldn't tell Ginny about Rachel's money. He wouldn't worry about Jane's baby, nor would he worry about Stephen's plans for fatherhood, nor would he worry about why Lillian was still here and when, in fact, she might take it upon herself to depart. He listened to Ginny clatter down the stairs, then listened to the ruckus in the kitchen. Stephen's voice had now joined the rest of them.

He closed his eyes. Ginny had shut the door behind her, and the sounds from downstairs were muted, distorted, the way sounds are when you hear them underwater.

※

"More flowers," said William. "These didn't come in a vase. Shall I bring them right up to Jane?"

"No," said Lillian. "Let's find a vase."

After she had settled the flowers in the vase William got her, and carried the vase into the dining room, and placed it in the center of the table, Lillian sat on the front steps and dialed Tom's work number. She shielded the phone with her body as if to hide the conversation from anyone who might pass by, but really it was unlikely that anyone would. Ginny and Stephen had taken Olivia and Philip to the playground at Oakledge. William had disappeared into the back garden with his weeding tools. Jane was in bed. Rachel had gone up to the shopping center for a pedicure.

"No more flowers," she said when Tom answered.

"You're very welcome. I'm glad you liked them."

That almost made her laugh — *almost* — but then a mental picture of Tom at work appeared, and that picture was quickly followed by an image of Nina sitting at her desk, sucking on a coffee drink and chomping on her gum, and those images together conspired to create inside Lillian a hot little ball of anger and indignity. "I mean it," she said. "They're expensive, and they're pointless, and my father can get better cut flowers from his garden any day."

Tom said nothing. Lillian, to fill the silence, said, "I'm surprised your little friend didn't answer the phone. What's her name? Nanette?"

"Nina," said Tom. "And she doesn't work here anymore."

Lillian gave a little shout of laughter. "Doesn't she? That's a lovely little detail."

"Come on, Lilly. You left in June. It's August. Don't you think this is getting a little ridiculous?"

"Maybe," she said. "But I don't know what else to do."

"What do you want?" said Tom. "You don't want flowers. You don't want apologies. You don't want me to come up there. You don't want to come home. What do you want?"

Lillian didn't know. She looked out at the street, at the sun beating down on the asphalt; you could almost see the drops of humidity in the air. Finally she said, "I want to turn the clock back. I want you not to have done it."

"We all wish that."

"Even Nanette?"

"Nina."

"Nina. Even she wishes that?"

"I don't know. Lillian! I don't know. I don't talk to her. I won't talk to her. I don't want to talk to her. You have to believe me on that. But I can't undo it. We can just move forward. Aren't you getting tired of all of this?"

She was. She was tired of digging through a suitcase to find her extra nursing bras. She was tired of getting in trouble when she didn't clean up after herself in the kitchen. Trouble! At age thirty-six! "I am," she said at last. "I'm tired of all of this. But mostly I'm just tired."

⁂

Rachel woke to find a stricken Olivia standing by the air mattress. She had been having a dream that featured both Marcus and Tess. Marcus was reading for a part in the film that Rachel had been supposed to cast, and which had surely been given over to the obsequious Stacy by this point. In the dream, Marcus was sitting at a long table with seven women, all beautiful, all greyhound-thin and each with one odd and arresting feature—big lips, high forehead, three-dimensional cheekbones — all fawning over Marcus, while Tess and Rachel sat somewhere off to the side, writing on a giant piece of paper with a green marker.

"What is it?" she asked.

"I had an accident," said Olivia. "I wet the bed."

"Oh, honey," said Rachel. She pulled herself up through the fog of the dream, as if up a giant rubber ladder, then hauled herself, commando-style, over to the nightstand to switch on the light.

"See?" said Olivia, turning to show Rachel her pajamas, with a darkened semicircle spreading across the back.

"Oh dear," said Rachel. "What do we do now?"

"I don't know," said Olivia, and a sob erupted from her small body.

Rachel cast about frantically for a plan of action. Sheets first, or clean pajamas? Where were Olivia's pajamas? Where were the clean sheets?

"Oh, Olivia. Don't cry," she said. "I'll go get Mommy."

But that only made Olivia cry harder, great, heaving sobs that seemed to come from the very soles of her feet. "No," said Olivia. "No, don't get her. You take care of me."

"Okay," said Rachel. She peeled the wet pajamas off of Olivia, then the underwear, then the wet sheets from the bed. She put the whole soggy mess in a pile outside the bedroom door. She opened the dresser drawers and began to look through the clothes. "There aren't any pajamas in here," she said.

"I know," said Olivia sadly. "Everything's dirty. The washing machine's broken."

"Oh, dear," said Rachel. She pulled out a pair of shorts. "You can wear these! With a T-shirt."

"No." Olivia shook her head. "I need real pajamas. I can't sleep in shorts."

Rachel pulled out a dress. "How about this?"

"A dress?" Olivia brightened visibly. "That's fancy."

"I know," said Rachel anxiously. "That will be fun, right? To wear a dress to sleep? Like a princess." Olivia nodded, and pulled the dress over her head. Rachel helped her work her arms through the holes.

When her head emerged Olivia said, "Do princesses wear dresses to bed?"

"Definitely," said Rachel. Then she said, "I'll be right back. I'm going to get clean sheets." She padded down the hallway and opened the door to the linen closet: no sheets. "No sheets," she reported to Olivia. "I can't remake your bed."

"What do we do?"

Rachel looked around the room, as though by looking she could produce clean sheets. Her gaze settled finally on the air mattress.

"Here," she said. "Climb in with me."

"With you?"

"Yes, with me. Or I can bring you down to sleep with Mommy."

Olivia considered Rachel. She worked her thumb into her mouth and pulled at a piece of her hair. "With you," she said finally.

Rachel pulled back the sheets on the air mattress, and Olivia climbed in, then Rachel slid in beside her. She had to get up again to switch off the light and when she returned Olivia was already asleep, one arm spread across Rachel's spot on the mattress. Rachel moved the arm carefully and regained her place, but she found that, owing to the slippery nature of the air mattress and her precarious position on it, she had to grip onto Olivia fairly tightly. Olivia moved toward Rachel, thrusting her body into her, breathing deeply, contentedly, and Rachel, though unable, for a long time, to fall asleep, was content herself, thinking that this was one thing she'd never before experienced, the sweet, wholesome weight of a child's body against hers, and that this, in fact, was worth abandoning the independent film, was worth fleeing the city, because it gave her a taste of what the future might hold, and also let her know that she wasn't ready for that future. She had thought that this was what she was missing, but it wasn't. Not yet.

*

"Polly is sick," said Olivia.

"I'm sorry to hear that," said William. He was on his way out to the garden; he wore his old green shorts and his Red Sox hat.

"Shoes on *outside*," said Ginny from the kitchen, where she was unloading the dishwasher. "I vacuumed up dirt all day yesterday."

"Got it," said William, holding both sneakers in one hand, winking at Olivia. "Hey," he said. "Do you want to come help Grandpa? I could show you which ones are weeds, and you could help me pull them up."

"No thank you," said Olivia formally.

"We could make a giant pile of weeds," said William.

"Why don't you go with Grandpa?" said Lillian.

Olivia sighed. "I can't. I have to take care of Polly. I can't leave her alone when she's sick."

"Who's this Polly?" asked William. "I'm not sure we've met."

"Polly is my friend," said Olivia.

"Her doll," interjected Lillian. She was organizing the children's clothes in the den. There was a small stack of pink underwear on the arm of the sofa.

"I'm going to put her to bed," said Olivia. "She's really sick."

Lillian said, to nobody in particular, "These baby socks are impossible to keep track of. What's the point of them?"

Philip, who was sitting in his bouncy chair and batting at a small stuffed bear, cooed.

"Oh, you *think* so, do you?" said Lillian.

"Be right back," said Olivia. She left the room and returned with a pink crocheted blanket, which she laid reverently over Polly.

"Shhh," she said imperiously. "Polly's sleeping."

227

"I didn't say anything," said Lillian. She shook out one of Olivia's T-shirts and began to fold it in thirds.

"*Shhh.*"

In the kitchen, Ginny clattered silverware into the drawer.

"Polly's *sleeping,* Grandma," said Olivia. "Quiet."

"Sorry," sang Ginny. "But the dishwasher doesn't unload itself, and if it did, it wouldn't do so silently."

Lillian loaded the clothes into a laundry basket and sat down on the couch.

"That's Polly's bed."

"I thought her bed was on the floor."

"No, *here,*" said Olivia. "On the couch."

"Fine," said Lillian, moving to the chair. She regarded Olivia. She wore pink shorts and a green and pink tank top; the tank top was decorated all over with pictures of fruit. Bananas, pears, apples, cherries, in an alternating pattern. Why was it okay for children to wear pictures of fruit or animals on their clothes but not for adults? Lillian would like to wear a fruit shirt.

Olivia touched the back of her hand to Polly's forehead. "Fever," she said.

"My land," said Ginny, coming into the den. "She's having a time of it."

There was a clatter in the hallway as the mail fell through the slot.

"Want to be the postman?" Ginny asked Olivia. Olivia shook her head. She was looking at Polly with an expression of bewilderment and consternation. "I think," she said slowly, "Polly needs medicine."

"Really?" said Lillian. She lifted Philip out of the bouncy chair and propped him on her lap. "Sounds serious."

"Yes," whispered Olivia. "It is."

Ginny, returning with the mail, opened the door to the deck

and called, "William? That health insurance form is here." She stepped out onto the deck, waving a pale yellow envelope.

"Mommy?" said Olivia.

"Yes, my little bunny."

"I know what's the matter with Polly."

"What's that?" Lillian was bent over, looking under the couch for one of Philip's toys that had rolled under. Philip watched her.

"She not regular sick. She's *homesick*."

"Oh, sweetie." Lillian put Philip back in the chair and he let out a little wail of protest.

"You're okay," Lillian told him encouragingly. "You're fine." Philip rubbed his nose with his fist. Then to Olivia she said, "Now, tell me more about what's wrong with Polly."

Olivia looked up to the ceiling. "She misses her house, and her daddy. She wants to go *home*." Olivia crawled onto the couch and then directly onto Lillian's lap, filling the space the baby had just vacated.

"Oh, honey," said Lillian. She was silent for a moment. She stroked Olivia's hair, the hair that in places was as light and as fine as it had been when Olivia was a baby. She rubbed Olivia's earlobe; this was how, when Olivia was Philip's age, Lillian had gotten her to sleep. She thought briefly of rocking her in the glider in their old house, the tiny house on Front Street with the little square of yard. She took a deep breath. "But we've got some more time to spend here, with Grandma and Grandpa. We're not going home just yet."

Olivia didn't answer.

"We've got lots of fun stuff to do still," said Lillian. We've hardly been swimming at all—"

"I've been swimming," Olivia whispered.

"We haven't been to the aquarium!"

"The kwaryum," Olivia repeated softly.

"There's lots more gardening."

"Yes," said Olivia.

"Don't you want to help Grandpa in the garden?"

"Yes. But." Her face was turned away from Lillian's, but Lillian felt a tear drop from Olivia's eye onto her bare arm.

"But?"

"But Polly is sick. And she misses her daddy. And she wants to go home."

⁂

Rachel, sitting by the lake in her bathing suit, heard her phone ringing from the depths of her bag. That would be Tess. August first had come and gone, and with it Rachel's opportunity to work on casting the independent film, and also with it her previous five years of work for the agency, and her opportunity to make an impact on the casting world. All of that had surely been given over to Stacy by now. Stacy, with her close-set, eager eyes, and the nervous tic that sometimes came upon her when she was particularly stressed or excited, must surely be thanking her lucky stars for Rachel's misfortune.

The little neighborhood beach was deserted despite the beautiful day. People must have struck out for beaches farther away, North Beach, or farther up, to the islands. And just as well: Rachel was happy to be alone. She rose from her towel and walked to the edge of the dock. She could see rocks beneath the surface; she could see small fish darting about; she could see clearly to the bottom of the lake, to the soft sand at the bottom. She sat on the edge of the dock, then lowered herself into the water. She swam once around the cove and when she returned to her towel she felt cleansed and invigorated—born anew.

Her cell phone was still ringing, or ringing again. How odd it was of Tess to call her now, after the deadline had passed. Tess was the type to move on without looking back. She dug in her bag and retrieved the phone. But it wasn't Tess. It was Marcus. She felt a little jolt in her body when she saw his name on the screen, a little tremble of fear or anticipation.

"Hello?" she said uncertainly.

"Rachel! I've been calling you and calling you at work. I must have left you hundreds of voice mails."

"I'm not at work. I'm in Vermont." A young mother arrived pulling two children in a little red wagon. Rachel felt resentment toward them, for disturbing her peace. *Can't you see,* she wanted to say, *that I am busy ruining my life?* "Why are you calling me?" She tried to make her voice sound stern and uncompromising, but in reality it was such a relief to hear his voice that she felt that her legs could no longer support her. She sat.

"Rach, the landlord called me."

"Why did the landlord call you?" Slowly the understanding began to dawn on her. There was another reason August first was important—not just Tess's deadline. Away from the city, swaddled in the family home, fed home-cooked food, idly passing the days, playing Go Fish with Olivia, she had completely forgotten to pay the rent.

"Shit," she said softly. "Shit, shit."

"Is everything okay?"

"No," she said. "No, not okay." *Don't cry,* she said to herself. But she could hear the strangled quality to her voice.

"Rachel?" It was something about the way Marcus said her name, and the question that dangled at the end of it, and the care she felt behind the question, that allowed it all to come out. She told! She told Marcus just as she'd told Lillian; in fact, it was as though that night in the kitchen had been a rehearsal for this, as though here, on the other end of the line, was her real audience.

"Oh, Jesus, Rachel," said Marcus at the end of it. "Why didn't you call me?"

In a small voice she said, "I don't know. There didn't seem to be any point. I just wanted to get away."

"Do you want me to come up there?"

Yes, she thought. She said, "And do what?"

"I don't know. Whatever you want me to do."

Marry me, she thought. Take me away. "No," she said. She thought of the full house, of her bunking situation with Olivia. Adding another person to the mix was hardly feasible. And besides, the worst of it had passed. Physically, she felt normal.

"Are you sure?"

"Sure." She paused. "Unless —"

"Unless what?" he said fervently.

"Unless you want to talk again, about what we talked about before."

"Before?"

"Before you moved out."

Silence. Then, "Oh, come on, Rach, we covered that."

"I know we did," she whispered.

"What? I can hardly hear you."

"I said, I know we did."

"So why are you bringing it up again now?"

"I don't know."

"Rachel —"

"I know," she said. "I *know*. I'm sorry."

"Rachel? Do you want me to come up, though, just to hang out?"

She felt as though time had stopped. She felt as though she had just jumped off the dock and was waiting, suspended, to hit the water. "No," she said, but she knew he wouldn't be able to hear that. She had said it too softly. So she said it louder, more forcefully, in a voice strong enough to carry to the mother with the wagon, to carry over the glittering surface of the lake. "No," she said. "No, Marcus, I'll be fine."

"Well, okay, Rach, but figure out what you can do about the rent. Don't get evicted."

"What do you care?" The words sounded more bitter than she meant them to.

"I care! That's a great apartment. And besides, I care."

"Okay," she said. She closed the phone carefully. The mother unpacked the children and spread out a striped picnic blanket. The children ran down to the water and the mother sat cross-legged on the blanket, watching them. Rachel watched the mother watching the children, and then after a while she lay back on the towel, her face to the sun.

※

Ginny knocked on Jane's door. She had a fresh pitcher of water and a plate with fruit and crackers. She didn't hear an answer so she entered slowly. She thought she would leave the food if Jane were sleeping. But Jane was not sleeping. She was sitting up in the bed, tapping away furiously on her BlackBerry, her concentration so complete that she didn't look up. Ginny put the water and the fruit on the dresser and didn't try to control the sharpness in her voice when she said, "What's all this about?"

Jane looked up. "What? Oh, Ginny!" She saw the fruit and the water. "Thank you. I'm famished." She smiled uncertainly. "What's all what about?"

"The working. I thought you had some time off."

"Oh." Jane looked back down and frowned. "Not really. No such thing. But."

"Jane."

Jane said nothing.

Ginny walked to the window and adjusted the shade. "Jane. Don't *do* this."

"Don't do what?"

Ginny thought that she must know already, that she was making Ginny spell it out for her. "Isn't it time to lay off a little bit? Prepare yourself for what's coming? This is so much more important."

"What are you saying, then?" said Jane with exaggerated politeness.

Ginny felt her heart beat faster. The air in the bedroom seemed to grow thicker and warmer; she thought she might have trouble breathing. *This is it,* she told herself. *It's now or never.* "I'm saying... well, I guess I'm saying that it seems to me that after the baby is born you're going to be putting a lot on Stephen." More quietly she said, "And I don't like it."

So unexpected was what happened next, so out of character, that, thinking about it later, in the quiet of her bedroom, where Ginny retreated after, it seemed as though it might have been a scene from a bad television drama. Because Jane flung the Black-Berry away from her and across the bedroom, where the battery dislodged and lay prone. It seemed to Ginny that Jane might actually spit at her, but she did not.

"If you must know," said Jane. "If you must know, I am on the brink of losing my job." Ginny opened her mouth to say something, but Jane held up her hand, stopping her. "So how does *that* sit with you? How does *that* make you feel about Stephen's future, and the baby's future?"

Ginny breathed in sharply. It seemed as though time had stopped. She said, carefully, "Not really?"

"Really. We all might. A lot us might. They say this isn't the worst of it."

"The worst of what?" Ginny's voice sounded hollow to herself. She stared into the plate of fruit. She felt her breath coming quickly.

Jane pushed her hair back from her face and looked down. "Oh, it's so complicated. It would take me hours to explain it all."

"Try me."

"No," she said shortly. "I won't. But I will say this. I have worked my *whole life* to get where I am. I worked like a dog, all through school, all through college. Business school. All of it. And I'm about to lose it all. And I don't need you or anyone else telling me what I'm doing wrong. For *God's* sake."

Carefully Ginny said, "Does Stephen know?"

Jane looked squarely at her, and shifted in the bed. "Of *course* Stephen knows," she said. "Do you think for a second that I would keep that from him?"

Ginny felt a sting behind her eyelids. It was a feeling she remembered from long, long ago, from childhood, of trying not to cry in front of the class after some humiliation or slight. "No," she said, trying to steady her voice. "No, you wouldn't."

"Exactly," said Jane. "So we are under enough pressure without anyone else adding to it. So thank you for the fruit, and thank you for the crackers, and thank you for the visit, if you can call it that, but I'd like to be alone right now."

※

Jane woke from a fitful nap to find an unfamiliar woman standing in the bedroom. At first she thought she was still dreaming; she mistook the woman, who had a mass of yellowish curls held back from her face with a tortoiseshell comb, for an angel. She thought, briefly, that if she was not dreaming then perhaps she had died. The midmorning sun coming in through the window was casting a golden glow in the room.

Then she saw Stephen standing slightly behind the woman, like a shadow, and she knew she was neither dreaming nor dead.

She rubbed at her eye and reached for her glasses on the bedside table; she had given up on her contact lenses weeks ago.

"Sweetheart?" said Stephen. "This is Jackie. She's a masseuse. She specializes in pregnancy massages." He was beaming—proud, it was clear, of having arranged for this stranger to be here.

"Hello," said Jane slowly. Her throat was dry. Her eyes were dry. Her lips were dry. She squinted up at the woman. She was very tall, and very thin, though thin in the inverted triangular shape of a swimmer or a volleyball player. She looked disconcertingly strong, but there was something gentle about the shape of her face, and about the expression in her wide brown eyes.

"Hello," said Jackie. "Your husband here tells me you've been a bit down."

Jane glanced at Stephen. "Under the circumstances—"

"Of course," said Jackie. "And who wouldn't be?" Her voice was soft and slightly accented, though Jane couldn't place the accent. Somewhere in Eastern Europe, perhaps, but she didn't know how (or if) that would account for all that golden hair.

"So—" said Stephen. "Happy birthday."

"My birthday's in October." Jane pushed herself up on her elbows.

"Happy Wednesday, then. Enjoy." He stepped out from around Jackie to kiss Jane on the forehead, smiled quickly at both of them, and disappeared through the door.

"He's lovely," said Jackie.

"Yes," said Jane reluctantly.

"Really lovely. So sweet!"

"I know," said Jane. She looked steadily at the ceiling.

"So," Jackie said. "Before we get started, let's talk a little bit about what's bothering you the most."

"It's *all* bothering me," said Jane miserably. "The whole thing."

"Of course it's extremely difficult, to be in your position." Jackie looked at Jane expectantly, the way Jane's mother sometimes looked at her if she'd had lots of sessions all in a row and forgot momentarily that Jane was her daughter and not a patient. "But what, specifically? It's so much better for me to know the specifics."

"My hip," said Jane. "This one." She pointed to her left side. "I think I'm getting a bedsore."

"Surely not!" Jackie laughed merrily.

"Like an aging animal. Animals get bedsores, don't they?"

"They do," said Jackie. "Sometimes, I think. But we're not going to let you get one."

"And also, my neck."

"Very common."

"And my back."

"No surprise there."

"Maybe it would be quicker if I told you what *isn't* bothering me?"

"Perhaps," said Jackie. She smiled.

Jane pondered this. Jackie had pulled out a CD from her bag and deposited it, without ceremony, into the CD player on the dresser. It began to play. Classical. Jane was pleasantly surprised; she had expected some sort of nature CD, with frogs and crickets.

"You know what?" said Jane finally. "There's nothing. There's not one single thing that's not bothering me. Bladder, elbows, eyeballs. All of it."

"That sounds terrible," said Jackie, nodding. "All alone, in this little room—"

"I know," said Jane. "I mean, they visit me, but it's more like... charity visits, you know? Or worse."

Jackie had her head down and was rummaging in an enormous

black shoulder bag for something, which turned out to be a bottle of pinkish oil.

"I sort of hate everyone right now. I feel *extremely* hateful. Can you fix that?"

"Not specifically," said Jackie. "But you know what masseuses say?"

"What?"

"Fix the body, and you've fixed the mind." She rubbed the oil on her hands and Jane wondered, briefly, if the oil would stain the sheets and if that would upset Ginny. It seemed like the sort of thing that might upset Ginny.

"Oh," said Jane. "Well, I hope that's true in my case. I feel like I'm feeding the baby negative thoughts through the umbilical cord."

"No," said Jackie. "I'm sure you're not. They're alarmingly resistant creatures, fetuses."

"I guess."

"Well," said Jackie briskly, losing the smile and allowing her features to drop into an expression of professionalism and concentration. "Let's get down to business. Why don't you roll over on one side. I'll start with your back."

"I've never had a massage before," Jane confessed, still looking at the ceiling.

"Never?"

"Never."

"Oh, massage is *wonderful*," said Jackie. "One of the few pure pleasures there is. Absolutely undiluted."

"I'm all yours, then," said Jane.

As gracefully as she could manage, she rolled onto her right side and Jackie stepped around the bed to stand behind her.

When Jane felt the pressure in her back, at first she thought Jackie had brought along some sort of instrument in the big black bag—a rolling pin was the first thing she thought of—but then she realized it was Jackie's elbow she felt, and then the flat palm of her hand. She realized too that Jackie had located *exactly* the trouble spot on Jane's back, as surely as if she had been given a map, and that as Jackie kneaded it and kneaded it the pain began to unknot slowly, to grow thinner and thinner, and then to disappear altogether.

"Just relax into it," said Jackie, and her voice sounded far away and softly muffled, as though it were coming from the ceiling or the closet. "Breathe right through."

So Jane breathed. She listened to the classical music, and she tried to pick out each particular instrument: the violins, the flute and the oboe, the tuba.

She imagined the baby, floating in the amniotic fluid, little fists raised to little ears.

She felt, for the first time in weeks—as she dropped off to sleep, she thought it was actually possible that it was the first time in her entire *life*—that she was in good hands.

�❈

Lillian met Heather at a nearly empty bar downtown. It was a Monday night. At the far end of the bar a couple of college girls were drinking something pink out of martini glasses. The bartender was studiously wiping down the bar with a white cloth. Heather had ordered a beer and was examining her cell phone, pressing buttons.

"An emergency already?" asked Lillian, sitting down.

"Oh. No," said Heather, looking up, smiling. "Just clearing off some old messages. It sounds silly, but I never get a chance to do that—"

"I know," said Lillian. "Kids down?"

"Yes. Yours?"

"Yes. I didn't dare leave when they weren't." Lillian picked up the drinks menu and studied it. "An espresso martini," she said. "I wonder which part of that would be more disastrous? The vodka or the espresso?"

"Both," said Heather. "And why didn't you dare?"

To the bartender Lillian said, "Beer. Same as she's having."

"Not the espresso martini?" asked the bartender. When she first entered the bar Lillian would have said he was rather plain, but she saw when he smiled that he had nice teeth, very white and straight.

"God, no. Too old for that."

"Oh, I don't think so." The bartender kept smiling, and continued to smile after he slid Lillian's beer over to her and went to check on the college girls.

Lillian said, "I didn't dare because they seemed irritated with me. Everybody seems irritated with me! Maybe I take up too much space, maybe that's the problem. Do you think we'll feel irritated when *we're* grandparents?"

"I expect so," said Heather. "I expect it's universal. Wanting your children to grow up and leave you alone, and then, once they have, wanting them around you."

"And then when they are around you—"

"Wanting them to go away again!"

They were silent.

"So," said Heather. "Total change of subject. But it's on my mind. I applied for a part-time job, at a law firm."

"You did! Good for you."

"No," said Heather. "I didn't get it. I think I blew the interview."

"Oh, Heather. I'm sorry. Were you really disappointed?"

"That's the thing," said Heather. "I wasn't, not really. I mean, I felt like an idiot. But I was relieved."

"Yeah?"

"Yeah. I was sort of... scared to join the real world."

"I could see that," said Lillian. "Liking the idea more than the actual. You know, having someplace to go every day. Wearing real clothes. *Accomplishing* something."

"Yeah," said Heather. "That was all appealing, for sure. But sometimes—" She folded her cocktail napkin into tiny squares, then unfolded it again.

"Sometimes what?"

"Sometimes I feel like I'm hiding from the world," she said slowly. "And I worry that when it's time to stop hiding I won't know how to be a real person anymore." She squinted at Lillian. "Do you know what I mean?"

Lillian nodded. "I do. But there's your mistake. You *can't* think about the big picture. The big picture is very, very dangerous."

"But... shouldn't we? Aren't the kids going to be grown up sometime? And then what?"

"Yeah," said Lillian. "I don't know. But I, for one, shouldn't think about the big picture. I can't. I'll go mental. I can't handle the big picture. I have to keep my picture very, very small."

"Because of Tom," said Heather.

"Of *course* because of Tom."

One of the college girls' cell phones rang. "Hello?" she said, mouthing something at her friend and pointing at the phone. "Oh my God, it's too funny that you called. What? I'm with Jess. It's so funny because her cell phone rang, and it was you, and then you called me—" She paused, nodding vigorously. "And we thought you were, like, driving by and you saw us."

"Oh my God. Are you serious?" The blond girl tipped the phone away from her mouth to talk to her friend. "She crashed into somebody's BMW convertible when she was eating her ice cream." They collapsed into giggles, leaning across the checkerboard table. "You're too funny," the girl said. "Like, what did you do next? Did you run?"

"What do you think you'll do?" asked Heather. "Will you forgive him, maybe?"

Lillian sighed. "I don't know. I don't want to forgive him. But I don't want to destroy my own life just to make a point either. I don't want Olivia to keep asking every day where her father is, and I don't ever want to have to tell her he's not coming."

Heather leaned forward over the bar. "It's just sex, you know. It was just once. Just bodies bumping together."

"Gross," said Lillian. "What a way to put it."

"But it's true."

"Is that what you would say if it were Geoffrey?"

"Oh, *Geoffrey*," Heather said. "I can't imagine that."

"But if it were?"

"Honestly?" said Heather. "Honestly, I don't know what I would do."

"Sometimes," said Lillian. "Sometimes I'm so angry with him that I can't even see straight. And then other times I feel like you do: it's just sex. But then I get mad all over again."

"Because on the other hand," said Heather. "It's *sex*."

"Exactly," said Lillian. "It's sex. It's *us*. You know?"

"I know," said Heather.

Lillian thought about Father Colin in the bookstore talking about forgiveness, talking about the feeling of warmth that had flooded through him after the boy beat him up. "Because maybe what he did with that horrible little slutty assistant only lasted a few minutes, and maybe he was drunk, and maybe he's sorry about it and wishes he never did it, but he still *did* it. He still was able, for a few minutes or an hour or two hours or whatever it was, to imagine life without me."

"I know," said Heather again, softly.

"Can you imagine what that feels like? He's the love of my life, the only one I ever wanted to be with. My knight! And he was able to imagine life without me. He was actually able to pretend I didn't exist. I never would have done that to him." Her voice cracked at the end of the sentence. She thought about Father Colin and his secret. He said he'd had to forgive someone as an adult. But he hadn't said whether he had done it or not. What if he hadn't? If Father Colin couldn't forgive everyone, how was Lillian supposed to?

"And that's why you're still here," said Heather. "I get that."

"That's why I'm still here." She thought of her parents' over-stuffed house, of the growing laundry monster in the corner of the den, of Olivia nursing her doll through a bout of homesickness. She thought of Jane up in Lillian's old bedroom: Jane, who would give anything to get out of there. And here was Lillian, able to leave anytime she wanted to, and refusing to do it.

Lillian sighed and circled her coaster in the wet spot the bottle had left on the bar. "Maybe I need revenge. Do you think I need revenge?"

"No," said Heather. They both looked at the bartender, who was sliding wineglasses upside down into the racks above his head. "No, you don't need revenge. That will just make everything worse. It's a myth that revenge makes you feel better. Don't do it."

"Oh, I don't know," said Lillian. "I don't want to talk about it. I want to talk about anything else."

"Such as?" said Heather.

"Let's see," said Lillian. "Oh! I know. Stephen's going to be a stay-at-home dad."

"He isn't!"

"He is, swear to God. Jane told me so."

"Now, *that's* interesting," said Heather. "He'll hate it."

"I don't think he will." Lillian emptied her beer and signaled to the bartender to bring two more.

"Don't you?"

"I don't."

"But it's so lonely! Right at first, with a baby. That's hard for a *mother,* never mind for a not-mother."

"Jane's worried that people will judge her," said Lillian.

"They will."

"Heather!"

"I'm not saying they should. But they will."

"But why?"

"They just will. They'll wonder why she didn't take a longer maternity leave. They'll wonder why she bothered to have a baby at all if she wasn't going to have a hand in raising it. They'll wonder all sorts of inappropriate things."

"Yeah," said Lillian. "I guess you're right. They won't *say* those things, though."

"No, but they'll wonder. And she'll sense them wondering. And then Stephen will get all sorts of credit for what he's doing, as though it involves some sort of heroism—"

"Right," said Lillian. "People will come up to him at the playground and say things like, 'How do you like being a full-time father?'" Here she talked in a fake voice, sounding rather like a Muppet. "But nobody ever asks *us* how we like being mothers."

"And," said Heather, "when the baby is really small, and he's carrying it around in a sling or something, and he goes for a cup of coffee, *everyone* in the coffee shop is going to go nuts over him. 'Oh, look at that dad with the baby.' Like it's really special. 'He must have taken the day off to be with the baby,' or some crap like that."

"Yeah," said Lillian. "You're right."

"It's annoying."

"It *is* annoying."

"But it's life."

"It's life." Lillian went on, "I was talking to her the other day, and it was strange. She seemed so . . . I don't know. Vulnerable. And frightened. I usually think of her as this powerhouse. Business woman, MBA, all those things I am not. But when I saw her in that little bed, *my* little bed, in her shorts and her big T-shirt, she just seemed regular. And scared."

"She should be scared," said Heather. "It's the scariest thing in the world."

"Yeah. I know. But maybe they've got it all worked out."

"I doubt it," said Heather. "Nobody does, not really, not until they've been doing it for a while."

"And even then—"

"And even then." Heather balled up her napkin and rolled it along the edge of the bar.

"But maybe what they *think* they have worked out will actually work out." Lillian looked briefly up to the ceiling. When she looked back down, she saw that the bartender was looking at them. She gave him a tiny smile and looked quickly away.

"Maybe it will. Stephen's a doll. If anyone can do it, he can."

"That's right!" said Lillian. "I'd forgotten. You and Stephen."

"Me and Stephen," said Heather. "Very funny." She rolled her eyes and grimaced.

"You know you had a thing for him."

"Did not! There never was a 'me and Stephen.'"

"Not officially," agreed Lillian. "But if he'd been a couple of years older—"

"Oh, stop it."

"Or not my brother."

"*Stop* it." Heather was smiling. She checked her cell phone for the time. "Shit. I've got to go."

"Curfew?" said Lillian.

"Something like that."

"Really, a curfew?"

"Of course not. I said I'd be back, that's all. So I plan to be back."

"And if you don't, you'll turn into a pumpkin?"

"Oh, shut up," said Heather fondly. "*You*, of all people."

"Right?" said Lillian. "I know. I've got no rights for criticizing other people's marriages—"

"That's not what I meant."

"Sure it is," said Lillian cheerfully. "But it's okay."

Heather hugged Lillian. "Call Tom," she said. "It's what you really want to do."

"I don't know," said Lillian to Heather's shoulder. "I don't know if I can."

"You do know," said Heather. "You can. Call him." She picked up Lillian's phone and scrolled through the numbers. "See?" she said. "It's right here. Home." Then she paused, looking. "Lilly!" she said. "What's this?"

"What?"

"This, under the *C*s. Colin. You have Father Colin in your *cell phone?*"

"Maybe." Lillian took the phone back and dropped it into her purse. "He gave me his number, just in case."

"In case of what? A religious emergency?"

"I don't know," said Lillian. "Just in case."

"Oh, sweetie," said Heather, and she hugged Lillian again. "This is not your summer, is it?"

"I know," whispered Lillian. "I know that."

After Heather had gone Lillian remained at the bar. She hadn't noticed the college girls go, but suddenly the bar was empty.

"Another?" said the bartender, coming over, white cloth now tucked into his belt.

"Sure," she said. "Keep 'em coming."

"Really?"

"No. But I've always wanted to say that. Just keep *one* coming." She studied her reflection in the mirror behind the vodka bottles. In this light, from this distance, she didn't look terrible.

"It can't be that bad," the bartender said genially. He had a dark, slender face; his hair was cut in a way that she was sure was meant to disguise the fact that it was thinning; his hands were small and almost feminine. And yet he had those perfect teeth, and when he smiled at her Lillian felt her cheeks warm and was thankful for the dim light inside the bar. He slid the beer toward her and took her empty glass.

"It is." Lillian was looking out the window, where she could still see Heather's figure retreating down the street. She watched her until she turned a corner and was swallowed up by the darkness. It was funny, wasn't it, that you could know someone so well for so many years of your life, and then you could live apart from them for so many more years, and when you saw them after a long absence you found that all along the two of you had been moving along on parallel paths and had arrived at the same point.

She turned back to the bartender, who was looking at her intently. "I'm here, right? I'm drinking alone. On a Monday night. I'm far from home. I'm living with my parents. On a foldout couch. It is that bad. It's worse than that bad."

She thought about Father Colin, about how the day in the bookstore when she'd opened up to him, and he to her, and how quickly he'd shut down. It was strange, the similarities between a priest and a bartender. Untouchable, somehow, both of them, and therefore safe.

That day in the bookstore she'd been worried that Father Colin was going to spout a Bible quote about forgiveness, or that he'd chastise her for her circumstances or for her feelings about those circumstances. But he hadn't: he'd just listened. He was a good listener. She thought that's what she needed now more than anything. Not someone to prod or solve or apologize or pontificate, but just someone to listen.

The bartender squatted to unload glasses from the dishwasher. She could see the top of his head, the way the hair on his crown grew in whirls, like eddies. It seemed too intimate a view of someone she didn't know and so she looked away, and as she put her hand just under her collarbone she thought she could feel a clot of rage and shame. What a relief it would be, wouldn't it, to have it gone.

She retrieved her phone from her bag and scrolled once again through the numbers. What would Tom be doing at that moment? Sleeping, probably. Or out! Maybe he went out every night, cajoling a neighbor or a friend to join him for a drink. Yes, probably he was out.

And Father Colin? *I'm a terrible sleeper,* he'd said. *A complete insomniac.*

She dialed.

※

When she pulled into the parking lot he was standing outside, fully dressed, hands in his pockets, backlit by the unsettlingly bright light on the rectory's porch. He could have been a suburban father watching a baseball game the way he stood there, with a casual and proprietary air. She took her time getting out of the car, locking it carefully behind her in what she recognized later, thinking back on the night, was probably an unnecessary action, and which probably helped reveal the fact that she did not have all of her faculties at her disposal. She walked unsteadily toward him and he tipped his head in her direction. "Lillian?" he said. "Have you been drinking?"

She made a small gesture with her thumb and index finger to indicate: a little. She motioned toward his clothes. "It's after midnight," she said. "Why are you up and dressed?"

"Come in," he said. "I'll make you coffee."

He led her into the kitchen she had passed the day she brought the paper for the bake sale. Same green Formica countertops, same aging appliances. She sat at the table, which was some sort of old wood, pocked and well worn. The kitchen chairs had those thin round cushions tied to the legs with fraying red threads. Grandmotherly, she thought, the way they slid around on you when you sat down.

Father Colin began fiddling with a coffeemaker on the counter. He looked at her severely as he filled the pot with water from the tap and said, "You shouldn't have been driving."

She bristled at that but she said, "I know." Under the bright lights of the kitchen, away from the bar, the bravado she had felt an hour before was beginning to disappear. She tapped her fingers on the table and said, "Do you drink?"

The coffeemaker spit and hissed. It too was old. "Not much," said Father Colin. "There's a tendency in my family for that to go badly."

"Oh?" she said. "Your father?"

"When he was alive. And my brother, when he's not careful, which is most of the time." He poured the coffee, then carried a mug to her. He poured himself a smaller amount. First the alcohol, and now the caffeine. She would have to pump and discard gallons of milk. Still, she felt the coffee begin to shore her up. "I'm sorry," she said. "I don't drink much anymore, since the babies. I don't think I can handle it."

He smiled, losing the stern look he had worn since she pulled up. "It's not a problem. I'm glad for the company. I haven't had many postmidnight visitors here."

"Did you in Boston?"

He shrugged.

"What were you doing? When I called?"

"Writing. A sermon."

"Oh." She rubbed her hands over the grooves in the table. She could never have imagined, back when she was studying for her confirmation with Father Michael, that so many years later she would be sitting in the rectory kitchen, slightly woozy, talking to a priest. She took another gulp of coffee. "How does that work? Do you just sit there and wait... for God to talk to you, or something? Tell you what to say?"

He laughed. "No. I wish it was like that."

It actually was terrible coffee, when you got right down to it, but she reminded herself, as her mother used to remind them when they were children, beggars and choosers, beggars and choosers. "What's it like, then?"

"Like any kind of writing. Like any kind of work, really. Hard. Torture, sometimes."

"What's this one about?"

"I'm still working that out."

She thought back to their conversation in the bookstore. "What about forgiveness?"

He looked searchingly at her. "They're all about forgiveness, in a way."

"That reminds me," she said, as though the thought had just come upon her. "You never told me. Who you needed to forgive."

"Ah." Father Colin rose from the table and brought his mug to the sink. He leaned over the sink, looking out the window into the darkness. He kept his gaze in that direction as he said, "The woman I told you about? Elizabeth?"

"Yes."

"Her husband."

She felt a shiver. She pulled at a hangnail. She said, very carefully, "What did he do? That required forgiveness?"

Father Colin returned to the table and faced Lillian. "He had a lot of anger. You could see the pain inside him, it practically pulsed. And who could blame him."

"Of course," said Lillian.

"But the anger was misplaced. He turned it on me."

"On you?" said Lillian, beginning to understand. "Because of the wife—"

"Right," said Father Colin. "Because I counseled her. He thought... he thought our relationship was inappropriate. He confronted me. Physically."

"He *hit* you?"

Father Colin smiled ruefully. "It was more like a punch. It knocked me over. He's a big man, very strong."

"So that's what you had to forgive?" Lillian was wide awake now.

"That, and then the fact that he brought his complaints high up the food chain. In effect, he's the reason I'm here."

"They sent you *away?*"

"Not forever, I hope. But to appease him, and because Father Michael got ill and they needed a pastor here."

"But did you?"

"Did I what?"

"Did you do what he accused you of?"

"Of course not."

She wished the lights weren't on. She thought it would have

been easier, in the dark, to ask her next question. She said, "But did you love her? Did you fall in love with her?"

He waited a long time before he answered, so long, in fact, that she thought that he might have forgotten her presence. Finally he said, "I don't know. I cared about her, for certain. And something about her grief, and my desire to help her, made me imagine that I had a power I didn't have, the power to make her anguish go away. But love her?"

"You did," she said softly. "You loved her."

There was a vulnerable bent to his shoulders then. He made her think of a little boy, waiting for praise or punishment. He didn't answer, but he rose when she rose, and she wasn't sure if he leaned toward her first or if she leaned toward him, and where the kiss started, but she knew where it ended, because he pulled away before she did.

"Lillian," he said.

Looking down, she said, "What?"

"You've been drinking. You're upset. You're confused."

"*You're* confused," she spat back. She knew that was cruel, but she was humiliated. "You're more confused than I am." Even though it was spiteful, and even though she said it to hurt him, she knew that it was also true, because thinking about it later, as of course she did, for the rest of the summer and even, sometimes, after that, she knew beyond a shadow of a doubt that he had kissed her back.

"Don't go yet," he said. "Lillian? Don't go. Stay here until you're ready to drive."

She stood as straight as she could and didn't meet his eyes when she answered. "I'm ready to drive now," she said.

"No," he said. "You need—"

She cut him off. "I don't need anything. From you, I don't need anything."

"Lillian, I care about you. But I am trying to do the right thing, whatever that is."

"Whatever that is? I thought you had all the answers." She could feel that her lips were pulled over her teeth in a mean and ugly way.

"I don't." He lifted his hands helplessly.

"So you're...pretending?"

He was silent.

"What would they say about that, your *flock?* Your woman in Boston, what would she say about that?"

He flinched at that. "Not pretending. Believing."

"But how do you know what you believe? How do you know there's anything to believe in? You don't even know when it's okay to love someone and when it isn't!" She knew her voice sounded bitter, but she was reeling.

He lifted his raised palm to the ceiling. "I just know. That's what belief is. You know I am here to serve the many, not the one."

"I know," she said. "Nobody's asking you to do anything else." She could still feel his lips on hers.

He ignored that. "But I'll pray for you and your family."

"Don't bother," she said. It was the worst thing she could think of to say, the most hurtful. "Don't do me any favors."

She forced herself to drive slowly, because her hands were shaking and, really, something in her very core was shaking. But she had to steady herself after she got out of the car at home because she could hear Philip crying as she walked rapidly up the front walk and she thought at first that he was alone in his Pack 'n Play, and hungry and frightened.

But of course he wasn't alone. Ginny was walking back and forth in the den with him. The windows were opened, which explained why Lillian could hear him from outside. Ginny didn't ask where Lillian had been, or why she was back so late, and though Lillian knew all that would come later she was grateful for it. Ginny said only this: "I can't get him to stop. I found some milk in the fridge, and I warmed up a bottle and he drank it down. But I think he needs you."

She passed Philip to Lillian and he settled almost immediately against her shoulder, breathing raggedly, then stuffing his fist into his mouth, and finally, while Ginny looked on, quieting.

*

Then the placenta moved.

William was loading a bag of grass clippings into the pickup to bring them to the compost facility when Stephen and Jane pulled up in Ginny's car. Stephen jogged around to Jane's side and opened her door. He grasped her elbow to guide her out of the car.

"Dad!" he said. He looked more upbeat than he'd looked in weeks. "Big news. We just came from an ultrasound. The placenta moved."

Jane stood next to him, smiling. Smiling! They were both smiling, grinning madly, even.

"Well, that's wonderful news," said William. He pulled off his work gloves and squinted at them. It was a hot, bright day, and the sun was directly behind Stephen and Jane, so their outlines were faintly smudged. They moved closer to William, and he saw the way that Stephen didn't let go of Jane. He always had his hand protectively on part of her body: her hand, her arm, her lower back.

"But. It's still low-lying," said Stephen. "We're not totally out of the woods."

"What's all the commotion?" Rachel, holding her book, wearing her sunglasses, walked around from the backyard.

"The placenta moved! And the baby is growing," said Jane. "I might be able to have a normal delivery."

"Now hold on," said Stephen. "Not so fast." He looked at his father and his sister and cleared his throat. "There's still a good chance of a C-section. The concern with a vaginal delivery is that the placenta can tear off the lower uterine segment."

"My brother, the obstetrician," said Rachel.

"That won't happen," said Jane. "It's going to be fine. It's going to be fine!" She smiled eagerly at William and Rachel. There was a new fresh look to her. It could have been the makeup she had put on for the appointment, or the clean pants and shirt she was wearing, or just the fact that she was standing outside in the sunlight, but to William she looked suddenly animated and vibrant. Reborn.

She turned to Stephen. "Can we go back to New York? I want to deliver at my own hospital."

"Absolutely *not*," said Stephen. "Not even an option."

"Let's talk about it," said Jane. "Let's just talk."

"You are going to sit down and rest," said Stephen. "And we're not going to talk about New York until we have that baby safely out of you."

"Says you," said Jane. But there was a new firmness and resolution to Stephen, William could see that. Stephen led Jane toward the front door, still guiding her by the elbow. Did William see her twitch her arm just out of his reach before he caught it again? Perhaps. Perhaps he did.

※

"Tom? It's Rachel."

Tom hadn't recognized the number on the caller ID, but the Manhattan area code was familiar, and because he had a few friends from college who lived in New York he thought it was one of them calling. It was eight forty-seven on a Thursday night. He was sitting on the sofa in the living room, the sofa that he and Lillian had chosen together soon after Olivia's birth, the sofa on which they'd sat together night after night until he had decided to dismantle their lives, their very happiness, with his carelessness and stupidity.

And drunkenness, he thought. Let us not forget drunkenness.

In front of him was a pizza box with a half-consumed pizza. It was yesterday's pizza, in fact, not a fresh one, and the previous night he had merely shoved the whole box into the refrigerator. Removing the box this evening, from its slanted, ill-fitting berth on top of a plastic grocery store bag of softening apples, he had felt a grim despair; when the refrigerator hadn't closed properly because part of the apple bag had slipped down and got itself stuck in the door, he had nearly left it there. There was no one, after all, who would be expecting fresh milk in the morning.

"Oh!" he said. "Rachel. I wasn't expecting you—"

"Were you expecting someone else?"

"No! No, of course not."

"Oh, you sounded strange, that's all. Like I took you by surprise."

"Nope! No surprise."

"I'm calling on behalf of Lillian."

He felt something lift in his stomach. "Why? Did she ask you to call?" Tom peeled a congealed layer of cheese off one of the slices, put an aging and withering olive into the center of it, and made it into a tiny wrap.

"Well. Not exactly."

Whatever had lifted now plummeted. "Oh."

"But I think she wants you to come up here." Tom took the dehydrated sponge from the sink, where it had lain for three days, and, without wetting it, worked at a spot of tomato sauce that had dried onto the counter.

"She does? She told me that she doesn't. She told me that she doesn't want to see me again, ever. She told me, specifically, *not* to come up." His throat clotted when he heard himself say that out loud. He thought of the way Lillian looked just out of the shower, eyes bright against the pale of her skin and her flaming hair. So many colors! How could there be so many colors in just one person?

"She's confused, of course," said Rachel. "And angry."

"She told you?"

"She told me. I had to wheedle it out of her, but she told me. And you were a total dick. Pardon my language, but you know that's the truth."

"I know that," he said morosely. "Believe me, I know that."

"A total schmuck."

"Rachel," he said. "I *know* that."

"So I don't think she wants to *tell* you that she wants you here, but I'm pretty sure that's what she wants."

"How do you know, though, Rachel? How do you know for sure?"

"Trust me," she said. "I know."

After Tom hung up the phone, he walked out the back door and onto the deck. The dog, taking his exit as an invitation to play, followed, ears lifted hopefully.

The previous summer he had sanded and stained that deck. Lillian, in the beginning stages of pregnancy, had been too exhausted to help, but he had given Olivia a massive sheet of white paper and a container of finger paints and allowed her to work near him, in the grass. It had taken the whole of Labor Day weekend, and he'd felt then a camaraderie and connection with Olivia that he had never experienced before or since.

It was eerily quiet on the deck now, and mostly dark. There were just a few threads of daylight remaining in the sky. From a house on another street he could hear the sounds of children yelling and somewhere, closer by, the sound of a baby crying. He thought of Philip, and the shock of hair in the very center of his head.

His neighbors, Mary and Parker, a middle-aged couple with grown children and a grandson on the way, were sitting on their deck with a bottle of wine.

"Bachelor for a while, are you?" called Mary. "I haven't seen your little angels around."

"Something like that," called Tom. "Visiting their grand-parents." He went back inside before they could ask him any more, and the dog followed, the tags on her collar hitting against each other. She settled herself in the corner of the kitchen with a sigh, regarding Tom as he moved around the kitchen.

He checked the phone for messages. He hadn't heard it ring, but it was just possible that if it had rung when he was outside he would have missed it. Unlikely, to be sure, but possible. Maybe Rachel was right. Maybe Lillian did want him back.

Nothing.

Then he checked the computer for e-mails. There was nothing there either, not even a stray work communication, not even a meeting announcement for the following day, or a piece of junk mail. Just: nothing.

He wandered through the rooms of the house, into Olivia's room, where the bed was made neatly and the animals that hadn't gone to Vermont were sitting sentry on the white shelf he had nailed into the wall shortly after they'd moved in.

Then into Philip's room, where the zoo mobile—the fuzzy animals with their odd, quizzical expressions—was silent. Although there was no reason to do anything, he drew the blinds, turned on the night-light on the dresser. A dried-out wipe was crumpled in the mouth of the diaper pail; he turned the blue handle, sending the errant wipe into the garbage bag that sat inside the pail. The sound of the diaper pail turning was startlingly loud in the silent room.

In the kids' bathroom, which he hadn't been into since Lillian had left, a middle-aged washcloth was balanced on the side of the tub; he picked it up and put it in the hamper in Philip's room.

The silence!

There were times after Olivia had become such a precocious talker, after Philip was born, that he had longed for just this type of silence. When he had invented an errand to get out of the house at certain chaotic times of the evening to achieve it. Times when he felt as if he and Lillian were jockeying for the silence so intensely that even talking to each other had destroyed it.

And now that he had it, now that he was surrounded by nothing but silence, and now that he faced *only* silence until he arrived at work the next morning, he didn't know quite what to do with it.

In the hallway he stood for a moment in front of a picture from his and Lillian's wedding; it was a black-and-white photo, but even so he could nearly see the red of Lillian's hair, which she had worn long and curling down her back, with a tiny jeweled tiara on top. She looked like a princess, as beautiful as any of the princesses Olivia now coveted and collected and talked about as though they were flesh and blood and living in the house next door.

He felt a *thump* in his stomach like the sensation one got traveling very fast downhill in a car. When Lillian had pulled out of the driveway, and told him not to call her, what was it that made him do as she wished? Part of it was honoring her, of course, because he had done wrong. But part of it was punishing himself by taking away what was most important to him: a form of self-flagellation.

᛭

"You might," said Ginny, as gently as she could manage, "pick up the den a little bit later."

They had driven with Olivia and Philip to the Laundromat. The washing machine, they had been told, was going to take two weeks to repair. A special part, whose purpose and exoticness Ginny didn't particularly comprehend, was on order. After the Laundromat they were going to take Olivia for a grilled cheese at the bakery on Pine Street and then, if Philip stayed in reasonably good spirits, to the playground at the elementary school for a bit of fresh air.

Olivia found a ball of dryer lint on the floor and was rolling it tighter and tighter, then tossing it in the air to catch it. The owner of the Laundromat, a stout, grumpy woman with orange lipstick three shades off from what would have been appropriate for her skin tone, watched her, frowning. She opened her mouth and then closed it again. The only other customer was an old woman, bent over like the letter *f*, who was sitting on a bench in the corner reading a newspaper.

"The den?" said Lillian. "Why?" She was sorting clothes into two giant carriages. In a basket from the house she had Philip's clothes, which she washed with the special baby detergent. She frowned at the label on the baby detergent. "I can't decide if I actually need this stuff still," she said. "Or do you think it's just a marketing ploy?"

Ginny ignored the second question. To the first she said, "Because the den is a pigsty."

"What's a pigsty?" said Olivia.

"A house for a pig," Lillian told her.

"Oh."

"It's not a *pigsty,*" said Lillian. She was wearing Philip in the BabyBjörn, having finally figured out how to adjust the straps so they didn't hurt her back. It annoyed Ginny suddenly, perhaps unreasonably, that Lillian had only *now* chosen to use the Björn, when it made little sense to have a baby strapped to her. Every time she bent forward to reach into the laundry basket Philip's head flopped awkwardly.

Olivia was looking back and forth between them. "Do pigs live in *houses?*" she asked breathlessly.

"Not exactly," said Lillian. "But sort of. It's more like a cage, a very messy cage."

Olivia was quiet, absorbing this.

Ginny was sorting through an enormous jar of change she had taken from her closet shelf. Looking up at Lillian, she said, "You might make the bed every now and then."

"Really?" said Lillian. "You mean turn it back from a bed to a sofa *every single morning?*"

"It would make the room feel more like a *room,* during the day, and less like a seedy motel."

Lillian rolled one of the carts over to a washing machine and began stuffing clothes inside. Ginny stopped herself from telling her she was overfilling it, though it was clear that she was.

"Your father is…unhappy with this arrangement." Ginny sighed. "And I'm afraid that when he's unhappy, it makes me unhappy too."

"I see. Isn't that just…old-*fashioned.*" She said it as though it were a curse word.

"Lillian!"

"I'm sorry!" said Lillian unapologetically. "But it is. And it's just like a man, after all. To criticize, but not to help."

Lillian sat down in one of the orange plastic chairs next to Ginny. Olivia had found, in the opposite corner, a bucket of old plastic toys. Ginny thought about telling Lillian not to let her play with them — really, they were very grimy, and who could say what germs might be lurking on their grubby plastic surfaces — but she could tell, even without looking, that Lillian was pouting.

She gathered every ounce of patience she could muster and said, in what she hoped was a gentle and conciliatory tone, "It's just that there are a lot of people in the house right now —"

Lillian had her wallet open and was pulling out dollar bills for the change machine. She spread them neatly beside her on the chair. Philip had caught his fist in her long hair and was twisting, twisting.

"This one's missing a piece," announced Olivia. She was holding a wooden farm puzzle. "The goat is missing," she said. "Where is it?"

"I don't know, sweetheart," said Ginny. "Why don't you go look in the box again." Olivia went back to the box and squatted on the floor in front of it. She poked through listlessly, but it was clear that her heart wasn't in it.

"Mom, what do you want me to do? Do you want me to leave?" Lillian untangled her hair from Philip's wrist and looked up at Ginny. Her eyes were suddenly, startlingly, wet. "I mean, I don't know what you expect from me."

Something cracked then in Ginny. Perhaps it was the way Lillian was looking at her, with an expression that reminded Ginny of every argument they'd had when Lillian was a teenager; it reminded her of every pout, every whine, every angry set of Lillian's shoulders as she crouched on the basement stairs, whispering into the phone.

It occurred to her that William was right, had been right to get angry the other day. It occurred to her that she did not welcome the intrusions and chaos in this stage of her life. She had not asked for them, and she did not particularly want to deal with them. She had, after all, already raised her children once. She did not want to do it again. Ginny rose, and stood over Lillian, who sat back in the chair and looked up at Ginny. The position intensified the feeling that Ginny had of talking to a child. She glanced quickly at Olivia, who was paying them no mind. She straightened her spine and said, "I expect you to act like the adult and the mother that you are, Lillian."

"*What?*"

Ginny thought of all the times over the past few weeks when Lillian had left either Philip or Olivia—and often, both—in Ginny's care. She thought of the diapers she had changed and disposed of, and the nights of sleep that had been interrupted by one or the other of them. She loved her grandchildren, of course she did, she loved them absolutely to pieces and there was no way she was going to pretend that she didn't, but enough was enough.

She said evenly, "I expect you to take care of *your own* children and stop expecting me to do it for you."

The color rose on Lillian's cheeks; this was the curse of the redhead, and had been a thorn in Lillian's side since she was very young. Her skin, beautiful but transparent, showed her emotions all too easily. "I'm not—" said Lillian.

"No. You listen to me. I'm not finished yet."

The lady with the orange lipstick had stopped cleaning lint out of a row of dryers to listen. Olivia, too, had stopped rooting in the toy box and was watching her mother and her grandmother. The old woman on the bench, undeterred, continued to read her paper.

"I expect—" began Ginny.

"What?" spat Lillian.

"I expect you to be grateful for the hospitality we've shown you over the past several weeks, and for the food that we've bought and prepared for you, and for the home that we've provided for you and your family—"

Lillian looked incredulous. "Is this about the *money,* then? I can't believe you." Her wallet was still open beside her on the chair. Quickly, she rifled through it. She grabbed a few bills and tossed them toward Ginny. "Here, take it. Is that enough? Take more." She reached for more. "Take my credit card. Take a *deposit.*"

"You're not hearing me!" Ginny heard her voice rise shrilly. "It's not about money."

"What's it about, then?"

"It's about *understanding.* Appreciation. Maturity."

"Well," said Lillian. "I'm sorry if I'm not acting perfectly mature right now, but—" She broke off, and looked down, then back up again. "But Dad isn't the only one who's unhappy."

Ginny turned toward Lillian. "What do you mean?" she said sharply. "Who else is unhappy?"

"*I* am," said Lillian softly, and she had her head down, her lips resting on Philip's head. When she at last met Ginny's gaze Ginny saw that she was crying, quietly, in earnest. Then she was crying loudly, great big gulping sobs. She cast an anguished glance toward Olivia, who had given up on the toys and was wandering among the washing machines, and said, more quietly, "I'm sorry. For making a scene. But I think my marriage is over."

"Oh, Lillian." Ginny sat beside her on the bench. Her heart lurched; she felt suddenly short of breath. "What do you mean?"

Lillian didn't answer at first. She leaned over and, as best as she could manage with the baby reclining on her chest, rested her head on her mother's shoulder and let the story come out, piece by piece. Finally Ginny said, "Well, I can't say I'm surprised."

Lillian lifted her head. "You're not?"

"Of course not," said Ginny. "I'm not an idiot. I knew something was going on. I've just been waiting for you to tell me in your own time." After a beat, she said, "Have you thought about your plans?"

"Plans?"

"What to do. About your situation."

Lillian shook her head, then looked steadily at the bulletin board to the left of the washing machines. LOST DOG, said one sign. PRENATAL YOGA, said another. "I thought," she began quietly, "that I might stay here for a while."

"Oh, *Lillian.*"

"What?"

"I mean, of course you're welcome to stay, as long as you want to."

"Am I?" said Lillian fiercely.

"Of *course* you are. But—"

"But?"

"But I'm not sure how much that would solve, hiding out like that."

"I'm not hiding."

"What, then? What would you call it?"

"You think I should go back," said Lillian. She met her mother's eyes.

"Well."

"Right?"

"I think you should hear him out."

"I've already heard him out. He's said everything he can say." She rubbed her fist in her eye. "You think I should go back."

"I think you should think carefully about what you might be giving up by staying away."

Lillian rose and walked over to the row of washing machines, peered in one. The woman with the orange lipstick watched her suspiciously. Lillian turned around and then said dramatically, "Jane thinks I should leave him."

"Oh, does she?" Ginny snorted.

"She does. She thinks it's black and white, just like that."

"I can't say I'm surprised about that either," said Ginny. She crossed one leg over the other.

"Maybe it is black and white," said Lillian. "Or maybe Jane thinks I have other options. But you... you don't think I do."

"Oh, come off it," snapped Ginny. She rose from the bench and opened one of the dryers. She attacked the clothes mightily, pushing them into the laundry carriage. "Lillian," she said.

"What?" said Lillian savagely.

"Stop it."

"Stop what?"

"Stop pretending. You and I, we're not as different as you want us to be."

"How do you mean?" Lillian gave her mother a small, cautious glance.

"I mean that once you become a mother... well, the rules you live by are different."

"Oh, *rules*," said Lillian, almost shouting. "I am sick to death of rules." The old woman rose and folded her newspaper carefully, in a manner that reminded Lillian of the way Ginny folded sheets.

"Nevertheless," said Ginny. "There they are."

"Fine," said Lillian. "If that's how you want to see it."

"It's not the worst thing in the world," said Ginny. She began to fold William's T-shirts, making a tidy stack on the laundry table.

"What isn't? Infidelity?"

"A stumble," Ginny said. "A bump in the road. These things

can be gotten over." She thought of Rachel slumped next to her in the car on the way home from the bus station. Ginny would have driven all the way to New York City to bring her home if Rachel had asked. She would have carried her home on her shoulders, all along the New York State Thruway. It all changed, once you became a mother. The lengths you went to. That became more important than everything else. Probably Lillian didn't know that yet. But she would, one day she would.

"Oh, *can* they?" said Lillian. "I'm so happy to hear you think so."

"Lillian —"

"*What?*"

"Don't be like that. I'm only —"

"I think you're wrong. I think it is the worst thing."

"Sweetheart —" Ginny stopped, then began again. "You're in pain, anyone can see that. But if you make a huge mistake, if you're *making* a huge mistake, then there's no going back. I've seen the way you look at him, you know."

"*Who?*"

"Father Colin."

"No," said Lillian, and her hands began to shake; she had to put them in her pocket to hide the shaking from her mother. "No. We. Are not having. This conversation."

Ginny rapped her knuckles quickly on the folding table. Her face became grim. "On the contrary. I think we should have it."

"Absolutely not," said Lillian. "You don't know what you're talking about. You don't know anything!"

She could see that that hurt her mother, that that would shut her up, and it did, and they folded in silence for several more minutes, folding and folding, stacking and stacking, while Olivia went back to the toy bucket and emptied all of the contents onto the floor, searching for the missing puzzle piece.

⚡

Rachel parked her father's car in one of the waterfront lots and walked along the bike path parallel to the lake. She passed a sign for kayak rentals. Maybe she should kayak! Did she even know how to kayak? It had been years since she'd tried, but she had a cobwebby memory of a long-ago camping trip with her parents and Stephen, but without Lillian, who had stayed behind for some teen-aged activity whose specifics Rachel couldn't remember but which she recalled being just fabulous and envy-inducing enough to make Rachel act like a total pill on the camping trip. God, how did they stand it, parents?

Rachel could see a few kayaks way out in the lake, the kayakers little black dots. The idea of joining them was appealing. She liked the thought of being out there with the birds and the fishes, close to nature and all of that. But she was not sure that she would be able to make it all the way to the middle of the lake (did Pilates muscles translate to paddling muscles?), and wouldn't it be just her luck to get stuck out there, requiring rescue. The headline in the *Free Press:* "Loser Old Maid Kayaker Rescued." No, no kayaking.

Bikes? There was a shop just ahead of her advertising rentals. *That* seemed like a good idea, riding as far as the bike path would take her. How far was that? She didn't know. Except she was wearing a skirt (another reason to eschew the kayaking) and it seemed stupid to spend money she didn't have to rent something that no doubt was sitting unused in her parents' basement or garage.

On to the aquarium, then. She passed through the turnstiles and joined the end of the line of tourists waiting to pay. The ten-dollar entry fee gave her pause, but she chalked it up to an educational experience and handed over her credit card, declining the cashier's offer to become a full-fledged, card-carrying aquarium member. "I don't live here," she told him. But didn't she, sort of?

She paused to take a drink from the water fountain near the cubby room, where strollers were lined up like soldiers. The cubbies were filled to bursting with diaper bags spilling out all manner of kid paraphernalia: boxes of crackers, little Sigg bottles with pictures of safari animals or dolphins. All children! This place, like every place, including her parents' home, was full of families with children. Was Rachel the only single, childless person in the entire building, in the entire world? It seemed just possible that she was.

She wound her way through the bottom-floor exhibit, studying the sturgeon, with their torpedo-shaped bodies. They depressed her. Remarkable, really, and yet here they were, behind a pane of glass, swimming listlessly around, probably wondering why the lake had suddenly gotten so much smaller. Did they deserve that? It was no wonder they looked so somber.

A sign to her left told her that at eleven o'clock there was going to be a live animal feeding. What kind of animal? The sign did not divulge that piece of information. Did she want to see a live animal getting fed? She didn't know. When had she become so indecisive? She didn't know that either. Was it only a few months ago she had had a life in Manhattan, a busy, fruitful life, a career? Where had all of that gone, and how was it possible for it to go so quickly?

She was grateful when the ringing of her cell phone interrupted her thoughts, and even more grateful when she saw Whitney's name in the caller ID window. She missed Whitney. She wasn't sure about all the rest of it, the hot sidewalks and the smells of garbage in the alleyways and the constant maneuvering around delivery trucks, but she missed Whitney.

"Rach?" Whitney sounded out of breath.

"What are you doing? Why do you sound like that?"

"I'm just walking on the treadmill at the gym."

"You *are?* Oh God, Whitney, hang up the phone. I hate when people do that."

"I know. I hate it too. I just…there aren't enough minutes in the day. Work is nuts, and then the wedding stuff. Anyway, I have one quick thing to tell you. Your bridesmaid dress is in."

"It is?" Rachel had nearly forgotten about the wedding. She had certainly forgotten about the dress.

"It is. I picked it up last night. It's *gorgeous*. I swear to God, Rachel, you're going to look amazing. You're going to look better than the bride!"

"Oh, shut up." But Rachel smiled. She did love the dress. But. There was one thing. "Hey, Whitney?" She tried to make her voice sound assured and confident, the way she did when she put out calls for actors for work, all business. "I paid for the dress already, right?" She closed her eyes and waited for the answer.

There was a pause. "You put down the deposit a few months ago. I just paid the balance when I picked it up for you. That's all, just the balance."

Rachel exhaled as silently as she could. "Jesus, I forgot all about that. How much was the balance?"

"Don't worry about it. Take care of yourself up there, Rach. You have shit going on. You've been through a lot. Pay me later."

Rachel felt an odd, weak sensation in her knees, and the edges of her vision began to blur. She located a bench and lowered herself slowly down onto it, next to a mother nursing an infant. She turned carefully away from the mother for the sake of privacy, but the woman didn't seem to care: she was proud of it, not even using a blanket to cover herself or the baby. Vermont, thought Rachel grimly.

"Rachel? It's okay, really. I'll take care of it."

Why was she the one who always needed taking care of? Whitney didn't. Whitney was fine. It sucked, being the underdog all the time. It just plain sucked. She knew she sounded short-tempered when she said, "Whitney, just tell me. What was the balance?"

"Two hundred thirty-three. That's with tax. But really, Rachel. I'm the one who picked out such an expensive dress —"

"I'll send you a check. I'm not a charity case."

"Rachel, seriously. It's *my* wedding. I don't want you to go broke over it."

But I'm already broke, thought Rachel. What's it matter, a little bit more? She said, "I'll send you a check. I'll put it in the mail tomorrow." Any check for that amount sent from her account at the moment was likely to bounce, she knew that. They both knew that. Perhaps she could pay Whitney through PayPal. That way she could put it on her credit card. Could you pay a friend through Pay-Pal? Was that done? She didn't know. But she was about to find out. She'd figure out the details later. "I'll get it to you," she said. "I'll get it to you ASAP." When had she turned into someone who said *ASAP?* She'd never been that person before.

After she released Whitney from the phone call she walked up the stairs to the second floor of the aquarium, where a gaggle of children had gathered for the live animal show. She took her place behind them, alongside the parents, and she studied the children, their plump, rapt faces. (All that collagen! They didn't know how lucky they were.) What was it her father had told her at the ice-cream factory? That she had a joy about her as a child. An ease with the world. Where had they gone, the joy and the ease? She wanted them back.

It was untrue, what she'd said to Whitney. No matter how she tried to spin it, it was untrue. She *was* a charity case.

※

Lillian and Ginny and Olivia made it to the bakery for grilled cheese but skipped the playground. Olivia, perhaps sensing something amiss, did not complain. Even though the trip home was only a few minutes long she fell asleep in her car seat, sucking rhythmically on her thumb.

"Poor thing," said Lillian, turning around to look at her. "Exhausted." She had composed herself somewhat in the car on the way home and had put on her sunglasses.

Ginny said, "Don't you think—"

And Lillian cut her off so quickly and certainly, raising a flat palm and saying, in a voice cold and hard, a voice that brooked no argument, "Mother. *Don't*."

Ginny couldn't remember when Lillian had last called her *Mother*, if in fact she ever had.

"Don't," said Lillian again.

So she didn't.

"What do you want me to tell Dad?" Ginny asked, pulling into the driveway and turning off the car.

Lillian sighed. "I don't know," she told her seat belt. "You can tell him, I guess."

"Okay. I mean, he might have guessed. We all wondered, of course."

"But not when I'm around."

"No," Ginny said. "Of course not."

Lillian carried Olivia in and brought her straight up the stairs, intending to put her down for a proper nap in her bed. Stephen was coming down the stairs as she was going up. Ginny heard him say, "Where were you?" and heard Lillian say, shortly. "Laundromat."

"You could have asked me. I've got clothes to wash."

"Oh, for heaven's sake, Stephen. You're an adult. Go yourself."

Stephen walked heavily down the stairs and stood morosely in the foyer, then sighed and ambled through the kitchen and out onto the deck.

"What's eating him?" said Ginny to William, who was standing at the sink, filling a glass with water. She put Philip's car seat on the floor.

"Go easy," said William. "I think they're fighting." He made a jerking motion toward the ceiling with his head.

"No! Them, too?"

"Why? Who else?"

Ginny waved her arm. "Never mind. A story for another time."

She unbuckled Philip and lifted him out. "Oh, *you*," she said. "You're soaked."

She brought him into the den and laid him down on the make-shift changing table on the floor. Her hips protested, and then her knees. "I am getting too old for these sorts of acrobatics," she said to Philip. He gurgled up at her, eyes wide and unblinking, and caught hold of his foot with both hands.

Ginny fastened the new diaper, then rummaged in a pile of clothes on the floor — clean, she suspected, though she certainly could not guarantee it — for a onesie. Really, the den was a tremendous mess. Since the last time Ginny had been here Lillian's belongings had migrated to the far reaches of the room. There on the desk was a mass of her makeup and hair elastics; in the corner was a pile of paperbacks that Lillian had unearthed from the basement or from the closet in Stephen's old room. Crime novels, mostly. She could see on the cover of one a black-gloved hand holding some sort of revolver.

She tried not to think of what Lillian had just told her. It was too upsetting to think about, her daughter nursing a broken heart all these weeks, sharing the news with nobody. Of course, as she'd told Lillian, they'd all suspected. But until it was confirmed Ginny had been able to believe that nothing was truly wrong, that Tom was, as Lillian said, simply caught up with work.

Her gaze returned to the desk, and she saw there a pile of bills that she had opened and looked through but had completely neglected to pay.

"Oh, Philip," she said reproachfully to the baby. "The electric bill! I forgot all about it."

She laid him carefully on the floor, and when he began to whimper she wagged a finger at him and said sternly, "Don't. Not now. If I don't get this bill paid we will all be sitting around in the dark while buckets of ice cream melt inside the freezer."

He turned his head to the side and rooted around his mouth with his hand until finally his thumb found its way in. It touched and heartened her somehow, this tiny person's capacity for self-comfort.

She watched him for a moment until his eyes closed. Then she turned her attention back to the desk. To clear a place to sit she had to move a package of diaper wipes and a copy of *Bear Snores On* from the desk chair.

She looked through the pile of bills until she located the electric bill, and then she found the checkbook and opened it to the register page. All of it was there, a record of the last year, written alternately in her neat straight hand and in William's slanted one, for they had not, despite Stephen and Jane's advice and promises that banking on the Internet was secure and convenient, moved in that direction. It wasn't the security Ginny was worried about; it was something more old-fashioned that she was reluctant to give up. She enjoyed the physical act of writing the checks. She liked balancing the checkbook with her little black calculator, licking the envelopes that held the bills, lining up a stamp in each corner, carrying the whole pile to the mailbox.

And there, in William's handwriting, was the record of a check written to one Rachel Owen earlier in the summer for twenty-five hundred dollars. Ginny paused. She considered. She looked away, then looked again at the register, as if it might have changed in the interim. Rachel Owen. Twenty-five hundred dollars. She looked at Philip and saw the way his eyeballs moved behind his eyelids.

Under different circumstances, perhaps any other summer, this discovery—the proof of a secret between William and Rachel, and an expensive secret, at that—would have caused her to raise her voice loudly, forgetting about the sleeping baby, forcing William to come running from the kitchen to see what was the matter. But this summer? No. Why shouldn't Rachel be able to ask her father for help when she needed it? And why shouldn't William be able to help Rachel in his own way, as she had in hers? "Why not?" she said aloud, and she wrote out the check for the electric bill while beside her Philip slept.

⁓

"That's it," said William. "We're going out to dinner."

"Really?" Ginny was on her knees in the closet, sorting through some old shoes. "Where will we go that will accommodate the children? Flatbread?" She tossed a pair of William's old sneakers out of the closet. "You don't wear these anymore, do you?"

He saw that she had a big black garbage bag at the ready. "I do, actually," he said, tossing them back into the closet.

She held up a pair of black pumps. *"These,"* she said. "I don't think I've worn these since Stephen's wedding. Good Lord."

"Save them for Rachel's wedding," he suggested. "They're beautiful shoes."

She rolled her eyes. "They will be long out of style by the time that day comes," she said.

"We don't know that."

"No," she said. "We don't." She sat back on her heels and pushed her hair out of her face. "Pizza sounds good, the more I think about it. Olivia will do well if we go to Flatbread. They have crayons—"

"No," said William decisively. "No pizza. No children. No any-body. Just us." He sat on the bed and looked at her.

Ginny frowned. "But what will the others do?" She tossed one of the black heels at him and nodded toward the bag. He didn't put it in; he held onto it, inspecting it. He supposed one could tell a lot about a person by considering a pair of shoes she had worn for an important occasion. There was a smudge along one toe, for exam-ple. Perhaps he had caused that smudge. He was notoriously clumsy on the dance floor.

"They will fend for themselves," he said. "The way that adults are meant to do."

"But—"

"No but," he said. "A nice dinner. Just the two of us."

Her frown deepened.

"You," he said.

"What?"

"You shouldn't look so upset! About being asked to dinner."

She smiled then, a lovely smile, and he was grateful suddenly for her, and for the house, and for the bits of the garden that he could see from the window. He was grateful for the dirt underneath his fingernails, and for the shower he was about to take, and for the meal he was going to have later with his wife. He would call for a reservation, someplace downtown, someplace nice like Trattoria Delia or L'Amante. They would have wine.

He tossed the shoe back at her. "Put on something nice," he said. "Wear these."

᠅

They did have wine, and she did wear the shoes, and as Ginny sat in front of fettuccine with cherry tomatoes, saffron, and white wine she looked across the table at William. They were seated near the window, and she watched him watching the passersby, the steady stream of people along College Street: teenagers, college students, young parents with strollers, slightly older parents with recalcitrant teenagers trailing behind them.

"What are you thinking about?"

"Nothing," said William. "Just looking at the people. Looking at how *young* everyone is."

Ginny looked. "It's a young town," she said. "Always has been."

"I know! But we were once part of the youth of it. Remember?"

"I do," she said. They were quiet for a moment.

Then, into the silence, she said, "Lillian's left Tom, you know."

"Oh, Jesus. Not really?"

"Really. There was —" She found she couldn't think of the right way to say it, almost couldn't say it all. She felt, even though Lillian had given her permission, that she was betraying her to talk about it. "There was an infidelity."

"On whose part?"

"His."

William set his lips in a thin and unreadable line. Finally he said, "Poor Lilly."

"I know," said Ginny. "She's devastated. Of course she is! Absolutely devastated. And keeping it from us all these weeks. Well, I just can't imagine how lonely it's been for her."

William was silent.

"William?"

"What?"

"I thought you'd be more...I don't know. More *angry* when I told you. I thought you'd want to kill him."

"I do," William said softly, and she saw then the set of his lips was not unreadable at all; she saw the tiny, angry vein pulsing in his forehead. He was furious.

"Poor Lilly," she ventured, echoing his words. The vein still pulsed. "And poor Tom," she added.

"Poor *Tom?*" He nearly spat it. He put down his fork.

"Well, yes. I'm sure he's aching with regret."

"He should be."

"Maybe. But."

"There is no but." He looked steadily out the window, then back at her. His gaze was unforgiving.

It occurred then to Ginny that she didn't know what she thought. If you removed yourself from the specifics — the sex, the physicality of all of it, the *mess* — then who knew what it all meant, to Tom or to Lillian or to their marriage? Who knew anything, really?

She drank from her wineglass. She had a vision of Lillian as a single mother, of Olivia growing up without a father. Of Philip in the yard five years hence, nobody to play catch with. It was unbearable, all of it: the thought of Lillian staying with Tom, and the thought of her leaving him for good. The thought of her staying with them indefinitely, and the thought of her not staying with them any longer.

They sat without speaking while the waitress cleared their dinner plates and poured the rest of the bottle of wine into their glasses. "Dessert?" she said.

"No," said Ginny.

"Yes," said William.

"I'll bring the menus anyway," said the waitress. "And you can take a look."

When she had gone Ginny took a sip of her wine and said, in a shaky voice, "William? Do you think we've done something wrong?"

"*What?* How?"

"That they're all so—unhappy?"

"They're not *all* unhappy." William's voice had softened. He reached across the table and put his hands on Ginny's. She forgot sometimes how big his hands were, how capable of covering her own completely, making them disappear.

"But they are. Stephen and Jane are *miserable*. Every time he comes out of that room it looks like they've been fighting—"

"Well, naturally. Jane has been confined to a bedroom for nearly six weeks, and not even in her own bedroom, mind you. And Stephen has to take care of her *in his parents' house*. Nightmare situation, really."

"Nightmare," agreed Ginny.

"But temporary. When the baby comes it will all be all right."

"But will it? Or will that just bring another set of complications, but different ones?"

"Well. Of course. But it's a *baby*. Complications are part of it. It's easy to forgive a lot when there's a baby in the room. You, of all people. You know that!"

"And Rachel—"

"Rachel is struggling. Also temporarily."

She thought of the check. "But they're all struggling! In one way or another they're all struggling."

He leaned toward her and tightened his hold on her hand. "And weren't we ever struggling, when we were their ages?"

Ginny lifted her head to look at him. "I don't know. It seems to me we had the basics."

He sat back and wiped his face. "*Now* it seems that way. But back then? Who knows! We were young. Poor. We didn't have the faintest idea what we were doing."

"Really?"

"Really. Remember that time Rachel knocked over an entire

can of paint on the kitchen floor? And we didn't notice until she'd crawled across the den?"

Ginny laughed. "I remember."

"And Stephen and Lillian watched the whole thing happen——"

"But they didn't say anything!"

"Because they wanted to see what knee prints would look like on a floor. How different they'd be from footprints."

"God," said Ginny. "I'd forgotten all about that. Disaster. One of many."

"You see? For all parents, sometimes." He sobered then, and squeezed her hand before letting it go. The waitress returned with the dessert menus, which were as elegant as wedding invitations. William squinted to read the tiny font. Then he put the menu down and looked sharply at Ginny.

"Why are you taking it so personally?"

She thought about that. Then she took a deep breath and touched her hair. She didn't look directly at William when she answered, because she thought that if she did she might begin to cry.

"Because they're my life's work."

He remained silent, watching her, listening.

"If they're not happy—if they're not capable of living on their own, and being *happy*—it means I've failed. I *should* take it personally."

"Oh, Ginny." He reached across the table and laid his hand on her cheek. She pressed it in closer.

"This is it," she said. "I'm sixty-three years old. This is what I've done with my life. They're my masterpiece, and they're broken."

"Ginny, Ginny," he said tenderly, and they sat like that for a while, and the waitress, coming back to take their dessert orders, must have sensed something momentous, because she backed away slowly and left them there, sitting by the window.

Rachel dialed the landlord's phone number. He was a squat Lebanese man with kind brown eyes and thick forearms. She pictured him surrounded by a large brood of similarly dark-haired, dark-eyed children, in an apartment in Queens, a place with lots of rugs with complicated designs and a spicy aroma emanating throughout.

She had deposited William's check in her account. But that money was long gone. She had owed a horrendous amount on her cell phone bill, and she was past due on her credit card, and now she owed Whitney for the bridesmaid dress: she was still short.

Breathe, she told herself. *Breathe deeply.*

She was willing to beg for mercy. She was willing to do anything. She would go on some sort of payment plan. She would babysit the brood of Lebanese children!

"It's paid," he said. "You're off the hook."

"What do you mean, paid?" Rachel felt a flutter somewhere behind her collarbone.

"Paid," he said. "You don't owe. August is paid. You're okay until September."

"Who paid?"

"I don't know," he said. "Got the check, cashed it, didn't look. Don't care."

Next she called Marcus. He was somewhere outside; she could hear the sirens, the squeal of traffic. Suddenly she missed the city, the noise and heat, the window air-conditioning units spitting onto the street. She missed the prim little dogs with bows in their hair. She missed the anonymity, the sense that at any point, if you wanted to, you could disappear.

"Did you?" she said immediately.

"Did I what?"

"Did you pay the rent for me?"

Silence. In the background she heard someone yell, "What the *fuck,* man?"

"I don't know," said Marcus. "Maybe, maybe not."

"Someone did."

"Well, then, I guess maybe I did."

"Why?"

"Why not? I had it, and you didn't. That's all."

"It's that simple?"

She thought again of her apartment, and how lonely, how half inhabited, it had seemed after Marcus left. How she dreaded being by herself. But now, after weeks on the air mattress, after nights listening to Olivia breathe while she struggled to get to sleep, after mornings elbowing for room at the breakfast table, the solitude she had eschewed seemed suddenly appealing. Because, after all, why did solitude have to be lonely? It didn't, of course. Not if you allowed your mind to focus elsewhere. New York City was chock-full of people living successfully on their own: fulfilled, engaged, even happy.

"It's that simple," said Marcus.

Maybe, after all, that was possible, for things to be that simple. What had Tess told her? *You're talented. You have a future here. You just need to focus.*

"Well," she said. "Thank you." She almost added, *I'll pay you back.* But then something stopped her. *Let's not take it too far,* she thought.

I'm on a roll, she thought. I might as well keep going. She dialed.

Tess answered on the first ring, and Rachel, taken aback by hearing her voice live after so many weeks — not on voice mail, not on the offensive—nearly panicked and hung up. *Breathe,* she said. She cut right to the chase: "Can I have my job back?"

"Rachel?" Tess said. "Rachel Owen, is that you?"

"Of course it's me."

"You have some nerve, calling me to ask me that."

"I know," said Rachel. "I'm sorry."

"You. You left me high and dry. All summer! High and dry."

"What about Stacy?"

"What about her? She sucks, that's what about her. She's gone."

"Really?" Rachel felt a surge of hope. "She sucks?"

"Terrible. She scheduled too many people, she scheduled the wrong people, she didn't have the head shots ready, she broke out in hives. You name it."

The hives sounded awful.

"We're postponing the whole thing for a month," continued Tess. "While we pull ourselves together."

"So," said Rachel carefully. "If it's postponed—"

"Just get the hell back here. Rachel? Get back here as soon as you can. Let other people take care of things there. I'm sure you've done your part. I need you here."

Family first, thought Rachel. That's the spirit.

"I'm on my way," she said. "I've got loose ends to tie up here. A couple of days, and I'm there."

✳

William crouched down in the garden and worked a weed out of the soil. There were a few more weeds, but they came out easily, the mulch having done its job all summer. The dahlias were in full bloom and he paused to admire their sturdiness, their simple squat beauty. They were perhaps his favorite flower. He planted them everywhere he had the opportunity. The trailing blue million bells and zinnias had grown to their full height, and in front of them, low to the ground, were the tender bunches of soft lavender ageratum. It was, perhaps, the best summer garden of his life.

He breathed in deeply, taking in the mixed scents, thinking ahead to the bulbs he would plant in the fall, the trimming he would do next week in the shrubs along the edge of the lawn, when a commotion from the house interrupted his thoughts. Lillian, coming out on the deck, arms waving cartoonishly, cheeks flushed.

"It's Jane!" she said. "It's Jane."

He felt, somewhere deep inside him, a drumroll of anticipation or dread: this was what they had been waiting for all summer. It was here now. Time.

"Her water broke!" called Lillian. "We've got to get her to the hospital. Stephen's not here. He went off with Mom." Behind her, mouth open, eyes wide and scared, stood Olivia.

"She peed," said Olivia. "All over her room."

"She didn't pee," said Lillian. "It's different."

"How?" asked Olivia.

"I'll explain later. Dad, can you keep an eye on the kids? I'll take her in. I tried calling Stephen, but he's not picking up."

But William found that for several seconds he could not look away from the garden. He was frozen in place, paralyzed.

"Dad?" said Lillian again. "Can you watch the kids? Let me just get my shoes."

"No," said William, and he could see by Lillian's face that she was as surprised by the authority in his voice as he was. He drew himself straighter. "No," he said again. "Lillian, you stay here and wait for Stephen and your mother. I'll take her myself."

In the car he tried not to look too hard at Jane. Every now and then she shuddered and pressed her hands to her belly. She looked very pale. Then again, she had been inside for the better part of the summer. Was this what a woman on the verge of labor was supposed to look like? He didn't know. Was this normal?

"Are you okay?" he said.

She shook her head. "No. I mean yes. I don't know."

He went up to Shelburne Road to turn left. That would be the fastest way, he thought, though he hadn't tested it out. Why hadn't he tested it out? Had anybody? All summer they'd had, to test it out. How unprepared they were!

"It's going to be okay," he said.

"William?" she said. "I'm scared."

At the stoplight he took her hand. It could have been Lillian's hand, or Rachel's, or even Olivia's. It seemed, in that moment, as though all of the females he'd comforted in his life were one and the same. "It's going to be okay," he said. "You have to know that."

They turned onto Pearl Street. "It's not far now," he said. But Jane knew that, of course. She'd been coming here for her appointments all summer long.

"William?" she said. "I did something."

"What?" They were on Colchester Avenue now, approaching the hospital. He glanced at her. She was staring straight ahead.

"I got out of bed. Whenever the house was empty, I got out of bed. I walked around. I went up and down the stairs. And I think that's why the baby's coming early. I didn't relax, I stressed out about work, and I got out of bed when I wasn't supposed to." Her lower lip began to tremble. "I did a bad job."

"Jane," he said gently, pulling the car up to the hospital. "You have kept that baby safe all these months. You have done a wonderful job. It's just ready to come out now, that's all. So what if it's a little early? Only a few weeks early, right?"

She nodded.

"It's ready. It will be fine."

※

"She's gone!" said Olivia excitedly, greeting them at the door.

Lillian appeared behind her. "Get to the hospital," she said to Stephen. "You left your cell phone behind. Or else we would have called."

Stephen felt his stomach drop. "What do you mean?" he asked, really, truly not understanding. "Who's gone?"

"*Jane*," said Lillian. "Her water broke. Just like that! And we called the doctor, and the doctor said to get there as soon as possible—"

"Nobody's *with* her?" he said. "She's there *alone?*"

"Of course she's not there alone!" said Lillian. "What do you take us for? Dad's with her. Someone had to stay with the children, and nobody else was here, and so we sent Dad."

"*Dad?* To the hospital? With Jane? In labor?" Even to his own ears his voice sounded strange, shaky and high-pitched.

"He wanted to go with her, he really did. You should have seen him peeling out of the driveway! It was like something out of a movie. And Jane, she was remarkably calm. It was amazing. I just heard this small voice coming from her room, and so I knocked on the door, and when I opened it she had this sort of panicked look on her face, but not *really* panicked, you know, not the way I'm sure I would have felt if I'd been her—"

But Stephen wasn't really listening. His mind had now clicked into gear and was rushing ahead of him. Lillian pressed car keys into his hands.

"Wait," said Ginny. "I'm going with you."

"No," he said. "It's okay. Dad's there."

"It's *not* okay," she said firmly. "This is a big deal. I'm going with you. I'm driving." She plucked the keys from him and opened the door.

"No," he said. "I'll go alone." He felt suddenly small, and alone, and as if he were about to cry. He looked pleadingly at Lillian, who was holding Olivia's hand and smiling at him in a gentle and encouraging way. "But it's too *early*," he whispered. "What if the baby isn't okay?"

"Go," Lillian said, taking him by the shoulders and guiding him gently out the door. "Everything is going to be fine. *Go.*"

"I'm coming down there," said Ginny when Stephen called two hours later. Lillian hovered near her. Jane had been admitted into a labor and delivery room. It was really going to happen. "I'm coming," said Ginny. "With Lillian. Rachel can watch the kids." Lillian nodded.

"Don't," Stephen said. "Just... do something else."

"What?"

"Wait. Pray. We don't know which way it will go. They might give her a C-section."

Ginny mouthed *C-section* to Lillian.

"Oh, poor Jane," said Lillian. "That's what she didn't want."

"How soon would that be? Stephen?" said Ginny. "Right away?"

"I don't know," said Stephen. "But just stay there for now. Please? Dad's here."

After she hung up, Ginny told Lillian that it took every ounce of whatever she had—willpower, fortitude—not to disobey him. She could not stop thinking, she told Lillian, of how he looked on his first day of first grade, waiting at the bus stop with his back curving under his navy blue backpack and his eyes big and scared beneath his baseball cap. Only twice in all of Stephen's life, said Ginny, had she felt such a need to protect him—that day, and today. "But we should stay here," she said, and Lillian heard the catch in her voice. "He doesn't want us." Ginny turned her face away and bent to pick up a crumb from the floor. I should hug her, thought Lillian. I should hug her and make her feel better. But she was hurt too, and she felt suddenly very tired, and the house seemed too small and warm to hold her mother's disappointment as well as her own long-standing, smoldering rage and resentment.

"I'll go out for milk," she said abruptly.

Ginny was looking out the kitchen window at the garden. William's weeding tools lay where he had dropped them to take Jane to the hospital. Lillian thought about going out to pick them up, but they seemed too far away, and the day too hot. Even the errand for milk she had just offered to run — air-conditioned car to air-conditioned store and back again — seemed like too much.

"Take Olivia," said Ginny. "Will you?"

"Sure," said Lillian. "But wouldn't it be easier if—"

"*Take* her," said Ginny. "I can't think with all the chattering."

Lillian touched her lightly on the shoulder as she passed. "It's going to be *fine,* Mom. People have babies all the time. It's going to be fine."

"I know," said Ginny shortly. "I know it is."

In the car Lillian saw her mother's point. Olivia kept up a running commentary on everything they passed, and some things they didn't. She ruminated on the state of her pink elephant's dress (it had a tear that needed to be fixed); she had a few questions about fairies (their diet, how long they lived, who taught them to fly); she wanted to know when her next swimming session at the Y at home would begin; she wanted to know when Tom would come up to bring them back to Massachusetts. To all of these, even (especially!) the last, Lillian answered with a series of noncommittal noises meant to convey wisdom and understanding without actually answering.

Then, with the milk on the seat next to her and Olivia returned to the safety of her car seat, Lillian looked in the rearview mirror and saw Olivia chewing on her fingernails.

"Olivia," she said sharply. "Stop that."

"Sorry," said Olivia, and continued to do it.

"Stop it. It's bad for your teeth and bad for your nails too."

"I'm thirsty," said Olivia, finally removing her hands from her mouth and tapping them on the window.

"I don't have anything with me. You'll have to wait."

"But I'm *thirsty!*"

"Olivia. I don't have anything." They were close to the house now. Lillian saw that all of the summer gardens they passed were drooping in the heat. It seemed as though everything around her was desiccated and dry, used up, on the verge of dying. Lillian thought she couldn't bear it: another conversation with Tom, the memory of her kiss with Father Colin and the shame that came with that, the effort required to continue the charade that everything was fine. And now, on top of it, the little voice chirping at her from the backseat. Needing, needing. Always needing. If not Olivia, then Philip. If not her children, then Rachel. Someone, always! Wanting, needing.

"But, Mommy." Lillian heard it from deep inside Olivia: the beginnings of a whine.

"Olivia!" she said sharply.

"What?"

"I can't stand it anymore. I can't listen to anything else. We're almost home. You'll have to wait, that's it." She made the turn onto their street.

Olivia began to cry softly. "This isn't home," she said. "This isn't *our* home."

Lillian turned into the driveway and pulled up hard on the

emergency brake. She reached back and unbuckled Olivia's car seat. She knew she was doing it too roughly, and Olivia jerked back and opened her eyes wider, startled. "Olivia. Just. Go. Inside."

"But—"

"No. Just go. Really, I need to be myself for a minute. Please. Just *go*."

She would be able to recall forever the look on Olivia's face, the expression of astonishment and betrayal and disappointment. Because no matter how hard you tried, there were some things you couldn't undo.

※

Jane writhed on the bed. This was nothing she could have imagined, nothing she could have prepared herself for, nothing she would ever be able to recall or explain later. The pain washed over her in waves, and just when she thought she might get a respite, it returned, stronger, again and again and again.

She gripped Stephen's hand so tightly that she could imagine clawing her way through the flesh, hitting the bone. And that's sort of what she wanted to do: make him hurt the way she was hurting.

Once she opened her eyes and saw a nurse standing near the bed. The nurse looked at the clock on the wall, then checked her cell phone, then checked the monitor hooked to Jane's stomach. It occurred to Jane then that this, this miraculous and tortuous birth of her child, was nothing but a regular workday to everyone else. It occurred to her in that one moment of lucidity that anyone who had had a baby had gone through some version of this, and that was astonishing to Jane, that something so brutal could be so common. That seemed wrong.

Another wave came. She thought she might die. She thought she would rather be dead.

Lillian ushered Olivia into the house, and she put the milk in the refrigerator, and then she got back into the car and without telling anyone she drove (too fast, recklessly, even, but it was the middle of the day and the streets were quiet) to the church.

She chose a pew in the center and slid into it, pulled down the kneeler. She knelt.

She was in that position, head down, resting on her folded hands, when Father Colin entered the church. She turned around, hearing his footfall, and her heart quickened. She told him then about Jane and the baby, and about the black cloud of dread in her stomach and the terrible things she believed it foretold. "I am trying to pray. But I don't know how. Am I going to hell?"

"Of course not." It was hard to believe that this was the man she had kissed. She thought of the kitchen in the rectory, with the aging, creaking appliances. It seemed like another person who had done that. A character in a movie, maybe. "Praying is just talking to God. There's no right or wrong."

"I don't know how to talk to God."

"Pray with me," said Father Colin. He sat beside her, then knelt beside her. He turned toward Lillian. He began, *Heavenly Father, hear us in our hour of need,* and without saying anything he put his hand over hers as he continued the prayer.

She acknowledged it then, that it was with that simple gesture, with the way his fingers closed around her fingers, the way she could have pulled away but didn't, the way she allowed her body to fall slightly toward his until their arms were touching, then their torsos, then their legs, that together they established what had gone on between them, and what still might.

The prayer ended and Father Colin sat back. He wasn't looking at her. He was looking straight ahead at the altar, at the giant crucifix and the two pots of flowers on either side. His face was open and expectant. There was something so intimate about the way he was looking at the altar that made Lillian feel as though she had intruded on a private moment even though she had entered the church first. She thought suddenly of this phrase: *receive the Word of God*. Perhaps this was what it looked like, receiving. She felt something blossoming in the general vicinity of her rib cage — not a pain, exactly, but not a wholly pleasant sensation either. A thrust.

It was then that Lillian understood what Father Colin was doing, what he had done that summer, not just that night in the rectory's kitchen but all summer long: he had transferred to Lillian his capacity for forgiveness, shoring her up, fortifying her.

"Thank you," she said softly, but Father Colin, who now had his head bowed, seemed to have retreated inward.

She thought of Jane in the hospital. She thought of the way her mother described Stephen on the first day of first grade. She thought of his fearful eyes when they told him Jane had gone. It *was* scary. It was terrifying, ushering a new person into the world. Things could go wrong in childbirth, even in this day and age, and Jane and Stephen's baby had been vulnerable.

Now she needed forgiveness herself. She had been terrible to so many people that summer: to her parents, certainly to Tom, and, not an hour ago, to Olivia. Thinking about that last one, about Olivia's face in the car, made her shudder. She had not been as nice to Rachel as she could have been, nor to her mother. She had been horrid, really, to Father Colin in the rectory kitchen that night. She may as well have bared her teeth, so willing was she to show the basest parts of herself. She had been taking, taking, taking, and not giving enough. Her heartbeat quickened and she felt a drumming behind her ears. If this baby dies, she thought, it will be my fault.

꙾

Stephen called back and Ginny's heart tumbled, hearing his voice. "You and Rachel stay there," he said, "but Jane is asking for Lillian. Can you send Lillian?"

Ginny put the phone down carefully on the counter and called Lillian's name. Once, twice. "I don't know where she is," she told Stephen. "Try her cell, or I'll send her when I find her."

Ginny lay down on her bed, on top of the comforter, and looked up at the ceiling. Then she closed her eyes, but the images she saw on her eyelids were brightly colored and bizarre—little pieces of confetti dancing around—and that was more disturbing than looking at the ceiling, so she opened them again. Send Lillian, Stephen had said. Lillian, Lillian, and not her. She tried not to be hurt by that, but she was.

She thought back to the births of her own children. Decades ago now, so far in the past that the specific sensations were buried in a subterranean section of her memory that she couldn't seem to access. Had she been scared? Certainly she had been, but she couldn't remember now what that fear felt like. She remembered a certain brightness in Lillian's eyes, the way they snapped open and looked at her. She remembered the first time Stephen fell asleep in her arms, and the abandon with which his arms fell back from his body. She remembered the thick black hair on Rachel's head, and how that had frightened her, until the nurse explained that that would most likely fall out and be replaced by hair that was softer and lighter. But specifically? The actual act of having them, the actual moment of childbirth? She didn't remember. How was it that she didn't remember?

Philip, who had been sleeping in the Pack 'n Play downstairs, let out a wail, long and low, and Ginny blinked a few times, preparing herself to get up and tend to him. But then Rachel called up the stairs, "I'll get him, Mom. I'll take him for a walk." Then she closed her eyes again, and this time she slept.

She must have fallen deeply asleep because when she heard the doorbell ringing it took her some time to pull herself wholly back into consciousness. She went to the window and did not immediately recognize the man who stood on the doorstep, his back to the door, rubbing one sneakered foot into the cement.

Of course she should have recognized him, but some trick of mind and vision and context played out in front of her all at once — the way, say, as a child you do not immediately recognize your fourth-grade teacher if you happen to see her at the supermarket, poking through the bin of day-old baked goods — and it took several seconds for his identity to take shape.

"Tom?" she said, opening the door, startling him so that he turned around and struggled to arrange his face into an appropriate expression. "Tom?"

⁻⁎⁞

They sat at the kitchen table and Ginny poured them both glasses of iced tea. Tom drank his quickly, gratefully, like a man who hadn't had a drink in two weeks. He looked around the kitchen expectantly, as though at any minute Lillian might emerge from a cupboard or from the deli drawer inside the refrigerator.

"She's not here," Ginny said finally. "So you can stop searching. She went off somewhere, I'm not sure where. And Olivia and Philip aren't here either. They went for a walk with Rachel."

Tom rubbed his finger on the glass. He picked the lemon slice out of it and placed it on the table beside him. Finally he looked steadily at Ginny.

"I'm not taking no for an answer. I'll sit here forever."

"Oh?"

"Yes."

Ginny rose, and gathered both of their glasses. From the sink, not looking at Tom, she said, "I could kill you."

"I know."

"I mean really and truly. I could kill you."

"Yes."

"For hurting my little girl."

"I *know*."

There was a thick and uncertain silence, and finally Tom said slowly, "You've never made mistakes, you and William?"

"Not *that* kind," said Ginny sharply. "Certainly not that kind."

"I know." Tom looked down. "I believe that."

"But you did."

"I did. But I'm here, hat in hand."

"Yes," Ginny conceded. "I guess that's true. But it took you long enough."

"She wouldn't let me come! She would barely stay on the phone with me. I thought if I gave her time..."

Minutes passed. They could hear, from down the street, a child yelling in a yard, then the *ting ting* of a bicycle bell. Ginny wiped the counters carefully, then straightened the dish towels on the handle of the oven door. Tom remained seated.

Finally she regained her seat across the table from him and said, softly, "You must miss the children."

"If I think about them too much," said Tom, looking at his hands, "I am going to lose it."

"I'm sure that's true," said Ginny. "They'll be back soon enough." Tom said nothing, so Ginny continued. "You're all she has, you know. You're what she has."

"I know," said Tom, blinking hard, giving Ginny a pained look.

"You did something so idiotic. So stupid, Tom."

"I *know*."

"You have to make it right."

"She's all I have too. She's everything. She's what I'm missing."

"So you have to make it right."

"I know," he whispered. "I know I do."

"Go away for a while and come back later. I want to talk to Lillian first, when she gets back."

"I don't know if I can stand to leave—"

"Then stay," said Ginny firmly. "But let me talk to Lillian first. I'm going to the hospital. I'm sure that's where she went. And I don't care what anyone says, I am going to be there when my grandchild is born. When Rachel gets back with the children you can have some time with them. And then we'll figure out the rest of it."

She was already in the car and about to pull out of the driveway when she saw Rachel walking down the sidewalk, wearing Philip in the BabyBjörn. Ginny watched as Rachel dipped her face down to kiss the top of Philip's bobbing head, and the gesture was so unconscious, so natural, that some trick of mind or light allowed Ginny to think for a split second that it was Lillian, not Rachel, that she was looking at. Babies, she thought. She's almost ready for her own babies.

But something was wrong with the picture, and it took her a few seconds to work out exactly what it was. When she did, she turned off the car and leaped out of the seat. "Rachel!" she screamed. "Rachel, where's Olivia?"

Rachel stopped short. "Olivia? I never took Olivia. I just took Philip."

"I thought you said you were taking *them* for a walk."

"No! *Him.* I said I was taking *him.* Philip. She must be in the house."

Ginny felt something twist in her stomach or her heart. "No.

That's impossible. Tom's here. She would have heard him. She would have come running."

"Then she must've gone with Lillian."

"She must have," said Ginny, and even as she said it she was running toward the house and into the kitchen, grabbing the phone from its cradle, dialing Lillian's cell phone number.

"She's not picking up," Ginny said frantically. They heard the downstairs toilet flush and Tom emerged from the bathroom. His gaze took in Rachel and Philip, and he made a move toward Rachel and held out his arms for the baby. Rachel began to undo the straps on the Björn, and Philip kicked his feet and waved his arms. Ginny hung up the phone and redialed. "She's not picking *up*," she said again.

"I'm sure Olivia's with her," said Rachel uncertainly.

"What do you mean?" said Tom, nuzzling his face into Philip's neck. "Olivia's where? What's going on?"

"She's got to be," said Rachel. "Where else could she be?"

Ginny's heartbeat picked up rhythm; her palms felt warm against the phone. "I don't know," she said. "But I don't think she's with Lillian."

Rachel said, "Mom," and Ginny held up a hand to stop her from saying anything more.

"What's going on?" said Tom again, but Ginny, who was dialing the number again, didn't answer.

※

"The doctor will be coming in to check your progress," said the nurse. She lifted Jane's head and gently repositioned the pillow under her. Another contraction came and Jane gasped and arched her back. The nurse held Jane's hand and watched her steadily.

"And then?" said Stephen.

The nurse put her hands on her hips and considered Jane. "Well, that depends. If the doctor is happy with how she's progressing, then we keep going like this, until we get a baby."

"And if she's not?"

"Then we consider the possibility of a C-section. Because of the placental issues, that's certainly not out of the question."

Jane let out a noise that she had never heard before. It seemed not to have come from a human being, this noise, and yet it had: it had come from her.

The doctor came in and pulled on latex gloves. "Hello!" she said brightly, maybe familiarly. There was something comforting about her short gray hair, and the wisdom and experience it implied. Jane couldn't remember if she had met her at one of the appointments. They had melted together, the faces and voices of all of them, into one bunch, the shadow of the long, hot summer. How long had they been in Burlington, she and Stephen? It seemed that they had lived there forever, that they might never leave. But what was the doctor doing—"Jesus *Christ,*" Jane said, loudly, because it was hard to know what was the worse, the contractions or the doctor's examination—and what was she saying?

"She's progressing," she said to Stephen. "But I'm not as happy as I'd like to be with the fetal heart rate. We're not going to do this much longer."

Jane heard herself say, "No!"

"Janey, we have to listen to the doctor."

"*No.* I want to deliver naturally. Please, Stephen? You have to tell them—"

Then the pain took over, and she felt it swirl around her and envelop her; she felt as if she were falling into a long, dark well of pain. The contraction eased, and she was so relieved to feel normal again that she took in great big gulps of air and opened her eyes to see Lillian in the doorway. "Tell her to come in," she mumbled to

Stephen, and that's all she got out before the next contraction began.

Lillian moved Stephen out of the way and took Jane's hand. Her hand was cooler than Stephen's had been, and she swept the hair back from Jane's forehead. "It's terrible, I know," she whispered. "It's awful. But it's temporary. Everything is temporary."

She heard Stephen say, "She doesn't want the C-section."

"Of course she doesn't," said Lillian. "Who would?"

"The doctor said—"

"I know," said Lillian. "The doctor knows what she's doing. They won't let it go too long."

Lillian took a cloth from the nurse and laid it on Jane's forehead. "You can do this," she said. "I know you can. But when they say it's time to stop, you need to listen. You've got to do what's right for the baby."

❋

When Lillian left the room she saw Rachel and William and Ginny standing in the hallway, talking intently.

"Wait," said Lillian, and they all turned toward her. "If you're here, Rach, and Dad's here, and Mom's here...where's Olivia? Where's Philip?"

William stepped up and took her arm. "Philip is with Tom. At the house."

Lillian looked around wildly. "Tom? At the house?"

"But Olivia—"

"*Tom?*" said Lillian again, not hearing him. "Tom is at the house? What's going on?"

"Listen," said William sharply. "Tom is at the house. Philip is with him. We thought Olivia came with you, but now we see that she didn't."

"So where is she?"

"That's what we need to figure out," said William, and it was when Lillian saw the fear in his face that she began to get scared herself. She couldn't remember, later, when she tried to, if she'd ever seen her father look so frightened.

"She's got to be at the house," said Lillian. "Did you call for her?"

"Of course we called for her," said Rachel. "We called, we screamed, we looked everywhere."

"Well, you must not have looked hard enough," said Lillian, and she was off down the hospital hallway, thinking about how she'd said those terrible things to Olivia in the car, and thinking about her daughter's small bewildered face, so hurt and confused, and about the way she could have made things right with her little girl but hadn't.

※

"Push," said the nurse, "we're getting close." And Jane had only a second to think how like television this was, except that on television the mothers-to-be looked brave and serene while she felt as if the entire inside of her body had been ripped open and laid out, raw and exposed, for everyone to see. But she didn't care who saw! She didn't care about anything, except whether or not the pain was ever going to stop. "On the next contraction," said the nurse, "push like there's no tomorrow."

So Jane pushed. With everything in her, she pushed. "Ah," said the nurse. "Now we're getting somewhere."

※

William and Rachel caught up with Lillian in the parking garage, and William gently worked the keys out of her hands. "Absolutely not," he said. "I'm driving." It was torture for all of them waiting in the line to pay the parking attendant, and torture again making their slow way down Shelburne Road, where every stoplight seemed to turn red just before they reached it.

Finally they arrived at the house, where Tom stood in the front yard, talking to a police officer and holding Philip over one shoulder. A police cruiser sat in the driveway, no light or sirens on. Lillian thought, *Why no sirens? This is a goddamn emergency.*

"Oh, Tom," she said, and she collapsed into him. Tom handed Philip to Rachel and put his arms around Lillian. The police officer, making notes on his pad, looked up briefly and then back down. "What do we do?" Lillian said, looking frantically from the police officer to Tom and back again. "How do we find her? How do we put out one of those AMBER Alerts? What do we *do?*"

"Well," said the police officer, and Lillian noticed a birthmark above his temple. Philip, in Rachel's arms, started to cry.

"I can't nurse him now," said Lillian, not turning around. "Give him a bottle, somebody give him a bottle."

"These things," said the police officer, "often turn out to be nothing. A misunderstanding, that sort of thing."

"No," said Lillian.

"Lillian," said Tom.

"First off," said the police officer, "I need to know what she's wearing."

Rachel and William and Tom and the police officer all looked at Lillian. "She's wearing…" She couldn't remember! She couldn't remember. She thought about looking at Olivia in the rearview mirror as she drove home from Shaw's. She thought about earlier, in the grocery store, when she rushed her down the milk aisle. *Hurry up,* she'd told her. Why had she been so impatient with her? What was the rush? What was she wearing? The red dress with the hearts on it? No, that was the day before. The green "Montreal

Love Bug" T-shirt William and Ginny brought her after their weekend there in the spring? No, she had put that in the hamper two days ago.

"I think it was a pink shirt—" ventured Rachel.

"No," said Lillian. "No. Not a pink shirt." When she pictured the view from the rearview mirror again she thought she saw yellow. She said, "Just let me think." She thought about that morning at breakfast, Olivia dripping yogurt onto the counter. Lillian had snapped at her for that too. She had been wearing her Tinker Bell nightgown. Lillian hadn't gotten her dressed. Who had?

"Who got her dressed today?" she asked.

"Not me," said Rachel. "I think she dressed herself."

"She dressed herself?" When they had arrived in Vermont in June, Olivia didn't pick out her own clothes, didn't get dressed without a series of nudges and prods. When had she become so independent? This seemed significant suddenly to Lillian, significant and heartbreaking, this detail of Olivia's self-sufficiency.

"That's okay," said the police officer. "I'll give you a moment." He stepped away and continued making notes on his pad.

"I don't remember what she was wearing," said Lillian. "I'm a terrible mother."

"Now, Lilly," said William tenderly.

"No, you don't understand." She looked at Tom, Rachel, all of them. "I was awful to her earlier. I said terrible things. She's running away from *me*." She turned toward the police officer. "Please find her. Please? You have to find her."

❧

Ginny sat up straight on the plastic chair in the hospital hallway. She tried not to think; she tried to keep her mind perfectly empty. She concentrated on the scrubs of one of the nurses standing in her line of vision, and on the drops of blood along her hem. Blood!

Whose? A messy business for sure, this childbearing. No wonder people died from it constantly in the olden days. No, she thought. Stop. Nobody's dying here.

Then the door to the labor and delivery room opened, and out came Stephen: sweating, gray, nearly limping, his hair plastered to his forehead, slumping onto a chair. But smiling! Smiling. Her son, the father.

"She's here," he said, taking Ginny's hand. "Baby Sarah. She's arrived! She's here."

⁕

When the phone rang, Lillian, who was holding it, answered. William and Rachel were out searching the neighborhood. She could hear them calling: "O-LIV-I-A! O-LIV-I-A!" And each time they called she felt her heart tear a little bit. Tom was sitting in a chair at the kitchen table, feeding Philip a bottle. She knew she needed to remind him to burp Philip when he was halfway through. She thought he was letting too many bubbles into the bottle. But she didn't say anything. She felt, somehow, that to take her attention from Olivia at all was to do wrong by her, would compromise the chances of finding her.

"Lillian? I expected to leave a message, I didn't think anyone would be home—"

"Father Colin!" she said, and Tom looked up quizzically.

"I was calling for news of the baby. I've been waiting, and praying."

"There's no news," she said. "But Olivia's missing."

"Missing?"

"Missing," she said, and her voice broke. "Missing. Gone. The police are here. We're all looking. We can't find her."

"Should I come over?"

"Yes," said Lillian. "No, don't. Yes, do. Oh, I don't know." She couldn't quiet the sensation of her blood moving too quickly through her body. "Come if you want. No, I don't mean that. We need you. Come, please."

She put the phone down. It rang again.

"What?" she said.

"Any news?" It was Ginny.

"No."

"Well, sweetheart, I know it's going to be okay. I just know it."

"I hope so," said Lillian dully. "How's Jane?" It seemed like days ago—months, even—that she'd stood in the labor and delivery room and held Jane's hand. It seemed like another lifetime. It seemed like her life had now been divided into two sections: before Olivia went missing, and after.

"The baby is here!" said Ginny. "Sarah. She's perfect. I just peeked in, but I'll leave them alone now, they're exhausted. I'll come home. Lillian? We're going to find her."

"I know," said Lillian, but she didn't.

❋

Later, when the nurse came in, carrying a bundle in a striped blanket, Stephen reached through a fog of fatigue and astonishment and thought, That's my baby.

"She's had her first bath," said the nurse briskly. She had a no-nonsense haircut and sturdy ankles just visible below her scrub pants. "She's going to need a feeding," she told Jane.

The baby opened her mouth and began to make small, chicken-like noises. Jane reached her arms out, and the nurse, passing over the baby, looked approvingly at Jane.

"You kept her safe, all those weeks. You did good."

Well, thought Stephen. You did well.

"She's perfect, right?" Jane said eagerly.

"She is."

Privately, Stephen was surprised by how imperfect the baby looked. Her head was very small and very red, and oddly shaped, like a plum tomato, and she seemed to be, if you judged by her expression, very angry. Stephen had been surprised, too, when he'd watched the baby get weighed and had seen her reddish and swollen genitals. All very normal, the nurse had told Stephen, something to do with Jane's hormones surging through the baby's body, but nonetheless unexpected and disconcerting.

Jane opened her hospital robe and the nurse pointed the baby's head, like a shuttle, toward Jane's nipple.

"There," she said. "She's on." Then, "Nope, she slipped. Here, try a little bit this way—"

"Ouch," said Jane, shifting her body, using her own hand to lift her breast toward the baby. Finally Jane made a wincing face and looked plaintively at the nurse and said, "Is that right?"

"Perfect," said the nurse. "You look like you've been doing it for years. She won't nurse for long now. Remember, she's new to it too, she's bound to get frustrated. So I can come back and bring her to the nursery in a few minutes if you want to get some rest."

"No!" Jane looked horrified. "Don't you dare. I'll keep her."

The BlackBerry, which had been in Jane's bag when she left for the hospital, began buzzing like a chain saw. Out of habit, Stephen made a move toward it.

"Don't," said Jane fiercely.

"I was just—"

"Throw it out the window." She shifted the baby and peered down at her.

"You don't mean *that*."

"I do."

"I wasn't suggesting that you call a meeting or answer an e-mail—"

"I know you weren't." Her face softened. "Look, Stephen. Her eyes are closed. She's sleeping!"

"Mmmm." He felt his own eyes grow heavy. In the hallway he could hear the nearly constant beeping and humming of people and machinery, nurses coming and going; it was comforting, in the same way that the sound of his parents eating dinner downstairs with friends past his bedtime when he was a child had been comforting.

He watched the baby's tight little fist, her tiny moving chest. He thought, *Someday I will know this person. Someday I will take her to a birthday party, or walking in Central Park. Someday she will call me Daddy. Someday I will say no to her about something, and she will cry.*

But just then it seemed impossible that the tiny red creature before him would be anything more than she was at that moment, tiny and red and concentrating so intently on living.

꙳

Twilight was coming on. Rachel noticed the folds of pink coming in under the blue. She reported that the police officer was outside in his car, talking into his walkie-talkie. Father Colin had just come in from driving around the neighborhood again. "Nothing," he said, and Rachel saw the way he touched Lillian on the shoulder. She thought Tom saw too, but she couldn't be sure.

Ginny was holding Philip, who was gurgling away, oblivious. "I suppose I should make something," said Ginny, and made no move to get up. "Is everybody hungry?"

"No," said Lillian.

"No," said Tom.

"No," said William. He was pacing in the den. He had called every neighbor he could think to call. "Maybe" he said carefully, "we should check Red Rocks. Before it gets dark."

"She wouldn't have gone *there!*" said Lillian, horrified. "She doesn't even know how to get there."

"There's that cut-through," said Ginny. "Behind that white house."

Lillian started crying again. "It's all woods in there. And the drop-offs to the lake. There's that cliff part, remember one summer, those boys? Oh, *God.*"

"I'll go," said Tom.

"No," said Father Colin. "Let me go. I run in there all the time. I know those trails. It's easy to get lost."

Lillian moaned.

"That's not what I meant—"

"I'll go with you," said Rachel.

"Don't we need dogs, or something, to search there? Why aren't there any dogs? Where'd the police officer go?" Lillian looked around. "Right? We need dogs. Why didn't he ask for something of Olivia's? A shirt she wore yesterday or something?"

"I'll get something," said Rachel. "Just in case."

"I'm going to see what's going on out there," said Lillian. "There should be dogs."

"I'll come," said Tom. He followed her, and William followed Tom, and even Father Colin and Ginny followed. The scene, Rachel thought, looking out the window of her childhood bedroom, would have been beautiful in any other circumstance because of the way the receding light was playing in the trees along the street, and the way they all formed a natural semicircle, shoulders nearly touching, as if they were waiting for something.

Which, of course, they were. For there, curled up, sleeping like a kitten in the clothes hamper inside her closet, was Olivia: tear-streaked, grimy, a stain in the shape of a jagged diamond on the front of her shirt. Olivia.

She stirred a little when Rachel lifted her and she flopped against Rachel's shoulder. It occurred to Rachel that she had never held a child this way, a sleeping child, with a thick and substantial body. Rachel carried her to the window and called out to the people on the lawn below. Lillian lifted her face first, and then Tom did, and then the rest of them, and Rachel stood there, holding Olivia like a prize, and she thought she understood, for the first time, the strange and terrible power a parent had over a child's happiness, and also how it worked in reverse.

❧

William went out to pick up pizzas from Flatbread. Olivia ate four pieces, minus the crust, never moving from Tom's lap. After the plates were cleared away, and the boxes had been folded and put out with the recycling, and the beers that William offered around were mostly empty, Ginny stood and said, "I'm exhausted. Sleeping arrangements? Everything sorted out?"

"No," said Lillian.

"Yes," said Tom.

They all looked at him. "I've got a reservation," he said. "At the Come On Inn." He shifted Olivia off his lap and picked up Philip, who had been in the car seat and was now beginning to stir.

"*That* place?" said Ginny. "Up on Shelburne Road? For heaven's sake, Tom, that's ridiculous. That place is a pit."

"I didn't know the Come On Inn took reservations," said Rachel.

"They do," said Tom defensively, as Philip flopped his head onto Tom's shoulder. "Recommended but not required. There's a pool—"

"Gross," said Rachel. "I wouldn't swim in there!"

"You'll stay here. We've got room," said Ginny. "You can stay in Jane and Stephen's room, or—"

"Oh, enough already," said Lillian. "He'll stay with me."

"I want a bubble bath," said Olivia.

"*I'll* get you a bubble bath," said Rachel.

"And I," said William, "cannot keep my eyes open any longer." He kissed Lillian on the forehead, shook Tom's hand rather formally, and followed the rest of them up the stairs.

"I have to feed Philip," said Lillian. She held her arms out to Tom.

"He's fine," he said. "Look! He's sleeping."

"No, I want to feed him. I do, at this time. This is what I've been doing all summer."

Wordlessly, he handed Philip over. Lillian moved to the den. She didn't tell Tom to follow her, but she didn't tell him not to either. He did. She settled herself in her usual spot on the recliner and he sat on the sofa, which, since the Laundromat scene, she had folded up and arranged semi-tidily every day.

"So," Tom began. "Will you come home now?"

She looked around the den, at the piles of her belongings, and Olivia's belongings, and Philip's belongings. And yet *she* didn't belong here, not really, not living in limbo in her parents' house like some college dropout. "I want—" She stopped.

"What?"

"I want to come back."

He smiled. She shifted Philip to the other breast. "But I want it to be like it was."

He stopped smiling. "It can be," he ventured.

"No, it can't. It's all changed. Forever."

"Lillian—"

"Well. It is, right?"

"Not to me."

"But it is to me."

"Listen, Lillian. I want you back. I want things to be good. I want to be a family again."

She shrugged. "Maybe as long as it's going to be different, it can be *better* different, not just different."

Tom waited, then asked, "How?"

"I want more help. From you."

Slowly Tom nodded. "Okay. For example?"

"I don't know yet. I just don't want to feel like I'm alone in all this, you know?"

"I know," he said.

"Do you really? Do you really know?"

"I think I do."

Then they heard Olivia's little feet working their way down the stairs and toward the den. Philip had finished eating and fallen asleep, so Lillian laid him carefully down in the Pack 'n Play and opened her arms to Olivia.

But Olivia shook her head! "I want Daddy," she said, and she went to Tom. Lillian's heart twisted a little bit at that. Then, watching Olivia wrap her arms around Tom and pat his back the way she'd done even as a baby, in imitation of what adults did to her, Lillian recognized something. She recognized that they were all battling—all of them, everyone in the family—to have their needs met. Ginny, William, Rachel, Stephen, Jane, all of them. Even little Philip. Clashing, every day, primal forces pitted against one another. And in the face of those battles her sorrow was not the biggest force. She'd learned that much when she thought Olivia was gone.

Olivia put her thumb in her mouth, and before five minutes had passed she was asleep, leaning sloppily against Tom.

"Okay," she said softly, to Tom, to Olivia, to Philip, and maybe even to the tired den furniture that had supported her throughout the summer, and on which she had cried and raged and threatened and sometimes—she could admit this now, though mostly to herself—laughed.

"Okay? Really?" Tom made a move toward her, but Lillian signaled to him to stay where he was because of Olivia.

"One more thing," she said. She saw him flinch so she said quickly, "This one's for us. I want us to get a babysitter. Once a week, date night. Guaranteed."

He smiled. "Yeah?"

"Yeah. More time for us."

"I like it. We need it."

"We do. *And.*"

"There's more?"

"I want Philip baptized."

"Really?"

"Yes. Before we go, in the church here."

"Don't you think there's a lot going on at the moment? We can get him baptized, if you want, but why not wait until we get home? I'm sure your parents will come down, and maybe the others will come up from New York—"

"Here," she said. "Not negotiable."

"Okay. If that matters to you."

"It does."

"Okay."

And they sat there for a long time, listening to the children breathe, watching Olivia's hair blow with each inhalation, listening to the sounds of the old house.

※

The next day Ginny drove to the hospital alone. Fall was still a couple of weeks away. Only yesterday it had been hot. But every now and then in August you got a day that made you remember how September would feel, and what the autumn light striking the trees would look like. This was such a day.

The others were going to follow. Already they were crowding into their various vehicles, sorting out seating arrangements and Rachel's luggage and which car seat belonged where. Rachel was going back to New York later that day. In a few days William would celebrate his birthday, his sixty-fifth. And then what? The rest of them would all head back, and she and William would be alone again.

The door to Jane's room was ajar. Jane was by herself, holding Sarah in one hand and the phone in the other. When she saw Ginny she said, "Mom. I have to go. *Mom.* I'll call you later." After she hung up she motioned to the chair beside the bed and said, "Sit down. Stephen went to find coffee." Then she rolled her eyes and said, "My mother keeps *calling*. She's in a panic that she wasn't here for the birth."

"Oh, but that's natural. I envy her these next months," said Ginny, sitting. "Watching your daughter become a mother for the first time...well, it's something."

"Yes," said Jane soberly. "I know."

"*No,*" said Ginny. "No, you don't." More softly, she said, "But you will, one day."

Sarah began to make little grunting noises.

"Shh," Jane said. "Shh, baby girl." To Ginny she said, "Apparently I'm supposed to nurse her almost constantly. Do you mind if I—"

"Not at all," said Ginny. Jane winced as Sarah latched on, then she closed her eyes and lifted her face to the ceiling. Watching the two of them, mother and child, Ginny felt a strange sensation of envy, like pinpricks all over her arm. To be *wanted* like that. To be *needed.*

"What I came here to say," said Ginny, "is that I'm sorry about that conversation we had, back at home. I never really apologized."

Jane waved her arm dismissively.

"But what will you do?" asked Ginny. "If it all goes the way you think it will?"

Jane lifted Sarah to her shoulder to burp her. It seemed to Ginny that she had not nursed her long enough on the first side. If Jane had been Lillian she would have told her so, but Jane wasn't Lillian, so she kept her mouth shut.

Jane moved Sarah to the other breast. "I don't know. *This,* I guess, for a while. And then we'll see. But I think we'll be okay. I really do. I just need Stephen to believe that too. And I'm not sure he does. Maybe you can help him? Help him see that?"

Ginny nodded slowly. "Listen, Jane—"

"What?"

"I know I haven't always—"

"Oh, stop it. I overdid it that day. I'm sorry too. I snapped. But I was tired. I was just so, so tired."

"It's okay to be tired," said Ginny. "We're all tired. Life is tiring."

Jane let out a short, abrupt laugh. "I *know,*" she said. "Isn't it, though?"

"But listen. There's something important I have to tell you."

"What?"

"You'll think this sounds silly, but I wanted to get here before the others. I wanted to talk to you alone."

"Tell me."

"It's about the knuckles."

Jane stared at her. "Whose?"

"Sarah's. Babies, all of them. When they go from pudgy to bone, when you can *see* the knuckles, that's when they're not your babies anymore. And it goes so *fast* from that point on, you have no idea."

Jane wore an expression of innocent bemusement; she looked like a child being taught a lesson in school. Finally she said, "I believe you."

"No. I mean, yes, I'm sure you do. But you don't know—you can't know—until it's too late. You have no idea."

"That seems very cruel," said Jane softly.

"It is. It's the cruelest thing."

Just then the door opened and Stephen came in. "There's a massive number of people out there waiting to see you," he said to Jane. "And you," he said to Sarah. He put down his cup of coffee and held his arms out for the baby. Stephen looked, thought Ginny, like someone who had been doing it for ages. He looked like a natural. He looked gentle and strong and determined and responsible and beautiful, her son, standing there holding little Sarah in the late-summer sunlight filtering into the hospital room. Then he sighed, a great, belly-deep, purposeful sigh that signified not boredom or irritation but a confirmation of the enormous responsibility that had settled on his shoulders.

Ginny blinked hard. "I'm going to let the others in. Brace yourselves. Then I'm going for a while, to see to things at home. I've got to get Rachel to the bus station by eleven. You," she said to Stephen, with as much manufactured gruffness as she could manage, because she thought that otherwise she might cry. "Take good care of this family of yours."

※

Stephen watched as they all came in. Rachel, who was dressed once again in her New York getup: smart skirt, heels, makeup, but carrying Philip, so that she looked like one of those thirty-something professional city mothers he saw all the time and whose existence had always seemed mysterious and otherworldly. William, holding the door open for the others and then stepping aside to let them through. Lillian next. Then Olivia, holding tightly to Tom's hand and leading him into the room. Olivia made an immediate lunge toward the baby, hands out. "Don't!" they all said at once, even Jane from the bed. Tom pulled her back and knelt down, one leg out, making a stool for her. "Sit," he said. "And be gentle."

"I *know*," said Olivia, and they could see that she did know.

Perhaps in a few minutes Stephen would want them gone; his impulse to protect Jane, to let her rest, and to protect little Sarah too, would outweigh everything. But for now he wanted them there. He wanted them! He watched as they arrived and took over the room: his wonderful, messy, imperfect family.

AFTER

The next week, after everyone had gone home, William and Ginny sat on the deck.

"I didn't expect this," Ginny said.

"What? The quiet."

"No, not that. I don't know what I mean, exactly." She had expected the quiet. But what she hadn't expected was the emptiness, the gnawing hole at the bottom of her stomach.

From inside the house the phone rang.

"That'll be one of them, needing something," said Ginny. She rose halfway.

"Let it ring."

"But maybe—"

"No," said William. "If it's really important, they'll call back. Sit down."

"But."

"Virginia Owen. Sit back *down*."

Ginny sat.

She and William stayed on the deck as late afternoon tiptoed out and evening quietly took its place. William closed his eyes and dozed, but Ginny did not. She was hungry, but she made no move to get up to prepare dinner. She just sat very still in her chair and waited, listening. This is what they didn't know about, the peace that came with having it almost finished. *This* you couldn't know about, ahead of time. She hadn't known, and wouldn't have believed anybody anyway, even if anyone had tried to tell her. She knew only now.

Finally the sunset came on, and then the darkness, and nobody moved and nobody made a sound and nobody called back.

Acknowledgments

First I want to thank Elisabeth Weed, my fabulous agent and a formidable editor in her own right, who took me on with such gusto, saw possibilities in this book that I had yet to see, and walked me through the revision process with grace and aplomb.

Reagan Arthur, whose first phone call to me I will forever remember as one of the happiest of my life, and everyone at Reagan Arthur Books, including Sarah Murphy, Andrea Walker, and Marlena Bittner, who have provided enthusiastic guidance along the way. And a big thank-you goes to Jayne Yaffe Kemp.

Iara Santos, au pair extraordinaire, without whose loving care of my children from mid-2008 to mid-2009 this book never would have seen the light of day. You are welcome in our home forever, and not just because of the chocolate balls.

Leslie Blanco, for candid, thorough, and invaluable editorial guidance at a critical time.

Dr. Jill Samale, who patiently answered all of my questions about childbirth and pregnancy complications (though any missteps I've made in those areas are mine alone).

Best friends Margaret Dunn, for explaining the nuances of the casting world to me, and Jennifer Truelove, for being an eager researcher in any subject matter, always. Also Susan Love, for the fortifying afternoon chats.

The members of the Newburyport Mothers' Club circa 2009: an amazing group of women who showed me, and continue to show me, how much it is possible to accomplish with small children in tow.

The Newburyport Public Library, whose air-conditioning (in summer), heat (in winter), and no-cell-phone policy (always) has kept me writing in comfort and concentration for some time now.

A book about families would be impossible to write without the top-notch families I'm lucky enough to be a part of. My parents, John and Sara Mitchell, and my sister, Shannon, nurtured a lifelong love of and enthusiasm for books that has led, finally, to this. My in-laws, Frank and Cheryl Moore, accepted my occasional absences at family gatherings during crucial writing times without question or complaint. The love and affection both families exhibit toward the pint-sized members make for a perfect model.

My beautiful daughters, Adeline, Violet, and Josephine, are constant sources of inspiration and laughter; their love allows me to explore imaginary worlds while their little chirping voices in my ear keep me happily and firmly grounded in my own very fortunate reality.

And finally: my husband, Brian, who always loves, always listens, and always understands. Without you there would be none of this.

About the Author

Meg Mitchell Moore worked for several years as a journalist. Her articles have been published in a wide variety of business and consumer magazines. She received a master's degree in English literature from New York University. She lives in Massachusetts with her husband and their three children. *The Arrivals* is her first novel.